Welcome to Sparkwood ...

where the drinks are cold, the eye candy hot, and the gossip is truly noteworthy.

For six months, I hated Asher Hammond.

And then I slept with him.

What started as one night turned into something neither of us expected—something real. Despite Ash's aversion to romance and my diehard belief in happily-ever-afters, we found our rhythm: my heart, his hands, and a passion that could burn down Sparkwood.

Between late nights at my bookstore, restoring my crumbling Victorian mansion, and falling for a man who swore love wasn't in his DNA, I let myself believe we were building something lasting. Even if Ash never said those three words, his actions spoke volumes.

Until she showed up.

The first—and only—woman Asher ever loved. The one who wrecked him, shattered his heart, and left scars deeper than any ink. And she's not here alone.

Ash swears it's over between them, but their shared history—and one too many secrets—make it impossible to ignore the cracks in the fragile foundation of our love story. I've been second best before, and I refuse to play that role again.

Walking away from the man I love is the hardest thing I've ever done. But just when I think I've found my footing, life throws me a twist I never saw coming.

Now, I have a secret, too—one that could bring us back together… or tear us apart forever.

Chasing Sparks

Sparkwood: Scenes From A Small Town
Book 2

M.L. Broome

Copyright

Sparkwood Series

\-

A Billion Sparks (Prequel Novella)
Secret Identity / Billionaire / Insta-Love
The First Spark (Book 1)
Enemies to Lovers / Forced Proximity / Opposites Attract
Chasing Sparks (Book 2)
Protector Role / Return of Ex / Surprise Pregnancy
Igniting Sparks (Book 3)
Fake Engagement / Age Gap / Forced Proximity
Sheltering Sparks (Book 4) *Preorder*
Friends to Lovers / Reverse Age Gap / Single Dad

A Billion Sparks *is exclusive to newsletter subscribers. Click the link to above to receive your free copy along with all the latest Sparkwood gossip!*

For my bookish babes who know exactly how to rock the tattooed heartbreaker's world… so he'll never be the same.

And they thought there was no point in our dirty books.

Ladies, time to show him ALL our skills.

A Note & Trigger Warnings

Ori and Ash have quite the journey.

Aside from the usual suspects: profanity (yes, they love their four-letter words) and open-door sex scenes, there are a couple of heavy topics.

The first is domestic violence. Now, it's **not** between Ash and Ori, but there is an off page reference to an abusive partner.

There is also a subplot surrounding sex trafficking. There aren't any details about the case and you don't meet any of the victims, but again, it's a hard topic.

I understand these themes can be difficult, so if you feel they might be too much for your heart right now, I completely understand if you choose to pass on this one.

Sending so much love, today and always.

Hold up, my gorgeous bookish babes!

*Did you read **The First Spark** yet? Now, it's not required reading or anything for **Chasing Sparks**, but since it's a continuation of Ori and Ash's journey (plus there are some seriously spicy scenes in there) I wanted to mention it before you dive in.*

*If you haven't read it and want to know how these two polar opposites first came to be, here's a link for **The First Spark**.*

The First Spark (Book 1)

Prologue: Ink & Old Scars

Ash

This prologue was originally exclusive to newsletter subscribers as a bonus scene but it's got some great Easter eggs, so here you go...

"Does somebody need more coffee?" Braden asks, a smirk coloring his mouth as I stumble into a folding chair next to our booth at the convention center.

"I need another gallon." Yes, I'm fucking exhausted, but last night was worth every second, even though I can safely say that woman wore me out.

Ori and I spent the entire night together, leaving me with just enough time to race home, toss my shit in a bag, shower, and make it to the airport on time.

I planned to sleep on the plane, but a screaming infant in the next row made that an impossible feat. Of course, the baby was smiling and laughing by the time we landed. I, however, was not in as happy a mood.

To add to the fun, our flight was delayed, so we had even less time to get everything set up for the convention, meaning I'm walking around like a zombie.

Or, in this case, sprawling across an uncomfortable-as-hell folding chair.

"Where were you last night?" my brother asks, waving a cup of joe under my nose. "You never came home."

"Do I have to run my personal life by you now?" I grasp the coffee and take a big swig. Pitch black, much like my humor today.

Braden shrugs and opens his tattoo gear case. "You're in a good mood, despite listening to a screaming baby for three hours, so I'm guessing you hung out with a certain bookstore owner. Am I close?"

I can continue evading Braden's questions, but what's the point? Judging by the smug expression on his face, he already knows the answer.

"Had to make sure Ori didn't forget me while I was gone."

Braden smiles, saluting me with his coffee cup. "Somehow, I don't see that happening to either of you."

The man speaks the truth, at least where I'm concerned. I never planned on Oriana Thorne, especially not now—not when my life had some semblance of routine and normalcy to it. Then she struts into my world and knocks everything, including me, on its head.

"You should have brought her along," Braden adds as he fiddles with the power cords strewn about the booth.

"No way," Zane pipes up, shooting Braden a dubious glance. "If he did that, he'd have to pass on all the ink bunnies, and you know Vegas is their prime hunting ground."

I snort into my coffee. Ink bunnies—a phrase I coined years ago for the women who hang around conventions, desperate for an after-hours piece of the action. These women are wild, too, and have a no-holds-barred attitude toward a good time. Let's just say that last year, my personal bunnies, a gorgeous blonde duo, brought along a suitcase filled with toys.

Did we use every one of them?

You better fucking believe it.

Like I said, no-holds-barred.

Most of these ink bunnies are normal, down-to-earth women for the other 51 weeks of the year, but in Vegas, the business suits come off and the sex kittens come out.

They pack an entire year of debauchery into one week, and the guys and I get to reap the rewards. It's a beautiful thing.

Plus, what happens in Vegas stays here. Once the convention ends, we go our separate ways.

It's beautiful, dirty fun.

But this year is different. I spent hours making love to Ori last night, coaxing several orgasms from her luscious body until she passed out on top of me.

No ink bunny can hold a candle to Oriana Thorne. Fuck, but that woman's pussy is magical. She's a siren, and I'll drown for her every time.

"The women this year are off the hook, and I know there's no way you're missing out on a week of fun. Right?" Zane asks, cocking a brow at me as he points to a few early arrivals.

"Eh," I mutter, taking another swallow of coffee.

"Wait a damn minute. You're playing it straight this year? Holy shit, what have you done with my buddy, Ash?" Zane shakes his head, a look of utter disappointment on his face.

"Relax. I'll be there."

Will I engage in any sordid behavior? Probably not, even though Ori and I aren't dating. Okay, we agreed to go on a date, but right now, we're in that gray friends-with-benefits area.

So, if I feel so inclined, I'm free to do what I want.

Hell, Oriana made a cheeky aside before I left this morning, warning me to play safe because she knows I play hard.

Which means she's not laying any claim to me... or she's got sordid plans of her own this week.

Well, fuck.

There's that damn jealousy again.

Maybe I should text her, just to let her know I arrived safely. Also, to remind her I'm thinking of her, which might put the kibosh on any of *her* planned extracurricular activities.

And then I realize I don't have her phone number. How the hell have I slept with her multiple times and not gotten her digits?

Unacceptable.

Glancing at the time, I realize she's working and *that* number I can locate.

I dial One More Page and hope to God Ori answers the phone, mainly because I don't want to give Mina any more gossip to chew.

"Good afternoon, One More Page." Ori's honey smooth voice melts into my bones.

"Fuck, I love your voice."

"Ash?"

"Yeah. Were you expecting someone else to call and say that?"

The answer had better be no.

"Hmm," she muses, "what day is it?"

"Tuesday. Why?"

"Well, depending on the day, I would know who was calling to whisper sweet nothings in my ear."

"Cut that shit out right now."

Ori laughs and I realize with every moment, I'm falling deeper under her spell. "How are you feeling?"

"Dead to the world, but amazing otherwise."

"That's what a night with me will do for you," she replies in a sing-song voice. "Try not to have too much fun out there, Ash."

"Ditto for you, Little One."

She huffs into the phone, but I hear the amusement in her voice. "Fine. I suppose you're worth the wait."

"Damn straight." Feeling eyes on me, I glance up and catch Zane's incredulous stare. "I better go."

"Bodyguard, over and out."

I end the call and shove the phone in my pocket. "What?" I ask, shrugging at Zane.

"Holy shit. The great Asher Hammond has fallen."

"Shut the fuck up."

"I'm serious. The first thing you do when you arrive here is call your girl? Damn."

"I let her know I'm alive. She's collecting our mail and watching over Black Lotus while we're gone."

"You sure that's all it is, *Little One*?" Zane asks, barely able to contain his amusement.

I didn't realize he heard my pet name for Ori. Apparently, he heard every word.

"Leave him alone," Braden interjects. "Looks like it will just be the two of us playing with the bunnies this year."

"I'll be there," I insist, my gaze volleying between them.

"Sure you will," they reply in stereo.

So glad they're enjoying this torture.

With a roll of my eyes, I push myself to a standing position. "I'll be back. I saw a vendor at the entrance that I want to check out."

What I need is to get out of this uncomfortable conversation and the implications they seem intent on making about Ori and me.

There is no Ori and me. We're just friends with the best damn benefits on the planet.

End of story.

Does that mean I'll take advantage of our status to sleep with some gorgeous, nameless women this year?

After hearing her voice, we all know the answer to that one, but it's not because I'm not *free* to do so.

I'm just not feeling it this time.

I stroll to a booth by the entrance of the convention center, run by a husband and wife duo who create tattoo designed book covers for the classics—a brilliant idea that I might have to put into play at Black Lotus.

Hell, Ori and I could team up, with me creating the covers and her selling them in One More Page.

Teamwork and all that jazz.

But that's not why I'm here now.

Ori's favorite book is *Jane Eyre*, which she divulged during our first night together. The woman is a diehard romantic, especially with the concept of true love overcoming all. She stands in direct opposition to my fierce beliefs about happily ever after.

But this isn't for me. It's for her, a token of appreciation for helping my dreams come true.

This booth has a copy of Jane Eyre, and it's exquisitely crafted, too. The dark color palette highlights a portrait of Jane in the center, with the gothic spires of Thornfield Manor behind her.

It's a perfect addition to Ori's collection of classics.

I grab my purchase and receipt before returning to our booth, thrilled I snagged a copy before they sold out.

But that happiness is short-lived because *something* is different, and I detect it the moment I step back into Black Lotus's booth.

My brother, so happy-go-lucky not ten minutes earlier, now wears a petulant scowl.

"What's the matter? Did something break?" I ask, glancing around the booth.

See, that's not unusual during a convention. Things get lost, broken, stolen, or any combination of the above, and it always makes the job tougher.

"Nope," Braden mutters, moving his cases from one table to another with excessive force.

"What am I missing?"

Braden pauses, his mouth turned down in a frown. "Are you a glutton for punishment?"

"What the hell are you talking about?"

He jabs a finger toward a young woman standing not three feet outside our booth.

"Who the hell is she?" I know I've never seen the woman before, no matter *what* she claims.

"Your first client."

I scrub my hands over my face, trying to deduce why this is pissing my brother off. "And?"

"It's a collab piece, right?"

"Yeah. I spoke with Scott at Steel and Stain about a month ago. The client approved my design, and Scott will work on the piece with me. He's a genius with dotwork, and that's what the client wanted as a border to her main ink. I don't get why you're mad. Did *you* want in on the collab?"

Braden walks over, pulling off his baseball cap and tugging a hand through his hair. "Scott is in the hospital with appendicitis."

Fuck.

I shoot another glance at the client, offering her a reassuring smile and a slight wave of my hand. "Okay. I'll do my part of the design, and she'll have to see Scott when he's out of the hospital."

Braden shakes his head, the frustration seeping from his pores. "Scott sent another artist in his stead. One who's equally brilliant with dotwork."

I nod slowly, trying to deduce what I'm missing in this puzzle. "That's awesome, then. Who did he send?"

"Your worst nightmare," Braden grits out.

What in the hell is he talking about?

"He means me," a gritty female voice says behind me.

I freeze as an ice-cold thrill shoots through me.

It can't be.

There's no fucking way.

It's been three years since I've last seen her and we agreed then to do our damnedest to avoid one another.

Sucking in a deep breath, I turn on my heel and face my nemesis.

The woman stands nearly my height in her knee-high stiletto boots, her curves wrapped in tight leather pants and a bustier. Her bright pink hair falls down her back and her bright blue eyes see right through me.

A hint of a smile plays on her full lips as she glides her tongue along her lip piercing, her tattoo bag slung over one shoulder.

No one would know it to look at her, but she's poison.

Don't get me wrong, she's also beautiful, but she's deadly on every level.

I should know.

"Scott sent you?" I grit out the words, feeling the bile rise in my throat. Seems like that black coffee might make another appearance all over her boots.

She nods as a smile breaks across her face. "Kismet, I guess. It's been a while, Ash. Too long."

"Not long enough," I grumble, feeling my insides twist at her proximity.

She motions to the bag in my hand. "What did you buy?"

We are *not* engaging in small talk.

I prepare to reply with a caustic retort, but I notice my client is within earshot. Correction: our client.

I pull the book from the bag and thrust it toward her. "*Jane Eyre.*"

She examines the cover, her long nails tracing the artwork. "Gorgeous. But you're not a fan of *Jane Eyre*. So tell me, who is she?" She cocks her head at me, her eyes wide and teasing.

"Nope, I'm not doing this." I stalk into Black Lotus's booth, trying to regain my balance.

Just when things were looking up.

Her boots click against the floor as she trails me to my station. "We're stuck working together, Ash, so can we make the best of it?"

Is she insane? I keep my back to her, willing my breathing to return to normal.

"Look, I know you hate me, but—"

"You know nothing about me," I snarl.

"That's not true. I know everything about you."

Whirling on my heel, I fix her with my glare. "Why are you here? And don't tell me Scott sent you. You could have said no. You *should* have said no."

She inches forward, her normally confident movements now timid. "I thought it would be a great opportunity."

"For what?"

"For us."

She's got to be fucking kidding me. My brain thumps in my head, and I swear I'm going to stroke out. Hell, maybe that's a good idea to get me away from this situation.

Ten years. Ten goddamn years and I'm still not past her. Still not past the lies and betrayal she heaped on my love.

Her hand touches my sleeve, and I yank it from her grasp. "Ash, please."

Tugging a hand through my hair, I finally meet her gaze. "What do you want, Lucille?"

"Another chance so that maybe you might like me again. Remember any of my good qualities."

"Do you have any?"

"You know I do, although I deserved that comment." She averts her gaze, fiddling with the arm of the portable tattoo chair. "I should go. I'll call Scott and let him know this was a bad idea. You want me to speak to the client?"

Lucille is offering me a way out, but how can I let this client down when I know her backstory? She flew five hundred miles for me to ink her dead fiancé on her skin. Correction: she flew hundreds of miles for Lucille and me to work together on this piece.

I know Lucille's skill and she'll do an exemplary job on the tattoo.

Trouble is, she might decimate my soul in the process.

Again.

You're a professional, Ash. You can do this. You survived Lucille once. How hard can it be this time?

"Ash?" Lucille prods, her voice more insistent.

"Let's go speak with the client." Grabbing my tablet with the approved design, I walk toward the young woman perched nervously on a chair, not bothering to check if Lucille is behind me.

The woman looks up, a tissue balled in one hand, her eyes red-rimmed. "Sorry. I thought this would be easier."

"Are you having second thoughts?" I ask, squatting by her chair.

Am I praying she says yes? Damn right I am.

"Not at all. Just want to ensure it's perfect because he deserves perfect."

So much for that idea.

I open the drawing program on my tablet and show my client the design. "I know you already approved it with Scott, but I added a bit more shading. How does that look?"

Her eyes widen. "Can you actually make it look just like him?"

"Asher Hammond is the best photorealistic artist in the business," Lucille states, standing on the woman's left. "I'd trust him with my life."

"Sounds good," the woman sniffles.

"You're a bit early, but I'll be set to go in about an hour." I stare over the client's head, connecting with Lucille's bright blue eyes, as any sense of equilibrium threatens to give way. "What about you, Lucille? Are you ready?"

"Absolutely." She pats the woman's shoulder. "Back in the day, Ash and I were the dream team. Some things never change. Do they, Ash?"

Figures Lucille would bring up that nickname, even though I haven't uttered it in over a decade. We worked together right after I opened Black Lotus and clients loved how our designs complemented each other. Despite the differences in our styles, they blended effortlessly.

Then again, at that time, so did we.

Until I learned the truth—that everything I believed in—was a lie. A carefully concocted story created by one devious woman.

A woman I now have to spend the next several hours with, in some sick sequel I never signed up for.

I realize I need to finish this tattoo and it needs to be perfect—not just for our heartbroken client, but for me, too. I need to prove to myself that I'm past the spell Lucille once cast over me.

That I've finally moved on and I'm free of the hold she had on my heart.

Let's not forget, I have an exceptional woman waiting at home. A woman who makes me feel things on the same level Lucille did.

A fear clenches my heart in a vise at that unspoken admission.

What if this is some caustic reminder to keep my heart safe and detached? What if the only thing I stand to gain with Ori is more pain?

There are so many variables now, and Lucille's sudden presence in my life has ripped open the bandages holding my emotional wounds closed.

Do I let them bleed? Do I allow Ori close enough to heal them? Or do I encase my heart in iron, so that no woman comes close to it again?

Something tells me, as I catch Lucille's gaze once more, that there is far more to her story, and somehow, I fear I'm going to get intertwined in her web of half-truths once more.

Chapter 1

It's Not Love. It's Hormones.

Ori

Fucking men.

At this moment, that derisive thought is aimed solely at my infuriatingly attractive, tattooed neighbor.

A neighbor who a week ago promised me dinner—and dessert—but has yet to deliver on either.

I get it, or at least the rational side of my brain does.

Ash is busy with business, and keeping his clientele happy at *Black Lotus* keeps the lights on in his upscale tattoo parlor. Plus, these aren't just *any* clients.

How do I know? Ash told me earlier today when he begged off our plans yet again. These women are not random inked hotties, desperate for some face time with Sparkwood's resident bad boy.

They're scouts for a major magazine.

Major, as in *life-changing*.

Ash needs to take this meeting, so our dinner date needs to simmer on the back burner while I stew next door.

The worst part? I hate being this way. I'm not the woman who gets all tangled up in fuzzy feelings because a man delivers an over-the-top orgasm—or several.

I'm the chick who plays it cool. No man gets under my skin, making me all hot and bothered.

No man until Asher Hammond, that is.

He's the first man I can't get out of my brain, and apparently, can't get back into bed.

Unacceptable.

Oriana Thorne does *not* go down like this.

Fine, I'm being a bit dramatic. It's only been ten days since Ash and I hooked up for a second time, right before he jetted off to Vegas for a tattoo convention. From the photos I saw online, there was a whole lot of partying and a crap ton of eligible females. Talk about some low-hanging fruit. The men of Black Lotus had a never ending buffet of beauties surrounding them.

In. Every. Photograph.

Do I want to know how many of them Ash bedded during those five days? No, because where that tattooed god is concerned, ignorance is bliss.

So, when Ash got home four days ago, I was champing at the bit to go out on a real live date. He seemed happy to see me, even brought me back a special edition copy of *Jane Eyre* with a custom drawn cover—all because he knows it's my favorite book. Then he informed me he was crazy busy playing catch-up, but we would have dinner together the following day.

That day came and went, along with a few others, and here we are.

I need a damn lobotomy.

I should be doing a million things, but here I am, leaning on the bookstore counter and straining to glimpse this evening's entertainment like some love-starved voyeur.

Am I in love with Ash? No, with a capital N. But I am in like. Big time like. Those very fuzzy feelings I swore I would never catch around him? I have them bad.

And that isn't good. Especially not with a man like Asher Hammond.

Too bad my heart doesn't care what my brain thinks about the subject.

A flurry of movement in my periphery catches my attention, and I swing my gaze to watch as three women, clad in little more than lingerie, approach the entrance to Black Lotus.

They must be the magazine scouts, and of course, they have to be hot as hell. They each possess an edgy appeal, but one is obviously the leader. Her skin is decorated with colorful ink, and her hair is styled into a long, vibrant purple mohawk. On me, that hairstyle would look ridiculous. On her, it's stunning—and I silently curse her and her future offspring under my breath.

See? This is why the idea of love with a man like Asher Hammond is *not* a good look for me. I apparently descend into madness—with little hope of escape.

There you go again with the L word.

I pause, realizing I've used the word love and Ash in conjunction one too many times for it to be a coincidence.

No, no, no. Get a grip, Oriana. Right now. You will not fall in love with a man incapable of the emotion.

Nope, I don't believe me, either.

From my perch behind the bookstore counter, I watch Ash saunter to the entrance of *Black Lotus* to greet the women, his sex-on-a-stick smirk at the ready.

When you've got it, flaunt it, and Asher Hammond has it *all* in spades.

I hate him for always looking so damn sexy, even though he's nothing like my usual type. Seems my hormones don't give a flying fig if I normally gravitate toward businessmen.

Ash is ruggedly handsome with permanent artwork covering every inch of his skin, all highlighting his muscular frame—and don't even get me started on his chiseled features or the way his neatly trimmed beard feels oh-so-damn-good against my skin. And his piercings? Damn, they take the pleasure to a whole new level.

But he's more than just wildly attractive. He's smart and pensive, with a quick wit and a reading habit that puts mine to shame. He's also the most talented lay I've ever had, and trust me, he's had some competition.

Sunday school teacher, I am not, but my reputation *pales* compared to Asher Hammond's.

Every woman Ash wants, he gets. That's not some egotistical aside that he spouts for effect. It's a fact. Just ask the women of Sparkwood—the man is a legend.

If I were smart, I would forget this cockamamie idea of dating Asher Hammond and focus on easier prey. I've had more than my share of requests for dates, but I've turned them all down.

I don't date for sport. In truth, I don't date. Who has the time? My bookstore, *One More Page*, keeps me hopping and now I've added a fixer-upper mansion to my to-do list—just for kicks.

Plus, I have a vibrator. A damn good one, too.

Not Asher Hammond good, though.

No one, and I mean *no* one, is that good.

That's the crux of my issue—he checks all the boxes. Everything I've ever wanted in a man, lover, life partner… dare I say, *husband*, he possesses, with one tiny flaw.

He doesn't believe in love or romance. Just ask him and he'll tell you all about it.

See? I should run for the hills and chalk up our two nights together to one too many whiskeys and one too few beds.

That's what a smart woman would do.

That's what I *should* do, but my brain cells have flitted away into the ether and it's all Ash's fault.

Like I said, fucking men.

A peal of laughter, tinged with one too many cocktails,

sounds from next door, pulling me from my self-imposed torment. I shift my attention back to Ash and his female companions, still lingering by the tattoo parlor door. As if on cue, the leader of the lingerie pack tosses her head back with a gleeful giggle, her hand resting on Ash's biceps.

He obviously told her something wildly witty and funny.

Of *course* he did.

With a grunt more feral than I'd like, I shove my jealousy back in its emotional cage. Time to focus on anything other than Asher Hammond—like my business, my new house, or reclaiming my sanity.

Twisting my long hair into a makeshift bun, I secure it with a pencil jabbed into the center.

Who cares what I look like? There's no one here to impress besides Mina, and she wouldn't give a crap if I wore a burlap sack to work.

A rap at the bookstore window grabs my attention. Jerking my head up, I meet Ash's wide-eyed gaze as he stands in the adjoining hallway, his menage flanking him like sentries.

Subtle, ladies.

But Ash isn't paying them any mind. He's too busy eye fucking me, or at least visually devouring the parts of me not hidden behind a wooden counter.

Peering down at my shirt, I realize what's caught the man's attention. Seems somewhere between inventorying paperbacks and restocking the coffee bar, a few buttons on my blouse popped open, offering quite a view of my lacy black bra.

Totally unintentional move, although I'm certainly enjoying Ash's reaction.

Ash bites his lower lip and offers me an appreciative nod. Then his sultry green-eyed-gaze travels back up the length of my torso while his fingers grasp his shirt lapels in a non-verbal cue.

How cute. He's trying to preserve my modesty.

But modesty isn't earning me drool worthy stares—my

breasts are. Plus, there's no one else here except his *friends*, and judging by their current attire—or lack thereof—they've clearly modeled their fair share of undergarments.

So, true to form, I opt to push Ash's buttons, which is fast becoming one of my favorite pastimes.

I yank the pencil from my hair and let the dark waves tumble over my shoulders before leaning on the counter and mashing my tits together.

Ash's eyes widen, flitting between the amused smirk dancing on my lips and my ample cleavage while I turn my focus to the packing list in front of me.

Your move, Asher Hammond.

I expect an exasperated shake of his head or even a snort of laughter at my inherent stubbornness.

I get neither.

When I glance up a few moments later, Ash is gone from the window, and the women are disappearing through *Black Lotus's* front door.

Not the reaction I expected.

With a huff, I twirl on my heel and freeze in my tracks.

Ash stands not a foot away from me and, judging by the smoldering expression on his face, I know just what he's thinking.

Time to feign innocent indifference—an infuriating and highly effective technique with men like Ash. "May I help you?"

Ash closes the distance between us, trapping me between the heavy oak counter and his muscled torso. "What do you think you're doing?"

"Whatever do you mean?" I bite my lip for effect, even pushing my glasses up my nose as I work the sexy librarian angle.

He slides his hands up my rib cage to cup my breasts, his thumbs dusting across my nipples. "These beauties are mine. For my eyes only."

"Says who?"

Any woman who claims she hates a man with a jealous streak is lying. I'm not talking about a full-on smack down for disobedience—I'd never tolerate an ounce of that shit—but seeing the muscle in Ash's jaw tighten at the thought of me sharing my lady parts with someone else is downright satisfying.

Not quite 'rolling in the sack with Ash' satisfying, but it's close, and getting a rise out of the man who claims to be immune to jealousy? Pure satisfaction, even if my wardrobe malfunction was totally innocent.

"Don't play with me, Ori," Ash warns, leaning in to glide his tongue along my throat. "I'll take you over my knee right here."

Walking my fingers along the firm column of his chest, I release a husky chuckle. "A delicious offer, but that would mean abandoning your guests for the evening because I won't settle for some quick fix. I'm craving an all nighter. So, I suppose playtime will have to wait… until *you* find ample free time."

He wraps his hands around my hips, hauling me flush against his erection. "Stick around tonight. My meeting shouldn't take too long and then I'm all yours."

"Tempting, Asher Hammond. Very tempting."

And it *is* tempting to cave to his demands and sit around whilst he entertains next door—though I shudder to think what his form of entertainment might involve with those sexy bitches.

Let's be real: I knew Ash's reputation *long* before we indulged in the horizontal mambo, and I dove in anyway. I'd be downright foolish to believe he'd hang up his playboy hat simply because of two fabulous nights with me.

I may be a romantic, but I'm also a realist. Still, a simple agreement to Ash's request is far too easy. Time to make him sweat a bit.

Besides, he owes me after canceling dinner and wrecking *my* plans numerous times.

"Is that a yes?" Ash presses, his fingers caressing my sides.

"Guess you'll find out when you're finished. After all, I have other ways to spend an evening that doesn't involve waiting around for you."

Ash groans, but I catch him biting back a grin. "Woman, what am I going to do with you?"

It's one of his favorite lines where I'm concerned, but I consider it a term of endearment. Plus, he's not wrong in his assessment. Stubbornness runs through my veins.

"Nothing good ever came easy."

"Not true," he murmurs, capturing me in a fierce kiss, his tongue tangling with mine. "I make you come really easy. Again, and again."

With every word, I fall deeper under Ash's spell. By the end, my entire body quivers from his touch.

Tilting my chin up, Ash forces me to meet his gaze. "Stick around tonight."

Then he's gone, his boots echoing across the wood floor as he returns to *Black Lotus*—to the trio of women waiting for him. Important women, wanting to discuss life-altering ideas. All while dressed in lingerie.

My little green monster is on a rampage tonight.

"Little predate action?"

I nearly jump out of my skin at Mina's voice over my shoulder. Spinning on my heel, I feel the flush rise to my cheeks as I re-button my blouse. "Not hardly."

"Sure looked that way."

"That would require us to actually go on a date."

Mina furrows her brow and shoots me a confused look before handing me a cup of coffee. "I thought you two were having dinner tonight."

Huffing out a noisy breath, I roll my shoulders back a few times. "So did I, but Ash canceled earlier today."

"Again?"

See? It's not just me. Ash's behavior is suspect, at best.

Still, being the cool and collected woman I am—at least on the outside—I opt to play it off.

No. Big. Deal.

Will Mina see through my facade? Without a doubt, but I'm going down with the ship on this one.

"It's a work thing. A few scouts from some magazine wanted to interview Ash for an upcoming issue."

"But you don't buy that reason." For someone so young, Mina certainly knows how to cut through the bullshit.

"You didn't see the way they looked at him… or the way he ate up every second." Scrubbing my face with my hands, I release a loud groan. "This is a bad idea. I should shelve any plans with Asher Hammond and return to my previously scheduled life."

"The life before the local tattoo god took up residence in your heart?"

"Sure isn't taking up residence in my bed," I mutter. "And don't let Ash hear you mention his name alongside the words love, heart, or happily ever after. You'll send him hurtling for the nearest exit."

Mina offers me a casual shrug as she pours herself a cup of coffee. "Maybe it's totally innocent, Ori, and those women aren't into Ash. People do have other reasons to visit *Black Lotus* besides drooling over the owner. You know, like getting pierced or tattooed."

I should fire my friend. It would be easier than enduring any more of this conversation. Figures Mina would throw logic into my emotional free fall.

But logic is not my strong suit when it comes to Ash. Mostly because I've let the man into my heart, and now, all bets are off.

And it's silly. Absolutely, ridiculously silly.

Ash and I spent one scorching night together, where we

moved from enemies to friends to lovers at warp speed. Then we toyed with each other for the next week until he stormed into my bookshop to claim he doesn't want to like me.

But he does.

He really, *really* does.

After a second night with the man, one that blew past all previously held expectations, he asked me out to dinner, despite telling me during the course of our lust-filled frolics that he doesn't date.

As in ever. Love and romance are not on the menu for Asher Hammond.

So, when he asked me, I knew it meant something.

Until it didn't.

And here we are.

"What do those women have that you don't, Ori? Not a damn thing." Mina waves her hand in the direction of Black Lotus.

"Not true," I grumble, gulping down a mouthful of coffee. "They have at least two cup sizes on me."

"Your boobs are fantastic, and you know it."

She's not lying. At the risk of sounding like a pompous ass, I have amazing tits. They're perky and just the right size. Plus, judging by his earlier reaction, Ash seems equally enamored.

Even if it's been ten days since he spent any time with them. Not that I'm counting.

"They also have about thirty more tattoos than me."

Mina considers my statement. "Do you have any ink?"

I shake my head before guzzling down the last of my coffee. "That's weird, right? Here I am, tattoo free and pining after a tattoo artist. We don't match."

"Opposites attract," Mina reminds me in a sing-song voice, no doubt trying to lighten the mood.

But do they? Can two people with nothing in common, save for amazing sex, actually build something when one half of the duo has zero interest in said project?

I rest my chin on my palm and release a huff. "Maybe he isn't that good in bed. Might have been a fluke."

Mina snorts and shakes her head, knowing full well my statement is crap. "Every time?"

See? Mina has never slept with Ash, nor has she shown a speck of interest in the man, but even she knows he's the most talented lover on the market. Word travels fast when you're a legend.

And Asher Hammond is the king of legends. He's perfect and perfectly unattainable. For some ridiculous reason, that combo is catnip to women.

Trust me, I know.

Lowering my head to the counter, I release a low groan. "I don't want to like him, Mina."

I shock myself with the veracity of my words, although I know each and every one is true.

Liking Asher Hammond is akin to dancing too close to the sun. I'm guaranteed to burn alive.

"But you do, and he likes you."

"Does he, though?"

Mina nods, shooting me a wink. "Deep down, he's always had a thing for you. That, no doubt, scares the shit out of a man like Ash. You always had a thing for him, too."

I bark out a laugh at her statement. "Not true. Not even remotely, in the smallest increment, true."

"You know you're lying."

"Did I think the man was good looking? Of course, but that's hardly newsworthy. I also thought he was pugnacious and pedantic, with an ego bigger than his biceps."

Another snort rises from Mina's chest. "He should put that on his business cards."

Trust me, I had *many* thoughts about Asher Hammond before our truce, but none of them involved him as a potential mate.

Mostly, they centered on his revolving door of women, with a seemingly new one every night.

Each of his conquests seemed so enamored with him as they batted their lashes and hung on his every word, all while hoping they would be the one to change his mind about love.

None of them even chinked his armor. Instead, he moved down the line to the next willing recipient with nary a thought to the pile of wounded hearts he left behind.

How do I know? He's honest about *that* facet of his personality, too.

Ash's beliefs are built on a foundation of heartbreak and jaded emotions, and it will take more than a talented tongue or hour-long blowjob to sway his opinion.

It will take a woman who's strong in her own right. Stubborn, like him, but able to turn him on his head and keep him guessing.

I thought I might be up for the job. Hell, even as a sort of experiment to test the limits of our neighborhood demigod.

Now, I'm not so sure.

The worst part? Asher Hammond is a nice guy, so long as you don't dare to fall in love with him. But if, or should I say when, you do, remember he warned you against such foolish notions.

"You know the real difference between you and those women?"

Once again, Mina's voice cuts into my internal monologue, but she's a welcome reprieve. My mind has dark corridors and rabbit trails, and when given free rein, there's no telling what stories I might concoct in my head.

"I told you already," I reply. "Two cup sizes, several dozen tattoos, and at least a few glasses of wine by now."

Mina slings her bag over her shoulder before turning toward the door. "It has nothing to do with tits or tattoos. All those women ask Ash out, but *he* asked *you*. That never happens."

"I asked him first, remember? He turned me down."

Mina shakes her head and wraps the scarf around her neck. "Fine. But then he asked you to hang out a few times, and you shot him down—or conveniently had plans with another man."

"A happily married man who has zero interest in me," I remind her.

She shrugs, pulling her keys from her bag. "Ash didn't know that, though, and it bothered the hell out of him. I'm telling you, Ori, you're not like those other women. See you tomorrow."

I marinate on Mina's words as I watch my friend stroll to her car, barely managing to stay upright on a slick spot caused by the falling snow.

We got snow on Long Island, too, but this is insanity. Every day it's either snowing or forecast to start within twelve hours. Such is the life in the mountains of New York.

Still, it makes for a beautiful landscape, and it is almost Christmas.

Shit! Christmas.

With all my afternoon musings over one tatted hottie, I forgot to finish preparations for Santa's visit to the bookstore.

I threw out the idea on a lark at a town council meeting, unsure if the residents would be interested.

Newsflash: they were.

We have over fifty children descending on One More Page in two days, and this store needs to look like a winter wonderland.

Since Mina has vacated the premises, it looks like I'm Santa's sole elf.

At least it will keep my mind off Asher Hammond and his platonic playthings next door.

An hour later, I've finished Santa's workshop, but Ash is no further from my brain.

I'm also still chewing on Mina's words about how I'm different from all those other women, although I call bullshit on that statement.

But the one overriding thought? I'm ready to eat the ornaments on the artificial tree to ward off the gnawing in my stomach.

A quick glance at the clock tells me it's way past dinnertime, which means Ash's time to get his happy ass over here is also up.

Apparently, he's having far too much fun with his ladies to wrap things up in a timely fashion, and I'm not sitting here all night like some besotted fan.

On to plan B.

I grab my phone and dial the local pizza place. My original idea? A cheesy Stromboli jam-packed with enough pepperoni to choke a horse.

But halfway through my order, a better idea hits me.

Ash wants me to hang around?

Fine, but there's a ticking clock for that request and if he knows what's good for him, he won't make me wait.

I stroll next door and shoot Braden a smile when he glances up from his desk. "Hey Braden, where's the man of the hour? Still entertaining?"

Yes, I'm testing the waters.

Sue me.

A grin splits Braden's face at my question. He looks just like his brother, but Braden and Ash are so different when it comes to their ideas on love.

Ash hates the concept.

Braden is open to the idea.

Neither one starves for female affection.

Such are the trials and tribulations of the Hammond men.

Braden jerks his thumb over his shoulder, toward the back of the parlor. "Come to rescue him?"

"Something like that."

Totally false bravado, but I need all the help I can get right now, and Braden is too much of a gentleman to call me out on it.

With a sigh, I toss my hair over my shoulder and follow the sound of laughter to the back seating area, earning a surprised look from Ash when he catches sight of me.

"Hey, Ori."

"Hey yourself." I nod at each of the women, but my smile doesn't reach my eyes. How can it when it's one hundred percent fake?

At least they're all dressed and sitting an appropriate distance from my man.

My man? What the hell is wrong with you, Ori?

Love. Do. Not. Recommend.

Terrible for the psyche.

Before my brain can pick apart my latest thoughts involving the L word, I plow ahead. The sooner I state my case and leave, the better.

The rest is up to Ash.

"It's late and I'm starving. I ordered a pizza from that place you like, and it will be here in thirty minutes. After that, both me and said pizza will be downstairs and I hate dining alone. I'm sure you'll be finished with your *interview* by then."

A scoff flies from one woman's mouth, but I pay her no mind.

Am I being forward? Damn straight, but like Mina reminded me, I have something they don't. Ash asked *me* out, not the other way around.

Plus, he admitted to having a mad crush on me *after* we slept together.

Sometimes, it pays to take chances. If it works, I have a dinner date. If it doesn't, then my love experiment, as it were, is finished and I'll wave the white flag of surrender.

Either way, it's an answer.

"I figured we would grab a drink," the woman with the purple mohawk protests, shooting me a side-eye as she slides the tiniest bit closer to Ash's side.

But Ash never wavers his gaze from me as a smile breaks across his face. I remember that dimpled smirk from our nights together, offered up right before he buried himself inside me and took us on the ride of our lives.

No doubt he's recalling the same memory, if the raw hunger in his face is anything to go by.

Sorry ladies, even if your tits are two sizes larger than mine, Ash's focus is singular—and it's on me.

Time to play this one to my full advantage.

"I'll be downstairs. Don't keep me waiting."

With that, I strut away, ensuring I toss in an extra hip shake for effect. Hey, my tits aren't my only asset, and Ash has a real fondness for my peach.

Let's hope it's enough to make him send those women packing.

Chapter 2

Pizza or Bust

Ori

Forty minutes later, I'm one pizza richer, but my dinner date is still nowhere to be found.

Seems Ash has made his decision.

At least I have pizza to fall back on. With a sigh, I open the box and inhale the tantalizing aroma. Warm dough and melted cheese might be a poor substitute for time with Ash, but it'll have to do.

I'm only three bites in, complete with drops of sauce on my chin, when the basement door opens and heavy boots smack against the steps.

Well, well, well—color me surprised.

"Thanks for waiting for me."

Glancing up, I wipe the sauce from my face and offer Ash a shrug. "I said thirty minutes. Don't keep a hungry woman waiting."

Chuckling, Ash grabs a slice, pausing to drop a kiss on my forehead. "Thanks for dinner, and the intervention. Those women wouldn't shut up."

"Too much fawning and pawing for one night?" I smirk, desperate to appear unaffected by his proximity.

"I'd prefer pawing from someone else. You interested?"

I quirk a brow at him, although I'm sure that line works on every woman in town. The man doesn't perspire, he sweats sex appeal—and he damn well knows it.

"Is that your way of wooing me into bed again, Asher Hammond?"

"I didn't hear you complaining the other times. In fact, all I heard was you yelling my name and screaming for more."

God, I hate how cocky he is.

Cocky and correct, as the case may be.

Still, he's not getting his kicks *that* easily.

"Maybe you got lucky. It was only two times."

My words unhinge him, but he recovers quickly. "Beautiful, it was *way* more than two times."

"Correction. I meant two nights." Slowly, I lift my hand to my mouth, gently biting the tip of my pinky finger. My tongue flicks out to tease it, a playful smile tugging at my lips. His eyes darken, tracking my every movement. "Although it has been a while. Maybe I'm building it up in my head."

That does it.

Ash tosses his pizza aside and pulls me onto his lap. With a disarming smirk, he plucks the slice from my hand and drops it into the box alongside his.

Then, his fingers go to work, deftly unbuttoning my blouse. "More than happy to offer you a refresher course."

"No can do," I reply, staying his hands.

"Don't tell me it's that time of the month. Figures I get five seconds free, and you're temporarily out of order."

"That's next week, actually."

"Good to know. I'll remember to bring you chocolate and maintain a safe distance."

"Aren't you hilarious?"

He chuckles at my perturbed expression, completely nonplussed by my fake show of anger. "So, what's stopping you right now? I see you, me, and a couch with which we are very familiar."

Here goes nothing.

As I sat in the basement, awaiting Ash's arrival, I made a vitally important decision.

Go big or go home has *always* been my motto. It explains why I now own a rundown manor house and why I uprooted my life in Manhattan to move to Sparkwood.

When I set my mind to something, I'm the most deter-mined woman on the planet. Dogged in pursuit of my dreams... even when those dreams play out far differently in reality than they do in my brain.

Ever since that first night with Ash, I've wanted something more with him, although I'm aware this is likely a fool's errand. But no matter how tempting, I refuse to become part of his friends-with-benefits rotation.

"No sex until we have a proper date."

The corners of Ash's mouth quirk upward as he bites back a smile. "Laying down the law, Ori? I like that. Take charge looks hot as hell on you."

Despite the man's ability to turn my insides into a fluttery mess with a single glance, I must maintain focus.

Ash needs to understand I'm not like all the other women in his life, content to possess a sliver of his time.

He has boundaries regarding love, and I have them regarding playtime, although I doubt Ash will accept the terms. He's not exactly hurting for female companionship, and he might chalk me and my rules up as being too high mainte-nance for his taste.

Still, I need to stay the course for *my* preservation and dignity.

We'll ignore my heart for the moment.

I rest my hands against his muscled chest, allowing a bit of distance between us as I meet his gaze. "I'm serious."

He raises a brow at me, but his smile never falters. Seems Ash is enjoying this game, although, per his own admission, he never backs down from a challenge.

Especially when he knows the stakes.

Hell, we're both fully aware of how magnificent our nights together were, which is *not* helping my current hormone situation.

What's a woman to do when her body wants to commit treason and cave to the enemy? An enemy who tastes delicious and feels even better? An enemy who *knows* he's God's gift to women?

I fall back on my last line of defense—sarcasm, my ever-reliable weapon in my arsenal of emotional survival.

I nibble my bottom lip with my teeth as I regard his chiseled face. "Don't give me that look, Ash, and think I'll fall at your feet. It might work on your other lady friends, but I don't suffer from that malady."

"I think you might."

A scoff flies from my lips. The gall of this man. Okay, he might be dead to rights, but that's beside the point.

Who goes around claiming no woman is immune to his charms?

Asher Hammond, apparently.

I suppose when your sexual escapades are the stuff of legends, you're entitled to a big ego.

I'm still not caving, though.

He locks our hands together, all the while edging me closer. "You like me way more than you're willing to admit."

Tell me something I don't know.

But I hold firm, hoping he won't notice my racing pulse. "Just because you claim it doesn't make it true."

"Just because you deny it doesn't make it false, either." Ash buries his head against my neck, his tongue hot as it dances along my skin. "Just say it. You want me as badly as I want you."

Arrogant bastard. Screw him for knowing me—and every weak spot on my body—so well.

How is that even possible after only two nights together? Most men take months to figure out a woman's sexual kryptonite. Years, even. But Ash? He's got every inch of me mapped out, and he's taking full advantage of that knowledge.

With each passing moment, my resistance weakens.

I know I'm losing this battle. We both do, but I'll make one last stand before I surrender to the passion coursing through my body.

"Perhaps, but I'm not giving this up for free. *This*," I motion along my body, "you'll have to earn."

Ash bites his lip, his fingers hooking in the belt loops of my jeans. "I always earn my keep."

He's saying all the right things, pushing all the right buttons, but that's what Asher Hammond does, right?

Is this what you want, Ori? A second encore?

Yes, please.

Another incredible night where nothing existed beyond the two of you?

Absolutely.

Even though that night ended with Ash jetting off to Vegas to party with copious amounts of alcohol and women?

Fuck.

My heart thinks Ash is perfection squared, while my head thinks my heart is an idiot who shouldn't be trusted.

But my libido is kicking sense and sensibility's ass right now.

"Do me a favor?" Ash asks.

"Besides buy you pizza and save you from the clutches of over-eager women?"

He reaches into his wallet and tosses a fifty on the table. "Now, will you do me a favor?"

"Sure, as long as it doesn't involve those over-eager women."

His eyes widen as a surprised huff flies out of his mouth. "Just you, beautiful."

"Go ahead."

Ash dances his fingers down my arm. "Strip down and let me get an up close and personal look at that sexy lingerie I saw earlier."

"How is this not going to end in sex?"

Ash's grin widens. "I'm not the one holding out. You stated your rules, and I respect them. However, after a long week away from you, I would love nothing more than to see those gorgeous curves again."

"That's not a good idea…"

The truth is, I have a bit of a kink for giving Ash spur-of-the-moment stripteases. Hey, it takes the man to an entirely new level of turned-on, which has served me well so far.

"Actually, it's the best idea I've heard all night. Let me make it easier for you. I'll sit on my hands. No touching, unless you ask for it. Ori, you're pretty much all I've thought about since that first night. Do with that information what you will."

My heart stutters at his admission.

How do I say no to that?

That's right, I don't.

It might be total bullshit, a smooth line to ply me into submission, but I choose to believe him.

Why butter me up when he has scads of women lining up to suck him off?

That's my theory and I'm sticking to it.

Besides, I do love playing with Asher Hammond—just to see what pops up.

With a mischievous smirk, I push myself to standing and slide my glasses off.

"No way. Put them back on," he demands.

Seems Ash gets off on my sexy librarian look. Who am I to deny him that basic right?

With slow, deliberate movements, I finger open each button before sliding the shirt down my arms. Kicking off my shoes, I turn around, giving him a front-row seat to my peach as I toss a coy smile over my shoulder.

Ash's smoldering gaze stays locked on me, and a thrill shoots through me when he adjusts himself with a low grunt.

Wiggling out of my jeans, I close the short distance between us, his heady stare trailing over every inch of me as I straddle his lap.

"Is this a close enough look for you?" I inquire, gasping when his hands cup my ass and push me against his erection.

"Not remotely."

"Gotten a lot of lap dances in the last few weeks?"

Why do I ask this question? Masochistic curiosity, I suppose. My willpower is hanging by a thread and hearing I'm one of many might be the cold water my libido needs.

Ash's eyes widen, but his grip stays firm. "Does this qualify as a lap dance when you're not moving?"

I roll my eyes and snort out a laugh. Arrogant bastard.

"Fine, how many stripteases have you received?"

"Ever? A lot."

Knew it.

I grunt, trying to push off his lap, but Ash tightens his hold, leaning in to steal a kiss. "Easy, little one. In the last two weeks? Just one. Only you."

I hate being jealous. I hate being that woman whose feelings are so transparent.

Damn Asher Hammond and his sexual mojo magic.

Ash leans back against the cushion, his thumbs tracing the edges of my bra strap. "Fuck, but you're pretty."

It's a line he's used on me before, but I can't help loving the way his eyes darken when he says it.

"A few less tattoos than your earlier guests."

"A few less tattoos than pretty much every woman I know." He slides his hands up my back, releasing the clip in my hair and letting the dark waves cascade down. "Like I told you before, you don't need them. You're perfect, just as you are."

"That's because I satisfy your sexy librarian kink."

"Damn straight you do."

"We're still not having sex."

Seems no matter what line I toss out, he sidesteps it with ease. "I know. But you're tense, so I'm going to help you relax."

"With a massage?"

"Exactly, but instead of my hands, I'm going to use my tongue." He winks before reclining back on the couch and crooking his finger at me. "Now bring that pretty pussy over here. I have something I want to discuss with her."

I climb up Ash's body and straddle his chest, making sure to maintain a safe distance from his decadently talented mouth. "What would that be?"

His gaze is pure fire as his hands once again grip the meat of my ass. "How much I love licking every inch of her sweetness and how desperate I am to taste her right now. That is, if it doesn't offend your moral compass."

A husky laugh escapes my lips as he drifts his fingers along the edge of my underwear, sending a rush of sparks through my body. "I'll let you slide this time."

Ash regards me with open amusement. "That was quite the fight you put up, Ori."

I toss up my hands, shooting him a mock scowl. "Give me some credit. I don't stand a chance against your talented tongue."

"Not if I can help it." He wraps a hand around the nape of my neck, bringing my face to his. "Now, get these off before I rip them from your body."

I slide off my underwear, gasping when Ash grabs me, lowering my pussy to his waiting mouth.

"Fuck, I missed you," Ash groans as he tastes me with

slow, tantalizing licks. His hands band tight around my thighs, his tongue slowly working me open, exploring every inch of me.

I clutch the arm of the couch, our gazes holding as he drives me out of my mind. When his tongue flicks my clit, I buck against him, earning another deep-seated moan from low in his chest.

"Don't you dare hold back," he warns me. "Fucking ride me, beautiful."

I rock against his face as he sheaths his tongue in me, desperate for more.

Desperate for everything.

But Ash isn't rushing my pleasure. Every time I get close, he slows down, drawing it out. Forcing me to ride that edge.

"Please," I beg, grinding against him as his tongue tortures my clit with short little licks.

I come with a cry, my fingers tangling in his hair and daring him to move his mouth from my skin.

My entire body trembles as I climb off Ash and grab him a towel. "You. Are. Amazing."

He gazes up at me with a grin before interlacing our fingers and pulling me down to rest against his chest.

"See? How relaxed are you now?" he murmurs, pressing a kiss to my hair.

"Hmm."

My truth isn't black and white. My body might be sated, but the bad thoughts linger in the back of my brain, eager to play on my anxieties.

How many women has he used the same lines on, knowing they would fall for them, just as I did—hook, line, and sinker?

That's the trouble with men like Asher Hammond. He's a bad boy with a face of an angel, and every woman dreams of being the one who convinces him to stay.

To settle down.

To change.

It happens, right? All the great romances throughout history can't be bullshit. There must be some shred of truth in there somewhere.

But I'm terrified to be another in the long line of women who fall for Asher Hammond despite his repeated declarations he has zero intention of returning the favor.

"Hey, earth to Ori. Where did you go?"

I trace lazy lines along his chest, feeling the hard muscles beneath the fabric of his t-shirt. "Just thinking."

Ash sighs, resting a hand behind his head. "Stop it."

"Stop thinking? I'm not sure that's possible."

He tangles his fingers in my hair, gently forcing me to meet his gaze. "Stop overthinking and analyzing every scenario. I know you're wondering if I ever plan on taking you out, but I promise I'm not looking for an escape route. Things came up —important things for *Black Lotus* and the speakeasy."

He's not lying—the man is juggling several ventures simultaneously, and somehow, he makes it look effortless. Much like everything else in his world.

Since I signed the lease agreement for the basement renovation, Ash has moved full steam ahead on fulfilling his latest dream—a private speakeasy beneath our businesses.

I'm thrilled for him, although a pang of sadness twists in my chest as I glance around the dimly lit basement, realizing that soon our secret hookup spot will transform into a glitzy hotspot.

No doubt it will be fabulous and sexy as hell, just like everything Ash touches.

No doubt it will also mean even less time together. We'll be drifting into negative numbers soon.

Not that I have any claim to this man. Hell, we haven't even managed a first date and yet here I am, pining for something that never was in the first place.

Get it together, Ori.

I seize on his mention of the speakeasy, redirecting the conversation to benign topics. Anything to pull the focus away from my overactive thoughts about this small-town tattooed legend.

"When do you break ground down here?"

"In a couple of weeks. The foreman figures it will take about two months to get her up and running."

I prop myself on my elbow, shocked by his words. "That quickly? Impressive. Can I borrow your guys once you're done with them?"

"You're opening a bar, too?" Ash asks, tucking a stray strand of hair behind my ear.

"Not hardly. I have my hands full with that house I bought, remember? I need to start renovations before she decays into the ground, but I've got zero experience in home repair. In hindsight, the purchase was a terrible idea."

Ash shakes his head, running his hand along his bearded jaw. "Not terrible at all. That house has good bones, Ori. All she needs is a little love."

"Sounds like someone else I know," I say the words aloud, realizing one second too late how it must sound to a man like Ash. Time to backpedal into safer territory. "Love and power tools I don't own. Seriously, will you hook me up with your contractors once they're finished?"

"No, because that's not their specialty. I can, however, offer my personal services to you."

I snort out a laugh, smacking him lightly on the chest. "Didn't you just do that?"

"More than happy to revisit again and again," he replies, a sexy grin once again dancing across his face.

"I'll have to keep that in mind. Maybe pencil in a standing appointment once per week. Purely for health benefits, of course. Nothing to do with liking you or anything."

Ash chuckles, knowing damn well I'm full of crap.

He knows I like him. I like him way too much and every second with the man only deepens the spell.

That's it. He's a damn witch. It's the only logical explanation.

"Can't have you like me too much," Ash jokes, cupping the back of my head and claiming my mouth in a leisurely kiss. "But for the record, my hands are not just for tattooing or sexual gratification. Braden and I renovated our farmhouse a few years back, and trust me, that was a monster of a job. There's little that can surprise me—construction-wise, anyway."

"Is there no end to your talents?"

He considers my question, then shakes his head, a smirk breaking across his lips. "Guess not."

"Arrogant ass," I laugh.

"How about I head out to your place this weekend and take a look? I'll bring the guys along, and we'll see what needs to be done. Work up a game plan."

"You have no time, remember?"

"For you, I'll make time."

But he hasn't. This entire week, all Ash has made is excuses for why he *lacks* time.

Still, I appreciate the sentiment, even if it's total bullshit.

Apparently, the sour expression on my face reads like a billboard.

"That's it," he murmurs, lifting my slight frame and sliding down on the couch until his mouth is once again level with my pussy. "You're overthinking again. Time to reset that gorgeous brain of yours."

But instead of caving for round two, I press a hand across his mouth, blocking his access. "While incredible, that is not the answer to everything."

"You sure about that?" Another chuckle rumbles from Ash's chest and I can't decide whether to smack him or let him proceed.

I'm leaning toward both. Possibly in tandem.

"I'm positive."

"Fine. Dinner tomorrow night at *Giuseppe's*. It's a great little Italian place a couple of towns over. I'll pick you up at seven."

Just like that, Ash lays down the law.

A law I already know I must break.

Figures.

"I can't tomorrow. I have to get the store ready for Santa."

I'm not lying. While I finished the back corner, there's still a ton of decorating to do before the festive gift-giver arrives to entertain the local kids.

Now it's Ash's turn to groan. "Thursday, then. Same time and place."

I bite my lip, realizing this might be how Ash has been feeling all week. "That sounds great, but I'm working late both nights."

Ash scoffs, his fingers digging into my ribs and eliciting a squeal. "Who's playing games now?"

"I'm not, I swear. I'd love to go, but I really need to get the shop ready for the holidays."

"Let me get this straight. I ask you out and get shot down. Twice."

A grin splits my face as I smack a kiss to his mouth. "To be fair, you've canceled on me three times, so I'm owed at least one more attempt."

Just like that, the heaviness and dread of the last two weeks fall away.

Maybe it's Ash's proximity or the afterglow of the mind-blowing orgasm he gifted me.

Maybe it's because he's trying to live up to his end of the deal.

Maybe it's that dreaded L word lingering between us—the one neither of us dares to utter.

All I know is that I adore every moment with him, with or without clothing.

My onetime nemesis has somehow become one of my favorite people.

Funny how life works out sometimes.

Ash pulls me into another fierce kiss, setting every nerve in my body alight. "Tell me, woman, when can I take you to dinner? Or do you need to consult *your* packed calendar?"

"I'll make you a deal. Since you guys are stopping by to look at the house, I'll treat you all to dinner."

Ash smiles, dragging a finger gently along my cheek. "Takeout will be fine. Besides, I'm on sexual timeout until we have a proper dinner, remember? A date shared with Braden and Zane is not my idea of a good time."

"Knew it was all about the sex."

"Not at all," he replies, his voice dropping. "Though feeling your tight pussy squeezing my cock is about as close to heaven as I've been."

I plant my hands on my hips and roll my eyes.

"What did I do now?" Ash asks, throwing up his hands in mock surrender.

"How many women have you used that line on? Be honest."

"Wait… let me think…" He averts his eyes, tapping his chin as he recounts the numerous women he's bedded over the years.

By the time he meets my gaze, only one of us is smiling.

Newsflash, it's not me.

"I've said it to one woman. A gorgeous librarian type who's glaring holes into me as we speak."

"Likely story," I mumble, feeling the flush climb my cheeks.

"True story."

The bastard and his romantic spoutings.

"*Good* story."

"I have my moments."

I drum my fingers against his chest, feeling his muscles flex beneath my hands. "One more thing."

Ash groans, scrubbing his face with his hands. "Only one?"

"This is business related. Don't lowball the price of the renovations. I want the house restored properly, and I have the funds. Don't cut me slack because I'm your…"

I trail off, unsure of what to call myself. His friend? Neighbor? Fuck buddy?

I know I'm not his girlfriend, although it is my end goal—even if that idea is probably more terrifying to Ash than a drunken monkey with a tattoo gun loose in *Black Lotus*.

"We'll figure it out. I'm not worried," Ash says, his voice steady as his eyes lock on mine. "I'll take care of you."

An emotion flashes in his green eyes. It's not love, but there's a protectiveness there, and I know he means every word.

And believe me, ladies, there is nothing like a strong, handsome man telling you he'll protect you to make you throw caution to the wind.

Trust me.

I skate my hands lower along his thighs, moving ever so slightly against his groin.

"Wait a damn minute," Ash says, gripping my hips. "You have to play fair, beautiful, unless you're planning to renegotiate the terms of our deal."

"Maybe I am." His cock strains against his jeans as I continue grinding against him, my moves slow and deliberate.

"I think someone's all fired up after round one and wants a repeat performance."

"I want *several* encores, Asher Hammond."

"Your wish is my command."

I scratch my nails along his cock, earning a low grunt of

approval. "When you say things like that, how can a woman say no? Want a down payment for services rendered?"

To my surprise, Ash shakes his head, threading his hands into my hair and pulling my mouth to his. "I'm taking you to dinner, Ori. My dick may hate me right now, but I'm doing this right."

"Doing what right?"

"Us."

Chapter 3

I'm Not That Guy

Ash

"Let me get this straight. You want me to give up a day of football and beer to work on Ori's house?"

My brother Braden is none too happy that I've volunteered him for duty this weekend, but I know I can finagle a yes from the guy.

"She's overwhelmed after purchasing the Dean Estate and I don't want to see her get taken advantage of by some sleazy contractor."

Braden snorts out a laugh as we walk over to One More Page for our mid-morning dose of caffeine. "Three weeks ago, you would have relished the idea of her losing her shirt to a scumbag."

"Times change. Besides, you like Ori."

"I always have but *you* felt a distinctly different emotion toward the woman."

I shrug, pulling open the door to the bookstore. "Like I said, times change. Are you in or not?"

Braden sighs, tugging a hand through his dark hair. No doubt he's adding this to my ever-expanding list of IOUs. "I'm in, but you're buying me coffee for the next week."

"Dude, I buy you coffee now," I volley back as we sidle up

to the counter, where Ori's co-worker Mina—her right-hand woman at the bookstore—is waiting with a grin. "Morning, Mina."

I scan the perimeter of the bookstore, but Ori is nowhere in sight. When I turn back to Mina, she's watching me with a sly smirk.

The woman knows exactly who I'm looking for and she's loving every minute of it.

"What can I get you two?" Mina asks, a hint of color climbing her cheeks when Braden offers her a dimpled smile.

What Braden and Mina need is a locked room and some private time, though my brother would sooner die than admit it. I know he's got a thing for the stunning blonde, but he'll never act on it—and I have no idea why.

Something to pick his brain about later.

"That Jamaican blend this guy loves so much." I jerk my chin in Braden's direction before pivoting to take another sweep of the store. "Where's your fearless leader?"

"She's not here yet, which is odd. Ori is never late."

But I know *exactly* why she's running behind. Our pizza picnic didn't end until after three in the morning, when we awoke curled up together on the couch. Despite the warmth of her arms, the cold had settled into the basement, and Ori said it was time to head home.

I begrudgingly agreed.

I rarely hang around long after the deed is done, but it's different with Ori. Something about her embrace just feels right.

Plus, we were busy.

I got that woman off several times last night. Damn, she's breathtaking when she comes. Don't get me wrong—any orgasm is an ego boost, but with Ori, she's on a whole different level.

Plus, she's fucking delicious. Getting her off gets me off, even if my cock and I aren't on speaking terms this morning.

Ori offered numerous times to lay aside her rule about dinner before coitus, but I stuck to my guns.

I *want* to take her out. For some reason, I need to prove I'm not the man she's so sure I am—even though she's had me pegged since day one.

I chuckle and run a hand along my jaw, remembering the taste of her honey on my tongue. "Cut her some slack. I wore the woman out last night."

Mina scoffs at my bold statement, but it's a gentle hip check to my right that steals my attention.

I glance down at Ori, grinning as she shoots me her favorite mock glower.

"Tell me, who did you wear out? Certainly not me, because I'm raring to go this morning," Ori teases, flashing a cheeky smirk.

"You slept well. Admit it," I whisper, leaning down to press a kiss to her cheek.

"Sure. Chamomile tea helps."

"My tongue helps," I volley back.

"Yes, it does," Ori purrs, her eyes fluttering shut as she bites her pouty lower lip.

Fucking tease.

Ori loves pushing my buttons, but what she doesn't realize is I'm more than happy to take full advantage of every perk that comes with our newly forged friendship.

She thinks I won't take her right here? Bend her over this counter and peel those pants from her luscious ass? Sink balls deep inside her as I mark every inch of her as mine?

That visual is enough to wake up *every* body part, desperate for some additional playtime.

I grunt and shift my leg to adjust myself, grateful for the baggy jeans. Without them, there'd be no hiding the effect Oriana Thorne has on me.

But of course, Ori notices. The woman notices everything.

Mina clears her throat, breaking up our flirtations as she slides a cup of coffee my way. "Sorry to interrupt your party."

A bark of laughter escapes my brother, and I realize that I'd forgotten anyone else was here besides Ori.

This isn't the first time, either. Hell, it's *every* time with this petite siren, which is far too dangerous a concept for my taste.

Ori shoots me an appreciative glance as she adjusts her glasses before giving me a playful punch in the arm. "Real nice. Getting me all hot and bothered. Don't you have work to do? Sexy women to ink?"

"Messing with you is far more fun."

She runs her fingers along the collar of her shirt. "You're just hoping for another wardrobe malfunction."

"Prettiest view in town."

She really is. Ori isn't my usual type, but she's exquisite. She's the living embodiment of a sex kitten librarian, and I'll fully admit I have a raging fetish for it.

And for her.

A confident grin splits Ori's face as she rests her palms against my chest. "You'd better go or else we'll have to discuss your behavior in my office."

Fuck, can we? Screw clients. I'd far rather spend the day screwing her.

"Please?" I chuckle, dropping a kiss on her forehead. "Before I forget, me and the guys will be up at your place on Saturday around nine."

Ori claps her hands together, thrilled I haven't forgotten my promise to inspect the damage at the estate house. "You're the best. Thank you for this. I know it's hardly a fun way to spend the weekend, but I'll bring lots of food and hopefully make it a bit less painful."

Braden waves his hand, dismissing her worries. "No problem, Ori. We're happy to help."

He means it, too. Although he'll give me some good-natured ribbing about it, he's fine with missing a few hours of football and beer.

Ori notices a well-dressed customer standing by the antique bookcase and waves toward him. "I have to run, but have a great day."

I watch her stroll over to the man, her face lighting up in a smile as he sets down his briefcase to engulf her in a hug.

A muscle jumps in my jaw as I observe their interactions. All I know is, if he tries that maneuver again, I'm breaking his hands.

Mina notices them, too. "He's been in a few times. Keeps saying he's searching for first editions, but I think he's gearing up to ask Ori out."

The fuck he is.

"Who is he?" I snap, taking a long pull of coffee to hide my irritation.

Mina shrugs. "I think his name is Kevin. Obscenely wealthy, judging by his outfit. That briefcase costs over ten grand."

"Fucking waste of money," I grumble.

I clear my throat, my eyes glued to them as they chat on the other side of the store. Why the hell is he standing so close to her? And why is she letting him?

Then the man glances in my direction as a sneer spreads across his face. Clearly, he's enjoying the reaction he's provoking in me, but if he doesn't back the fuck up, he's going to end up with a pair of black eyes.

"We'd better go," Braden says, nudging my arm. "I don't have bail money."

Swallowing down my jealousy, I huff out a breath, forcing a smile for Mina. "You let me know if he bothers you two. I'll handle it personally."

"Thanks for looking out for us." Mina bites back a smile as she hands us a few muffins from the case. "On the house. Oh, and Ash, I wouldn't worry too much. Seems Ori has a type and he's not it."

I nod and rock back on my heels. "Who said I was worried?"

Mina lets my question lie, but her smile speaks volumes.

And she's not the only one.

From the corner of my eye, I catch my brother's knowing smirk as we stroll back to *Black Lotus*, but I refuse to acknowledge it.

I know what he's thinking, but he's wrong.

Grabbing the tablet at the front desk, I open the appointment app and check over the damage for the day. Shit, we are booked solid.

I was supposed to leave early today, but when Ori told me she had to work late, I opened my schedule back up. Hey, some extra cash is always nice, but I didn't expect *this* in a few short hours.

"Have you seen this?" I hold up the tablet, determined to steer our conversation to neutral waters. "Apparently, the three of us believe there are twenty-eight hours in the day. We need a receptionist, because at this point, there's no time to sleep, eat, or shit. Don't even get me started on extracurricular activities."

"Mm-hmm." Braden's response sounds innocuous, but it's the way he's watching me. No matter how long I linger by the reception desk, I'm not escaping the noose of this chat.

With a grunt, I slug down some coffee. "I know what you're thinking. Don't even say it."

Maybe if I play off my situation with Ori like it's nothing, my little brother will believe me.

No such luck, judging by the shit-eating grin on his face.

"Fucking stop before I beat you."

"What?" Braden throws up his hands in mock surrender. "I'm happy for you."

"There is nothing going on between Ori and me." I

scratch my chin, reconsidering my words. "Okay, there's something, but not what *you're* thinking. We're hanging out. That's all."

"Right," Braden drawls, biting back a laugh. "That's why you're skipping out on your day off to help her repair her house… because you two are buddies."

"Exactly."

"And you only go next door half a dozen times per day because the coffee is so good."

"You said it."

"And you damn near lost it when that guy hugged her."

"Yeah, because he's a sleaze bag and should respect her personal space. Someone has to look out for her—she's tiny, okay?"

"Fucking liar. All I can say is it's about damn time, Ash," Braden retorts.

Crossing my arms over my chest, I pivot to face him. My first appointment isn't for another thirty minutes, which gives Braden plenty of time to give me crap about Ori. "What is that supposed to mean?"

He furrows his brow, clearly perplexed by my question. "You and Ori. It's a good thing. She's a great woman, too. She'd have to be, to coax your ass into settling down."

I slice my hand across my throat in a cutting motion. "Whoa, whoa, whoa. Easy there, killer. No one is taming me or tricking me into settling down. That's not how I roll. You know that."

I expect my stern response to end this chat.

It doesn't.

Instead, Braden perches on the green velvet couch in the reception area, a wary look flickering across his face.

He's going to get into it.

Even though I've told him—nay, warned him countless times to *never* bring it up, he's going digging.

Son of a bitch.

"Ash, it's been over ten years, man. You've got to let it go. Lucille wasn't worth the energy then, and she sure as hell isn't now."

"This isn't about Lucille." Total fucking lie, but it's the only comeback I have at the moment.

"Isn't it? Haven't the last ten years been all about Lucille? She was a heartless bitch, and you're lucky you didn't get caught in her web."

One thing about Braden—he knows how to hold a grudge against my ex.

He also had Lucille pegged from the start, but even after what she did, he never threw it in my face. Never once did he say, 'I told you so,' or remind me how he warned me.

Not that I don't blame myself daily for not realizing the truth sooner. I still do, and nothing can change my mind.

I won't allow it.

Emotional distance keeps me safe, and that's the way I like it.

Now, if only I could convince Braden of that.

"You're right. I'm damn lucky to have slipped Lucille's clutches and I will *never* wind up in that position again. I'll be in my office if you need me."

I make it four steps before he throws out a comeback.

"There's something to be said about a serious relationship with the right woman."

With a choked laugh, I pivot on my heel. "Says the man who's not in one."

"If I met the right woman, I would absolutely consider it. *You've* met the right woman."

"I meet lots of women."

"And you've fucked even more, but are you happy? What Lucille did to you was beyond messed up, but when are you going to stop blaming every woman out there for her indiscretions? When are you going to stop blaming yourself?"

"Dude, if I wanted a therapy session, I'd still be screwing

my shrink." A callous comment, no doubt, but I need Braden off my back about this love stuff.

My brother doesn't get it. His heart has never been decimated.

Mine has, and I'll be damned if it happens again.

Besides, I've been completely up front with Ori about my lifestyle. She knows exactly where I stand on relationships.

I'm honest with *every* woman—no confusion, no false expectations. That way, no hearts get entangled, and no blame gets thrown my way when I have the audacity to stay true to my word.

I keep it simple and straightforward. Any woman who doesn't like it knows where the door is, and I wish her the best in finding a man who can fill that role.

I really do.

Because I'm *not* that guy.

Braden can tell from the set of my jaw that I'm done with this conversation, but although he might walk away now, I haven't heard the last on the subject. When he latches onto an idea—no matter how ridiculous—he's like a dog with a juicy bone. Fucking relentless.

"You're an idiot," he mutters, tossing his coffee cup into the garbage.

"Why? Because I'm telling the truth?"

"You're so mired in past grievances you don't know what the truth is."

That's where he's wrong. I know exactly what the truth is. And it fucking terrifies me.

Will I admit that? Not a chance. Even admitting it to myself takes serious effort.

But Braden sees the difference between Ori and all the other women who have drifted in and out of my life.

I see it, too, and that's exactly why I *must* keep my wits about me.

The raw, unvarnished truth?

The thought that won't stop bouncing around my brain, no matter how much I try to reason it away as insane and impossible?

I don't want to like Oriana Thorne this much.

I don't want her running through my thoughts on an endless loop or her image tattooed in my memory.

And it's not just the sex, though I know that's what Ori believes.

It's everything.

Her smiles, her snarky wit, that husky laugh—even her infamous eye roll when I've stepped in it yet again.

I invent reasons to be near her, even if it's only for a few moments. How I felt like a fucking king when she walked into *Black Lotus* last night and staked her claim on me.

It's all the little moments when she doesn't think I'm paying attention.

And it's exactly why I need to keep her at a safe distance.

I've been down this road before, and I know how the ride ends.

Trust me, it's not pretty, and I'll be damned if I fall down that rabbit hole again.

Not even for Ori.

No matter how tempting the idea.

It must be a full moon.

That's the only explanation for the string of cockups throughout the day. Nothing major, thank God, but countless minor inconveniences in an already swamped day.

First, the phone lines went down. Then the ink delivery I'd been waiting on for days ended up at the wrong address—

again. And when one of the hydraulic chairs gave out mid-session, I was damn near ready to throw in the towel and take up bartending instead.

By the time I finally heed the gnawing hunger in my stomach, it's almost three o'clock. My morning coffee is *long* gone.

On the plus side, I finished a side piece, which took over twelve hours to ink. It was worth every second, judging by the woman's excited squeal when she saw it in the mirror.

A gorgeous woman, too, her extensive ink adding to her already gothic vibe. Turns out the admiration was mutual—she pressed a cash tip and her cell number into my palm before blowing me a kiss and strutting out the door.

"Another number? How many does that make this week?" Zane asks, giving me a slap on the back.

Zane has been at *Black Lotus* for years, so he's well-versed in my dating habits. But let's be real—the man isn't exactly hurting for female companionship, either. Three is his favorite number, and he's never short on takers.

"Five, I think? It's been a slow week." I rub the back of my neck, trying to work out the kinks. "I'm starving and my head is blasting. Want to call in a pizza?"

"No need," a familiar voice chimes in from over my shoulder. "I saw you guys were swamped, so I brought in some fuel for your fires."

A grin breaks across my face when I turn to see Ori standing in the reception area of *Black Lotus*, her arms loaded with bags.

"You didn't have to do that," I say, though I'm so damn glad she did.

Ori shrugs, setting the bags on the table. "No big deal. I stopped at the deli and got several sandwiches, a few sides, and some drinks. Then I swung by the liquor store to grab an after-hours treat for you three."

"You brought us food? I'm so marrying you, Ori." Zane

grabs one bag and peers inside, groaning at the delicious smell.

I know the man is joking, but something about the appreciative looks he's giving my petite brunette irks the fuck out of me.

Hold up. Did I just refer to Ori as mine?

I shoot Zane a stern gaze. "Nice try. Hands off."

"Yeah, I think she's already been claimed," Braden chimes in, giving Ori a high-five before snatching a sandwich from the bag.

"I'll leave you guys to fight over the food. Have a good afternoon. Don't have too much fun with the whiskey." Ori winks at me, flashing a glorious smile before strolling toward the exit.

"Like I said," Braden murmurs, grabbing me around the neck, "you're a fucking idiot if you let her go."

I brush off my brother's comment, but deep down, I know he's right.

Women like Ori don't come along every day and she deserves the best of everything—all the romance, all the trappings.

And sadly, that's something I can't give her.

Thanks to Ori saving our asses—and stomachs—the rest of the day passes without a hitch. Before I know it, the world is dark, and our final customers have vacated the premises.

Time for that after-hours treat.

I stroll to the water cooler and grab three cups, but my gaze lands on a Maybach parked on the opposite side of the now-empty street. The only reason I notice it?

He was there earlier today, too. My money says this car belongs to the asshole in Ori's store this morning.

But her store sits locked up tight, so why is he still here?

Time to shut this situation down, even if it's all in my head.

I unlock the front door and step onto the sidewalk, crossing my arms and pulling myself to my full height. My gaze locks on his vehicle, making it clear I'm onto him.

Sure enough, the engine turns over seconds later, and he pulls onto the street. But he's in no hurry, barely crawling along at ten miles an hour.

When he's parallel to me, the window lowers a crack—just enough for me to glimpse his beady eyes. Then he revs the engine and guns it down the street.

"Asshole," I mutter, shaking my head as I retreat to the warmth of *Black Lotus*.

I grab a cup of whiskey, my gaze drifting to the darkened interior of One More Page.

Ori is gone for the day. Judging by the hour, she's probably asleep by now.

I wonder what she'd do if I dropped by her place.

Then it hits me—I have no idea where she lives. She owns the Dean Estate, but it's uninhabitable. For some reason, not knowing where she calls home doesn't sit well with me.

What if she needs help? Or someone to reach a box on a top shelf?

What if she's lying there right now, thinking of me, hoping I'll make a midnight visit?

What the hell is wrong with me?

Scrubbing my face, I take another sip of whiskey. Have to hand it to the woman—she's got great taste in single malt.

Then again, she's got great taste in everything.

Retreating to my office, I settle in to work on a custom design, but my mind keeps drifting to Ori, curled up in bed, her naked curves begging to be explored.

A woman with the tightest pussy and sweetest taste on the planet.

Get a fucking grip, man. She may be hot, wicked smart and a goddess in bed, but she's still just a woman.

Nope, I don't believe me, either.

She's not just some woman, and if Lucille hadn't ripped me to shreds all those years ago, Ori would be perfect wife material.

I did not just think that.

But I did, along with a million other thoughts centered on Oriana Thorne.

Too bad she didn't stroll into Sparkwood eleven years ago, when my heart was still capable of love.

But Lucille ended any chance of that.

The shop phone rings, and I grab it, assuming it might be a client. Hey, they call at *all* hours.

It's not.

"Hi, cowboy."

My hand tightens on the phone, a death grip to match the unease surging through me. "Lucille?"

Is this some kind of sick joke?

Her husky laugh, so unmistakable, carries through the receiver. "Bingo. What's shaking, bacon?"

Is she serious? My ex is calling me out of the blue to have a casual conversation?

The gall of this woman.

"What can I do for you?"

"Where do I begin?" she replies, her levity grating on my nerves.

"Are you drunk?" That has to be it. Drunk dialing explains a lot. I down the last of my whiskey, knowing I'll need it to get through this call.

"No, I'm not drunk." Her voice softens, the giddy edge fading. "Sorry, I was nervous about calling you."

Lucille? Nervous? That's a first.

I scrub my face with my free hand and groan. "What do you want? I'm exhausted, and I want to go home."

Her voice drops to a whisper, muffled like she's covering the receiver. "I can't talk to you over the phone. I don't know who might be listening."

What in the hell has she gotten herself into now?

"Are you in some kind of trouble?" And if so, *why* are you calling me to discuss it?

"Do you have a free hour or two this weekend?"

Typical Lucille—ignoring my questions and bulldozing me into conceding to her demands.

Sorry, love. I don't play by your rules anymore.

"For what?" I ask, drumming my fingers against my desk. "Is this about that custom piece we did in Vegas?"

"Umm… not really, no," she says, her voice so low I barely catch it.

"Not really? That's a yes or no question, Lucille."

I'm losing patience fast.

"Hang on." Her voice fades, muffled by some garbled exchange in the background.

Honestly, I'm tempted to hang up, because I'm in no mood for her variety of bullshit.

She comes back on the line, the background noise now a dull roar. "That's better. I walked outside."

Why do I care? Better yet, why am I still on this call?

Consider it morbid curiosity.

"So, this weekend? Are you free?" she presses.

"I'm not. I'm helping a… friend with her house. Why do you ask?"

But Lucille continues with her cloak and dagger game. "I need to talk to you, but it has to be in person. Please, Ash, I wouldn't ask if it wasn't important. Do you have time next week?"

She has *got* to be kidding me.

"Of all the people in the world, why are you calling me? Don't you have some friends who can help you?"

"I can't trust them, Ash. You're the only one I can." Her voice wavers, thick with emotion.

Don't do it. This is a terrible idea.

But despite my brain's warnings, I huff out a sigh and relent to her request. "Fine. I can find an hour or two next week. You want to give me your number or—"

"I'll call you. It was great hearing your voice."

The line clicks dead, leaving me staring at the phone.

"Don't tell me that was a last-minute addition to tomorrow's schedule, because my hands are aching." Braden stands in the doorway, massaging his palm.

I lean back in the chair and release a noisy exhale. "That was Lucille."

"What the fuck does she want?"

"To talk."

"Maybe she should have done that ten years ago. You know, told you she was married before she started fucking you?" Braden snarls.

"Good point."

"You told her where to shove her request, right?"

I shrug, pouring another finger of whiskey. "She said it was important. That she can't trust anyone else."

Braden yanks off his ball cap, running a hand through his hair. "Ash, come on, man. You know she's not worth it. Don't do this to yourself."

"I'm not, Braden. She asked to see me this weekend, but I told her we're busy helping Ori."

"Good. I'm glad you told her no."

I run my tongue ring along my teeth, unsure I want to say anything more.

But my brother knows me too well. He reads my silence like a book.

Braden narrows his eyes, his disgust palpable. "You didn't tell her no."

"I told her I'd find time next week. She said it was important," I mutter, sounding like a broken record.

"What's important is getting your head out of your ass before you wind up right back where you were ten years ago," Braden snaps before storming off, throwing up a hand for effect.

There is no love lost between my brother and my former lover, but can you blame him?

Braden had a front-row seat to the nuclear meltdown of my one and only romance.

In the beginning, he loved Lucille, too. She was wild with a devil-may-care attitude that made her fun as hell.

She'd do anything on a dare—including riding topless down the streets of Sparkwood on the back of my bike. Per Lucille, she was in love with all the richness life offered.

Turns out, she was also in love with another man, and that man was her husband.

I learned this valuable piece of information *after* I blew my savings on a diamond ring for the two-timing bitch.

My family and friends rallied around me, but they don't know the whole story.

Everyone thinks Lucille and I ended that night.

We didn't.

A stupid move? You fucking bet. But I was in love with Lucille for a long time—and in hate with her for even longer.

So, when she approached me at a tattoo convention, desperate to talk, I played it to my full advantage.

She wanted a second chance, but I had no intention of giving her my heart.

Not again.

I'd done that one time too many.

I wanted revenge.

And so it played out over the next several years. We'd hook

up occasionally, but it never went beyond the cheap motel room. She was my dirty little secret, always on the down-low, and no one but us was the wiser.

But even that lost its appeal.

When my ex cornered me last week at the Vegas convention, desperate for a little side action, I flat-out refused.

This time, I wasn't interested.

This time, I had Ori waiting for me at home—a fact which really piqued Lucille's curiosity. She asked about my new woman, but I ignored every inquiry.

Ori is none of her business.

A realization settles over me as I acknowledge I don't want to speak to Lucille—not about anything. I don't care if I ever see her again.

Lucille is no longer a part of my life, and that's exactly how it's going to stay.

Braden is right. Any further contact with her is asking for trouble, and Lucille has already brought enough of that to last a lifetime.

"Are you ready to go?" I ask, poking my head in my brother's office. "My headache is back, and I'm ready to call it a night."

Braden meets my gaze, but he doesn't smile. He's still fuming over Lucille's attempt to worm her way back into my world. "Sure. We can go."

"Hey, you're right about Lucille. She's not my problem anymore."

His eyes widen, suspicious of my one-eighty. "You mean that, or are you blowing smoke up my ass?"

As soon as he asks, I know the answer. "I mean it, Braden. She's my past and she's fucking staying there."

"I'm glad. You've got a good woman next door. Don't mess that up."

Braden is right—Ori is spectacular, the total package. But

no matter how many feelings swirl in my gut for that sexy librarian, I know I can't give her what she needs.

Lucille's phone call serves a taunting reminder from the universe that love can't be trusted and that I was played for a fool once.

Love is no longer an option for me. Lucille made sure of that.

Chapter 4

Power Tools Can't Fix This

Ash

"We need to stop for coffee immediately," Zane grumbles as he climbs into the backseat of my truck.

I throw a smirk at my hungover friend before thrusting a travel mug into his hand. "That'll teach you to be out until three in the morning on a work night."

"May I remind you, this was supposed to be a day off? I'm doing your ass a favor, so keep the coffee coming."

"Fair enough," I chuckle, pulling onto the highway.

Ori's recent acquisition, the Dean Estate, sits perched on a ridge about fifteen minutes up the mountain. In her prime, she was the beloved summer home of a real estate tycoon, but years of neglect have dampened her glow.

Here's hoping the work is mostly cosmetic and that rodents and mold haven't gotten a foothold. Otherwise, Ori has one hell of a project on her hands, and, per her own admission, the woman doesn't know the first thing about power tools.

Or hand tools.

Or blueprints.

The list goes on and on.

That's where I come in, along with my two begrudging assistants.

Gazing into the rearview mirror, I toss Zane a lopsided grin. "Which one was it? The brunette or the redhead?"

"Both."

I snort at Zane's deadpan response, knowing full well the man isn't joking. Like I said, three is his favorite number.

"What about you?" Zane asks. "What was your final tally?"

He's referring to this stupid game we play, where the person with the most digits at the end of the week wins.

Look, we're single guys and these women are more than happy to part with their phone numbers, but we never ask for a number. Not only is it unprofessional, but it also strictly violates the rules.

When they offer, though? That's an entirely different section of the rulebook.

I shrug and crack the window, allowing the cold air to filter into the truck's interior. "A handful."

"How many have you called?"

"None."

A gravelly chuckle rises from Zane's chest. "You were right, Braden. She's gotten under Ash's skin."

Once again, I bristle. Time to play dumb. "And who might that be?"

Braden and Zane exchange glances before laughing.

"Who do you think?" Braden says. "The woman whose house we're going to right now. Ms. Oriana Thorne."

I shake my head, drumming the steering wheel in an erratic rhythm. "What a load of garbage. I'm helping a friend because I'm a nice guy. That's all this is."

"Right," Zane drawls, locking gazes with me, open amusement dancing in his eyes. The man is having way too much fun at my expense.

"I told you—" I growl out, but Zane throws up a hand, slowing my roll.

"Relax. I'm fucking with you, although Ori is hot as hell. Just saying."

I'm tempted to reach behind me and grab my buddy by the collar to issue a stern warning about keeping his eyes off Ori, but I swallow it down.

My going apeshit will only solidify their belief that I've fallen into love's trap, and I know for damn sure that won't happen again.

Once is more than enough for this lifetime, thank you very much.

"Ori and I are not dating," I mutter.

We're not anything, aside from newly established friends who have engaged in the greatest sex this world has ever known.

We are the quintessential friends with benefits.

It's a perfect scenario with zero obligation and full-on balls to the walls orgasms.

So why do I feel like an asshole admitting that fact aloud?

"Relax Ash," Braden says, his gaze focused out the window. "After hearing Ori the other day, I realize you two agree when it comes to dating."

Excuse me?

"How the hell do you know?"

And why do I care so much?

"When Ori dropped off the food, a woman pulled her aside and asked if you were single."

"That takes balls."

Braden nods. "I guess she could tell we were all friends and figured she would get the dirt from Ori. Woman to woman or some shit."

"What did Ori say?"

Now Braden's eyes spark with amusement. "That you were single and very popular."

I smack the steering wheel with my palm. "Why the hell would she say that to a complete stranger?"

My brother shrugs, but the smirk never leaves his face. "Maybe because it's the truth? All I'm saying is, you've got nothing to worry about with Ori. She knows where you stand."

Then why does this knowledge bug me so much? Ori's not wrong, but still…

"Fucking hell," I curse under my breath, returning my focus to the road.

Thankfully, I know exactly where this place is, because the entrance is overgrown with vines, completely obscuring the address marker.

I pull down the long, winding driveway that leads to the Dean Estate, trying my damnedest to avoid the potholes which have taken up residence over the years.

"Ori told us to meet her at the carriage house, which I think is around here." I drive around the house to a smaller structure that sits alongside an overgrown English garden. "I guess this is it."

Braden's eyes widen as he takes in the surroundings. "Holy shit, man. It's been years since I've been here. Still can't believe Ori bought it."

"Me, neither. Did I ever tell you I considered buying this place?"

"Seriously?" Zane asks.

"I even mentioned it to Kiki, but she told me it had sold only a few weeks before at auction."

Zane claps me around the shoulder. "And now, our friend owns it. Talk about a small world. I'm bugging her to throw a party once it's restored. It will be sick."

Seems we've beaten Ori here. Might as well take advantage of the free time and poke around the house.

It doesn't take long to complete a quick once-over, but I can see why this project is intimidating to a layperson.

All Ori sees is peeling paint, broken windows, and over-grown shrubbery.

I see potential, and tons of it.

Plus, despite the cosmetic damage, there doesn't seem to be any real structural issues with the house. She'll have to upgrade the electrical and plumbing to meet code, but that's normal in this type of restoration.

She got lucky with this purchase. Now it's time to convince her of that fact.

Ori's truck sits parked outside the carriage house as we round the corner from the front of the estate. Looks like the little lady is finally here.

"Ori, where are you?" I call out, my boots crunching across the gravel path.

"In here," she replies from inside the carriage house. "Sorry I'm late. There was a huge line at the deli. I picked up breakfast and coffee. Help yourself."

I find her in the main room of the carriage house, perched precariously on a rickety ladder, her face a mix of fierce determination and barely contained terror.

Braden and Zane make a beeline for the food, but I have a different destination: getting Ori off the damn ladder.

"Are you kidding? You hate heights. What are you doing up there?"

She clutches the ladder with one hand and points toward a few books on the top shelf of the bookcase. "I think they're first editions."

"I don't care if they're the original printing of the bible. Nothing is worth you getting hurt." I grab her around the waist, pulling her to safety.

"Thanks for the save, cowboy." Ori giggles, reaching up to stroke my jaw, but I freeze at the term of endearment.

It's not because I dislike her use of nicknames, but because Lucille used the *exact* same term with me.

I step back from Ori, cracking my knuckles as I realize my

five-minute chat with my ex-girlfriend the other day has done more damage than I care to admit.

It's triggered an avalanche of memories I spent years trying to forget.

Memories of when I still believed in love and happily ever after.

I force a smile as I struggle to regain my emotional center.

Braden is right. I need to stay as far away from Lucille as possible.

It's not just my heart on the line, it's my sanity.

Ori picks up on the shift in my disposition.

"Ash? Are you okay?"

"Actually, I'm not."

She clears her throat, the smile falling from her face. "Uh-oh. Did I do something?"

Since I refuse to dive into the abyss of my life with Lucille, I decide to focus on something directly involving Oriana.

"Did you tell some woman to give me her number?" I ask, crossing my arms as I lean against the bookcase.

"The other day?"

My jaw slackens at her response. "Has there been more than one?"

Ori rolls her eyes and offers me a casual shrug. "Truthfully? It's a daily occurrence. But no, I'm not giving anyone your number or telling them to hand off theirs. I'm fully aware of your bachelor status, but I draw the line at helping you field women."

At least this topic annoys her, because it sure as hell annoys me.

"You're pawning me off on other women?" I push off the bookcase, narrowing my gaze at her.

Ori huffs out a breath, clearly aggravated. "Hardly."

"Then why talk to them?"

"Because they ask about you. Constantly." She throws her

hands up in exasperation. "What should I tell them? Tell me what to say, so I'll know for future reference."

"Tell them I'm not interested."

The side of her mouth quirks upward. "Blanket statement? Regardless of how hot or sexy she may be?"

"Yes."

"Really? Okay."

I cup her face, tracing my thumbs along her cheeks. "No more hunting dates for me. If someone wants to approach me, they can ask me directly."

Definitely the wrong response.

A muscle jumps in Ori's jaw. "Got it. Did you guys look at the house?"

She's desperate to change the topic. I'm desperate to provide her some reassurance.

"I'm not calling her, Ori."

But my words don't have the intended effect as she averts her gaze. "She will be bitterly disappointed, I'm sure."

Zane walks over, waving around a half-eaten sandwich. "I can't believe you got meatballs and eggs. Best sandwich ever."

"I overheard you saying something about it the other day," Ori says offhandedly. "I hope it's good."

"Amazing," Zane replies, shoving another bite into his mouth. "Ori, how about you forget this guy and marry me instead?"

A grin breaks across Ori's face at his offer, but I'm not smiling. I glower at my buddy over Ori's head. Doesn't matter if he's kidding. This is the second time he's mentioned stealing Ori from me.

He'll learn the hard way I don't share.

As if picking up on the tension, Ori points to the table and chairs in the center of the room. "Come on, guys. I know you're putting your social lives on hold to help me out, so let's not waste anymore of your weekend."

We gather around the table and dig into our breakfast. Figures the woman would bring us a gourmet feast.

"I'm going to ask the question that we're all wondering," Zane proclaims, pointing a finger at Ori before stuffing the rest of his sandwich in his mouth. "How in the world did you afford this place? Are you secretly a queen of some small but wildly wealthy land?"

"Of course," Ori replies, not missing a beat as she waves her hand with a regal air. "An evil queen, to be sure, and you're all now my captors."

Then she laughs and I realize how different she sounds from Lucille. While both women have smooth voices, Ori's laughter is lilting. Kinder.

It stirs something in me, along with pretty much every other facet of Ori's personality.

If only…

Ori wraps her hands around her coffee cup, her expression pensive. "I received an inheritance from an estranged relative. I held onto the money for the first year because I had no clue what to do with it. Part of me wanted to cash it in and set it all on fire, but that seemed silly and dramatic—plus a total waste of lighter fluid."

"Next time you come across a pile of cash you don't want, I'll take it," Braden offers with a grin.

"Deal." She shakes her head as she glances around the carriage house. "My parents used to bring me here as a little girl for the fall festival and every time, without fail, I made them drive past the Dean Estate. When I moved here, I asked Kiki about the place. Just as a lark, you know? She told me about the auction and before I could think through my crazy scheme, I bought it. Pissed off some developers big-time in the process."

"Damn, woman. That's impressive." I loop my arm around her shoulder, pulling her into my embrace.

But Ori slips from the cocoon of my arms and begins

pacing the wooden floor. "Enough stalling. Lay it out for me. Was this a good purchase or the dumbest idea of my life?"

"It's not that bad," I state, but my words do little to reassure her as her gaze falls on my brother.

"Is he just saying that?"

Braden chuckles, shaking his head. "It's going to take some work, but at first glance, she's solid. No evidence of mold, which is a huge plus."

"Granted, we won't know the full extent until we tear out the walls, but I'm telling you, this house has good bones."

"Just needs a little love," Ori sighs, playing with the end of her long braid. "Don't we all?"

I don't respond to her comment, although I'm fully aware she's repeating my words back to me.

However, her version has a far different meaning attached to it.

Look, I get it. Ori is the type of woman who wants the whole happily ever after scenario. I want her to have it, too.

Even if it kills me to know it's not a possibility with me.

But I have no desire to dive into that sticky conversation. Far safer to keep us on task and focus on the house.

I grab my coffee and move to the far side of the carriage house, leaning against the wall with a sigh. "Here's the deal: the main house is going to take months, maybe even a year, of full-time restoration. It'll require all kinds of skilled craftsmen to pull it off."

Ori buries her face in her hands. "That bad?"

"Hey." I walk over to her and put a finger under her chin, forcing her to meet my gaze. "I haven't gotten to the good part yet. They turned the carriage house into a two-bedroom apartment probably twenty years ago, so it won't take much to make this space livable—buy some new windows, cabinets, appliances, polish the floors and throw on a fresh coat of paint."

I mean my words to soothe her, but the furrow creasing her brow only deepens with every sentence.

"So basically, a total overhaul? What was I thinking?" Ori swings her arms, her eyes bright with tears. "I must have been certifiable that day at the auction to think I could move to a new town, open a store, and renovate a dilapidated mansion all in one go."

"Nah, just determined. Like I said, I'm glad you bought it. I was afraid some investors were going to tear it down and build condos."

"Trust me, they're lined up, hoping I fail."

"But you won't."

"How do you know?"

I lock my arms around her slight frame, smiling when she melts into my embrace. "You, Oriana Thorne, don't fail when you set your mind to something."

"Does that apply to you, as well, or are you exempt from that equation?" A teasing grin lights up her face as she lightly smacks my chest. "Don't look so stricken. I'm just playing. So, what's the plan? Can you refer me someone to start the work?"

I nod, stealing a quick kiss from her pouty lips. "Absolutely, and we're here now. Let's break some shit."

Demo work is fun work. Plus, it gets out a ton of pent-up frustration and rage. Trust me, after Lucille's phone call, I need to beat the piss out of something.

A few hours later, we've demoed the kitchen and bathroom, working up quite an appetite in the process. Have to hand it to Ori. She plays with the big boys—guess she's working out her frustrations, too.

"Shall I order some pizza for us or would you rather I give you cash, and you get the hell out of here?" Ori asks, wiping the sweat from her brow.

Fuck, but she looks amazing right now—her skin glistening, tiny pieces of drywall in her hair, her cheeks flushed with color.

Pretty sure she'll disagree with my assessment, but there's something about a woman who doesn't need to get dolled up all the time.

Doesn't hurt that I know exactly what deliciousness lies beneath her clothes, either.

Braden checks the time on his phone. "As amazing as pizza sounds, we're meeting some people at the bar."

Ori bends at the waist with a loud groan. "Thank God. I'm so glad you said that."

We gather our tools and stow them in the truck. Ori meets us outside the carriage house and hands Braden and Zane a couple of hundred-dollar bills apiece.

"Thank you for everything."

"This is too much," Zane argues, but Ori waves him off. "Ash, can I please take her home? She's gorgeous, funny, smart, and generous. They don't make women like this anymore."

"Back off, Romeo." I slam down the lid to my toolbox, shooting a death stare at Zane.

His persistence is beginning to piss me off.

"Last but certainly not least," Ori says, pressing some cash into my hand. "Thank you. I'll be right out. Just have to lock up."

"Wait a second." I catch up to her and pin her against the exterior door. Then I slide the money into her back pocket, resting my hands against the swell of her ass. "Keep your money. That's not the payment I want."

She gazes up at me through her dark lashes. "What would you prefer?"

"Dinner and then you for dessert."

Ori bites her lip, considering my request. "Do you want to come over tonight? Skip out on football and spend the evening with me? I'm a hell of a cook, so I can whip us up some dinner, we can have some wine, and then maybe a bubble bath. What do you think?"

It sounds fucking perfect, much like her, which is why turning her down sucks.

"That sounds incredible, but I'm working tonight."

Her eyes widen behind her glasses. "I thought your shop was closed for the holidays."

"I have a custom piece to finish. Raven called last night and asked if I could squeeze her in. She's filming in Vegas next month and wants it fully healed before then."

Ori leans against the door, her face a careful mask of neutrality. "Raven. She's the Snow White-Jessica Rabbit mashup from the holiday festival, right?"

"Yeah."

A sense of unease settles over me, which is stupid, really. I'm not doing anything wrong and yet, it feels that way.

Plus, I know Ori doesn't hold Raven in high regard, and I don't blame her. Raven messed with her head in an attempt to land a spot in my bed.

Didn't work out in her favor, but despite my claims that nothing happened between me and the adult film star, I get the sneaking suspicion Ori doesn't buy it.

Ori shifts her gaze to her ring, spinning it around her finger. "Have fun. I know she enjoys… spending time with you."

I shrug, desperate to play it off. "It's just work, you know."

"Does she know that?" Ori waves her hand, as if dismissing the question. "Ignore me. It's none of my business."

She's right, so why doesn't that make me feel better?

Because she's right about *all* of it—she knows Raven wants to sleep with me and if my reputation is to be believed, she knows I'll take her up on it.

But will I act on that offer, should Raven make it?

I don't think so, and I need Ori to know that.

"Enough talk of work. What about tomorrow?" Yes, I'm being forward, but I can't leave here like this, with this ever-widening emotional space between us.

She cocks her head up at me. "For what?"

"That home-cooked meal you promised."

Ori releases a slow breath as she fiddles with her keys. "Umm… sure. Six o'clock work for you?"

The uncertainty lining her voice kills me, making me feel even more guilty about my appointment with Raven later tonight.

"Actually, could we do something earlier? How about three-thirty?"

Yes, it's ridiculously early for dinner, but there's a method to my madness.

Ori wipes a hand across her brow, growing more agitated by the second. "Why not?" She jerks her chin toward my truck. "You'd better go. The guys want to get some food and beer in them."

Trouble is, I don't *want* to go. I'm happy spending the next week leaning against this door with Ori's body mere inches from mine.

And I feel like an asshole about the whole Raven situation, even though I'm not doing anything wrong. I *am* working, even though Ori and I both know Raven wants some playtime afterward.

But Ori and I aren't exclusive. Hell, we aren't even dating.

Ori is well aware of my dating habits—with no commitments or hearts involved—so why does this feel so fucking wrong?

I could have lied and claimed I was going to the bar with Braden and Zane, but isn't that worse?

"Hey," Zane yells from the truck, "today, dude."

Ori forces a smile. "Drive safely, and thank you for today. You're a great guy."

"Right," I mutter.

Truth is, I'm a heartless cad who fucks women because I'm incapable of love—or letting anyone love me.

"I'm serious. You've helped me so much with this house and not just the demolition, although that was beyond therapeutic. You gave me an honest breakdown of the repairs needed, along with an idea of price, so some contractor can't take advantage of me." Ori rests her palm against my chest, rises on tiptoe and presses a kiss to my cheek. "Now get out of here. I'm going to spend a few minutes in the atrium before calling it a night."

With a tired sigh, I trudge back to the truck and slide behind the steering wheel.

Braden, as always, picks up on the subtle change in my mood. "Are you two okay?"

Huffing out a breath, I tug a hand through my hair. "Yeah… I just… let me get you guys home."

I don't want to get into it. Mainly because I don't know what I'm feeling right now.

Ori let me off the hook. Even wished me a good time with Raven tonight. I don't owe her anything, so why do I feel like the biggest asshole on the planet?

"Hey." Zane reaches up from the backseat, giving me a friendly punch in the arm. "You want some women to get under your skin. It's not always a bad thing."

That's as far as he takes it, but he's said enough. His words hit their intended mark, and he's right. Ori has gotten not just under my skin, but into every cell of my body.

I'm just not sure what to do with that knowledge.

"Listen up, handsome. I have an empty suite just waiting for some serious action." Raven shoots me a coy wink as I put the finishing touches on her tattoo. "I also brought along some special lingerie and a few toys for the occasion."

Raven is a guaranteed good time. A woman with no strings attached and with moves that have captured the adult film industry's imagination.

A woman I can't sleep with—not tonight or any night.

About a million men would kill to be me right now—and yet, I'm not thinking about Raven, at least not beyond her ink.

My mind has been on Ori the entire evening, and the hurt in her eyes knowing what I *might* be doing right now.

A hurt I plan to rectify tomorrow.

"Ash, are you listening?" Raven asks.

"I heard you."

A small smile quirks her red lips. "But… you're still hung up on your little librarian, aren't you?"

I chuckle as I rest my machine in its holder. "Pretty much."

"And I can't convince you otherwise?"

I shake my head. That's a solid no. "I don't think anyone can."

Chapter 5

You're in the Friend Zone, Man
Ori

I need to stop. I've checked the food fifteen times in as many minutes. At the rate I'm going, it might be done by Christmas.

I'm so nervous I can't think straight, which is laughable in and of itself. Why be nervous? I'm cooking for a man who has legions of women at his disposal.

Including one adult film star, who no doubt showed Ash a plethora of positions last night… while I brooded about it alone in my bath.

Oh, and the icing on the cake is that no woman stands a chance at bagging the comely artist. Ash doesn't believe in the concept of love or romance or any of those silly trappings.

What am I doing? I hardly need to cook for him if I want to get laid. All I have to do is ask, and I'm sure Ash will fit me into his rotation.

I swallow back the bile rising in my throat at that visual.

Doesn't that sound delightful? Right up there with Lucifer's Christmas display.

I don't know what I'm trying to prove. Per everyone who knows Ash, which is everyone in Sparkwood, he's a wonderful man, so long as you don't expect him to drop to one knee.

Both knees? That's a possibility.

Hey, I speak the truth. Anything sexual is on the menu. Intimacy? That's off limits. It's not just hearsay, it's a verifiable fact regarding Sparkwood's infamous bad boy.

But here I am, the eternal optimistic romantic, ready to serve dinner to a man who has told everyone in our town that love is for idiots.

"Ori, snap out of it. You knew all this. Ash is a good time. You can't look for anything beyond that."

The words taste bitter in my mouth, no doubt because I want to choke on every one of them. I don't believe a word I'm saying.

Correction, I believe Ash is only in it for a good time, but I want more.

Somewhere along the line, I morphed from an optimist to a masochist, apparently.

The proof being that I watched him drive off to spend hours alone with an adult film star—a woman who's desperate for a slice of Ash's pie. And she's not some run-of-the-mill hottie. No, Raven Scarlet is *the* it girl of the adult entertainment world—and trust me, I watched enough of her videos last night to commiserate. She oozes sex appeal and is apparently double-jointed everywhere to bend into some of the pretzel positions she manages on-screen. She's bedded a legion of men and women, all beautiful in their own right.

Now Ash is among them.

Oh, he claims it was 'just work' but come on. I may have been born at night, but it wasn't last night.

Plus, she's the bitch who intimated Ash only slept with me because of the speakeasy. She took great delight in it, too, and even though Ash negated that theory, part of me believes there is truth in her words.

Something else came of that knowledge—a comparison between the woman he spent last night with and the woman staring back at me from the bathroom mirror.

Total opposites. Literally, nothing in common.

I know I'm fun in bed, but I'm not swinging from the chandelier level. Plus, my boobs and ass are of normal proportions, which next to Raven likely appear downright miniscule.

But tonight isn't about any of that. It's simply a thank you to Ash for yesterday. He's earned this dinner because he was a tremendous help with my pet project.

Yes, my fixer-upper mansion has a new nickname, and at least it's better than 'what the hell was I thinking,' which is what I originally called it. Ash assured me the house was structurally sound, and that I made a good investment.

Once I slog past the gazillion items on my to-do list, I'll have one hell of a mansion—in between running my store and trying *not* to compare myself to porn royalty.

Ori, what the hell were you thinking?

Seems to be a running theme in my brain these days.

But Ash and I are just friends, which feels safe. Now I just have to convince my body that friends don't always equal benefits—because benefits, while terribly enjoyable, also tend to muck up my heart.

Best to leave Ash in the friend zone and rely on my vibrator for orgasms.

Good plan.

The doorbell rings and my gaze cuts to the clock. Right on time. No doubt he's running a tight ship, with at least one other woman lined up after our afternoon soiree.

Lovely thought.

I pause by the foyer mirror and bite back a laugh. I look ridiculous, with my hair perched atop my head in a crooked bun and flour crisscrossing my chin and cheeks.

Don't even get me started on my outfit.

"Screw it. This will have to do," I mutter before swinging the door open. "Hi, there."

As always, the butterflies cut loose the moment I lay eyes on him. Can you blame me? Ash cuts one hell of a figure in his tight-fitting jeans and leather jacket, and he knows it, as evidenced by the smirk on his full lips when my gaze finally travels upward enough to meet his. "Hey, yourself. Am I early?"

If I had spent three hours getting ready, he wouldn't notice. But when I look like a hot mess? He picks up on it instantly.

"Here I thought this look upped my sex appeal. Come in."

Ash pauses on the threshold, grasping my chin with his hand. "You're always sexy, Ori. But if you're worried, lose the clothes and I'll gladly reassure you."

See? Anything my sexual little self desires, so long as it never, and I mean *never*, includes my heart.

Far too dangerous a game for me to consider.

"Get in here."

I lead him into the kitchen and motion to the stove. "The food will be done in just a minute. Would you like a drink?"

Ash pulls two bottles of wine from a paper bag. "How about one of these?"

"Look at you, bringing options."

"Always come prepared."

In more ways than one.

Since we won't drink more than one bottle, I can only assume the other one is for his dessert date later this evening. Wonder if his favorite porn star is still in town?

Time to pump up the volume on our friendship angle. "Wow. These are nice bottles. Did you pick these or did the hot little number in the liquor store help you?"

Ash chuckles, but a hint of flush crawls up his cheeks. "What hot little number?"

"Asher Hammond, we both know she's hot. No need to pretend you haven't noticed."

Why am I bringing up other women in front of him? Probably my ego's way of putting up a shield. The classic preemptive strike—let Ash know I'm well aware of his reputation, so he doesn't have to pretend to be anything different.

Besides, friends don't stand on ceremony. We can be upfront, brutally honest. That's what friends do, right?

After all, Asher was brutally honest with me yesterday when he told me of his plans for the evening.

I hate playing this game. I'm no good at being friends with a man I have a mad crush on. You'd think in thirty-nine years I would have figured it out, but no, I'm still as clueless as ever.

"The cashier was about seventy-five… and a guy." Ash pops the cork, passing the bottle under his nose. "And I chose these wines."

Interesting. "Didn't peg you for a wine connoisseur."

"There's a lot you don't know about me."

"Well, I'm about to cross one item off my list. Let's see if you like my cooking."

I'm a damn good cook, but that wasn't always the case. For years, I subsisted on granola bars and protein shakes, but after learning how terrible most of those aforementioned foods were for my body, I decided to go organic. Turns out, I have quite the knack in the kitchen.

Who knew?

"It sure smells amazing in here," Ash comments, settling into a kitchen chair. "Anything I can do to help?"

I push a stubborn stray from my face and shake my head. "It's all done. The only thing that isn't ready is me, but you're going to have to deal with my less than stellar appearance. Give me five minutes to clean up?"

Ash nods, his gaze traveling the length of my form. "Need some help?"

If he'd made that offer yesterday, I would have jumped at the opportunity. But somehow, knowing the identity and notoriety of the woman he bedded last night has tarnished the glow.

That and I know I can't swing around a shower rod like

Raven did in one of her videos. I stand under the spray like a normal person, which is quite boring in retrospect.

Friend zone, Ori. Keep it in the friend zone.

"Sure. How about you light the candles and find us some music? I have a ton of vinyl." I nod toward the record case, leaning against the far wall.

"Any artist in particular?"

"Surprise me."

Ten minutes later, I emerge from my bedroom, looking only slightly better than before. At least I managed to wash off the lingering scent of flour and onions from my four-hour cooking spree. I decide to forgo any real makeup in lieu of comfort—leggings, an oversized blouse, and a bun that now sits centered on my head.

I pad into the kitchen and grab the glass of wine Ash left on the counter, smiling when I hear the familiar strains of Frank Sinatra playing over the speakers. "You have good taste. Great wine, great music—"

"Great company," Ash interjects, stepping in front of me and plucking the wine glass from my hand. His palms glide up my sides, leaving a trail of sparks in their wake. Framing my face with his hands, he leans in, his mouth brushing mine. "You smell good enough to eat," he murmurs, his voice low and teasing. "Too bad we'll have to wait until dessert."

I push my glasses up my nose, trying desperately to tamp down the feelings flooding my core. "You brought dessert, too?"

Ash leans against the counter, his eyes devouring every inch of me. "You *are* dessert, Ori and I plan on having a few helpings tonight."

God damn, but he's so good at that. Each line, carefully crafted to shoot straight to a woman's pussy, all while completely short-circuiting her ability to think of anything beyond him.

This is why I nicknamed him the Pussy Whisperer.

It's voodoo of the highest order.

It's also why it's imperative for me to maintain some sense of focus. Keep my heart on a shelf far from Ash's clutches—not that he wants that part of my body, regardless.

Time to regain control of this conversation train and steer it to safer—albeit far less enjoyable—waters. "Let's see if you like dinner well enough to stay for dessert first. Have a seat."

Ash's eyes widen at my abrupt pivot away from sexy time, but he follows my command and settles into a chair.

"Hope you're hungry. I made garlic focaccia and chicken saltimbocca."

"When you said Italian, I figured you meant spaghetti and meatballs."

I pause, the spatula hovering midway between the pan and the plate. "Would you rather have that?"

"Hell no. I'm just surprised."

I hand him a plate, a grin splitting my face as he inhales the fragrant goodness. "Why? I told you I could cook."

Ash gestures to the food. "You did, but this is gourmet level. And it's a traditional Roman meal."

"Is that a problem?"

"Did you know my grandmother was born in Rome?"

I rest my chin in my hand, giving him a slight shrug. "I had no clue. Did she make these dishes for you when you were growing up?"

"She did, but it's been a long time." Ash leans back in his chair, swirling his wine as a flicker of humor dances in his eyes. "You really didn't know? Braden didn't give you a heads-up?"

A bolt of irritation flashes through me at his egocentric remark. "Oh, I see. This is how women woo you, isn't it? Ply you with a genuine Roman dish hoping to win your heart?"

"It's happened once or twice," he murmurs, his gaze steady and intent on me.

"No doubt *way* more than that." I hold back a laugh

at the surprise flickering across his features and turn my focus to my plate. Taking a bite, I release a low moan of satisfaction. "While I admire their efforts—futile as they may be—mine is pure coincidence. I took cooking classes from a woman who hailed from Roma. She taught me a few tricks, although I suppose you'll be the judge of that."

Ash stays silent for a few beats before setting his glass on the table. "Huh. You're full of surprises, Ori."

"That's probably because you know nothing about me, Ash." I gesture toward his plate with a smirk. "Now, less talking, more eating."

"Don't have to tell me twice." Ash takes a bite, and a low groan escapes him as the flavors hit. "Damn, little one. You've outdone yourself. This is spectacular. My grandmother would've been proud."

"That was the goal. You liking it? That's just a bonus."

This time, his laugh is genuine. It's strange because I've only really known the man a couple of weeks, but I know his different laughs.

There's one for the public—affable and polite. Another for his close confidantes, a sharp snicker that borders on mischievous. And then there's this one, warm and unguarded, like an embrace without the use of his arms.

I've only heard that laugh when we're alone and I like to think it's something special.

Am I reading too much into it? Likely, but a girl has to get her romance somewhere.

"To amazing food, incredible wine, and exquisite company. Thank you. This may be the best meal I've ever had."

I sputter my wine at his statement. "Don't say that too loud, or your grandmother might come back to haunt you."

"She probably would—and then join you in the kitchen to whip up a feast. She would've loved you." He shifts in his seat after saying the words, like he's just let slip something he hadn't meant to.

"I'm sure I would've loved her, too," I reply softly, leaning in. "Could've picked her brain for all her culinary tips. Tell me about your family. I want to know all their deep, dark secrets."

"We're not that interesting," he says with a faint smile, deflecting.

"Now that's a lie, isn't it, Asher Hammond? I'm certain you have scads of stories. Time to sing for your supper."

But Ash doesn't want to talk about his family. He has something else on his mind.

Leaning his arms on the table, he fixes me with his piercing green gaze. "I think it's time you told me about *you*."

"What about me? Compared to your life, I'm the definition of staid and boring. Look it up in the dictionary, and you'll find my picture."

"Not a chance." His lips curve into a slight smirk. "Can I cut through the bullshit and be brutally honest?"

I click my tongue against my teeth, unsure I want to traverse this path. "Sure. Wait—let me grab more wine for this conversation."

"It's not that bad."

"Says the man who just announced he's about to be brutally honest," I shoot back, raising a brow.

"No, I'm asking *you* to be brutally honest."

I wave my hand, dismissing him. "Tomato, tomato. Go ahead, ask me."

"You said you bought the Dean Estate with money from an inheritance. I'm assuming your parents?"

"Something like that," I reply, averting my gaze out the window.

Ash nods and helps himself to some more food, but his gaze finds mine again, silently prompting me to continue.

I think I'd rather discuss his night with the porn star.

"You don't have to tell me. I just want to know you, Ori."

Damn it. With a line like that—so earnest and real—how can I not empty my skeletons out of the closet?

"My father died. I didn't even know it happened until a week after he passed."

"You weren't speaking?"

"Not for years. My twelfth birthday surprise was that my father had another family and was leaving my mother and me to live with them. His mistress worked with him at the law firm, but it was hardly an overnight affair. They had been in love since high school—at least, that was his claim. Only hiccup was my father was married with a small child. Not that it stopped them. He carried on a secret affair for a decade, with all his extra money going to support her and *their* son. When I turned twelve, I was apparently old enough to know the truth. Happy birthday to me."

Ash runs a hand through his hair, leaning back in his chair as he exhales a slow breath. "Holy shit, Ori. I'm so sorry. I didn't mean to open that can of worms."

"It's fine."

But Ash doesn't buy my blasé response. "No, it's pretty fucking far from fine."

I fiddle with my napkin, folding and unfolding it along the crease. "You're right. Betrayal like that never goes away—it hardens you, turns you against what, or who, you used to love. You never fully recover."

Ash stiffens, a strange look passing over his features. "That's the damn truth. You're never the same."

He's speaking about his first love, the one who destroyed him years ago—the one he can't move on from, and the reason he hates love today.

But I won't press him for details about her. The last time I asked, that first night in the basement, I saw the scars on his psyche—and they're deep.

They might be deeper than mine.

"How could your father abandon you? How could any father abandon their kid?"

I take a swallow of wine, grateful for the warm flush it provides against this cold conversation. "He tried to reconcile with me several times, but I didn't want to hear it. I was too angry to realize that forgiveness was the only way to release the hurt. Open that safety valve, you know? His last letter told me how sorry he was for what he did, how proud he was of me, and how he wanted to do right by me. It arrived with a notice that I was the beneficiary of his life insurance policy. Two million dollars."

"I see now why you wanted to burn it."

"I'm glad I didn't, although it was mighty tempting at the time." Grabbing the wine, I top off my glass. "Can we switch to a lighter topic of conversation?"

Ash nods, refusing my offer of more wine. "What's that big, sealed box by your record player? The one with the stickers all over it."

A rush of color climbs my cheeks, and I shake my head, biting back a smile. "Next question."

"Is it that embarrassing?"

"Yes."

"Now you *have* to tell me." He leans over, squeezing my knee. "Is it a box of sex toys or something?"

I burst out laughing, covering my mouth with my hand. "Absolutely not. If it were, if sure as hell wouldn't still be sealed."

A smirk dances across his face. Clearly, he doesn't believe me.

"What? It's not sex toys," I insist.

"Damn. That's disappointing, because those are mighty fun to play with."

"You would know," I volley back.

Ash stands and drops a kiss on my forehead before

carrying his plate to the sink. "Apparently so would you, considering you have a box of the damn things."

"It's a wish box."

Ash narrows his gaze at me. "What the hell is that?"

"Items I've gathered over the years for my wedding, my first baby, my first home. That sort of thing."

Ash nods, marinating on my words. "Kind of like a scrapbook."

"Sort of, but for memories that haven't happened yet."

"So, no vibrators in there?" Ash asks with a wink.

I chuckle. "With the right man, I won't need a damn vibrator."

"I'll volunteer as tribute," Ash says, realizing in the same moment I do the weight of his words. "Just saying, I've been told by a certain someone that I'm the Pussy Whisperer."

"You love that nickname, don't you?"

"Wouldn't you?"

Just like that, his humor softens the edges of our earlier conversation.

Although, he does seem eager to move this dinner along.

He's cleared half the table and glanced at his phone three times in the last ten minutes.

A girl can take a hint.

I point toward the door. "You can head out. No need to wait for me to finish. I like to take my time with my wine."

Ash rests his forearm on the table, shooting me a stern look. "Where do you think I have to go?"

"A date, I presume."

"That's what you think?" he scoffs, running a hand through his hair. "That I'm rushing out of here to see another woman?"

"It makes sense. You wanted an early dinner. You brought two bottles of wine. You're watching the clock."

Ash takes my free hand, his lips brushing softly across my knuckles. "You are way off. I brought two bottles because I wasn't sure what you were cooking, and I'm watching the clock because I have somewhere to take us—and the sun sets so damn early this time of year."

I frown, glancing down at my leggings. "I'm really not dressed to go out."

"Put on pants, then."

"See, that was code for I don't want to leave the warmth of my apartment and go sit in some bar. No offense."

Ash grabs the back of my chair, pulling it gently from the table. "Lucky for you, I'm not taking us to a bar. Now go throw on some jeans. In fact, I'll help you. Wait, on second thought, I better not—if I strip those off you, we're definitely not leaving."

"Sounds like you're still hungry, Asher."

He bends down, his breath warm against the back of my neck as he nuzzles the skin there. "For you, I'm always hungry."

Universe, hold up a damn minute.

I stop dead in my tracks when I meet Ash outside and see him waiting on his motorcycle.

Yes, I'm aware he owns one, but I assumed we were taking something with windows and a roof, especially since it's a brisk forty-five degrees and falling fast. Never mind that I'm a motorcycle virgin.

"I don't have a helmet."

Ash pulls one from his saddlebag and places it on my head. "I've got you covered."

"But I've never ridden before," I stutter, worrying my lower lip with my teeth.

"If you're my girl, little one, you've got to ride. Trust me—I won't let anything happen to you."

I don't know if it's the way he uses my pet name or the quiet promise in his eyes that melts my hesitation, but I nod in agreement. With a deep breath, I push aside the fear and take his outstretched hand.

Time to trust the man.

Fifteen minutes later, Ash steers down a narrow road, stopping at a rocky outcropping. The winter sun kisses the horizon, spilling a breathtaking blend of pinks and purples across the sky.

"It's incredible," I murmur, offering Ash a grateful smile as he helps me off the bike. I step closer to the edge, letting the view steal my breath. "The most beautiful sight ever."

"Yes, it is."

But Ash isn't looking at the overlook. His green-hued gaze is locked on me, hunger blazing in its depths, undeniable and all-consuming.

I could cave to his intimations, which is exactly what my body is begging me to do, but my heart isn't on board with being just a helping to his several-course dinner.

Best to keep our conversation on the straight and narrow. "Do you come here often?"

"Yes, but I never bring anyone with me."

An odd response. "How come?"

He sighs, his gaze fixed on the valley below. "I'm afraid they'll ruin it for me."

I wander back to the bike, my fingers brushing over the smooth lines of the handlebars. "Why did you bring me?"

He catches my hand, his fingers wrapping gently around mine. "Because somehow, I know you never will."

His sweet words resonate with my heart. No matter his long-term intentions, Ash trusts me, and that feels special coming from a man who walled off his heart years ago.

I straddle the bike seat and press a soft kiss against his

cheek. "I never will. Thank you for entrusting me with this place."

His hands settle on my thighs, giving them a light squeeze. "I wanted to come by your apartment last night."

"Really? I assumed you and Raven…" I trail off, unwilling to dredge up any more mental images of them together.

Ash shakes his head. "I finished her tattoo and went home."

Well, this is an interesting turn of events, because I know Raven would love a piece of him. "Guess all that demo work caught up with you."

Am I sorry about this hiccup in his plans? Not in the slightest.

Ash huffs out a breath, his focus shifting back to the mountain view. "I wasn't too tired. I just… didn't want to hang out with her."

He doesn't say more, but somehow, it's enough.

Reading between the lines, I know I'm the reason—and I hate how warm and fuzzy it makes me feel.

"So, why didn't you come by?"

Ash chuckles, his hands gliding along my legs before slipping beneath my ass. "Because I felt like an asshole. I knew what you thought was going to happen with me and her, and I felt stupid for not doing a better job reassuring you it wasn't. That nothing was going to happen with her—because I had someone *far* more important to see today. But I really wanted to see you last night. The idea of you, wine, and a bubble bath sounded spectacular."

Looping my fingers around his neck, I shift closer, draping my legs over his. "How about you make it up to me and *show* me how spectacular I am?"

His brows shoot up at my bold statement. "Right here? Okay."

I'm glad he's on board for a little public display, even if the chill is biting harder by the second. "Fabulous idea, but I might freeze my tits off if we do it right here. How about taking me home and giving me that dessert you promised earlier?"

Ash narrows his gaze at me, his fingers squeezing me tighter. "See, that's not the deal, remember? I have to take you out to dinner first."

In my mind, it's semantics.

I dust my mouth against his, teasing his lower lip with my tongue. "Fuck the deal. How about you fuck me instead?"

Ash pulls back just a fraction and slides his hands along my jaw, cupping my face. He presses a tiny kiss to my nose, then each cheek, before settling on my lips. "I don't like that term."

"What term?"

"Fucking. It's too caustic. Too raw."

My heart flips at the tenderness in his eyes as he speaks the words.

Even if he can't say it outright, I am different. I see that now.

With a soft smile, I steal another kiss. "It is a bit crude, isn't it? How about this—forget the dinner deal and spend the rest of tonight making me feel so damn good I forget my name? Does that work for you?"

A smile cuts across his face as he claims my mouth in a slow, drugging kiss. "That I can do. But first, turn around."

I oblige, shifting closer when he wraps his arms around me, his chin settling on my shoulder.

"Let's hang out just a minute more," he murmurs, his breath warm against my ear. "I want this memory."

Chapter 6

Maybe He Feels It, Too

Ori

"You need to stop being so damn happy," Mina teases, giving me a playful elbow to the ribs as we tidy up the main counter area.

I cock a brow at my friend. "You prefer me scowling and surly?"

"Hell no. And thanks to Asher Hammond, you're pure sunshine."

Planting my hands on my hips, I pivot toward her, praying my poker face holds steady. "What makes you think my good mood has anything to do with Ash?"

She leans in with a conspiratorial wink. "Because every time you see him, you light up brighter than a damn Christmas tree. Admit it, you're in love."

Okay, that might be a bit of an overstatement. Ash and I have been dating for the last month, and it's been perfect. But is it love? Am I ready for that idea with a man who claims to have shelved the concept a decade ago?

Better question—do I even have a choice in the matter when my heart has already made up its mind?

"I'll admit no such thing," I scoff, straightening a few items on the lower shelf.

But my firm denial doesn't faze my friend. "I love the idea. You two hated one another and then, after one magical night —poof—true love finds its mark. It's a fairytale, just with a bit more leather involved."

"I never should have shared my thoughts on true love," I mutter. Serves me right for waxing poetic while we unpacked antique books full of love stories last week.

"I love your romantic ideals. It's refreshing in a world filled with jaded hearts."

Call me a fool, but I'm a diehard believer that Prince Charming exists—and if you believe hard enough, and wish on enough stars, one day he'll ride in and save you from a life of loveless drudgery.

I know I've read way too many romance novels, but what if Mina's right? What if my prince has arrived? Only his horse is a Harley and he's sporting a few more tats and piercings than my original vision?

"I thought, per you, no one tames Asher Hammond."

Mina shrugs at my statement. "Every man's a player until he meets the right woman. You told me that, Ori, and you were right."

"Since when do you listen to me?"

"I always listen to my elders."

That's it. I'm drowning her in the bathroom sink. Elder, my ass.

But despite my snort of indignation at a twenty-five-year-old doling out relationship advice, Mina's words resonate.

Dating is a game until you find someone who makes you want to play with a new set of rules. Ash never planned on me and I sure as hell didn't see him coming, but maybe that's the point.

Maybe, just maybe, he feels the same way.

He's never outright said how he feels in the love department, but he shows me in a ton of little ways—dropping off my favorite foods when I'm working late, bringing me a vibrant Christmas cactus from the greenhouse at his farm, cleaning the snow off my truck so I'm not stuck scraping ice after dark—the list goes on.

Most importantly, it's the absence of something—or should I say, *someone*. Over the past month, Ash has split his free time between *Black Lotus*, downstairs with the speakeasy crew, or at my apartment. There hasn't been a hint of another woman, and that's a big deal in Ash's world.

We've never spoken about exclusivity, and I know Ash's reputation all too well. He never settles down with one woman. Okay, maybe one woman a night, but never a monogamous, committed relationship.

Not his style—his words, not mine.

And I haven't asked him.

The truth is, I'm a chicken-shit—terrified to find out we were special only in my head and unable to be angry because we never had any other type of arrangement.

But maybe I don't have to ask. Aren't his actions enough?

As if in answer to my question, my gaze falls on a package sitting by the front cash register. Like most deliveries, it's addressed to me, but this one is different. I'd recognize Ash's artistic penmanship anywhere.

Snatching up the package, I find a note tucked under the twine holding the burlap wrapping closed.

> When I realized this book existed, I had to grab a copy for you.
>
> Good bones, Ori, just like I told you. Take a peek at her former grandeur and tell me she isn't worth every second and cent.
>
> XOXO
>
> Ash

I cut the twine, a smile stretching across my face as I hold up the book. It's from a local printer, and they spared no expense with the embossed leather cover and gold leafing. But it's the title that catches my attention.

"The Grand Dames of the Catskills," I murmur, thumbing through the pages. Thanks to digital advances, photos once available only in black and white are now vibrant, showcasing the historic mansions that dot these mountains.

Then, I see them. Pages 45 to 61 contain photographs of my house—the one currently in a state of upheaval and disarray—captured in all her former glory.

Lavish gardens enclose the courtyards, where a fountain sprays water into the air. Soft lighting illuminates every corner, beckoning exploration. Each room sits adorned with rich wood paneling, polished floors that gleam like glass, and frescoed ceilings depicting Celtic mythology.

She's stunning. Absolutely stunning.

"Wow," Mina breathes, peering over my shoulder. "Is that your house?"

"Well, it was at one time."

"It will be again. How are the carriage house renovations coming along? When can you move in?"

All good questions, but ones I don't have solid answers for yet. Ash and Braden have finished demoing the interior, but between their other obligations, progress has stalled. With the speakeasy opening in a couple of months, Ash needs to focus his energy there, even though I know he feels like he's letting me down.

Ash swears that once things calm down, he'll focus on finishing the two-bedroom apartment, but there are only so many hours in a day—and he's just one guy.

Plus, it's barely crept above freezing for weeks, and space heaters aren't exactly cutting it.

"Ash is stretched a bit thin lately, so not much is happening right now," I admit. "I'm interviewing a few contractors who specialize in this type of restoration. That way, Ash can stay involved, but he doesn't have to do all the heavy lifting. It's a big project."

"That's an understatement," Mina chuckles. "The place is enormous. The carriage house is twice the size of my mom's home. You could fit ten of her houses inside the main dwelling."

"So much space," I murmur, tracing a photo of the once-magnificent gardens. "I can't believe I own this place."

Mina leans against the counter, flipping through a few pages. "Just think, soon you'll have your dream home. I think your dad would be happy knowing that."

Anger flares in my chest at the mention of my father. Mina is only trying to help, to soothe the wounds still festering in my soul from his absence.

But forgiveness feels impossible—now more than ever.

"I know you hate him, Ori, but whether he gave you the money out of guilt or love doesn't matter as much as the fact that you were in his thoughts before he passed. I choose to believe he left that money as an apology, hoping you'd do something fabulous with it. And you have."

"You're right," I admit, though my tone is hesitant. "Although I don't know if she's my dream home. She's a bit of a nightmare right now."

Mina waves away my concern. "Once you find the right contractor, you'll be amazed at how quickly the renovations happen."

"Let's hope so. For now, I'm happy with these photos of her in her former glory."

"She's magnificent. Where did you find that book?"

"I didn't. Ash did. He's been telling me from the start that the house has good bones and all she needs is a little love. These photos certainly prove his point."

"Proves my other theory, too."

"Which is what?"

Mina shrugs, a sly smile tugging at her lips. "That you're not the only one in love."

"Will you stop with all the love and romance talk? I swear, if Ash hears you, he'll run away screaming."

"Or maybe he'll surprise you," Mina counters. "Maybe he feels exactly the same way, but worries that telling you will make *you* run away. Ever thought of that twist?"

I nibble my lip, her words sinking in more than I'd like to admit.

Maybe she's right.

"I'm going to run next door and thank Ash for the book. Should I bring Braden back here as a gift for you?"

Mina gives an exasperated huff and turns away, but not before I catch the flush climbing her cheeks.

I love messing with her—and trust me, she gets her digs in, too.

I stroll next door to Black Lotus and pause at the reception desk, craning my neck to see if Ash is available. Unlike my store, there's a high degree of intimacy and privacy involved in the parlor, and random intrusions are generally unwelcome.

Braden catches sight of me as he exits a room and shoots me a smile. "Hey, Ori. Everything okay?"

"Of course. I just wanted to thank your brother for a gift. Is he around?"

Braden glances over his shoulder at the clock on the wall. "To be honest, I have no clue where he is. In fact, he hasn't been at the farm for a few days, either. Any idea where he's been hiding?"

I feel the color climb my cheeks because Braden knows damn well where his brother has been hanging his hat. But it's far more fun to play coy.

With a shrug and an innocent smile, I turn toward the exit. "How should I know? The man's a legend, remember?"

"In his own mind," Braden replies, snorting out a laugh. "I'll have him call you when he gets here."

"Thanks."

I push open the door, nearly colliding with another woman.

"Sorry about that," I murmur, holding the door for her.

"No problem. Have a good one."

I step outside but can't help glancing back. The woman strides into the parlor with the kind of confidence I envy—like she owns the place. She waves to Braden before slipping into Ash's office.

Odd. Braden wouldn't let a client waltz into Ash's inner sanctum when he wasn't around.

Unless… she isn't a client.

I scan my memory, trying to place where I've seen her before.

Then it hits me—she's an editor or photographer for a top tattooing magazine.

She's also gorgeous and busty, because of course she is.

The same woman who interviewed Ash for her magazine while attempting to ply him with drinks—a plan I spectacularly derailed with one supreme pizza and a very amateur lap dance.

So, why is she back here again?

I shrug off my curiosity, reminding myself there are plenty of facets to Ash's job that I know nothing about.

Still, I'm not entirely thrilled about her comfort level with my man—professional or not.

And now I sound like a crazed, lovesick stalker.

Gah. I need to go.

Mina glances up as I walk back into *One More Page*, a look of surprise crossing her face. "That was fast."

"He's not there."

"Is he playing hooky?"

"Likely. Braden didn't know when he'd be in, but my guess is soon, since he has someone waiting. Either way, I'll have to thank him later."

"I'm sure you'll come up with all sorts of interesting ways."

I chuckle and shake my head, but I don't deny a damn thing. "Sadly, you and I are working late tonight, remember? He'll have to wait for his thank-you gift."

"I bet if he knew what you were offering, he'd find a way to make sure you closed early."

Chapter 7

Cue the Lube & Handcuffs

Ash

"The prodigal son returns." Braden shoots me a smirk as I stroll into Black Lotus. "Where the hell have you been all morning?"

I roll my eyes at my brother, flipping through today's mail. "I was at town hall, getting permits for the speakeasy. If you'd checked my schedule, you'd know that."

"How's that going? You on track to open on time?"

"Yep." I am, too. The transformation—or shall I say, restoration—of our basement back to its original glory as a 1920s speakeasy is moving along without a hitch.

My crews aren't thrilled about working overnight shifts, but it can't be helped. The basement sits under Ori's shop, and the grinding of power tools isn't exactly great for business.

So, they work through the night, and I pay them accordingly.

Doesn't stop them from bitching about it, though.

"And did you settle on a name?" Zane asks, leaning over the counter, a bottle of water in his hand.

"*Rum & Ruin.*"

"Good choice," Braden replies, dusting his nails on his shirt.

Of course he says that—it was his first choice for a name.

Still, I can't argue. It's a great name, and damn, does she roll off the tongue, which is *exactly* what you want. If a name is catchy, people remember it—not that anyone will forget *Rum & Ruin* once she opens.

She's going to be fabulous.

I feel eyes on me and glance up, my gaze shifting between Braden and Zane. Okay, something's up, because these two look like the cat who ate the canary.

"Did I miss something?"

Braden bites back a grin. "You haven't been home the last few nights."

I scoff. "What are you, my mother?"

"I'm just curious where you've been. Helping the contractors?" With every word, his smile widens because my brother knows damn well that's not the answer.

I cross my arms over my chest and rock back on my heels. "I crashed at Ori's place. Is that okay with you?"

"You owe me twenty bucks." Braden snaps his fingers at Zane.

"Damn it," Zane mutters, pulling a twenty from his wallet and handing it to my brother.

I motion between the two men. "Wait a minute. You're placing bets on where I've been sleeping?"

Braden shrugs, like it's the most normal thing in the world. "Not where, so much as with whom. Zane figured you were changing it up, but I had a feeling you were with Ori every night."

"You two need a damn hobby. What made you so certain I was with Ori, anyway?"

Braden rolls his shoulders, stretching his arms out. "You've been in a good mood the last few weeks. You're always in a good mood around Ori."

Huh. I didn't realize it was that obvious. But being in a

good mood is a good thing, right? Far better than being aggravated and uptight.

I click my tongue against my teeth, glancing toward *One More Page.* "What can I say? She's a talented woman."

Braden snorts, shaking his head. "You're a dick."

"What? It's a compliment." I snatch a few bucks from the register and motion toward Ori's shop. "I'm grabbing a coffee. You want one?"

"Your girlfriend is going to have to wait," Zane says, jerking his thumb toward my office. "You've got company."

"Who?"

Please don't tell me someone from the zoning board has decided to drop by unannounced. That would kill my good mood quick.

Zane smirks. "Casey Rinbauer."

Also known as the lead talent scout for *Ink Spot.* The woman who, along with two of her friends, interviewed me last month for the magazine. The same woman who dropped plenty of hints about wanting to get to know me on a more *intimate* level—right before Ori burst into the room to stake her own claim.

To be honest, I'd forgotten all about her.

"What does she want?"

"She claims it's a business proposition, but judging by her outfit, I'm not sure what kind of business she plans to conduct." To emphasize his point, Zane mimics cupping an invisible chest, a smug grin plastered on his face.

Well, well, well. This should make for an interesting afternoon.

I stroll into my office and smile at the buxom beauty sprawled across my armchair. "Aren't you a surprise?"

"A good one, I hope." She slides off the chair, her voice a low purr as she perches on the corner of my desk.

"Always." I play it cool, but I'm no fool—I smell trouble.

Casey is gorgeous and used to getting what she wants. And right now, judging by the bedroom eyes that she's flashing my way, she wants me.

Tricky, tricky.

Why? Because over the past month, I've been asked on about two dozen dates—give or take a handful. I've gone on zero. The renovations on the speakeasy have eaten up most of my free time. What little I have left, I spend with one woman —Ori.

Hey, I wasn't kidding. She's superbly talented—both in and out of the sack. Suddenly, other women don't feel like a temptation anymore.

But Casey Rinbauer isn't just any woman. She holds the keys to the proverbial city, and while I loathe the idea of singing for my supper, I'm not one to bite the hand that feeds me. A headlining feature in *Ink Spot* would be one hell of a feast for *Black Lotus*, putting the shop on the national map.

Still, maybe I'm getting ahead of myself. Just because most women around here seem to want nothing more than an evening with me between their thighs doesn't mean that's Casey's deal.

Time to check my ego and hope her visit is purely professional in nature.

Casey leans over, dragging her nails down my arm. "I'm taking you to dinner tonight. There's a business prospect I want to discuss with you. Trust me, you don't want to miss it."

She's not asking, but rather demanding my presence, which hopefully means it really is only business.

"I'll be back around six. Have a great day, Ash."

Do I watch her ample assets sway out the door?

Fuck yes, I do. I'm not dead. I'm a single guy—kind of single—hell, I don't know what I am anymore.

But for some reason, this dinner date doesn't sit well with me at all.

Braden walks into my office uninvited and drops into the

chair across from me, stretching his arms over the backrest like he owns the place. "Well? Was it a business or social call?"

I scratch my chin, frowning. "She asked me to dinner tonight to discuss some business proposition."

"What kind of business?"

"She didn't say."

Braden rolls his eyes, crossing his arms. "Be careful. The woman's fine as hell, but she's trouble."

"It's a business meeting."

"Sure, it is. Does Ori know?"

"We made plans five minutes ago."

"Let me rephrase. Are you going to tell Ori?"

I tilt my head, resting my hands on the desk. "I don't have to clear business meetings with Ori."

Braden stays silent, his raised eyebrow saying everything.

"Aren't you going to offer some brotherly advice? Maybe smack me upside the head?"

"Nope." Braden shakes his head, staring at the far wall. "If you're that fucking stupid, you deserve what you get."

"I haven't done anything."

"Yet," Braden adds, shooting me with a finger gun.

"Braden, Ori and I aren't exclusive. We're just hanging out."

"Does she know that?"

"I made it clear the first night."

Braden rubs the back of his neck, his expression shifting. "Well, that changes everything."

"How so?"

"I can't tell you how many guys come in here asking about Ori. I've been telling them she's hands off, but I was mistaken. Seems she's fair game, and that'll make a lot of them happy."

"What the hell does that mean?"

"The next time one of them asks, I'll let them know she's single… because she is, right?"

I hate my brother sometimes. "Stay out of my love life."

"We aren't talking about your life, Ash. We're talking about Ori. Seems if you're on the prowl, she should be, too."

I lean forward, my jaw tight with anger. "Don't you say a fucking word to any of these guys. I don't trust them around Ori."

"You mean your girlfriend?"

I'm going to kill Braden. Son of a bitch won't rest until I admit how I feel about Ori. And I *can't* admit it—to him or myself.

Ori and I have been hanging out for a month, and it's been bliss. She's perfection—beautiful, smart, sweet, sexy as hell, and with a mouth that could wreck a man in the best ways possible.

If I were the marrying kind, she'd be it. But I'm not. So here we are.

Maybe one day, I'll believe the bullshit I'm spinning in my head to cover the fact that I'm crazy about her. Wildly, wickedly, over-the-moon crazy about her. And that terrifies me. I swore I'd never walk that plank again. I can't let my guard down—not even for Ori.

Especially not for Ori.

So, we keep things cool. The woman never pushes the issue. It's as though she understands I'm like a cornered animal with the L-word. Any mention of it and I'll be scoping out the nearest escape route.

We hang out, have amazing sex, and leave love to other people. Why mess with a good thing?

Still, this dinner with Casey feels wrong. And it shouldn't.

I groan, tugging at my hair. "Braden, please don't start. I'm not doing anything wrong. I'm having dinner with a business associate who could help Black Lotus. I'd be a fool to pass up the opportunity."

"Maybe." Braden shrugs, pushing himself from the chair. "But some would say you're a fool for passing up your *other* opportunity."

At the door, he gives the wall a couple of taps. "Be careful, man. I love you and want you happy. But Ori's my friend, too. Don't play her. Just be straight with her."

"This place is fantastic," Casey gushes as we stroll into the trendy seafood restaurant.

She's not lying.

"It's been a huge hit. They even get people from the city up here to sample the chef's wares."

Casey pivots, running a finger down the button-front of my shirt. "I know some other wares I'd like to sample."

Oh fuck. Here we go.

Two months ago, I would have dragged her to the nearest bathroom and ripped that skintight sheath of a dress from her body.

Now, all I can manage is an uncomfortable laugh as my brother's warning swirls in my head.

Did I tell Ori where I was going? Sure, I mentioned I had a last-minute business meeting.

Did I offer specifics? Not a one.

Why borrow trouble when I don't know how tonight will play out?

But as Casey links her arm through mine, it seems *she* has a really good idea, which only serves to further addle my brain.

Is Casey attractive? Without a doubt. She's hot as fuck, and I'll put money on the fact that she can work her body like it's nobody's business.

But somehow, the idea of sinking inside any woman besides Ori just isn't appealing anymore.

My best option is to play it cool and keep it professional.

That is why Casey requested this dinner meeting, even if we both know her reason is bullshit.

We settle into a booth, and right off the bat, she orders some wine—an overpriced luxury blend that's no doubt one of Casey's power moves, designed to loosen me up in all the right ways.

Hate to break it to her, but I can afford the bottle, too.

She clinks her glass against mine, a smile spreading across her face. "It's been too long, Asher Hammond. You've been too damn busy."

"You know I'm opening the speakeasy. Time is at a premium these days."

"Sure there isn't something else usurping your time? Or should I say, someone?"

"Casey, I highly doubt your bed has been cold."

"Not as warm as if you were in it."

Her words should excite me, but they only make me want to leave.

I lean my forearms on the table, a snicker slipping past my lips. "You told me this dinner was about a business proposition. What kind of deal are we discussing?"

She smirks and trails her foot against my pant leg. Subtle, she is not. "Who says it can't be both? Work first, then play later."

I lean back with a sigh, running a hand over my jaw. All the while, Braden's voice echoes in my head, reminding me I knew better—and I did it, anyway.

Best idea? Cut this dinner short with a strategically placed call from the shop or the farm and get the hell out of here before Casey strips me down tableside.

Part of me can't believe I'm actually running away from this.

Ash, you've truly lost it this time.

Thankfully, our server brings out our appetizers, interrupting Casey's foot play and offering me some much-needed breathing room.

"This looks amazing," I state, popping a shrimp into my mouth.

"Here." Casey offers me an oyster, tipping it up to slide it into my mouth. "One of the world's great aphrodisiacs."

The oyster should go down smooth, but with her gaze locked on mine, it feels like swallowing gravel.

God help me, I'm never making it through this dinner.

"Are you attached to Sparkwood? The New York area?"

Casey's sudden segue startles me, though I'm grateful for the shift to a benign topic.

"Yeah, my shop is here, along with the speakeasy."

She nods, sliding another oyster into her mouth. Licking her lips, she fixes me with a gaze that dares me to take the bait. "True, but there's a whole world out there, full of artistry and excitement. What if you got a seat at that table?"

"I'm not sure what you mean."

"After your piece in *Ink Spot*, we got a ton of calls. Mostly about how gorgeous you are—which I agree with—but several about your linework and portraiture skills. People from all over the world want you to ink them."

"Awesome. Send them to *Black Lotus*."

Yes, it's an ego boost to know that not only do people admire my outer wrapping, but they're damn impressed by the creativity that flows from the inside.

"But sending them here to Sparkwood isn't your idea, is it?"

Casey shakes her head, inching closer to me, her foot once again brushing against my shin. "I want to take you on the road, to all the best shops in the world, where you'll have lines of fans clamoring for you."

"*You* want to take me?" I clear my throat, moving my leg out of her reach.

"*Ink Spot* does, but I'll be your traveling companion. Imagine all the fun we'll have."

"Tons," I murmur, my emotions a tangled mess.

See, Casey's offer is the stuff of legends. Every artist dreams of that kind of recognition, and I'd be a fool to refuse it.

But what about *Black Lotus*? What about *Rum & Ruin*?

What about… Ori?

"What do you think?" Casey purrs, dragging her nails along my thigh. "Sound good so far?"

"It does. So," I state, swirling the wine in my glass and trying to find my center, "give me the details. Where, for how long, that sort of thing."

"Hmm. Wherever you like, for as long as you like."

Her hand creeps further up my leg. With a nervous chuckle, I grab her hand and place it back on the table.

Jesus Christ, she's persistent. Never thought that would be a turnoff.

"Seriously, Casey. I need details."

"Cut to the quick. No foreplay for you." Casey leans back, a bemused smirk on her darkly stained lips. "Just the way I like it."

"You're asking me to upend my life, so I need a bit more information. And for the record, I'm a huge fan of foreplay."

Just not with you, Casey.

I should have said the words out loud, even if they were biting, because now she's kicked it into high gear.

"Why don't we get our food to go, and I'll tell you all the details at my hotel suite? I'll order another bottle of wine and then show you all the goodies I brought along. Handcuffs, flavored lube—one for every mood. What do you say?"

"Yes, Asher, what *do* you say?"

At this moment, *fuck my life* seems an appropriate sentiment.

No need to turn around. I recognize that husky-edged

tone anywhere—the voice of the tiny bookstore owner I've spent the last month with.

What are the chances? Hell, I'd throttle Braden for ratting me out, but he had no idea where Casey and I were headed tonight.

This is one of those freak coincidences, also known as the universe fucking with me.

That Casey was discussing extracurricular activities when Ori walked up? Icing on the cake.

Sucking in a breath, I turn to face my executioner. But instead of rampant anger, Ori's face is a sea of calm.

That fact scares me way worse. It means one of two things: either Ori doesn't give a crap that I'm out to dinner with a woman who wants to fuck me, or she's going to slit my throat while I sleep.

Trouble is, I don't know which option is worse.

Best to aim for levity and hope Casey plays along. After all, nothing has happened besides some sexual innuendo—and that was all from Casey's end.

It's not like I agreed to shack up with her.

It's totally innocent… right?

I shoot Ori a smile, waiting for her face to register an emotion. Any emotion.

No such luck.

"Ori, you're a surprise. What are you doing here?"

She holds up a bag of food containers and nods toward Mina, who stands beside her, glowering at me. "Mina raved about their crab cakes and insisted we have some for dinner. I called your shop to ask if you wanted something, but Braden mentioned you were out. Small world, isn't it?"

Beyond fucking tiny.

The silence blasts out as the seconds roll by, each one feeling like an eternity.

Ori's gaze meanders to Casey, who has—thankfully—returned all body parts to her side of the table. With a forced smile, she extends her hand in Casey's direction. "I know we've met before, but I'm terrible with names."

Time for me to jump in.

"Ori, this is Casey from *Ink Spot* magazine. She interviewed me several weeks ago. You remember."

Ori forces another smile. "That's right. I thought you looked familiar when I saw you earlier."

Casey snaps her fingers, pointing at Ori. "You're the chick with the pizza, right?"

"Casey, these are my friends Ori and Mina. Ori owns the bookstore next to *Black Lotus*. She looks after me, especially when I forget to eat."

I mean it as a sweet sentiment, because Ori has taken care of me. Hell, she takes care of everyone at *Black Lotus*, like a mother hen.

A mother hen with the finest curves on the planet.

But my words miss the mark by a mile.

I shoot Ori an endearing smile, just in time to watch hers slip from her face.

Meanwhile, Mina looks like she wants to drop me in a pot of boiling water alongside the lobsters.

Now *what the hell did I say?*

I don't need to wait long for the answer.

Ori straightens, averting her gaze to the floor. "Yep, that's me. His friend from next door who force-feeds him pizza and coffee on occasion."

Mayday, we have derailed.

Ori motions to Mina, who hasn't stopped glaring holes into me. "We better go, or our food will get cold. Let's leave our *friend* to his dinner. Have a good night."

Then they walk away without a backward glance.

"Wow," Casey says, swirling her wine. "That was dramatic." She tilts her head, her smirk creeping back. "So, about those handcuffs…"

Her words barely register as I sit in stunned silence.

What the hell do I do now?

Do I run after Ori and explain my situation?

I don't even know my situation—or if we actually have one.

I swear, women are so much more difficult to read than men. All men need is food and sex, and not necessarily in that order.

Women need... damned if I know, if recent events are anything to go on.

I toss down my napkin, intent on chasing Ori down, but Casey reaches over to stay my hand. "The food is here. Plus, she's already gone. I have a clear view of the parking lot, and I saw her truck pull out."

The server sets our plates down with a flourish, but I've lost my appetite.

Ori is hurt, and it's all my fault.

I'm not sure how much she heard of Casey's ramblings about sex toys and room service, but I saw the light flicker out in Ori's eyes when I introduced her as my friend.

Add in this business dinner facade, and you've got my current clusterfuck.

"So, is that who you've been spending your nights with?" Casey inquires, popping a piece of food into her mouth. "No doubt she wants you all to herself, but that would be so unfair to the rest of us."

"It's complicated."

"Bullshit," Casey snorts. "It's complicated because you got caught. Otherwise, it would be as simple as you, me, a bottle of wine, and hours of casual sex."

I pivot in my seat, a flash of anger rushing through me at her presumptions. "Was that your plan? Does the deal currently on the table hinge on how many orgasms I dole out to you tonight, or is it based at all on my talent as an artist?"

Casey's eyes widen as she takes a slow sip from her wine

glass. "Don't get mad at me for doing exactly what you've done all these years."

"And what exactly is that?"

"You're gorgeous. Oozing sex appeal. Beyond talented in the bedroom. You know it, and everyone who knows you knows it. It's hardly a secret. In fact, you pride yourself on a constant rotation of beautiful women, but you're not a dick about it. You're always honest with your intentions and always deliver on your lady's sexual fantasies. You are the quintessential definition of a great fucking time. I'm the female version of you."

Damn it. She's right. I've spent years winning at this game, so why does it suddenly feel like I'm losing everything?

"That still doesn't answer my question about your supposed business deal."

"The world tour is based on your talent, Ash, but let's be honest. Your model good looks are good for business. Women love a bad boy, and you fit the bill." She finishes her glass of wine and motions to the server. "As for the extracurricular activities, I thought we hit it off well last time. Really well, and I got the impression you'd like to see me with my clothes off as much as I'd like to see you."

I rub my hand across my brow, a massive headache brewing in my temples. "Casey—"

"If she's just your friend, what does it matter what you do after hours?" She holds up her hand, cutting off my answer. "I saw your face when she walked over, but more importantly, I saw hers. That woman doesn't consider you a friend. I feel bad for her."

"Why?"

Casey shrugs, smiling as the server refills her glass. "She was stupid enough to fall in love with you."

Her words hit against my emotional armor, and trust me, it's already taken a beating tonight.

"Why is that stupid?"

And why do I care so much that Ori might be in love with me? Plenty of women have told me they were falling for me. Each got gently but firmly reminded of my position on the topic. Then, to save future awkwardness, I began pulling away.

It was the best thing for them.

And the easiest thing for me.

But Ori isn't like these other women, and I can't imagine my world without her in it.

"Because you don't return her affections," Casey reminds me. "Come on, let's finish dinner, and then you can hash it out with Ori—although I'm pretty sure the damage is done."

Sadly, I'm pretty sure she's correct. But I can't give up so easily.

"I'll be right back." I push away from the table, phone in hand, and stroll to the entrance.

A blast of Arctic air greets me, though it's likely far warmer than Ori is right now.

Sure enough, she doesn't answer when I call, and after a few minutes, my text is still unanswered.

Read, but unanswered. The words stare back at me, a silent confirmation that I've screwed up royally. What the hell am I supposed to do now?

"Fuck it," I mutter as I walk back inside, sliding into my seat and motioning to the server. "A glass of whiskey, please."

Then I turn to Casey, my arms crossed on the table. "Give me the details of this world tour."

"Here or at my hotel suite?"

The woman doesn't know when to stop.

"Here," I bark. "I'm busy tonight."

A hint of a smile plays on Casey's mouth. "I'll be damned."

"What now?"

"You love her, too."

"No, I don't. She's a great woman, but—"

"Keep denying it, but your face says it all. Just like hers did. If she's such a great woman, don't leave her dangling out there for some schlep to scoop up. Better claim her for yourself before someone else does."

But I know the truth. Love isn't real. It's a story people tell themselves to feel less alone. But Ori? She's real. And damn it, she's mine.

I just hope I'm not too late to fix this mess.

Chapter 8

Find Your Place—Now

Ash

I now understand how people must have felt as they crossed the threshold to certain death.

Am I being dramatic? Obviously. But there's a chill to the air surrounding Black Lotus, and it's more than the arctic temperatures outside.

I'm jonesing for coffee, but I'm fairly certain my favorite java haunt won't be too amenable to me this morning.

And then there's Ori. I'm desperate to speak to her, although I have zero idea how to broach the topic of last night.

Nothing happened. Sure, Casey threw out a few more offers before I dropped her at her hotel, but I held firm. For the first time in forever, I had no urge to take a beautiful woman up on her offer of illicit fun.

Why?

Because Casey, although sexy as fuck, isn't Oriana Thorne. That woman has invaded every corner of my psyche.

The thought running on repeat in my brain isn't a ready-and-willing Casey handcuffed to a bed; it's Ori's face when I introduced her as my friend. The look of dejection that washed over her has lodged in my heart like a splinter I can't remove, no matter how many needles or tweezers I try.

What a fucking disaster.

And I know I'm in the doghouse with my petite librarian because the texts I sent her last night are still unanswered more than twelve hours later.

Yes, texts. As in more than one.

When I neared Ori's apartment en route to the farm, I texted her—again—and told her I was around the corner and would love to drop by for some late-night snuggling.

I used the term *snuggling*, for Christ's sake.

I figured my message was twofold: reassure Ori I wasn't sleeping with Casey and earn some face time with my favorite lady.

But it was radio silence from her end. Not even a thumbs-up to acknowledge the text, which, in hindsight, is a loud enough message on its own.

With a final glance through One More Page's windows, I walk into Black Lotus, rubbing my hands together to ward off the chill.

Braden looks up from the desk, shooting me a gaze that's equal parts irritation and curiosity. "Look what the cat dragged in."

"Cut the shit. I was home before nine, which you damn well know."

Yes, I'm speaking at an abnormally loud volume. I want the entire shop to hear me, so I can deaden this issue right now.

"Much to Casey's chagrin, no doubt." Braden smirks, motioning toward a cup of coffee. "Grabbed you one while I was next door. Figured it might be safer for you that way."

I release a groan, dragging a hand through my hair. Some part of me had hoped I was imagining the severity of my situation.

No such luck.

"That bad?"

Braden holds out the coffee, motioning to the empty seat next to him. "What did you expect? You and I both know that even if nothing happened with Casey, it looks bad, man. Really bad."

Funny, I never pegged Ori for a gossip, but it doesn't take much in a town like Sparkwood. Small towns are powder kegs, and a lover's quarrel is the match to set the whole damn thing alight.

Plus, hell hath no fury, right?

I settle into the chair with a grunt. "That's the thing, Braden. Ori knows the score with me. I've been upfront since the beginning about my stance on dating."

I can't be sure if Braden meant for me to see the eye roll or not, but I'm tiring of the nth degree.

That, and the more I think about the situation, the worse I feel… about hurting Ori and possibly losing her in my life.

"You act like I'm the asshole, but I didn't do anything. Hell, I've only slept with Ori since that first night, and that hasn't happened in forever. Give me some credit."

"For keeping your dick out of other women and being monogamous?"

"Exactly."

I've been asked. I've said no.

In my book, that counts for something.

Apparently, Ori disagrees with my sentiment, considering she's spouting off to my brother about what a lech I am.

Judging by the flash of exasperation crossing Braden's face, he agrees with her take. With a snort and a shake of his head, he returns his gaze to his current project, thus ending our conversation.

But I'm nowhere near done.

"What?" I bark. "Just say it."

Braden sighs and sets down his tablet. "Ash, I've seen countless women dog you, but this time, I thought it was different. You two had something together. Fuck, you were content and settled for the first time in years. I figured it was because of her and how you felt about her."

The truth? I feel so much for Oriana Thorne, but no one, and I mean no one, will hear me admit that fact.

I don't even like admitting it to myself. The last time I dared to care about someone, I got my heart returned to me on a bloody platter.

Since then, my heart has been safe.

At least until that night, with Ori in the basement.

Now, up is down, wrong is right, and those settled feelings my brother mentioned are all but gone, replaced by a nagging suspicion that I've fucked up so badly I can't repair the damage.

I avert my gaze, focusing on the trees swaying in the wind outside. "I'll speak to Ori. Hopefully, she'll understand and stop dragging my name through the mud to anyone who'll listen."

Do I deserve said treatment? Probably. Although for business's sake, I hope she might cease and desist.

Braden's brow furrows. "Ori hasn't said a word about you."

Wait just a damn minute.

I toss up a hand, my gaze snapping over to my brother. "Then who—"

"Mina would like to see you drawn and quartered. That's the only reason I know anything about last night."

"Ori didn't say anything?"

"She waved and said good morning. Does that count?"

All these dramatics, and Ori hasn't said a word about running into me.

Now, why doesn't that make me feel better?

I run a hand over my beard, releasing an annoyed huff. "Huh. She didn't say *anything*?"

Braden smirks at my continued digging. "Who knows? Maybe she's not that into *you*, either."

I click my tongue against my teeth, shooting daggers at my younger brother. "Go fuck yourself."

"Love you too, brother." Braden swigs the last of his coffee and tosses the cup into the trash. "So, are you ever going to tell me about Casey's business proposal, or was it all just a front to get laid?"

"Well, she asked, but I let her down gently."

"You're such a dick."

I roll my eyes, snorting out a laugh. "I speak the truth. Anyway, that interview in *Ink Spot* garnered crazy attention. Worldwide attention. They want to send us on a tour to some of the finest tattoo parlors around the globe to work as traveling artists."

Braden bolts upright in his chair, his booted feet hitting the ground with a thud. "Us? As in, all of us?"

Not exactly, but I'm not disclosing that piece of information.

Yet.

What I told Casey, in no uncertain terms, is that my decision hinges on Braden and Zane tagging along. They're my guys, my chosen family, and I wouldn't be here without them.

Either we all go, or none of us do.

Casey figures the bigwigs will need some convincing, but I told her that with Zane's black-and-gray, Braden's neo-traditional, and my photorealism, we'd cover all the bases.

A tattoo lover's wet dream. Or orgy, whatever they prefer.

"That's the goal, but there are a ton of moving parts, and who knows if it'll come to fruition."

A ridiculous grin breaks across my brother's face. "Holy shit, that's huge! When do we leave? How long would we be gone? What countries are we hitting? Are we going to Italy because I'd kill to see Rome."

The questions fly from Braden's mouth like bullets, his excitement impossible to miss.

No doubt Zane will be equally enthused.

Too bad I don't feel one iota of their ardor. The idea of leaving Sparkwood doesn't sit right with me—something about uprooting everything, even for a once-in-a-lifetime opportunity, just feels off.

Or maybe my head is still screwed from last night.

"Try to curb your enthusiasm," Braden remarks, pushing himself to his feet. "I'm grabbing a refill. You want to come along? Face the firing squad?"

With a snort and a light smack to the back of his head, I trail him into the bookstore.

Mina glances up as soon as we cross the threshold, her face lighting up with a smile when she sees Braden.

That same smile morphs into a scowl the second her gaze lands on me.

"Back again so soon?"

"You make excellent coffee," Braden replies, settling onto a stool. "Plus, I'm starving."

Mina leans against the coffee counter, her smile once again front and center for my brother. "We make pretty good food, too. What can I get you?"

She takes his order, her demeanor warm and inviting, before turning away.

Guess I'm not eligible for service.

"What do *you* want?" she hisses, not bothering to face me.

"Just your sunny smile," I volley back.

I get it. Mina loves her boss like a sister, and in her eyes, I'm a bona fide asshole.

Still sucks to be on the receiving end of Mina's anger. I much prefer the googly eyes she normally shoots in my direction, even if she'd rather die than admit to it.

"I'm not a mind reader, Ash. What do you want?"

Suddenly, coffee is the last thing on my mind.

Something else has caught my attention.

Or should I say someone.

Across the store, seated on one of the overstuffed sofas, is Ori.

Right next to her? Some young punk who's way too close for my liking.

They're leaning over a book, smiles lighting up both of their faces as Ori flips the pages, carefree as can be.

When her lilting laugh reaches my ears, I see red.

Ori has the best laugh on the planet, bar none. It's deep and husky and washes over you like salted caramel. Absolute perfection.

It's also mine, and I don't give a damn how ridiculous that sounds.

"Who the fuck is that?" I mutter, earning a snort from Mina when she follows my gaze.

"No idea. They've been back there for over an hour, but when he's that hot, who cares?" Her smirk tells me she knows exactly what she's doing, and it's grinding me further.

Enough of this crap.

I clap my brother on the shoulder and make a beeline across the floor, catching the smirk dancing on Braden's face out of the corner of my eye.

Fuck you, man. You'd do the same damn thing if it was your woman.

And she *is* my woman, even if she doesn't realize it yet.

"Hey," I say, stopping a few feet away from Ori.

Best to start simple, right? Feel out the situation before knocking this guy on his ass.

Ori glances up, the smile faltering on her lips. "Hello, Ash. Come for your coffee fix?"

At least she's speaking to me, though I can feel the chill from six feet away.

Baby steps.

"Can't live without your coffee."

Normally, that line would earn me a smile or a sexy smirk.

Not today.

Strike one.

"I've got some free time this weekend," I murmur, stepping closer to her side, my voice easy, like I'm testing the waters.

Ori nods, her lips thinning into a hard line. "How odd for you."

And there's strike two.

Managing an uneasy chuckle, I run my hand over my beard. That frosty temperature is dropping by the second.

Time to break out the big guns.

"You and your smart mouth. I figured if the weather clears like they say, I'll be able to get the sheetrock up in the carriage house."

Ori takes the book from the guy seated next to her and pushes herself to standing. "Thanks. That's a really kind offer."

"I have my moments."

She snorts, waving her hand at me in a dismissive fashion. "We'll talk about this later. Eddie and I are heading out for an early lunch."

So that's his name.

My glare fixes on the guy as I thrust out my hand, all the while willing down the anger boiling inside me. "I assume you're Eddie."

He stands, shaking my hand with a calm, measured grip. "You assume correctly."

"I'm Ash."

Then I wait for the flicker of recognition to cross his face, proof that Ori has mentioned me.

I'll be waiting a long damn time.

"Nice to meet you."

Nothing in his tone, not a single glimmer of interest, indicates he has the slightest clue who I am.

And that knowledge makes my blood boil.

"How do you know Ori?"

Am I pressing? Damn right I am. That lump lodged in my throat since last night is growing by the second, and if I don't get some answers—and fast—I'll have no problem laying this kid out.

"Eddie owns a contracting company that specializes in old house restoration," Ori interjects, her tone clipped but composed. "When he learned I'd bought the Dean Estate, he reached out to see how I was faring. I've hired him and his team to finish the repairs."

Shaking my head, I pin my gaze on Ori. "What the hell? Without mentioning it to me?"

I know I have zero claim to her house, or the work being done there, but until this morning, Ori and I discussed every facet of the repairs. She ran everything by me, respected my input.

We were a team dedicated to restoring that home to its original glory.

What a difference a day makes.

"Eddie, would you give us a moment?" Ori grits her teeth, though her smile never falters.

"Sure. I'll meet you in the car." With a last nod in my direction, he exits the building.

If he's smart, he won't come back.

The second Eddie steps away, Ori lets her exasperation loose from its cage. Her jaw tightens, and her arms cross over her chest as her steely gaze meets mine.

"What was that?"

"I was about to ask you the same thing. Who the fuck is that guy?"

"Like I told you, he's a reputable contractor. He's worked on dozens of homes like the Dean Estate."

"So he claims."

"I've checked his references, and they're impeccable. He

helped restore Benjamin Hartwood's estate and consulted on Aurum Ridge. If a billionaire tycoon can trust the man, so can I. Anything else, or are we done with this lecture?"

Time to try another tack.

I grasp her shoulder, giving it an affectionate squeeze. "I worry, Ori. The last thing I want is for some guy to take advantage of you."

You know those moments when you realize one second too late that you've said the worst possible thing on the face of the planet?

This would be one of those moments.

Ori's gaze hardens, and she shirks from my grasp. "Funny how that's a concern to you now."

"Ori—"

"I'm not having this argument. I need to get that house restored. The longer it sits, the worse the damage. Those are *your* words. Now, I may not be an expert in the field of construction, but I'm a damn fine businesswoman, and I checked this guy out. Thoroughly."

I can keep pushing, but Ori's emotional walls rival my own, and every word I say will only make them higher.

"Like I said, I worry about you." My voice is softer now, gentler, an attempt to reassure her that my concern is genuine.

But it's a moot point.

"Well, don't. I'm a big girl, Ash." She forces a smile as she pats my arm in an awkward, dismissive gesture. "I have to go. Eddie is waiting."

Releasing a noisy sigh, I shove my hands in my pockets. "Where are you two eating? The burger joint?"

Ori shakes her head, grabbing her coat from the hook behind the counter. "We're headed to *La Belle Étoile*."

Any semblance of calm washes away the second she mentions the French bistro.

Why? Because I planned on taking Ori there. Hell, the woman's been talking nonstop about it since it opened a few weeks ago. Per her, she was a French food virgin, and I was all too happy to pop her cherry.

"That's fucking great," I bark, dragging a hand through my hair.

Her eyes narrow. "What's your problem now?"

"You know I wanted to eat there."

"I planned on taking us this weekend."

Instead of softening, her expression grows colder. "Sure, you did. Just like you promised to take me to that seafood restaurant, only instead of me, you took another woman."

"It was a business dinner," I hiss, my composure slipping with every word.

"One that involves handcuffs and lube? Spare me your bullshit stories, Ash. I don't believe a word out of your mouth."

"I've never lied to you," I snap, fully aware Mina and Braden are both watching from the sidelines.

Normally, I keep my personal life under wraps, but the anger coursing through me has taken on a life of its own.

"You're right. You told me from the beginning who you were. I was a fool to believe anything different. There, I admitted it. Are you happy now?"

"Not fucking hardly."

Suddenly, we're right back where we started months ago —nose to nose, toe to toe, glaring holes into each other.

And I want her now as badly as I did that first day.

I want to swallow her kiss, wrap those slender legs around me, and back her against the picture window in full view of the street so everyone in Sparkwood knows she's taken.

They'll know Oriana Thorne belongs to me, and any man who steps too close will get their bones broken at every joint.

But before I can make good on that internalized threat, my phone rings.

With a huff, I pull it from my pocket and groan. It's Casey. "Fucking perfect timing."

Once again, I step right into it.

I silence the call, but not before Ori's expression shutters. She knows exactly who's calling, and it's salt in a festering wound.

"I have to go," she says, turning toward the door.

"We're not done talking, Ori."

My phone rings again, and Ori's glare sharpens like a blade. "Better answer that. Seems Casey doesn't take silence as an answer. She's probably ready for round two with you… or is it round ten by now?"

"Nothing happened. It was business." I lean in, my mouth hovering against hers, the energy between us crackling like a live wire.

Blood pounds in my ears, and I'm two seconds away from dragging her to her office, ripping every stitch of clothing from her body, and sinking so deep inside her that the only words Ori can form are my name as I make her come again and again.

But I don't get the chance.

Ori steps back, throwing her hands up in surrender. "Not my business who you're doing business with, Ash. You reminded me of my place last night. Kindly find yours."

She turns on her heel and storms out the front door, the bells clanging against the wood.

With a strangled grunt, I smack the counter before stalking outside to my bike.

No idea where I'm headed, but I need some air.

For the first time in forever, I can't breathe.

After freezing my ass off on an hour-long ride, I return to Black Lotus. This time, Braden doesn't bother to hide his amusement at my predicament, but I'm not in the mood to talk.

I'm still too damn mad.

Thankfully, I have a packed afternoon, which keeps me physically occupied.

My brain? That's another story.

Sometimes, I want to call my ex, Lucille, and ream her out for what she did to me—how she tore me apart and left the pieces to rot.

But that would mean admitting how she broke me, and I'm damn sure not walking that path. Never again.

Hell, I never even heard from the woman again after that random, late-night phone call. Should've known she was drunk dialing, because after our brief chat, she promptly fell off the map.

She's good at that. Really good.

Not that I care. I feel nothing for Lucille.

But it's easier to focus on my ex than on my current situation.

Why?

Because I feel too damn much for Ori.

And that idea scares the hell out of me.

Ori gave me an out earlier, so why don't I take it? Return to the life I've led for the last decade and forget the one hot month with the petite bookshop owner.

Because I never want to forget a moment with Ori.

I want more moments, tons of them, all centered on her—her laugh, her scent, the feel of her body against mine.

I want them all. But that means giving up the life I knew before and diving headfirst into the unknown. An unknown I swore I'd never enter again.

Is Ori worth that risk?

Hell, for all I know, she's relieved by my stupid antics from the night before.

But I need to know for certain.

"Fuck this," I mutter, peeling off my gloves after finishing with my last client.

Luckily, I'm not known for much bedside conversation. Still, a bit of small talk might've helped fill the abyss of my current mindset.

"Hey. Phone call for you." Braden taps me on the arm, snapping me out of my thoughts.

"Who is it?"

"Casey. She's still in town. I wasn't sure if you'd want to talk to her, so I said I had to check to see if you'd left. Are you still here?"

Glancing outside, I spot Ori's truck in the lot. "No, I'm gone."

Braden smiles knowingly. "I kind of figured. Good luck."

"Think I'll need it?"

"I think you both will. Either that or a little less stubbornness."

Mina manages another scowl when I walk into *One More Page*, but I'm in no mood for her extended grudge.

I smack the coffee counter with my gloves, locking eyes with her. "Nothing happened. Stop acting like something did."

"Ori told me to forget about it, but I'm still mad at you."

"That's apparent."

Mina huffs out a breath before sliding a cup of coffee down the bar to me. "Why Ori? Why did you have to choose her?"

"Why the hell not? She's gorgeous, brilliant, an all-around amazing person. Why wouldn't I choose her?"

"Because she's too good to be part of your harem."

"My what?"

"Don't act like you've never heard that term used in conjunction with you before."

"Never from you."

But Mina barely hears me as she barrels on with her diatribe. "I stood up for you. When Ori figured she meant nothing to you, I negated her statements because I saw how you looked at her. I pushed her to pursue you, and I feel terrible about it."

"Wait just a damn minute. She didn't want to pursue me?"

What the fuck?

Mina manages a strangled laugh. "She thought you were hot, but so does everyone. And after that night together, she was prepared for it to be the end. Not because she didn't want more, but because she knew how you were—per your own admission. I convinced her it was different with her. Imagine my surprise when I see you dining with another woman."

"Nothing happened."

"But would it have happened if we hadn't shown up? That's the rub, Ash."

Her words stop me cold as they sink in.

Would I have slept with Casey if Ori had never walked through the restaurant door?

If I knew Ori would never find out, would I have acted on Casey's offer?

It only takes a second to know my answer.

"Where is she?"

"Out."

"A few more details, please."

"Why? So you can lure her back only to hurt her again? Ash, I should have listened to everyone in town when it came to you."

"What the fuck is that supposed to mean? I'm a good guy, Mina. I don't hit women, abuse animals, or even drive above the speed limit, for Christ's sake."

"I know. You *are* a good guy. A hell of a nice guy. But you don't believe in love or relationships. You've always been that way for as long as I can remember, and you have zero plans to change. I see that now, but more importantly, Ori does, too."

"Fucking hell," I grunt, tempted to smash the glass counter with my fist. "Please, just tell me where she is."

Mina crosses her arms, her glare unwavering. "Give me one good reason."

I realize that if I don't bare my soul to Mina, she won't tell me where to find Ori—and I can't go another minute without knowing where she is.

I meet her gaze, my voice low but resolute. "Because I can't lose her. Not like this."

Chapter 9

A Tale of Breadfruit

Ori

"Care for another?"

Bartender, you have no idea.

All I manage is a slight nod, keeping my focus glued to the hockey game blasting from the television above the bar.

Too bad I don't know a damn thing about hockey. All I see are two teams chasing a puck across the ice, and half the time, I couldn't tell you where the puck is if my life depended on it.

Apparently, I understand hockey about as well as I understand Asher Hammond.

Not. At. All.

At least I'm not home sulking. No way was I letting that happen—not tonight—especially knowing Ash is probably out with one of his many lady friends.

I am such an idiot.

I've never been here before—deep in unrequited emotion—and let me tell you, it's not a locale I plan to visit again.

Sure, my bruised ego wants to create a voodoo doll in Ash's likeness and add a few more holes to his pierced cock. But my brain, ever the voice of reason, reminds me that the man's behavior isn't suspect.

It's just who he is.

Not based on the whispers of the townsfolk, either. No, this came straight from the horse's mouth.

Asher Hammond doesn't believe in love or relationships.

Period. End of story.

He hasn't mentioned his stance since our first night together, but Ash likely figured it didn't bear repeating.

As a master's-prepared, highly intelligent woman, I surely understand his words apply to me, too.

Now, if I can only convince my heart to detach from the northeast's most notorious playboy, I'll be all set—especially once the warm buzz of alcohol takes hold and soothes my wounded soul.

Mina offered to tag along with me to the local watering hole, but I declined, particularly since she spent most of the afternoon outlining all of Ash's shortcomings.

I love the woman. I do. And I know she feels terrible about the situation, even though none of this is her doing. Don't tell that to her temper, though—Ash better check his coffee for the next couple of weeks.

She wanted him to be for real, for us to be real.

And I suppose, as reality goes, we were—if only on one side of the equation. But on his side? The numbers never even added up.

A steady stream of locals drifts into the bar, no doubt many of them running from the same emotions I'm trying to avoid. I'm not sure who decided grouping us together into a sodden, soused mess was a good idea, but here we are.

Now all I need is for a bar brawl to break out, and my week will be complete.

I wonder where Ash is now.

With a quick shake of my head, I try to derail that train of thought. I don't want to know, though my morbid curiosity can't help but wonder how many other women coexisted alongside me during this last month.

When did the man fit them in? He must run on twenty-eight-hour days or something.

At least we were always careful. Protection was a must, even if my stupid, emotional side occasionally dreamed of throwing caution to the wind.

In my mind, we were making love. Hot, sweaty, sticky love, sure—but love, nonetheless.

For Ash, I was a good fuck. A reliable lay.

Maybe that's why he never took me to his farm.

Hell, I always assumed it was because of our ridiculously packed schedules, made even tighter by the holiday rush.

Truth be told, I'm not one for bars and late-night parties, so it never occurred to me I was being kept on the down low.

So much for not thinking about it.

"This seat taken?"

I bite back a groan.

I am so not in the mood right now.

Sucking in a deep breath, I slip on my emotional armor before pivoting to meet Ash's golden-green gaze.

"There's only one seat available. Where will your lady friend sit? Oh wait, I guess she can straddle your lap. That'll do."

Friendly and accommodating, I am not.

But it's more than my discovery last night that has my temper flaring. It was Ash's tantrum earlier when I dared to eat lunch with another man.

A man I've hired to fix my house.

Unless Casey was working on Ash's plumbing last night, this is not the same situation.

Of course, she likely *did* work on his plumbing. Ugh.

Ash ignores my heated barb as he slides into the chair and flags the bartender. "Whiskey, neat."

Then he returns his gaze to me, and I catch the thinly veiled amusement dancing in his eyes.

That's enough to send my temper careening into the red.

So glad the man finds this situation amusing.

"What's so funny?" I demand, sipping my whiskey.

"You." He clinks his glass against mine, a smile already tugging at the corners of his mouth. "Me. The last twenty-four hours. We need to talk."

"Not now, we don't. I'm busy."

Ash huffs out a sigh, biting back a chuckle. If he doesn't stop laughing at my expense, I'll bite something on him—and trust me, he won't be laughing then.

"Busy doing what?" he asks, leaning closer. "Drinking at this shit hole?"

"It's not a shit hole," I lie, inching back from him.

"We both know that's not true."

I glance around the dimly lit interior at the patrons hunched over the bar, nursing their drinks. Most wear hats pulled low over their eyes, as if they too don't want to be seen here.

I shrug and down another swallow of my drink. "Fine, it's a crappy place, but it serves its purpose."

"Which is what?" Ash presses.

"I'm having a drink and watching the hockey game."

"Oh, yeah? Who's playing?" Ash grasps my chin, turning my gaze from the screen.

Damn him for knowing me too well.

I try to jerk my chin away, but he holds me fast. "A… red team and a blue team?"

Ash laughs and swoops in to steal a kiss. "The Dr. Seuss league is on the ice tonight, I see."

With a defiant glare, I wrest free of his embrace and wag my finger under his nose. "No, you're not doing that anymore."

"Doing what? Kissing you? I sure as hell am, actually." Ash drags his hand along my spine, counteracting any attempt I make to move away. "Let's get out of here. I need some time with my girl."

I scoff into my whiskey glass, trying not to fall prey to his ministrations. Again. "You mean your girl for the evening? Sorry, Ash, I've relinquished my spot on your rotation, although I'm sure you'll fill it soon enough."

The angrier I get, the more amused he becomes, and that alone is enough to send my temper skyrocketing.

"Are you done now?" Ash asks.

"No, I've got plenty more if you're interested."

"Always interested where you're concerned."

"While I appreciate this faux show of concern, I'm fine. Honestly, I don't even know why I'm surprised by last night. We both know I'm not your type. Casey is far more your speed."

Ash's gaze narrows, his amusement fading. "Who spouted that nonsense?"

"You did. That first night."

Ash snorts out a laugh. "Since when do you listen to me?"

"Since yesterday."

He inches closer, his presence overwhelming as his voice drops, rough and insistent. "No, you're not my usual type. You're sexier, smarter, and cooler than all those other women combined."

"Sexier, huh?" What a load of bullshit.

"Way sexier." His lips brush my neck, sending an unwelcome shiver down my spine.

I place my hand against my neck, blocking Ash's access. "Does Casey know this piece of information?"

Ash's mouth quirks in a wry smile, but his eyes remain fixed on mine. "I forgot one more quality. You're also way more of a pain in my ass."

"I consider that a positive trait," I retort, my voice sharp despite the warmth creeping up my cheeks. "Still didn't answer my question."

"Ori—" Ash exhales heavily, running a hand through his

hair in obvious frustration. He doesn't want to get into it. He'd rather gloss over everything and pray I forgive him.

Not happening.

I throw up my hand to cut him off. "You know what? Forget I asked. It doesn't matter, anyway."

Another noisy exhalation escapes him, and he shifts his weight. Seems the man about town doesn't enjoy being scolded.

Too. Damn. Bad.

Normally, I'd hear him out, but the truth is, Ash doesn't owe me an explanation. I built our relationship—if you can even call it that—on dreams of my own creation.

He told me how he operated that first night. No uncertain terms. No hedging.

He hasn't changed.

I have.

Any further discussion is just salt in an already festering wound.

I don't want to see the gleam of sympathy in his eyes, that look of pity when he realizes I've fallen into the same trap as countless other women.

Women who love Asher Hammond.

Women he doesn't love back.

Promises he never made. Feelings he never had.

The list goes on, and now I've joined their ranks, despite every determination that I was different.

To see that look in his eyes and realize I was wrong?

No. Just no.

Some things are better left unsaid, and this is one of them.

Hell, for all I know, this past month was one giant ploy to ensure the speakeasy project moved ahead without a hitch.

You know that's not true, Oriana.

But honestly, I'm not on speaking terms with my heart right now. Following its dumb lead is exactly what landed me here in the first place.

Heart, at this point, I hold your estimations in very low regard. If you were a sullen employee, I'd fire your ass for being so very far off the mark.

But none of it matters. Whether our time together was a ruse or a passing fancy, it's all water under the bridge.

We're friends—just like Ash said last night.

I only wish I'd gotten the memo before his newest flavor of the month.

Although, to be fair, Casey is certainly a better fit—definitely his type of woman. Me? I'm an outlier. One of those, dare I say, exotic fruits you try once and decide doesn't pack quite the flavor you'd hoped for.

I'm breadfruit.

Yep. I'm going to need way more whiskey to shut my mind off tonight.

"You need to stop being mad," Ash says, his voice low as he tucks a strand of hair behind my ear.

"I need a lot of things." I jerk away from his grasp, hating how right it feels when he touches me.

Even though everything else is so, so wrong.

Ash tugs gently at my sleeve, persistent. Seems the more I want him to stop touching me, the more determined he is to do the opposite. "Let's go home."

"I don't want to go home. I'm sick of my apartment."

"Fine. Let's go to my place. We barely spend any time at the farm."

"As in *any*?"

"Come on, we have privacy at your place. It's also two minutes from our shops. It's not like I have women stacked up in my bedroom waiting for my return."

His piss-poor attempt at levity earns him a scowl, but Ash is undeterred by my stringent stance.

"Why would I leave with you, anyway?" I ask.

That sensual smirk—the one that undoes all the ladies in

Sparkwood—stretches across his face. Too bad for him because it no longer works on me.

"Because I'm asking nicely, and I promise I'll make it worth your while."

"And I'm telling you no nicely. Besides, I don't fuck my friends."

"God damn it, Ori," Ash mutters, scrubbing his face with his hands, frustration etched across his features.

"It's cool, Ash. Just go." Do I want to dally in this dark pub that reeks of stale beer? Not at all, but I refuse to cave to Ash's whims simply because his dance card has an opening.

"I'm not leaving without you," Ash states as he pushes himself to his feet. "So, stop arguing."

"I'm capable of sitting in a bar by myself."

Ash leans over me, pointing toward a darkened table. "See those guys? They've been drooling over you since I walked in, and they're not subtle about it. Then there's that guy who's stripped you naked in his mind at least a dozen times in the last minute."

Twenty-four hours ago, his actions would have been endearing. The big, powerful protector looking out for me.

But a lot can change in twenty-four hours.

"Good for me. I have fans."

"Ori, you're a tiny woman, alone in a bar, surrounded by men who would do anything to have you. What kind of man would I be if I knew that and didn't keep you safe?"

What kind indeed.

I cross my arms and shoot him a glare. "One whom I didn't hire to be my bodyguard, but thanks ever so much for caring."

He levels his gaze at me as anger and frustration replace any remaining amusement.

Looks like we're going to have to discuss our situation-ship.

Or non-situation-ship, as the case may be.

I sigh and slide off my glasses, pinching the bridge of my

nose. Time to end this ruse, so I can deal with my heartbreak in private. "Ash, it's fine. Really. I read into something that wasn't there. That's on me. We're on the same page now. So, if you don't mind, I'd like to finish my drink. Have a good night."

Then I turn my body back toward the screens. My attention, however, is firmly on Asher Hammond.

Hard to miss the holes he's burning into me.

Ash leans closer, his tone dropping. "Don't make me carry you out of here."

I snort, rolling my eyes. "You wouldn't dare."

His green gaze pins me in place, serious and smoldering all at once. "Beautiful, where you're concerned, there's nothing I wouldn't do to keep those men away from you."

My breath hitches, but I quickly recover, waving a hand at him. "Just go. I can handle my fan club."

Ash straightens, tossing some cash onto the bar. "Screw this."

Guess he finally took the hint.

I keep my gaze glued to the television, pretending his departure doesn't twist my already tangled emotions into knots.

But then he spins my barstool around, his hands bracketing me in place. He frames my face and crashes his mouth against mine, pulling me into a heated kiss.

Before I can protest—or react—he pulls back and hoists me over his shoulder like a sack of potatoes.

"What the hell are you doing?" I yell, pounding my fists against his back.

"Taking what I want, caveman style." To drive the point home, he sinks his teeth into the meat of my ass.

A surprised yelp escapes me. "Did you just bite me?"

"Damn right, I did."

"Put me down, Ash," I demand, my voice sharp as I struggle against his iron grip.

"I warned you, little one." His tone is more amused than angry as he pivots toward my so-called fan club. Tightening his hold around my thighs, he looks directly at the men staring at us. "She's gorgeous, isn't she? She's also mine."

The barroom door bangs open as he strides into the cold, a frigid blast stealing my breath. Then he sets me down by his Harley and steps back, a smug smirk on his face.

I yank my shirt back into place, crossing my arms as I glare at him. "This is ridiculous. *You* are ridiculous."

"What's the matter now?" he asks, cocking his head, his smirk never faltering.

Spinning on my heel, I toss up my hands. "All of this! You can't play both sides, Ash. It's not fair, and life doesn't work that way. You can't have dinner with a woman who wants to fuck you—if she hasn't already—and then throw a fit when a man shows me some attention. It's a two-way street. You want your footloose and fancy-free life? You'd damn well better extend me the same courtesy."

"Wait a minute, Ori." Ash's voice hardens, his jaw clenching. "I didn't sleep with Casey. I've never slept with her."

"Not for her lack of trying," I snap, crossing my arms over my chest.

"You want me to lie and say she didn't offer me a nightcap at her hotel? She did. I declined."

"Bully for you," I bite out, my tone razor-sharp. "Must have been difficult to turn her down. But hey, you can take her up on her offer tonight. There's still time."

"Will you stop?" He clenches his fists, frustration radiating off him in waves.

"I grew up believing in fairytales. That one day I'd get my happily ever after. I never dreamed I'd fall for a man who won't even consider the possibility. Or is it you won't consider it with me? It doesn't matter, anyway." I turn toward the bar, my chest tightening with unshed tears. "I'm going back inside. Goodnight, Ash."

Before I can move, his hand clamps around my arm, pulling me back to him. His gaze burns into mine. "I freaked out, Ori. We have this great thing between us, and I didn't want to ruin it. I needed to pump the brakes because it felt like everything was moving so fast."

"Too fast?" A bitter laugh escapes me. "At the rate you're going, I'll be collecting social security before you consider the idea of a relationship."

His face falls, but I press on, the ache in my heart fueling my frustration. "Consider us stopped."

"All I could think about at that dinner was you," he says, his voice softening. "And the look on your face when you saw me with Casey. I never want to hurt you, Ori, and the idea that I did—it kills me."

His words twist like a knife as I draw in a shaky breath. "I hated seeing you with her, but I needed to see it. I needed that truth to slap me out of my daydream and back into reality. And the reality is, you don't believe in relationships. You don't believe in monogamy. You don't believe in us. Those are all things I need on my end, so here we are, at an impasse. I don't see there's much else to say."

"I told you I didn't want to like you," he grumbles. "I'm not built for relationships."

"Fine. Message received." My throat tightens as I take a step back. "My mistake was thinking I was an exception to that rule. Can I please go back inside now?"

"Will you stop?" His voice rises, raw and desperate. "I'm trying to say—"

"Want me to say it for you?" I cut him off, my voice breaking despite my best effort to hold it together. "You're sorry you don't feel more for me, but you think I'm a really great person and you've enjoyed fucking me."

"You're way off."

Then, to my horror, amid all my anger, the tears come. I

bury my face in my hands, releasing a growl of frustration. "What do you want, Ash?"

"You." His voice is low, steady. "I want you."

His words hit me like a punch to the chest—so sincere, each syllable wrapped in raw emotion.

Ash crooks a finger under my chin, gently forcing me to meet his gaze. "Nothing happened. I swear it. You're the only woman I want, Ori."

Swiping at my tears, I shake my head, trying to regain control of my runaway emotions. "Look, I thought I could handle this casual thing between us, but I can't. I—"

Ash slides his hands along my jaw, capturing me in a tender kiss. When he pulls back, his voice is just above a whisper. "I want you. I don't care what you call it—dating, a relationship, whatever you prefer. I just know I want to call you mine, and I promise I will never take you for granted again."

Do I believe him? I desperately want to, especially since there's a softness in his eyes I've never seen before.

"But what happens when the next hot chick comes onto you?" I ask, my voice trembling. "Are you going to tell them all no? That's not your style, Ash. Those were *your* words."

"You act like women are always hanging on me."

I snort, shooting him an incredulous look. "Seriously?"

He exhales sharply, throwing up his hands in mock surrender. "Fine. They can look, but they can't touch."

"How long until that gets old for you?"

His sexy smirk makes a comeback as he straddles his bike, motioning for me to climb on behind him. "That depends entirely on you."

"How so?"

"As long as you're by my side, there's not a snowball's chance in hell I'll ever get bored." His gaze softens again, his voice quieting. "I'll gladly spend all night talking, but can we do it somewhere warmer? It's freezing out here, and the snow is about to start."

"Figures you'd ride your bike in a snowstorm."

"I thought it was going to miss us, and I'd get one last ride in before spring. Come on, we'll leave your truck at the shop. No one will touch it."

"Why don't we drive the truck and leave the motorcycle?"

I think it's a valid question, but the look of sheer horror crossing Ash's face at my suggestion is laughable.

"I'm not leaving my bike unprotected in a snowstorm. Besides," he says, reaching into his saddlebag and pulling out a helmet. "I've got something for you."

"You brought this with you after our fight earlier today?"

Ash shrugs, offering me that maddeningly casual grin. "I knew I wasn't leaving here without you."

I roll my eyes and scoff. "A bit presumptuous, don't you think?"

"No. Hopeful." His voice drops as he averts his gaze. "I may not have a horse, Ori, but I'd like to try to finish that fairytale for you."

Maybe it's a line. Maybe they're all lines. Or maybe, just maybe, I don't have to walk away from the biggest love my heart has ever known.

I rest the helmet on his motorcycle seat and grasp the lapels of his coat, tugging him closer. "You, sir, are maddening."

He cocks his head, his eyes alight with mischief. "In a good way, though, right?"

With a giggle, I brush my lips against his. "In a damn good way, yes."

Although I instigate the kiss, Ash is quick to take control. He pulls me effortlessly onto his lap and guides my legs around his waist as his hands firmly grip my ass. His mouth crashes down on mine—urgent, possessive, reclaiming every inch of me as his.

His beard scratches against my cheeks as I thread my fingers into his hair, our shared desperation growing by the second. I bite back a whimper. But Ash has no intention of letting me go until he's damn good and ready. His tongue slides against mine in a slow, seductive rhythm, every movement brimming with hunger.

It matches my own.

A few whoops and cheers erupt from the bar patrons, reminding us we're not alone.

Ash buries his face in the crook of my neck, his teeth grazing the soft skin of my throat. "Let's go home."

I nod, conceding defeat. "Follow me to the shop, and then we'll take your motorcycle. Can't wait for an icy ride in the snow."

"We'll beat the snow," he says, a sly grin tugging at his lips as he sets me to rights. "Did you see it?"

I furrow my brow, unsure of what he's referring to. "See what?"

"On the helmet."

I bring it under the light and my breath catches when I notice it—my name etched neatly across the side.

Another wave of tears threatens to spill, but I tamp it down, opting for levity instead. Pivoting with my hand on my hip, I arch a brow and motion to the helmet. "How many women named Oriana do you know?"

"One," he growls, his tone low and dangerous, "and she's about to get her ass spanked for the entire bar to see."

"Promises, promises," I shoot back, unable to suppress the grin spreading across my face.

Chapter 10

Truth Over Easy

Ori

"**D**o you forgive me?" he asks.

I release a sound somewhere between a chuckle and a sated moan as Ash rolls off me and pulls me to him.

"I don't know. Your idea of a tour sucks."

I speak the truth. After freezing my ass off on the ride to Ash's farmhouse, I wanted to make a beeline for the wood stove to thaw out.

Ash had a different idea. No sooner had we walked inside than he scooped me into his arms and carried me to his bedroom.

I will say this for the man—despite losing all articles of clothing, he certainly warmed me up quickly. And maybe, just maybe, I didn't mind too much.

"You'll get the full tour in the morning—greenhouses, grounds, everything."

"Ooh, well, that changes things."

"So, I'm forgiven?" he presses.

"I suppose I'll let it slide. This time."

"Lucky me." He shoots me a lazy grin, his arms warm around me.

It should be enough, but a niggling voice in the back of my mind urges caution—to fight the urge to move full steam ahead into love with this man.

"You *are* lucky, so don't you forget it." Propping my chin on his chest, I trace the outline of one of his many tattoos, his muscles flexing beneath my fingers. "You really didn't sleep with her?"

Ash's eyes widen at my segue. "Are you asking me about another woman five seconds after I was inside you?"

"Why not? Seems as good a time as any." I deliver a light smack to his chest at his guffaw, fully aware I appear needy and ridiculous.

Hey, I still need answers.

"Well?"

Another snort escapes his lips as he grabs me close and seizes my mouth in a fierce kiss. "What am I going to do with you?"

Apparently, not answer me.

With an exasperated huff, I turn away from him, shooting a petulant pout over my shoulder for effect. "Fine. Don't tell me."

But he's on me immediately, his hands becoming more presumptuous by the second as his lips nuzzle my shoulder.

The man has memorized every sensitive spot on my body, no doubt a testament not only to his sexual prowess but to his dogged determination to deliver multiple orgasms every time.

Trust me, he succeeds.

Ash links our fingers together before pulling me into a bear hug, his hard chest firm against my back.

"You're a problem, Ori. Remember what I told you after our first night together? How you played in my brain on an endless loop? It's only gotten worse the longer we spend together. My addiction to you has grown exponentially, and I don't think there's any help for me."

Turning in his arms, I reward his answer with a hungry

kiss, my tongue dancing along the roof of his mouth while my hands glide along the planes of his stomach, trailing downward to brush against his cock.

"I should have warned you. Once I sink my claws into you, there's no turning back."

"Now you tell me," Ash murmurs, his voice a husky whisper.

It's not a direct answer, but it's an answer, nonetheless. I realize emotional intimacy is terrifying for Ash, and we have to baby-step our way along this journey.

At least we're on the same path.

Besides, even if he partook in extracurricular affairs this past month, we turned over a new leaf tonight—although I pray, I'm keeping the man sexually satisfied.

I sure seem to be.

"Couldn't give you a chance to escape," I purr as I wrap my hand around his shaft, dancing my thumb across the sensitive tip.

Ash's eyes drop closed as he bucks against my hand. "If this, right here, is prison, lock me up and throw away the key."

"You and your fabulous responses tonight. Maybe I should reward you for such exemplary behavior."

"I love where this is heading."

"I bet you do."

Ash, like every other man on the planet, loves getting head. Lucky for him, I love his cock, and I especially love the way I own him when I drop to my knees and take him in my mouth.

But when I sit up, determined to take my man on a ride, he grasps my arms and rolls me onto my back.

He drifts his hand between my thighs, and I bite back a moan, my pussy still tingling from the last round.

"You're so fucking wet. So ready for me again."

I grind against his hand as he curves his fingers to stroke me from the inside. "Ash—"

Ash grasps both my wrists in one hand and holds them above my head, locking me in place. "Let it all go. I want everyone to hear how good I'm making you feel."

He's relentless, his thumb circling my clit while his fingers continue to work me open.

Ash's gaze never shifts from my face, his eyes locked on me as I fall apart beneath him.

I fist the pillow, the only thing within reach, and hiss as the overpowering emotions rip through me.

"Fuck, fuck." It's all I can manage as I writhe against his hand, my muscles squeezing around him as I desperately seek my release.

"That's right. That's my good girl," Ash murmurs, a ravenous hunger awash in his face as he frees my hands.

I blink my eyes closed, but he twists his fingers in my hair, urging them open. "Eyes on me. Watch me claim what's mine."

Ash spreads my legs, the warmth of his body overpowering me as he buries himself deep inside. A keening cry escapes my lips, the sound raw and unrestrained.

His gaze holds me captive as he moves slowly, each thrust deliberate, coaxing me closer to the edge. "Nothing feels as good as you, Oriana."

I tighten around him, drawing him deeper, knowing damn well he's barely holding on.

"You say I'm yours? Show me. Claim every inch of me."

"You're driving me insane," he growls, his movements growing desperate, almost frantic, as he slams into me again and again. "I can't wait to take you raw. I'll come so deep inside you, you'll never fucking recover."

The words hit me like a spark to kindling, igniting every nerve. His stare anchors me, unrelenting, pulling me under as my body tightens, the tension snapping like a cord.

And then I'm gone. My body convulses, every inch of me trembling as wave after wave of pleasure crashes over me.

Ash wraps his hands around my hips, his thrusts hard and unyielding as he chases his own release.

He lets out a rough shout, collapsing against me as his breathing comes in ragged bursts against my ear.

I drag my tongue along his sweat-slick skin, letting my fingers trace lazy patterns along his scalp as his breathing evens out.

Ash props himself on his forearms, his skin gleaming in the dim light. He presses his forehead to mine, a slight smile tugging at his lips. "Every time with you is better than the last. How the hell do you do that to me?"

"Simple." I smile, pressing a soft kiss to his mouth. "I'm magic, remember?"

"Yes, you are."

"Want to take a shower?"

He nods, a flicker of tenderness crossing his face. "Sure, but give me a second to just look at you. You're the prettiest thing I've ever seen."

His words knock the air out of me more than any dirty line ever could. Sure, his filthy talk turns me on, but moments like this, when he lets his guard down and shows me exactly how he feels, these are the ones I'll replay in my head for days.

Tracing my fingers along his beard, I steal another kiss. "Lucky for you, I'm all yours."

"Damn lucky, all right."

I'm awake before Ash, but that's nothing new. The early morning light streams through the window, and despite the frigid temperatures outside, there's nothing as beautiful as a winter sunrise blazing across the sky. The vibrant streaks of orange and pink bathe everything in a rosy hue.

Or maybe that's just the look of love.

After a few minutes admiring Mother Nature's handiwork, I pull on my clothes and drop a kiss on Ash's cheek. "I'm off in search of coffee."

"Okay," he murmurs, his face buried in the pillow. "I'll be down in a few minutes."

I'm halfway to the door when he calls to me. "Hold up a second. Braden is home."

My stance stiffens, wondering if, despite everything, I'm still a secret to the outside world.

"So?"

"Don't go downstairs naked," he grunts. "That gorgeous body is for my eyes only."

"Not a problem. In fact, I might steal a few more layers before the morning is out." Chuckling, I walk downstairs, following the aroma of freshly brewed coffee to the kitchen.

I wave to Braden as I walk into the room, nodding toward the coffeepot. "Is that—?"

"From the store? You bet." Braden slides a mug of coffee across the counter to me. "I made a full pot, since I knew you were here."

Oh. My. God.

We didn't see Braden when we arrived last night, so if he knew I was here, it's because he heard us.

My cheeks flame as I try to hide my face behind the coffee mug. "Did we keep you up?"

Braden chuckles. "You weren't quiet."

I set the coffee aside and bury my face in my hands. "Oh, God. I'm sorry."

"Don't be. I just figured you'd need the fix this morning, and I know you love your coffee."

"How did you know it was me and not some other woman?"

Braden cocks his head, a slow grin spreading across his features. "Ash never brings anyone here, except for you."

His blunt admission damn near brings me to tears, which would no doubt confuse the younger Hammond brother. But he doesn't realize how much my heart needed the validation that I'm different. Special.

"It's about time, too," Braden continues. "Ash kept saying he wanted to bring you out here, but your apartment is so much closer to the shop."

"Two minutes up the road, which is nice when it's single digits outside."

"I didn't see your truck."

"No," I laugh, taking another sip of coffee. "Ash insisted we had to get his bike home safely before the storm. Figures he'd choose the coldest night of the year to take me on a moonlit ride."

"We love our ladies."

"Only if they're carved from steel."

"Touché," Braden replies, clinking his mug against mine. He straightens and peers toward the doorway, no doubt waiting for Ash to make an appearance. "Are you two okay?"

"I think we're better than okay. We had a bit of a break-through last night, which is far superior to the breakdowns we experienced earlier in the day."

Braden leans on the counter, tapping his fingers against the ceramic surface. His green eyes lock on mine, serious now. "He really cares about you, Ori. I know he sucks at showing it sometimes, but trust me, he does."

"Now you tell me. Where were you yesterday when I was a hot mess, thinking he slept with Casey?"

"Right next door, as usual." He shrugs, a small grin tugging at the corner of his mouth. "But don't worry. Nothing happened there. It's not Ash's style."

I sputter my coffee, sure I heard him wrong. "Juggling multiple women isn't Ash's style? Since when?"

"When Ash gets serious about someone, it's like blinders go on. Nothing else matters."

I wrap my fingers around the mug, considering his words. "I thought he didn't get serious. Ever."

"Not in a long damn time, but you seem to have changed his mind."

Have I, though?

Despite stepping forward, Ash remains wary about the concept of love. All I know is some woman broke his heart and did a bang-up job of it.

How do you help someone trust in love again when they've already decided it's a losing game?

"What are you two talking about?" Ash asks as he strolls into the kitchen and grabs a mug of coffee, pausing to drop a kiss on my forehead.

I give him a nonchalant shrug. "You. Obviously."

"Shit. Here I thought it would be a good morning."

Braden laughs and motions toward the door. "I'm heading into the shop. I have a custom piece later this morning. You two behave."

"No promises," I giggle, swatting at Ash when he slides his hands under my shirt to squeeze my boobs.

"Be nice, mister, or I won't make you breakfast."

"Just appreciating the chef," he teases, grinning as I swat him away. "Although far be it from me to stop you from taking over the kitchen."

"I can teach you how to cook, you know."

Sadly, although half Italian, the man could burn water.

Come to think of it, he likely has.

The further away he stays from the oven, the better off we all are.

"How about you cook, and I'll clean up afterward?" Ash offers.

"Deal." I grab some eggs from the fridge and crack a few into a bowl.

"What were you two saying about me?"

Should have known the man wouldn't let that statement lie.

"Why? Are you paranoid?"

"No, but I'm curious what shit my little brother was spouting."

I set the eggs aside and hop onto the counter, swinging my legs slightly as I plant myself directly in front of Ash. "He said you were over-the-moon cuckoo for me."

Okay, Braden didn't exactly say that, but it's a good opening, and it may be enough to convince Ash to talk about his past.

"I knew he was spouting shit." Ash laughs at my look of mock horror, wrapping a hand around my nape to steal a soft kiss. "I like you okay, Ori. You'll do."

I fan myself, shooting him a side-eye. "Who says romance is dead?"

Yes, I'm playing it off and volleying back banter, as is our norm. But I know Ash well enough to realize that his humor is simply a bandage for the pain.

How do I know? Because I've been there. After my dad walked out on my mom and me, I became a pro at pretending I didn't care. If I could fool everyone else, maybe I'd convince myself too.

Still waiting on that one.

"You know I'm not a big believer in romance. It's all superficial, surface-level bullshit. Don't get me wrong—if you want flowers, I'll get them for you. But I hate the idea that how I feel is measured by how big a bouquet I buy."

I slide off the counter and dump the eggs into a pan. "I get that."

But apparently, Ash doesn't think I do. He steps closer, his face a mix of conflicting emotions. "You know I'll get you flowers, Ori. I'll get you whatever you want."

"I can buy myself flowers, but I appreciate the sentiment."

I pause, letting the air between us grow thick before adding, "Although I do have one request."

Ash stops in his tracks, his hands sliding into his hair as he exhales sharply. "I may live to regret this, but go ahead."

I stop stirring the eggs and face him. "Tell me about her."

Ash's brow furrows. "Who?"

"You know who."

His eyes scan the far wall, squinting in the morning light. "Casey? I told you, nothing happened between me and her."

"Not Casey. The woman who changed your mind about love."

"Shit." He mutters the curse under his breath, pivoting away from me. "I don't want to talk about her."

But I'm not willing to let the subject drop. Not this time.

The first night, I barely knew the man and allowed his past to stay firmly corralled within the confines of his mind. But now, we're an integral part of each other's lives. This isn't about prying—it's about understanding him.

Most importantly, understanding if *we* have a fighting chance.

"It's impossible for me to fight the ghost of her if I don't even know what I'm up against."

"It was a long time ago, Ori."

I shake my head, pointing toward the floor. "No, she's still very much here—in every day and every moment. Look at it this way: maybe if you tell me about her, I'll understand why you hate intimacy and romance and the dreaded L word, and I'll leave you alone about it."

"Doubtful." Ash scrubs a hand over his face, his jaw tight as if holding back words he's not ready to say.

I reach out, giving his arm a gentle squeeze. "Always a chance. Come on, talk to me. You know I'm a good listener."

Ash huffs out a sharp breath, his nostrils flaring. He doesn't want to discuss this topic, but he realizes I need him to.

"Trust me, I don't want the details of your sex life. Just a basic overview of the relationship."

"Details of our sex life would be less painful to discuss."

"Maybe for *you*." I turn my attention back to cooking, flipping the eggs and bacon in the pan with practiced ease.

He encircles his arms around me, depositing a series of slow, shivery kisses along my throat.

It feels like heaven, but I know exactly what he's doing.

I wiggle against his muscled form. "You're stalling."

"Damn straight."

"Guess you're not hungry then," I reply as I turn to him, holding the plate of eggs and bacon just out of reach.

I raise the plate higher, smiling sweetly as his gaze narrows. He sighs, running a hand over his jaw as if genuinely debating whether tackling me for the food is worth it.

Finally, he relents and settles into a kitchen chair before holding out his hand. "Give me the damn plate, and I'll tell you my tale of woe."

Score one for the home team.

He snatches the plate, scarfing down a few bites. "You really are the most amazing cook."

"Stalling," I retort in a sing-song voice.

"You first. Who broke your heart the worst?"

"That's easy—my father." I swallow hard, the familiar ache rising in my chest. "He took an enormous piece of me with him when he left, and I didn't know how to process the pain of his abandonment. My mom was no help—she didn't understand it, either. So, I wore a mask every day, pretended I hated my father, and stumbled through life."

The words spill out faster now, like they've been waiting too long to be spoken. "But when the one man who shouldn't ever break your heart shatters it to bits, your view of men becomes skewed. I opted to create this incredible love story in my head with this unbelievable man. Of course, since it was a fairytale, no one ever came close."

I duck my head, my fingers curling around the edge of the kitchen table. Admitting the next part feels like stepping into the light after years of hiding in the shadows. But if I want Ash to be real with me, I owe him the same courtesy.

"Until you. You're the first man I want to open up and be vulnerable for."

A muscle jumps in Ash's jaw at my declaration—my brutal and beautiful admission. He runs a hand over his beard, his gaze fixed on some distant point as he processes my words.

"Damn." His voice is low, gruff, but there's a flicker of disbelief in his expression. "Thank you."

I'm not sure what kind of response I expected, but that certainly wasn't it.

To be fair, I never planned on spilling *my* guts this morning—I wanted Ash to spill his. But here I am, baring the parts of myself I swore I'd keep hidden.

With a shrug, I focus on my breakfast, certain I've said too much and overstepped the boundaries of our fragile new relationship. No doubt my admission might send Ash scurrying away—back to the arms of his waiting harem.

Sometimes, you need to stop while you're ahead.

"You want some more?" I ask, rising from the table, eager to escape the awkwardness brewing in my stomach.

But Ash grabs my wrist, nodding toward the chair. "Stay."

I sit down, facing him expectantly.

"It was eleven years ago. I'd hung out with all kinds of women, but I was so busy getting Black Lotus up and running that I didn't have time for a relationship. Then I met Lucille, and within five minutes, I knew I wanted to spend my life with her."

Okay, maybe this was a bad idea.

"That fast, huh?"

Ash nods, swigging his coffee. "It was immediate and powerful. She felt it too—or so she claimed. Everything in my life revolved around her—work, play, my present, my future. I wanted to marry her, but I didn't have the cash for a ring, so I sold the bike my grandfather gave me."

"Was he angry?"

Ash shakes his head, wincing as if the memory still stings. "He'd passed a year earlier. My dad and Braden wanted to kill me when they found out, but I didn't care. I knew what I wanted—I wanted her."

"Sounds like you were very devoted."

"I was very *stupid*," Ash bites out. His fingers drum a sharp, uneven rhythm on the table. "I bought this big-ass ring, dropped to one knee, and asked her to marry me. That's when she told me the truth."

Oh boy, this is not looking good.

"She was married. Want to know the icing on this shit cake? I sold my grandfather's bike to her fucking husband. He didn't know about the affair, either—at least not at that point."

I release a slow exhale, buying myself a few seconds. "Holy shit, Ash. That's beyond messed up. I'm so sorry she did that to you."

"The worst part? I never saw it coming. My friends and family warned me about her, said she wasn't what she seemed. But I was blind to everything. I saw what I wanted to see— that she was perfect."

"No one is perfect."

"She wasn't even close," he snaps, his fingers stilling as he presses his palms flat against the table.

"What happened after that?"

"I told her I never wanted to see her again and chucked the ring over the side of the mountain."

I clap my hand over my mouth. "You didn't."

Ash nods, his expression pained. "I did. I went from dumb to dumber in thirty seconds flat. So, I had no girl, no bike, no ring, and no money. I had to go to my father and tell him what happened."

"What did he do?"

"He hugged me and wrote me a check to buy a used truck to get me around. He saw how broken I was. But it got worse. Her husband was one of the head guys in a local MC."

"Christ."

"I figured I'd end up riddled with bullet holes. It was just a matter of time. Then one night, I saw him in a local bar where I was drowning my sorrows. I didn't say a word. Just got up and left. Figured this was it, you know? I planned to pull over and let him take his pound of flesh, but a drunk driver got to him first. Ran him off the road."

I jerk upright. How can this story get any worse? "That's terrible."

"Part of me wanted to leave him there, just like the drunk driver did. But I couldn't do that. I got most of the plate and called the cops. Waited with the guy—he was barely lucid. Told him he'd be okay, and that I wasn't going anywhere."

"Did he survive?"

Ash nods, fiddling with his fork. "He spent six weeks in the hospital and a few more months learning to walk again. But Trace is a tough son of a bitch. He fought back. One day, he knocked on my door, and I thought he was there to finish the job. He wasn't. He handed me the keys to my bike and said he hoped he never saw me again. Then he thanked me for saving him and left."

I'm not sure what kind of tale I thought Ash would have, but this story is the stuff of nightmares. Only for Ash, it's his waking reality.

"Whatever happened to Lucille?"

Ash clears his throat. "She disappeared for a while. Popped back up a couple of years later at a tattoo convention."

"She's a tattoo artist, too?"

Ash nods. "Yep, a damn good one. Too bad she's a heartless monster."

"A lot of talented artists are terrible people. Were you angry when you saw her?"

"I don't know what I was, Ori. I felt everything and nothing at the same time. Anger, rage, sadness, longing—everything. She insisted on taking me to dinner, and we talked. Mainly she did, apologizing and trying to explain her side. I told her it didn't matter."

"But it did."

"I wasn't going to let her know that. After falling for her, I swore I'd never allow another woman into my heart. In that way, you and I are exactly alike. The people we trusted the most betrayed us."

But we're not, Ash, because I'm willing to let you into mine.

Knowing what I do now, though, I realize it's going to be a tougher road than I originally believed.

"So, that's it? She apologized and walked away?"

"No. God, I wish." Ash hesitates before answering, his voice quieter now. "We slept together after the breakup. Actually, we hooked up quite a few times over the last several years."

I blink, absorbing the new information. Seems the woman still has her claws in him, which is not good news. "Huh."

He shakes his head, as if regretting his admission. "I never told anyone that before. Lucille was this dirty secret because everyone I knew hated her."

But you didn't.

I skew my mouth to the side, at a loss for a response.

Ash reaches over and grabs my fingers. "I shouldn't have said all that about us hooking up. I'm sorry."

Waving my hand, I dismiss his concern—even though it gouges me like a dagger. "It's okay. I get it. I was like that with a guy I dated. We were toxic together, but there was comfort in it. I knew his body. He knew mine."

Ash waves his hand. "Nope. Stop talking."

"About my ex?"

"No, about any former sexual partners. The thought of you being with another man drives me crazy."

My eyes widen at his jealousy. "Why? It was ten years ago."

"I don't care. As far as I'm concerned, you were a virgin before I came along."

"Too bad I can't play that card," I reply with a smirk.

"Trust me, I don't want to talk about my past relationships, either." He leans over, grasping my fingers. "Are we okay?"

It took so much courage for him to open up like that—to share the dark recesses of his soul.

And even though his admissions hurt to hear, mainly because Lucille got the version of him I'll never have, I know he needs my reassurances that we, such as we are, are still on solid ground.

Besides, I asked. Don't go digging in a litter box if you don't want to find some shit.

And Ash is worth it, even if he believes he's broken beyond repair. Maybe, by loving him and demanding nothing in return, he'll come to realize that, too.

"Just so you know, if I ever meet this Lucille, I'm punching her in the mouth."

A smile splits Ash's face as he leans in to kiss me. "Thank you, my little warrior. Am I done spilling my guts now?"

I'm more than satisfied. He was brutal in his honesty, and now I understand the pain behind his eyes.

"Won't stop me from trying to change your mind about love, though," I reply, flashing him a teasing grin.

But the smile fades from Ash's face as he looks away. "I don't know, Ori. I'm pretty set in my ways on this one. The last thing I want is you expecting something I can't give."

Chapter 11

My Woman Loves Surprises

Ash

I'll admit, Ori's calm and collected response to my story about Lucille surprised the hell out of me—especially when I reiterated how I had no plans to change my opinion on love and marriage.

But she just smiled and carried on with our day. And what a day she made it—filled with laughter, a delicious home-cooked meal, and several rounds of mind-blowing sex.

The best part, though? When she fell asleep on me while we watched a movie, with my cat, Merlin, curled up beside us.

In those moments, just like on our first night together, I let my walls down and allowed myself to bask in her presence.

I may not be the man who can give her the life she dreams of, but she's the one woman I'm willing to go the distance for —even if I have no idea what that looks like.

At first, I braced for Ori's inevitable breakdown, convinced she'd sit me down and tell me that, after thinking it over, this relationship wasn't what she signed up for—and I'd have to let her go, knowing it was what she deserved.

Even if it killed me.

But it never came.

After a couple of weeks, I stopped waiting for the other

shoe to drop and focused on all the good in my life—and, damn, there's a lot.

The speakeasy finally looks like a bar again, even if it's still missing plumbing and seating. The polished oak counter stretches the length of the room, and the walls, painted a deep emerald green, glow softly under vintage sconces.

Every day, my team of contractors edges *Rum & Ruin* closer to completion.

Let me tell you, I never thought this dream would come to life, but here it is—the embodiment of the spirits which I believe still roam the streets of Sparkwood.

Black Lotus is busier than ever, thanks in part to Casey's article in *Ink Spot*. And just the other day, I got another call from her—no, not *that* kind of call. Turns out, she meant it about the tattoo world tour. Now, it's just a matter of hashing out cities and dates to ink in some of the finest parlors around the globe.

Talk about living the life. I've got a gorgeous woman, a thriving business, and a soon-to-be Sparkwood hotspot.

The only downside? The frigid temperatures which seem intent on sticking around until spring—and *fucking Eddie*.

I tried to convince Ori to hire someone else—someone who doesn't grate on my nerves simply by existing—but she insisted on having Eddie restore the Dean Estate.

Sure, the guy has solid credentials, and his restorations in the area are impressive. But that doesn't mean I have to like him. There's just something about the way he always seems to be hanging around Ori that drives me nuts.

I get it. My woman is beautiful. But back the fuck up, okay?

He does not need to drop by *One More Page* every damn day. That's why phones, email, and, hell, Morse code exist. Pick one.

At least the work he's done on the carriage house is up to snuff—and trust me, I've checked. His crew has rewired and re-plumbed the entire place, and they'll be ready to start hanging sheetrock soon.

Not soon enough, though. And even once the carriage house is done, I know he'll be around for at least another year working on the main house.

Fucking joy of joys.

But today? I'm not worrying about Eddie or his dogged persistence.

Today, I'm celebrating—and it's not just any celebration. Ori's going to love this.

She has no idea what's coming, but I can't wait to see the look on her face.

A scowl replaces my smile when I walk into *One More Page*.

Once again, Eddie is here, and this time, he's bent over the counter, examining an old book.

He looks up, shooting me an affable smile. "Hey there, Ash. How are you doing?"

I jerk my chin toward the book in a pseudo-greeting. "You should wash your hands before handling that—better yet, wear gloves."

Eddie frowns, glancing down at the book. "Gloves? Seriously? Why?"

"The oils from your hands can seep into the pages and mess with the ink over time. That's a first edition, and it's worth a small fortune. Your fingerprints could wreck the value. Just saying."

He straightens, his smile dimming slightly. "Didn't know you were such a book expert."

"Neither did I." Ori walks over, a surprised smile lighting

up her face as she tips her head up for a kiss. "Since when do you know so much about antique books?"

"Since my girlfriend owns a bookstore." I shrug, pulling her slight frame against me and claiming her mouth in a hungry kiss.

Do I throw in some extra tongue action and an ass grab for Eddie's benefit?

Damn right I do.

I meant what I told Ori—any man comes near her, and I'm breaking them into tiny shards.

No, it's not love, but it is a fierce protectiveness if anyone dares to take what's mine. And Ori is the most precious thing in my world, even if I don't have the balls to tell her.

So, I'll show her instead.

"Aren't you spicy today?" Ori teases, licking her lips and giggling as she brushes a strand of hair behind her ear. "How are things coming along with *Rum & Ruin*?"

"Why don't you walk downstairs and have a look? We can take the newly restored bar for a test drive."

I glance over Ori's shoulder at Eddie, who's looking increasingly uncomfortable. Good. Time for the old boy to take the hint.

"Sorry. Just can't resist with her," I say, squeezing her tighter to my chest, my grin as unapologetic as it gets.

Eddie shrugs, shifting his weight from foot to foot as he averts his gaze. "Have at it, man. Hey, it's almost time to hang new light fixtures, and Ori mentioned you'd like to select them?"

I tighten my arm around Ori, a small, satisfied smile curling my lips. As much as I can't stand Eddie, I love that Ori and I are working on the Dean Estate together. It feels like we're building something real—even with him as the unwelcome third wheel.

"You saw the pendant lights I set aside in the main

house?" I glance down at Ori, brushing a thumb across her cheek. "You like those for the apartment, right?"

She tilts her head to the side. "The Tiffany glass ones?"

"Yeah."

"Those are beautiful. Can you hang those, Eddie?" Ori asks, her voice sweet and unassuming.

A broad smile stretches across Eddie's face as he looks at her. "Anything for you."

Seriously?

I grumble under my breath, refusing to be one-upped by a thirty-year-old contractor.

"Hey, little one," I say, turning Ori's attention back to me, "I need you to go home and pack."

Her brow furrows as she glances up at me, confusion flickering in her eyes. "What for?"

"I have a surprise for us."

Ori releases a nervous laugh as she bites her bottom lip. "I have a huge inventory due in a week."

"I know," I reply, not missing a beat as I brush a stray strand of hair from her cheek. "Mina said she and a few of the other girls will handle it."

Her arms cross over her chest, her curiosity building. "What am I packing for, exactly?"

"Five days and four nights in the Keys."

Her eyes widen as her jaw drops. "You booked us a trip?"

"First-class accommodations all the way," I reply with a grin as I wrap an arm around her waist. "From the plane to the resort. Only the best for you."

Her lips part, clearly trying to process the information. "What is this for?"

I shrug, my tone softening as I tilt her chin up to meet my gaze. "I could say it's for Valentine's Day, but it's really because we deserve a break—and because I want to spoil you a bit. So, what do you say?"

"Who's going to watch the store while we're gone?"

"Braden and Mina. I've already spoken to them."

"You really did plan this for us."

"Imagine that. Now, I'll ask one more time—yes or no?"

She jumps into my arms with an excited yip, her hands wrapping around my neck as she peppers kisses across my face. "That's a *hell* yes. Five days to work on my tan. Nude sunbathing, here I come."

I smile, but then her words register. "No, no, no. You're not showing this body off to anyone but me."

Ori rolls her eyes, her lips curling into a mischievous smirk. "Fine. Is a dental floss bikini acceptable? Ash, I have a fantastic ass. I need to show it off. You can wear a Speedo."

I narrow my eyes, recognizing the teasing glint in hers. She loves getting a rise out of me. And I love putting her right back in her place.

Lowering her to the ground, I deliver a firm smack to her ass, well aware our buddy Eddie is still lingering.

But this time, it's not just about sending a message to the overly friendly contractor.

Every day, I find it harder and harder to resist the tiny woman at my side.

Maybe you should stop trying.

For once, the thought doesn't fill me with dread.

Maybe it's time.

"What did she say?" Braden asks the second I stroll back into Black Lotus.

"It's a go. You sure you don't mind watching the store, too? I know it's a lot, but I really need the downtime before the craziness of the speakeasy opening."

Braden rolls his eyes. "You need a tropical vacation with your girlfriend."

I wave my hand in agreement as I black out my schedule for the next week. "That too. I'll mail you a palm tree."

"Just send some blasted sun. I never thought I'd say this, but maybe Mom and Dad had the right idea, moving to Florida."

"Spring will be here soon, and all will be right in the world. We just have to muddle through the shit until then."

"Says the man boarding a plane to the Keys tomorrow." Braden grabs a sticky note, waving it toward me. "Hey, change of subject—Lucille called and left a message for you. Wants you to call her back. Are you two talking again?"

"Not at all."

It's the truth. After her random, insistent call begging to meet up several weeks ago, she dropped off the face of the earth.

To be honest, any thought of the woman had slipped my mind—completely.

Huh. That's never happened before.

And I know why—because of one tiny librarian who usurps my every thought. A tiny siren who has plans of strolling a beach wearing a dental floss bikini.

No way we're ever leaving the hotel bed if she tries that. I'll tie her gorgeous ass up and find a million ways to keep her occupied.

Braden shakes the piece of paper with the phone message under my nose. "What should I tell Lucille if she calls again?"

I shrug, not caring. "Tell her I'm on vacation and she'll have to wait. Feel free to throw in a comment about Ori's numerous assets, if you'd like."

A slow smile lights up Braden's face as he leans back in his chair. "Hallelujah. You're finally past her."

"I've been past her."

"Bullshit. You pretended you were, but Ori got you past her. I could kiss her for that."

"Don't you dare touch my fucking woman."

Braden smirks. "Look at you all possessive and shit. Just remember, I am not wearing a tux to your wedding."

I shoot him a scathing glare. "Slow your roll. We're going on vacation. I'm not marrying her."

"Aww, here I thought I might have ignited the closet romantic in your soul."

Fuck. The last person I needed hearing that line is the one now standing behind me.

Pivoting on my heel, I flash Ori a sheepish grin. "I didn't mean it like that."

She cocks a brow, crossing her arms as her lips twitch into a knowing smirk. "Yes, you did, but I'll let it slide because you are taking me to paradise tomorrow."

See what I mean? Without a doubt, the coolest chick on the planet. Hey, for all I know, maybe she's good with our arrangement, too, and doesn't want anything more.

Great times. Great sex. Tons of laughter. No need to muck it up with love and contracts.

So why do I hate that she heard me say those words?

Because you don't mean them and maybe one day…

Braden cuts my thoughts short. "Hold up. You're letting my brother get away with that?"

Ori shrugs, brushing her fingers over the counter. "Yep, although romantic guys get far more loving than ones who don't believe in the concept. Pity for you, I suppose, Ash."

She's joking… I think. "I'll find ways to convince you to cross to the dark side."

"I've been on the dark side since we started hanging out together. Lucky for you, I kind of like it here."

I pull her into an embrace, letting my arms linger around her waist as I nuzzle her neck. Her scent wraps around me— soft, warm, and forever inviting.

"I'm the lucky one," I murmur, the thought slipping out unbidden.

Her gentle laugh vibrates against my chest, and for a moment, I wish I could keep her there forever, the rest of the world forgotten.

"What do you need, beautiful?"

"Something you can't give me, so I'll have to settle for the time of our flight tomorrow. Are we working part of the day?"

I shake my head. "Only on our tans. Our flight leaves at six-thirty."

"Perfect, although I'm warning you, I'll be running on sunshine and caffeine tomorrow, since tonight is all about packing." She pecks my cheek and pulls from my embrace. "See you later."

"Hey." I grasp her fingers, giving them a gentle squeeze, my thumb brushing over her knuckles.

"Yeah?"

"What did you mean when you said you want something I can't give you?"

Do I have a good idea what she meant? Of course, I'm not stupid.

But maybe I need to hear Ori say it to finally break free of the chains tethering me to my past. Maybe if she lays down the law and demands every part of me, I'll stop being afraid of a future.

Or maybe hearing it will only heighten the fear.

Doesn't matter either way, because my beautiful lady has no intention of spilling her secret.

Her only answer is to blow me a kiss and walk out the door.

Chapter 12

If I Pee On It, It's Mine

Ori

Turns out Mother Nature doesn't care about first-class tickets. Despite our upgraded travel accommodations, we're flying on the same plane as everyone else —a plane that currently sits empty on the tarmac.

Seems New York has no desire to let us escape. If she's stuck with this miserable weather, so too should all her residents.

Our flight is delayed due to icing, but Ash assures me we're getting to the Keys, even if we have to drive the whole way. I'm praying it doesn't come to that, though a road trip with him might be its own kind of adventure.

Hell, this entire relationship is an adventure.

It's hard to believe that just a few months ago, I hated Asher Hammond. Now, he's whisking me away to a tropical vacation.

I glance over at him, his fingers drumming against his thigh in sync with the erratic tapping of his foot.

He's aggravated, that much is clear. Things aren't going according to plan, and even though no one—not even him—can control the weather, it's eating at him.

I get it.

But luckily for him, I'm the roll-with-the-punches type. Shit happens, and I'd much rather err on the side of caution in this nasty weather than tempt fate.

As long as we eventually arrive safe and sound on the sand, I'm good.

Until then, I'm making the best of it. Spotting a table in the first-class lounge, I head straight for it. Time for some grub.

"It's not so bad," I say, releasing a moan of contentment as my French toast arrives. "I really wanted this fat-filled feast, and now it's all mine."

Ash chuckles, swiping a piece off my plate before I can stop him. I gasp in mock indignation.

"What? Your food came out first," he says with a smirk.

"You're lucky I like you." I smile, retaliating by snatching a piece of bacon from his plate the second it arrives.

"You more than like me, Ori." Ash winks before diving into his omelet, but his words linger, wrapping around me like a warm hug.

He's right.

I do more than like him.

I'm in love with him—a fact which hit me a week ago as we snuggled in front of the fire at his house. Maybe it was the light snow falling outside the window, the way his hand interlaced with mine, or the way his eyes softened when he looked at me. Perhaps it was the whiskey warming my veins or the simple comfort of the chicken dinner I'd cooked for us earlier.

Maybe it was all those things. Or none of them.

Maybe it was just the undeniable, bone-deep truth that I am devastatingly, irrevocably in love with Asher Hammond.

The urge to tell him flares, even though I know he doesn't believe in love—or at least, not for himself.

The romantic in me argues that he's changed. He's far different from the man I met that first night, when the lines between us were drawn in sarcasm and challenge.

There are moments—so many moments—that whisper I'm not like the others who came before me. This vacation is one of them.

Maybe it's enough.

Maybe he'll stay forever.

"Earth to Ori. You okay?" Ash waves a hand in front of my face, pulling me out of my thoughts.

I snap from my reverie and offer him a rueful smile. "Just thinking."

"Always dangerous where you're concerned. What's up?"

Since there's no way I'm sharing my actual inner dialogue, I opt for a safe subject. "Do you think the cold will hamper the progress on the carriage house?"

It's a legitimate question—Eddie's crew has been moving at a snail's pace lately. I get it; the finer details take far longer to complete and don't offer the same wow factor as a new bathroom or kitchen, even though they're just as important.

But Ash, my unofficial partner in crime throughout this renovation, insists on period-appropriate accents and splashes. He has strong opinions on everything from wall sockets to drawer pulls, but I know it's because he's thinking of me. Plus, his taste is impeccable.

After all, he's dating me, isn't he?

Yes, I'm allowed a few moments to bask in triumph. There are hundreds of women who want Asher Hammond, and he chose me.

Take that, mean girls.

Ash sighs, his focus shifting to his plate. "It likely will. Batteries on the power tools don't last in extreme temperatures. But it's supposed to warm up in the next few days, and good old Eddie will get back to work."

There's no mistaking the sarcasm in his voice.

"Why do you hate Eddie so much? Has he done something to you?"

Ash shrugs, his gaze dropping to his food. "I just don't like the guy," he mutters, his fork pausing mid-air.

I know that tell, and I plan to milk it for all it's worth. "Are you jealous of my relationship with Eddie?"

It's a joke. There's nothing between Eddie and me, but the muscle twitching in Ash's jaw tells me I've hit a nerve.

"You *are* jealous," I say, leaning back with a sigh. "I know you're a brilliant tradesman, but Ash, you're so busy. The house would never get done if I relied on you and Braden to do all the heavy lifting. There aren't enough hours in the day."

"I know," he mutters, stabbing at his eggs without meeting my eyes.

"Then what's the problem? Eddie does great work, and you know it."

Ash tosses his fork down and finally meets my gaze. "I don't like the way he looks at you. Like he sees something I don't deserve."

My chest tightens, the rawness in his voice unraveling me.

"I haven't noticed that."

"Yeah, well, I have. Trust me, he's been analyzing me, too —like he's waiting for me to screw up so he can swoop in and steal you away."

I reach across the table and squeeze his hand, letting my thumb trace over his skin. "No one is stealing me away from you. Besides, you only have one guy to fight off. I deal with an entire legion of Asher Hammond fans on a daily basis."

Do I love that he's concerned about another man homing in on what's his? Absolutely. It's the proof I need that maybe, just maybe, he's in the same emotional place as me.

A smile cuts across Ash's face, and he leans over to kiss me. "No other woman stands a chance."

"I like that. Still, I'm going to keep staking my claim. It's too bad that humans can't operate like dogs. If I pee on it, it's mine."

That does it. Ash throws his head back in a laugh, the

sound rich and unguarded, before sliding into the booth beside me and wrapping me in a hug. "I have fetishes, but that is not one of them."

"Duly noted."

The announcer calls out our flight, and Ash tucks a stray lock of hair behind my ear, his touch lingering. "You ready for some fun in the sun, little one?"

"Born ready."

Stepping off a plane from single-digit weather into balmy sunshine feels like magic.

I inhale deeply, the air sweet with the lush, heady aroma of hibiscus and frangipani, their perfume mingling with the salty tang of the ocean breeze. Tossing my discarded sweatshirt over my shoulder, I shoot Ash a grin and skip toward the baggage claim.

Sue me. This weather is bliss.

Ash shakes his head, but there's no hiding the grin spreading across his face. At the baggage carousel, he grabs my hand and pulls me into his arms, pressing a kiss to my shoulder before nuzzling the crook of my neck. "Someone's happy."

"Are you kidding? This is paradise. I think I'll just stay here. Want to join me?"

"Do you promise to parade around in bikinis daily?"

"No."

His eyes widen, and I laugh. "Who wants to wear that much clothing in this heat?"

He tightens his hold, pressing a kiss to my cheek. "Remember what you said? These curves are reserved for a select few. As in me. Only me."

I blink, caught off guard. I can't believe he remembers me saying that at the holiday fair. Seems he was paying more attention than I realized.

I plant my hands on my hips and give him a mock scowl. "Are you acting the part of the possessive boyfriend?"

"Absolutely. You're mine. End of story."

Damn, but I love how that sounds. I love being his.

And I truly believe we have a future together. What that future looks like is anyone's guess, but I'll play it as it comes. Ash may be reserved when it comes to love, but I know how much he cares about me.

Hell, giving up every other woman in his life says more than words ever could.

Ash's phone rings, and he answers it with a smirk. "Let me guess—your maternal radar went on high alert the second my feet hit Florida. Am I close?"

Ah, Ash's mom. I know they're close—he's always showing me their latest sailing or restaurant adventures on social media —but this feels different. Does she know I exist? And if she does, what does she think of me?

"We're here for four days. That's all the time either of us could take off." He glances at me with a smile. "Mom says hello."

"Hi, Mrs. Hammond," I reply, feeling oddly self-conscious.

"Ori says hi," he relays into the phone. "Yeah, I wish Tampa was closer, too. I miss you. Love you, Mom." He hangs up just as our luggage comes down from the carousel.

He grabs my suitcase before I can reach for it, his movements casual but full of purpose. "I bet she was hoping to see you while you were in Florida," I say, testing the waters.

Ash shrugs, the corner of his mouth tugging into a small smile. "I think she was hoping to see you, actually."

"Me? How come?"

He claims his own suitcase and pulls up the handle,

motioning toward the rental car station. "Why do you think? Might have something to do with the fact that I've told her about you."

My heart skips at his words, but I'm determined to play it cool. "You have? What did you say? That I'm amazing and a goddess in bed? Please tell me you didn't say that last part."

"Definitely not discussing our sex life with my mom," he replies, his smirk growing. "But I did tell her I like you a little. That you keep me entertained."

I roll my eyes, even as a laugh escapes me. I know he's messing with me—his shit-eating grin serves as proof. I also know that any kind of public declaration is difficult for Ash, so while some women might find his words underwhelming, I realize what a big step it is for him to have mentioned me at all.

To anyone outside his immediate circle in Sparkwood.

"Thank God," I sigh dramatically, grinning at him. "I was worried you told her I'm the greatest woman on the planet. That's far too much hype to live up to. I prefer striving for mediocrity."

"Little one," he says, his voice a husky growl, "you haven't been mediocre a day in your life."

Looping my arm through his, we walk to the rental car counter and hand over our reservation paperwork. "Some might say the same for you, Mr. Hammond."

"You're just saying that because I stole you away from the ice and snow."

"It sure as hell didn't hurt your cause."

Ash grabs the keys from the agent, and we stroll to our ride for the next few days—a sporty convertible, perfect for soaking up every drop of tropical air. "If that's the case, then just wait until you see the hotel," he says, a hint of mischief in his tone.

I wrap my arms around his waist, resting my chin on his

chest as I gaze up at him. "Don't need to. This is already one of the best days ever."

He tilts my chin and presses a soft kiss to my lips. "Just you wait, beautiful."

The moment we arrive at the hotel, I understand exactly what Ash was referring to. It's stunning—a high-end resort nestled on the beach, complete with onsite restaurants and luxury boutiques for when the shopping bug strikes.

The second I open the door to our temporary home, I freeze. Tropical bouquets burst with color in every corner of the suite, their perfume a lush mix of sweetness and spice, mingling with the faint saltiness carried in from the ocean breeze. Rose petals lie scattered across the bed, a box of decadent chocolates sits on the side table, and a bottle of champagne chills in an ice bucket, glistening with condensation.

It's breathtaking.

"They think of everything. Talk about setting the mood," I murmur.

Ash steps behind me, wrapping his arms around my waist as he lifts my bag from my shoulder and tosses it onto a nearby chair. "They didn't think of this. I requested it."

I twist in his embrace to face him. "You did all of this?"

He shrugs, his eyes warm as he leans in to kiss me. "I wanted it to be as special as you are."

My chest tightens as I take it all in—every detail he arranged, every thoughtful touch. Blinking back tears, I rise on tiptoe and kiss him hard. "Any chance you might want to explore this bed before we explore the resort?"

A slow smile spreads across his face as he eases me onto the soft mattress, his hands cradling me with care. "No, but I will gladly explore every inch of *you*."

Chapter 13

Sex On The Beach

Ash

"That's it. I'm never leaving." Ori stretches out on the lounger, basking in the eighty-five-degree heat, her skin glowing under the sun.

I lower my sunglasses, letting my gaze sweep over her with zero subtlety. "As long as you keep dressing like that, we can stay here forever."

Her blue bikini, though thicker than dental floss, covers just enough to fuel my imagination. She knows exactly how to work those curves, too, adding an extra hip shake or ass wiggle every time we stroll along the beach. She's trouble, and she knows it.

Hell, I nearly came to blows with some asshole at the bar last night when he thought it was a good idea to get a little too friendly with her.

But Ori just grabbed my hands, pulling me onto the dance floor, her lips finding mine as if to remind me—and everyone else—exactly who she belongs to.

Trust me, I didn't hesitate to return the favor.

I damn near lost it right there on the dance floor, in front of the entire crowd. It's insane how much I want her, every second of every day.

Back home in New York, it's easier to keep my emotions in check. I stay guarded, determined not to let myself get swept away by what I feel for her. But here, surrounded by sun and strangers, I don't need the mask I wear to protect myself.

Here, I can just be me.

And allow myself to feel *everything* for her.

Ori reaches over, her fingers brushing against my arm as she flashes me that soft smile of hers before returning to her book. That single touch sends a jolt through me, the kind that lingers even after her hand is gone.

I lean back, close my eyes, and let the sun warm me down to my core.

Damn, but I needed this trip. And there's no one I'd rather be here with than Ori.

She's the perfect traveler—never complains, always ready to try anything. I've got the photos of her kite sailing to prove it. She makes even the smallest moments feel monumental.

All the little things mean the world to her.

Like this morning, when I ordered breakfast delivered to our room. Sure, on its own, it's hardly noteworthy, but I made sure it included all of Ori's favorite treats—fresh pastries, fruit, and cappuccino. They set it up on the suite patio before she even stirred from the bed.

But when Ori woke up and saw the table laden with goodies, she threw her arms around my neck and kissed me like I was the most incredible man on the planet.

And in that moment, I felt like I was.

I excuse myself and duck inside our suite to call my brother. Look, I know the man's totally capable, but I worry. There's a lot happening back in New York.

"You're the worst," Braden says as soon as he picks up.

"Shit. That bad?"

"No. Everything's fine. But you're in paradise, and we got ten inches of snow yesterday. So yeah, I hate you. Nothing personal, of course."

I chuckle, leaning against the sliding glass door to watch Ori wade into our private pool. The sunlight catches the curve of her shoulders, making it impossible to look away. "I can lie and tell you it's terrible. Does that help?"

"No, because I know it's a lie. Are you two having fun?"

"Best time ever."

The second I say it, I know it's true.

"Anything I need to know about?" I ask.

"Contractors are waiting on some custom tile to arrive so they can finish the floor, and Ori got a massive shipment of inventory yesterday, but other than that... oh, wait."

My stomach tightens. "What's up, Braden?"

He sighs into the phone, and I can already tell I'm not going to like this. "Fuck, I don't know if I should tell you this."

"Now you *have* to tell me."

"Lucille's been calling almost every day. She's relentless. I told her you're on vacation, and she keeps hinting around, asking where you are and if she can have the number."

"Please tell me you didn't."

"Of course not. But prepare yourself for when you get back."

I pinch the bridge of my nose, trying to stave off the irritation building inside me. "I'll set her straight. Sorry that she's bugging you."

"Nah, I enjoy telling her to fuck off."

I laugh, shaking my head as I grab two bottles of water from the fridge. "I'll bet you do. Alright, I'm out of here. See you soon."

What is it about my ex? The woman seems to know, intuitively, that I'm ready to move on and decides now is the time to throw a wrench into the process.

Not happening, Lucille. You will not screw up what I have with Ori.

But, like an earworm that won't relinquish its grip, thoughts of my time with Lucille flood my brain. It's not a fond mashup of memories, but rather a comparison of the two women who have turned my world upside down.

Not that Lucille and Ori are similar in any fashion.

Lucille was, in many ways, a female version of me—enjoying the motorcycle and tattoo life—a bit raucous and extremely raunchy. Especially between the sheets.

She was adventurous but not cultured. Lucille didn't give a shit about designer names or labels. She was fringe and proud of it.

Actually, I don't know who the hell she was. And now, I never will.

Then there's Ori. I never saw her coming. She's a tiny powerhouse with the biggest brain I've ever seen and a mouth that is as talented at telling you off as it is at sucking you off.

But there's something so fragile about her, too. Ori truly believes in fairytales and happy endings, and not just in her books. She believes in them in everyday reality, for everyday people like us.

Hell, she's making me believe it, too.

"I wondered where you'd gone." Ori looks up at me, shielding her eyes with one hand, her lips curving into a soft smile. "Thought you might be planning your escape."

"From you? From here? Not a chance." I sink into a shaded lounger, my gaze raking over her, lingering on every sunlit curve.

"Good answer, sir." She pulls her legs from the pool, water trickling down her skin, and saunters toward me, her fingers slowly loosening the strings of her bikini top. "See something you like?"

"Everything. Every damn inch of you."

That sex kitten smile of hers? It wrecks me every time.

She straddles my lap, her bikini top sliding down as her bare skin presses against me. Her hands tangle in my hair, her lips brushing my ear as she whispers, "Show me."

I'm with Ori. We're never leaving.

Today is our last full day here, and somehow, each moment outshines the last.

The food. The sun. The cocktails.

The sex.

Holy shit, the sex is out-of-this-world *phenomenal*.

There's something about this place—the tropical air laced with the scent of jasmine, the sun melting into the horizon, the way Ori looks at me like she's daring me to give her everything I have and then some.

The rules feel different down here.

Or maybe it's me who's changed.

Ori told me she loved me the other day. It was barely a whisper as we drifted off to sleep, so faint I almost convinced myself I'd imagined it.

But her words have been on a constant loop in my head ever since, haunting me in the best and worst ways.

And just as I started to believe it was nothing more than a dream, she said it again.

This time, it was undeniable—her voice soft but certain, her breath warm against my ear as I collapsed on top of her, our bodies tangled in sticky, sated bliss.

Once again, I stayed silent.

I don't know what's stopping me. Maybe it's the way she looks at me, her eyes so full of trust and hope. She believes in all of it—love, forever, happy endings.

I want to believe in them, too.

Am I chicken shit? Maybe. Probably. Hell, I'm a whole lot of things, including scared shitless of what those words mean and everything they demand.

What's next after *I love you?* A ring? Marriage, if we get that far? A baby?

Ten years ago, I wanted all those things more than my next breath.

But Lucille cured me of that delusion. She ruined me for other women—and not in a good way.

"Hey, no scowls today. Only smiles for our last day in paradise." Ori settles next to me on the edge of the pool, her hand tracing a gentle path along my spine.

"I seriously get why people move to Florida now," I smirk, skewing my mouth as I shoot her a look. "Think I might invest in a place down here."

Ori nods, her lips pooching slightly as she gazes over the private pool area. "Can I come visit?"

"Damn straight. Open invitation." I nudge her shoulder gently.

She sighs, her expression turning wistful. "Look, I'm just going to say it again, even though I know you heard me the last few times. I love you."

Well, that's direct.

My heart races into my throat as I glance at the water and nod. "I did hear you, but I don't say those words, Ori."

She cups my chin, forcing me to meet those dark, soulful eyes. "Doesn't mean I don't. Doesn't mean you can't acknowledge that I have."

I drag a hand through my hair, my thoughts knotting into a mess I can't untangle. "How the hell am I supposed to respond without sounding like a total asshole? Thanks? I know?"

Ori smirks, her eyes sparkling with humor. "All valid responses."

I blow out a breath, shaking my head. "None of them are, and I don't want you angry that I don't say it, because I care about you. You know that, right?"

"Ash," she whispers, her voice steady but unyielding, "I'm

not saying it because I expect you to feel the same. I know you don't, and trust me, the day I can't handle that anymore, I'll walk away. But today's not that day. Right now, I'm embracing all these overwhelming emotions and felt like sharing them with the man who made me feel them. That's all."

Instead of answering, I slip into the warm water and wrap my arms around Ori's waist, pulling her into me.

Her curves melt against me as I tease her lips, coaxing her to grant me access to her talented mouth.

With a soft sigh, she relents, and I slick my tongue against hers, tasting her sweetness, her fire—everything that makes her Ori.

She smells like sunshine and a hint of everything I could have been had I not given my heart to the wrong person the first time.

I wind one hand into her hair, tilting her head to deepen the kiss, my mouth never straying from hers as I lift her effortlessly out of the pool. Her breath hitches, her nails grazing my shoulders as I carry her inside, dripping water onto the polished floor.

She told me she loved me.

I couldn't say it back.

But as I gaze into her deep brown eyes, I know I feel so much for Oriana.

I'm lost in her and I never want to be found.

I lay her gently across the bed, our skin still damp and glistening in the filtered light.

I pull the strings free on her bikini top, tossing it aside as I lower my mouth to tease her pert nipples, my hands gently cupping her firm breasts. My tongue drags along her slick, sun-kissed skin, and I press kisses down her abdomen, desperate to map every inch of her body as mine.

Only mine.

Ori moans softly, her back arching beneath my leisurely exploration, her body yielding to my touch.

I stand at the edge of the bed, hooking my fingers into her bikini bottom and dragging it down her legs, revealing the delicate curves I crave. Grasping one shapely leg, I press a soft kiss to her instep, letting my lips linger.

Higher and higher, I climb, my mouth depositing soft kisses along the smooth curve of her thigh, my breath warm against her skin.

Our eyes lock, and I see the hunger radiating in her gaze—a reflection of the need burning through me. But I won't rush.

Not this time.

This time, she needs to feel everything I can't say.

My cock aches with the sharp pang of restraint, every nerve in my body screaming for release, but I can wait. Ori reaches forward and wraps her fingers around my length. The sensation almost undoes me, but I catch her hand and gently press her back to the mattress, asserting my control.

Leaning forward, I spread her thighs wide, my mouth descending as I drag my tongue along her pussy in a long, deliberate lick.

She tastes like heaven. Every time, it's better than the last—like honeyed perfection meant only for me.

My hands slide under her ass, lifting her closer as I devour her. Her sweet moans fill the room, blending with the faint crash of waves outside. Her fingers tangle into my hair, holding me tight, and I swear she's the most addictive thing I've ever known.

She's everything.

She's fucking everything.

Ori whimpers, her thighs trembling as she chases her release. Her nails scrape down my shoulders, her body arching closer to mine, but I keep her teetering on the edge. Every time she gets close, I shift just slightly, slowing the rhythm and drawing it out.

She deserves every ounce of pleasure I can bring her.

"Please," she begs, her voice a whispery velvet, beckoning me closer. "I need you."

And I believe her. I trust in that need—that quiet desperation. But there's something more as my gaze locks onto hers, so vulnerable and full of trust.

Huffing out a breath, I glance toward the nightstand and the box of condoms. It's within reach. My safety net—our safety net. But when I look back at Ori, everything changes.

Her trembling fingers trace the planes of my face, her touch tentative yet sure, as if she's memorizing me. Her body quivers beneath me, completely open, completely mine.

"I need you," she whispers again, her voice a soft, desperate plea.

God knows I need her, too.

I know the risks. I know what this means. But in this moment, it feels like more than just skin against skin—it feels like giving her a part of myself I've never given anyone.

She loves me, even though I can't say the words back. Maybe this is how I show her I'm trying, that I'm hers in ways I can't articulate.

With my heart pounding in my chest, I toss the condom aside, letting it hit the floor. My mouth crashes to hers, a kiss full of everything I can't yet say. My entire body trembles as I let go of my last reservation.

"You're so beautiful, Ori," I murmur against her lips. "How did I ever get this lucky?"

I pull her slight frame closer, sliding into her warmth, burying myself to the hilt. A low moan rumbles from my chest as I feel every inch of her connecting to every inch of me.

Her body welcomes me, wrapping around me as I pause, overwhelmed by a bevy of emotions.

I damn near lose it right then, as her tight pussy clenches around me.

But there's no way I'm caving—not yet.

I move slowly, pulling almost all the way out before sliding back in, building a torturous, sensual rhythm.

Over and over I plunge into her heat, her pussy growing wetter by the second, her back arching as she meets each thrust.

Fuck, nothing has ever felt so good.

My cock threatens to override my brain, but I hold back, tamping down the need coursing through me.

Right now is all about Ori.

Feeling her.

Feeling us.

Feeling *everything.*

Call me shallow, but this is my love language—an unending adoration of her body that is so much more than just a physical act.

It's how I share everything I feel—the emotions, the need, the fears.

I pray Ori understands. Even though I don't believe in love as a concept, I believe in her.

I believe she might make me whole someday.

I want that with her.

But saying the words, breathing life into them, feels like jumping out of a plane with a parachute I know is faulty.

The last time I did that, I crash-landed in a brutal reality my heart didn't want to see.

Even now, Lucille's specter lingers—not because I want her back, but as a reminder of what happens when I entrust my heart to someone. Chances are, they won't want it.

Even if Ori claims otherwise.

After all, Lucille said all the right words but never meant them. If she had, she wouldn't have spent months lying to me.

Every time I step forward with Ori, it's like the universe waves a red flag, warning me to stay on my guard.

But when I look at her, feel her wrapped around me, I want to give her *everything.*

More than I ever wanted with Lucille.

That knowledge terrifies me because if Ori has the power to love me, she also has the power to destroy me.

The only thing tethering me at this moment is Ori's legs wrapped tightly around me as she urges me on, demanding more.

My time. My body. My loyalty.

I pray it's enough—because it's all I have to give her.

My heart is off-limits.

"Hey, where did you go?" Ori whispers, her voice soft and searching.

Smiling, I shove my jar of doubts onto a shelf deep in my mind. "I'm right here, beautiful. You okay with this?"

She nods, her lips curling into a gentle smile as she pulls me into a kiss. "Are you?"

"You're perfect. How could I not be?"

I start moving inside her again, losing myself in the connection—the purest, rawest need imaginable.

Ori wants me in this moment, and at *this* moment, I can give her everything.

We Have A Problem

Ori

"How was it?" Mina asks, resting her elbow on the counter.

"I would tell you, but then you'll hate me because you had to survive a blizzard while I sat poolside, sipping tropical beverages."

Mina rolls her eyes, but I see the grin threatening to explode across her face. "You're right. I hate you."

She doesn't, of course. First, because the woman doesn't have a mean bone in her body, and second, because she adores the idea of Ash and me together. Something about the undeniable attraction of polar opposites, which, I have to admit, isn't entirely off base.

We are from opposite ends of the spectrum, but somehow, we work. I glimpsed us reflected in a storefront in Key West, and instead of looking ridiculous, we looked... fabulous together. Like we were made to fit.

Of course, it could be love talking—a love only I feel... for now. Still, I'm glad I said it. I'm glad he heard me.

I knew he wouldn't say it back—he's told me enough times he doesn't believe in love—although some wisp of my romantic soul hoped he might surprise me.

No such luck. Not with words, anyway.

But then there was *that* moment. The one where he tossed the condom aside as though it didn't matter anymore—his movements deliberate, his eyes locked on mine. Emotions flashed across his face—feral desire tangled with an unshakable certainty. There was no hesitation. I didn't stop him. I couldn't.

And it didn't end there. The hunger in Ash was different after that—more intense and all-consuming. Something shifted in the man, and he couldn't get enough of me. We caved to our carnal desires several times that last day, each time more urgent than the last, as if waiting was no longer an option.

Hell, he dragged me to a far corner of the first-class lounge at the airport, caging me in his arms as he pressed his length against me, his lips voracious against my neck as he whispered all the filthy things he had in store for me.

But he wasn't content simply to tell me his plans.

"Turn around," he demanded, twisting his hand in my long locks. "Place your hands on the wall."

The devious glint in his eyes screamed trouble, but I couldn't resist him. My breath hitched as I obeyed, my palms flat against the cool surface, anticipation thrumming through my body.

I gasped when his fingers slid beneath my skirt, plunging inside me with a deliberate, possessive rhythm.

The more I squirmed, the tighter he held me, his free hand bracing against my hip as he pushed me closer to the edge.

I don't know who saw us, and Ash claimed he didn't care.

He's always possessed a healthy sexual appetite, but this was a whole new side of the man—ravenous, impatient, reckless. And I'd be lying if I said I didn't love it.

There were the little moments, too. The sweet gestures which, in my heart, added up to love. As we walked through the airport, he kept his arm tight around me. During the plane ride, his hand never left my lap. And I caught the expression on his face as he watched me while we waited for the plane.

He didn't think I saw him... or maybe he did. Maybe it was his way of letting me know I wasn't totally alone in this. That he feels it, too.

Either way, it was a fabulous vacation.

The bells chime over the door, jerking me back to the present moment. Glancing up, I smile as Kevin Duncan strides toward the register. The man has become a bit of a regular here, and despite his obvious wealth, he seems pleasant.

"Hello, Mr. Duncan."

His gray eyes fix on me as he places his briefcase on the counter. "Please call me Kevin. Look at you—stunning color. You've escaped New York, haven't you?"

"I have. Spent a few days in the Keys."

A muscle jumps in his jaw, his smile tight. "How interesting. I hope you had amenable company. I own a glorious home down there. Next time you're thinking of a trip, let me know."

I'm not sure what the man is offering—his home or his company as my escort next time—but either way, it doesn't sit right with me.

"We stayed in a beautiful resort."

"Of course you did. Nothing but the best for you, Oriana."

Time to steer this chat back to business topics. "What can I do for you? Hunting for another first edition? I got a few in last week." I motion to the display case standing against the back wall. Each prized book nestles on velvet stands, high-lighting their ornate leather-bound covers.

"No, actually. I have something for your friend, Asher." He pulls a wrapped book from his briefcase, the leather-bound cover peeking through the tissue paper. "Would you be so kind as to see that he gets this?"

"Sure. He's right next door, you know."

"I know, but something tells me he'd far rather see you than me." He snaps his briefcase shut and offers a stiff smile. "I'll be making more regular visits to see you—I mean, your wonderful book collection. Until next time."

The door swings shut behind him, leaving me standing there with the package in hand.

"What was that about?" Mina asks, eyeing the book curiously. "He brought you a gift?"

"Not me. This is for Ash."

"Strange, I didn't think they knew one another."

"How do you know?"

"When Kevin was here another time, Ash was none too happy with how friendly he was toward you. But he didn't act like he knew who he was when I mentioned his name." She gives me a gentle nudge and a knowing look. "Then again, Ash is *always* jealous where you're concerned."

"Not hardly," I reply with a roll of my eyes. "Although I will run this over to him. But first, tell me about you. Was it truly terrible while I was gone?"

Look, I know it's no picnic to work short-staffed while knowing the person you're covering for is lounging in the tropics. But I hope having Braden here to assist her made it a worthwhile undertaking.

Plus, I gave her the same number of days off I was away. Sure, she didn't get to frolic on a beach, but she avoided blizzard number two, which swept through Sparkwood two days ago. Fair trade, right?

"Braden was a tremendous help. He dug out my car when it snowed and even followed me home."

"Did he now?"

"He didn't come inside," she rushes to add, her cheeks flushing.

"Well, that's just silliness on your part. Imagine the fun you two could have had."

Despite her obvious beauty, Mina is the world's worst flirt. She's friendly and sweet with everyone else, but with Braden, she's painfully shy—like a high schooler with a crush. If things are to move forward, it's clear he'll be the one holding the reins.

"I could barely speak to the man. Not everyone has the ability to spout such sinfully wicked things as you, Ori."

"Imagine if they did? What a world it would be," I reply, blowing a kiss to Ash as he scurries past the shop window. "I don't know where he gets the energy."

No joke. Since our return a week ago, I've only seen Ash in passing.

Apparently, the contractors needed him to make several decisions about Rum & Ruin's renovation, and our vacation threw a wrench into their plans. To atone, Ash has been working on *their* schedule—which means he's been running on caffeine and a prayer.

Judging by his hurried pace as he disappears downstairs, he hasn't slowed down since.

I'll admit, a small part of me wonders if my confession of love struck fear into him. Maybe he's pulling back emotionally and using work as an excuse for the distance.

But a bigger part of me trusts him. Deeply.

Even if he can't say the words, I know he cares about me.

Either way, I miss him. And I'd give anything to see him for just five minutes.

Lucky for me, I have something he wants and needs—coffee.

I smooth my blouse, steadying my nerves, and glance toward the door. "I think I'll pop downstairs and have a look at the progress on the speakeasy."

"Don't tell me you can't go a few hours without speaking

to the man," Mina snorts, her smirk cutting through the morning quiet.

"A few hours? I haven't spent any time with him since we landed."

"Really? He's that busy?"

Something about Mina's wide-eyed gaze doesn't sit right. It stirs up the fear I've been trying to shove aside—the nagging thought that maybe, despite all the trust I've placed in him, Ash doesn't know what to do with my declaration of love.

Best way to handle it? Bring him coffee and be my usual snarky but lovable self. No need to spiral into paranoia when I can take action instead.

"So he claims," I reply with a casual shrug, popping a lid on an extra-large cup of coffee. I tuck the book from Kevin under my arm and motion toward the door. "The least I can do is bring him a refill. Poor man was relegated to gas station java this morning. The horror."

"Likely story."

"One I'll keep telling," I call over my shoulder, flashing Mina a grin before disappearing down the basement steps.

When I hit the floor, I do a double take. This can't be the same basement. It just can't.

The concrete walls are now paneled in a rich cherry wood, the kind that gleams under the soft, recessed lighting, casting a warm, inviting glow into every corner. What isn't paneled is painted a deep emerald green that feels both luxurious and daring. The original oak bar has been restored to its former glory, every inch polished to a mirror-like finish, glistening proudly along the far wall.

There's even a small stage at the front of the speakeasy, framed by delicate sconces, where no doubt any number of sexily clad flappers will entertain the masses. The room practically hums with anticipation, as if it's already alive with laughter, music, and the clink of cocktail glasses.

It's beautiful. Breathtaking, even. And for a moment, it

feels like I've stepped back in time—only better, because Ash has left his mark on every inch of this space.

This is *Rum & Ruin*, and it's going to be a triumph.

"What are you doing down here?"

I pivot, shooting Ash a smile as I motion to the stunning restorations around us. "This is incredible. Well done, you."

"It's not bad, is it?"

I smack his arm, shaking my head at his downplayed reaction. "Not bad? It's every F. Scott Fitzgerald novel brought to life. You did it, Ash. You really did it."

"Hard to believe." His gaze drops to the coffee in my hand. "Is that for me?"

"You know it is. Black like your soul."

"Cute, little one." His eyes roam the length of me, his smirk widening as he takes a sip. "Thank you. I needed this."

"No problem. Also, this came from one of my customers." I hand him the package from Kevin.

Ash eyes it warily, his expression tightening ever so slightly. "Really? Who?"

"Kevin Duncan. He asked me to bring it to you."

Ash sets the coffee on the bar and opens the package, his brows furrowing as he inspects the contents. "Huh. Interesting."

"See? You're the talk of the town. Everyone's champing at the bit to get a drink here."

"Funny thing is, I don't know the guy," Ash says, setting the package aside. "But I'll check it out later."

"So, is *Rum & Ruin* almost ready for her first guests?"

It's strange. Although he's giving me a blatant eye fuck, he hasn't kissed me or even hugged me. After a week apart, I kind of hoped he'd miss me more. Maybe he's too tired to do anything beyond work. At least, that's what I'll keep telling myself.

"Not yet," Ash replies, running a hand over the polished

bar. "There have been a few hang-ups, so it's not going to open for another month or so."

"I'm sorry. Is it because of our vacation?"

"Partly." His mischievous smirk returns. "But you're going to make it up to me."

"I am? Ash, you've seen me with home repair. I'm dangerous with a hammer... or any tool, for that matter."

"Then we have a problem."

The playfulness drops from his voice, his face stern as he stares at me, unblinking, arms crossed over his chest.

"We do?"

Uh-oh. What did I do now?

Trust me, I ask myself that question a lot. My mouth has gotten me into hot water more times than I can count.

"Big problem. Huge."

Ash grips my elbow, his grip firm as he leads me toward the back of the basement. "We'll be back, guys," he calls over his shoulder.

Although there isn't an overabundance of space, Ash had the crew fashion a small office in the back corner of the speakeasy, complete with a leather settee, wood desk, and a tiny private bath.

"So, what kind of problem do we have?" I ask, my brows raising when Ash latches the door behind us.

But Ash doesn't say a word as he lifts me into his arms and deposits me on the desk. His hands hike my skirt up as he tears at my tights, pulling them down in one rapid movement.

"Oh, we have *that* kind of problem." I purr out the words, twining my fingers in his hair.

He cups my face, his thumbs brushing my cheeks as his eyes lock on mine. "I can't stop thinking about you."

"A woman likes to be missed."

He buries his head against my skin, his mouth latching onto the sensitive spot just below my ear, and I gasp, the heat of his breath and the scrape of his teeth sending a shiver down my spine. His hands grip my thighs, firm and possessive, guiding them around his waist until there's no space left between us. "It's more than that. I can't fucking breathe when you're not here."

He drags his head up, his gaze locking on mine. "I need you, Ori. Tell me I can."

There's something so intense about his energy—this raw need all directed at me.

Nibbling his lower lip, I murmur, "I'm yours."

That's all he needs to hear. Ash loosens his belt and jeans, letting them fall to his ankles. He slides his hands beneath my ass, and, without hesitation, thrusts inside me, his body trembling as he pauses.

"You feel too good," he rasps, his voice husky with want.

"I told you that first night, we're a perfect fit."

His movements are slow and deliberate, his eyes never leaving mine. His hands anchor me as his rhythm builds, each thrust sending waves of heat through me, driving me closer and closer to the edge.

The faint sound of workers talking on the other side of the door presses at the edges of my mind, but Ash doesn't seem to care. His focus is entirely on me, his pace steady, his breathing rough.

I bite back a cry, my teeth sinking into my lip as my body tightens around him.

"Ash," I manage, my voice breaking.

His fingers slide into my mouth, and I circle my tongue around them, watching the desire flame in his eyes and knowing in this moment, at least, I own the man—body and soul.

The slow burn builds between us until I catch fire, our bodies trembling with the intensity of release. Ash collapses onto his forearms, his ragged breaths warm against my ear.

"You're everything, Ori." His words emerge in a whisper, so faint I can barely hear them.

Perhaps my mind is imagining things, although one thing is for certain—we didn't use anything. *Again.*

Ash glides his thumb along my lower lip, a strange smile on his face. "You're really fucking pretty."

I chuckle and shake my head at his personal brand of compliment. Since almost our first night together, that's been his signature—where I'm concerned, at least.

Ash stands and walks to the bathroom, returning with a small towel. Then he wipes me down, setting me to rights after our illicit tryst.

And now it's time to address the elephant in the room.

"We're tempting fate." I worry my lower lip with my teeth as I pull my tights up and smooth my skirt.

"I just don't care. I guess I really like you," he replies, his tone casual and matter of fact.

For a man who claims he doesn't believe in love, moments like this make me wonder if he's lying to himself—or both of us.

I snort out a laugh. "Wow. That was almost romantic."

He grins, his familiar cocky edge softening. "I was thinking hot and sexy, but romantic works, too."

"Don't worry. Your secret is safe with me."

"Would you like me to refrain from doing that again?" Ash leans casually against the desk, but his gaze never wavers, cutting through the space between us.

Do I? No, I don't. Some might call it mad, but I feel so connected to him now. Plus, we had the talk about safety and getting tested *long* before this aspect came into play.

Look, I'm a romantic, but I'm not an idiot.

"Just warning you—we're playing with fire." I walk into the bathroom and use the mirror to twist my hair into a loose bun, pulling a few strands free to frame my face.

Ash joins me, resting his head on my shoulder, his green eyes meeting mine in the reflection. For a moment, the world fades away—just him, me, and the crackling heat between us.

"Ori, I've been playing with fire since our first night together," he murmurs.

"You know what I mean."

"I do—and I told you I don't care. So, I guess I must really like you."

"Or you really like the way my pussy feels," I reply as a smirk tugs at my lips.

His laugh is low and rough, but he doesn't miss a beat. "Smart ass," he murmurs, pressing a kiss to my cheek. His tone softens, quieter, more vulnerable. "You, Ori. I really like *you.*"

That settles it. He's the best medicine in the world, and sex with Asher Hammond will definitely cure what ails you… although I'll cut any woman who goes near him now. Just saying.

"Are you free tomorrow?" Ash asks as I return to his office.

"I am. Why?"

"I have a surprise for you." He rubs the back of his neck, his gaze darting to mine before glancing away.

"Another one?" Not that I'm complaining—the Keys were heaven.

"What can I say? I love surprising you." He shoots me a wide grin. Seems he's not disclosing any additional information.

Works for me.

"I love being surprised, so keep them coming, big man."

"Be ready tomorrow at eight, okay?"

"Done and done." I step closer and steal a kiss from his soft lips. "I'm really proud of you. You had a dream, and you brought it to life."

"There've been a lot of dreams coming true lately," he murmurs.

A knock at the office door breaks our moment, but not

before I catch the look in his eyes—nervous, yes, but also hopeful.

I'm not just another good time.

Even if he can't say it now—possibly ever—I'm pretty damn certain he feels it. At least some degree of it. I'm clinging to that hope… along with the glorious orgasm my man just gifted me.

"What were you doing?" Mina asks the second I return to *One More Page*.

"Giving Ash coffee, which is exactly what I told you I was doing."

She clears her throat, pulling a shred of paper from my hair. "And what was he giving *you*?"

My cheeks burn as I wave her off and walk to the opposite side of the counter. "Behave."

"Well, someone has to." Mina motions to a well-dressed man by the coffee bar. "He wants to speak with you."

"What about?"

"He wouldn't say, but insisted on waiting for your return, so he's not a customer."

"Wonderful," I mutter, heading toward the man.

"May I help you?"

The portly gentleman smiles and stands, extending his hand. "Ms. Thorne?"

"Yes."

"I represent McGwyer Holdings, and they would like to make an offer on your property."

"I don't own this building."

"But you own the Dean Estate."

Fuck, he's another seedy investor. They're like cockroaches —you smash one, and ten more pop up.

I straighten my shoulders, refusing to let this man see any sign of weakness. "I do, and I've no desire to sell."

The man, unfazed, pulls some papers from his briefcase. "I think you'd do well to consider their offer. Miss, it's a lovely house, but it will require extensive renovations. The costs will be considerable, and I doubt you'll recoup it when you sell. McGwyer can take it off your hands."

"I'm not concerned about the cost. I considered that when I bought it."

"You're a single woman. What in the world do you need all that space for?"

"Excuse me?" My voice rises, sharp and cold.

Who the hell does this man think he is?

I open my mouth, ready to put this arrogant prick in his place, but a low, familiar voice cuts through the air behind me.

"First, that's none of your damn business."

Ash steps into view, his broad shoulders practically blocking me from sight. His arms cross over his chest, and the man takes a small step back under the weight of Ash's glare.

"Second," Ash continues, his tone hard as steel, "just because she's single now doesn't mean it will always be that way. Hell, she wants like a dozen kids."

I'm not sure which shocks me more: the brazenness of this stranger or Ash's defense, boldly stating I'm not bound for a life of spinsterhood.

"But how will she afford the repairs?" the man persists, clearly grasping at straws.

"Again, none of your business," Ash fires back, his voice carrying an edge that leaves no room for debate. "Between Ori and me, there are more than enough funds. Are we done here? I think we are."

The man stammers something unintelligible, straightening

his tie like that will save face, then quickly gathers his papers and scurries toward the door.

As the door swings shut behind him, I glare at the space he left behind, my pulse still pounding.

Ash smirks, his eyes softening as they meet mine. "He's a piece of work."

"He's not wrong about the costs." I mumble out the admission, hating that there is truth to that asshole's words.

Ash steps closer, brushing a strand of hair from my face. "Doesn't matter. You don't have to face it alone. Not anymore."

The blood pounds in my ears, so loud I can barely hear his next words.

He glances at the clock. "I have to run, but I'll see you tomorrow. Don't worry. We've got this, Ori."

"Damn, but that was hot." Mina walks over, joining me at the coffee bar, her grin as wide as the Hudson.

"Are you talking about that smarmy investor? If so, we need to work on your taste in men."

Mina waves her hand, a look of disgust passing over her features. "Not him. Ash and his full-throttle defense of you."

"I didn't even hear him walk in."

"You should have seen his face when he overheard what that jerk was saying to you. Stormed over like he was about to strangle him."

"It was impressive. My own personal bodyguard." I'm trying to downplay it, but Mina is right. Ash's tongue lashing hit me in *all* the feels.

"Way more than that. Did you hear him? She won't always be single. She wants twelve kids. Ori and I will handle the expenses." She hops onto the counter, her face alight with mischief. "I just need to know. When's the wedding?"

"For God's sake," I mutter, grabbing a stack of books to return to the shelves, hoping to smother the blush creeping up my neck.

"I'm serious. Ash doesn't behave that way—ever. I told you, Ori. He's different around you."

"You barely knew the man before."

"I knew *of* him, and trust me, that's enough to know this isn't typical behavior. He wants a future with you."

"I highly doubt that."

"Why?"

I stop mid-step, as the bluntness of her question catches me off guard, and the raw truth bursts from my mouth before I can stop it. "Because he doesn't love me."

The room falls quiet. My voice trembles as the words hang in the air, stark and painful. I grip the edge of the counter, my knuckles white.

Mina tilts her head, her expression softening. "How do you know?"

"I told him I loved him, and he reiterated that although he cares for me, that emotion isn't in his wheelhouse."

"Hmm."

"What?" I snap, hoping my friend will take the hint and switch to a less painful subject.

"Actions speak louder than words, right? For someone who doesn't believe in love, he sure acts like he does." Mina gives me a soft smile before hopping off the counter, as if she didn't just drop the most casual bombshell in history.

Then, in typical Mina fashion, she waltzes away, leaving my mouth agape and my emotions fluttering.

Why do her words affect me so? Because they echo my own thoughts—the idea that Ash, despite his arguments to the contrary, has fallen as hard and fast as I have.

Maybe I'll bring it up tomorrow. After all, Ash did mention having a surprise for me.

The man is full of surprises, and so far, I've loved every single one.

Chapter 15

Trouble Comes Calling

Ash

That fucking piece-of-shit investor.

I hate when wealthy men try to take advantage of people, assuming just because they're young, poor, or female, they're incapable. But I think I showed him exactly where he could shove his proposal.

I didn't know who the guy was as I walked through our shared hallway, but I saw how Ori was reacting to him—her head bowed, her hand rubbing her brow. She was upset, and that was enough to make me see red.

So, I left Braden hanging mid-sentence and rushed into *One More Page* to protect my girl.

I think she appreciated it, too, even if I didn't intend to say all that aloud.

Now, it's back to work. Or, as I lovingly call it, the insanity of my life.

"Everything okay?" Braden inquires as I walk into Black Lotus. "You rushed out of here like your bike was on fire."

"Shut the fuck up. Why would you put that out there?" I shoot my brother a look of death, shuddering inwardly at the very thought. After everything I've gone through with my ride, I'm getting buried with her. No joke.

"Just saying. Relax."

"Some sleazy property investor came to speak with Ori about selling her house. I intervened."

"Does she want to sell?"

"No, but she gets overwhelmed. Who wouldn't, right? I assured the schmuck that Ori and I have it covered."

Braden's grin widens. "Knew it."

"Knew what?"

"You've fallen for Ori."

"Whatever, man."

"That's not a no." He chuckles, dodging the paper cup I lob at his head.

The truth is, I have fallen for her. Hard and fast, and there's no going back. I tried everything to avoid love, but it turns out love is one hell of a huntress.

I hate I couldn't say it back to Ori when she told me she loved me in Florida, but I had to let it sink in. Marinate on the idea that I could love again like I did with Lucille.

That's not right either, because this is bigger than that love. Deeper.

I'm so fucked.

But maybe not. Maybe this time will be different because I'm different. Ori is different. She's not Lucille, and she's never given me a reason to doubt her sincerity.

Granted, neither did Lucille—until the day I proposed. And look how that turned out.

See? This is the shit circling my head. All. Day. Long.

But tomorrow night, I'm biting the bullet. I'm not ready to admit that I'm in love, but I am ready to reassure Ori that I don't want any other women—ever. Period. End of story.

And if any guy comes near her, they're going to wind up as dog food.

Not even kidding. The possessiveness I feel toward that petite ball of fire grows exponentially by the day. Pretty soon, it will consume me, much like everything else about Ori.

Then, I'll tell her how I want us to grow a life together. Working on the Dean Estate, pooling resources, and building something real.

I think she'll be on board.

It's going to be good.

"Hey," Braden claps his arm around my shoulder, his characteristic grin lighting up his face. "I'm thrilled for you. She's a good woman. A damn good woman."

"I take it you're a fan of Ori?" Truth is, I know my brother loves her. He's also got the hots for her employee, Mina, but that's a story for another time.

"I enjoy seeing my brother happy after so many years of watching you miserable."

"I wasn't—" But I stop myself because, despite the devil-may-care facade I wore as I played with countless women, I was deeply unhappy.

Now, for the first time, I see a future that isn't just me, my bike, and some one-night stand. I see a life with Ori.

"Am I right?" Braden nudges me, pushing as usual until I cave and admit he's been correct all along.

"Damn it, dude. You're right, okay? She's amazing, and… I'm crazy about her."

"Was that so hard?"

Actually, it was incredibly easy.

Maybe I *can* tell Ori how I feel.

Maybe this time, my heart won't get ripped apart.

So much crap to do, and there just aren't enough hours in the day.

I head downstairs, giving a quick once-over to the day's work before sending the guys home. They're busting their asses, and *Rum & Ruin* is coming together quickly.

Not as quickly as I'd like, but hey, Rome wasn't built in a day, right?

Settling into my office, I pull out some designs I've been working on, my mind already running through the changes I want to make. My gaze drifts, landing on the book Ori delivered earlier.

I still have zero clue why some random guy would give me a book, but perhaps it's like Ori said. Maybe he's excited about the speakeasy opening, too.

Leaning back in the chair, I flip through the pages. The scent of old paper fills the air, and I must admit, the book is pretty damn cool.

A piece of paper slips out, landing in my lap. Frowning, I unfold it, expecting some notes or a misplaced receipt.

It's neither.

It's a letter.

And it's addressed to me.

Ash,

You've got yourself a nice setup here. Oriana's quite the prize.

I wonder, does she know about the skeletons you keep?

Or is honesty still a luxury you can't afford?

Good luck keeping all your cards in play—someone always has a better hand.

— Kevin

I tug a hand through my hair, my emotions spinning. What the fuck? I don't even know this guy, and yet he's threatening me?

Oh, hell no. Time for me to track this bastard down and show him that keeping your mouth shut and out of other people's business is always the best move.

Then there's his mention of Oriana. I knew this piece of shit was after her. I don't know what game he's playing, but if he thinks I'll stand by while he messes with her, he's dead wrong.

I crumple the letter and toss it onto the desk, reaching for the bottle of whiskey in the drawer. Screw the glass. I twist off the cap and take a long pull, the burn doing little to temper the fire in my chest.

"Skeletons." The word rolls bitterly off my tongue. I've had enough of them. I'm tired of being haunted by ghosts I didn't invite.

Deep breaths, Ash. Focus. He's just trying to get in your head, and you can't let him win. He's got nothing on you. Hell, he doesn't even know you.

The vibrating hum of my cell phone slices through the tension, the unknown number flashing across the screen. My gut tightens as I stare at it. Instinct tells me not to answer. Logic tells me it could be important.

Pick up the damn phone.

"Yeah?" I bark into the receiver, still on edge, wondering if it might be my new nemesis on the other end.

It's not.

"Ash." Her voice trembles, raw and barely audible.

"Lucille?" My grip on the phone tightens, and I push out a sharp breath. Of course, it's her. "How the hell did you get this number?"

She sniffles, her voice cracking. "I need your help."

I scrub a hand over my face, the weight of the day pressing heavier. "What's going on?"

"I can't explain over the phone. Please—it's important."

"Lucille, you can't just—"

"Please," she interrupts, her voice desperate, trembling with fear. "Don't say no."

My jaw clenches, torn between frustration and an ingrained sense of duty. I don't owe Lucille anything, but the terror in her voice sets alarm bells ringing in my head.

"Where are you?"

She rattles off an address I recognize immediately: *The Camelot Inn.* A goddamn cesspool.

"Stay put. I'll be there soon."

I stride to the front door five minutes later, pulling Braden aside. "I need you to take my consult for the afternoon, okay?"

"What's going on?"

"Lucille called, and she's begging me to come get her at a motel a few towns over."

"Why you?"

"No idea, but she's hysterical. I'm going to get her and bring her wherever she needs to go."

"I don't like this, Ash. Last time you got mixed up with this woman, you damn near got killed."

"Not getting mixed up with her. Just giving her a lift."

I can tell by the set of my brother's jaw that he's not convinced, but he also knows better than to push the issue. Smart man.

"Be careful," he mutters as I walk out the door.

Trust me, brother. With this woman, careful is my middle name.

Lucille sure can pick 'em. I drive into the parking lot of *The Camelot Inn* just as the sun is setting, noting how the derelicts and drug addicts are just starting to stir, searching for their nightly fix.

The seediest motel for three counties—renowned for all

manner of debauchery—and this is where my ex-girlfriend winds up? Never a dull moment with Lucille, that's for sure.

I knock at the door of room #7, my skin crawling just being here.

"Ash?" Lucille's voice comes from the other side, shaky but unmistakable.

"It's me."

The sound of bolts sliding and locks turning assuages my ears before she pulls the door open, grasping my arm and tugging me inside.

What the fuck? I do not want to stay here a minute longer than necessary.

"Thank you for coming."

My jaw drops as I take in the faint bruise covering her upper cheekbone and the half-healed split in her lower lip. I pull her under the flickering light, studying the marks more closely.

"What the fuck is going on? Who did this to you?"

"A bad man."

"That's an understatement. Is this the first time?"

I already know the answer. Sadly, most women don't leave the first time. Or the tenth. Hell, some never leave, powerless to escape the abuse as society turns its head away.

Total bullshit.

I'm not in the mood for a knock-down, drag-out fight, but it looks like that's what this is gearing up to be.

No one hits a woman.

No. One.

A heavy knocking reverberates through the room, and my gaze flits between Lucille and the door. "Did he tail you?"

Lucille shakes her head, peeking through the keyhole before swinging the door open.

On the other side stands Trace. Also known as Lucille's ex-husband, the guy I unwittingly screwed over a decade earlier.

Lucille, what the hell are you doing?

I tense, the weight of old grudges mixing with fresh confusion. Maybe these two dragged me here to settle some decade long grievance.

All I know is—I should have listened to Braden.

Trace notices my stiff stance and extends his hand. "Easy, brother. I come in peace."

Now I know this is about to get messy.

I stare at his outstretched hand, still not trusting the situation—or either of them.

"Trust me. I'm not here for you."

Although Trace might be full of crap, I'll give him the benefit of the doubt. What other choice do I have? He's standing between me and the door, so if I want to get past him, I'll have to go through him.

With a sigh, I shake his hand before swinging my gaze back to Lucille. "Want to tell me what the fuck is going on?"

"I don't know about you, Ash, but I need a drink." Trace pulls a bottle of whiskey from his coat pocket, sloshing the liquid inside. "You game?"

"Why the hell not?" I mutter, my eyes bouncing between Trace and Lucille like a pinball on speed.

He grabs two disposable cups from the counter and pours out the amber liquid.

He hands me the shot, and I nod toward Lucille. "Where's yours?"

"I'm on the wagon."

At first, I figure she's drying out, but then I notice the slight swell of her belly.

There's no way.

"You're pregnant?" I choke out.

A feeling I'm not familiar with shoots through me—a jealousy that she's having a family. Lucille never wanted kids, but I was champing at the bit to have a few. That is until she eviscerated my heart.

After that, I shelved the idea, right next to love and all its trappings.

Now, *she's* having a kid?

Fucking figures.

Lucille rests a protective hand on her belly. "Fifteen weeks. Hard to believe, right?"

"That's an understatement. Are you the dad?" I motion toward Trace. Anything seems possible at this point.

Trace snorts into his glass. "Hell, no. That would be too easy."

I grab my keys from my pocket, jerking my thumb toward the door. "Look, Lucille, Trace is here. He can take care of you, okay? I've got to go."

"That's not why you're here," Trace replies, motioning for me to take a seat at the battered wood table.

I scoff, growing more irritated by the second. "Then someone better tell me why the fuck I am here."

"Because we need your help." Trace's voice is firm, unyielding.

"We? As in you two?" I wag my finger between Trace and Lucille.

Trace shakes his head, his expression unreadable in the dim light. "We, as in the United States government."

I rub a hand across my eyes, certain this is some crazy fever dream concocted by my sleep-addled brain. "Wait, are you—"

"I'm with Homeland Security." His tone is matter of fact, but the words knock me off balance.

"I thought you were part of an MC."

Trace waves his hand dismissively. "Never mind that. Look, Lucille has gotten involved with the wrong man."

"I can tell."

"And now, through no fault of your own, you're also involved."

"Wait a damn minute." My voice sharpens as I lean

forward, pointing to myself. "How the hell am I involved? I don't even know the asshole she's dating."

Then it hits me. Maybe I do know the son-of-a-bitch. Who else has been sending me veiled threats?

I slump against the chair. "Kevin Duncan."

"Yep." Trace takes another sip of his whiskey, his foot tapping a steady rhythm against the dingy carpet. "Guess you've had a few dealings with him?"

"You could say that." My jaw tightens as I glance at Lucille. "He left me a note, intimating he was going to reveal the skeletons in my closet. Some such shit. Not sure what he thinks he has on me, though."

Lucille leans forward, her fingers drumming nervously against the table. "He thinks you're my baby's father."

My entire world tilts on its axis, her voice reaching my ears like it's traveling down a long, dark hallway. "Excuse me?"

Those are the only words I can manage, and even they feel like a monumental effort.

I scrub my hand over my face, as the cloudy, seemingly random moments—the book, the note, Kevin's car loitering outside my shop, and his dogged interest in Ori—form a horrifyingly clear picture.

Now I get it, although I'm not sure how Kevin made such a ridiculous leap.

"How the hell did he reach that conclusion?" I finally manage, my voice hollow with disbelief.

"He suspected something was up between us after he found pictures from the convention in Vegas. I denied it, but Kevin was convinced we were sleeping together."

"Yeah, I get that." The words bite as they leave my mouth, my head pounding. "So why didn't you set him straight? Or better yet, ignore his bullshit accusations and leave?"

"It's not that simple." Her voice cracks, tears spilling down her cheeks. "Kevin is dangerous. And it's not just about me— it's about the women at the club."

"What club?" I snap. Nothing they're saying makes any sense. They might as well be speaking Chinese.

Trace clears his throat, his calm demeanor further stoking my irritation. "Kevin owns a high-end sex club. We've been monitoring it for months, and we believe it's a front for trafficking."

I whirl back to Lucille, incredulous. "I'll ask you again. Why the hell didn't you leave?"

"Because she's been working with me." Trace's tone is firm, the syllables clipped.

"Are you Homeland Security, too?" The sarcasm drips from my words.

"Of course not," Lucille snaps. "I worked reception at Kevin's club a few nights a week. I always surmised something was happening there, but I chalked it up to paranoia and too many crime dramas. A few months ago, I saw Trace at the club, but I avoided him, as I've done for the last decade. The next day, he showed up at the tattoo parlor where I work. Told me who he was and how I could help him."

"You didn't know he worked for the government?" My skepticism is palpable. Hell, Lucille and Trace were married— how does someone hide that integral piece of information?

"There was a lot I didn't know about my husband." Lucille's voice is calm, but there's an edge to it—a resentment, or unfinished business, maybe both.

"That worked both ways," Trace mutters, shooting her a side eye. "Anyway, Lucille offered to be our eyes and ears in the club—monitoring which girls came in and, more importantly, which girls vanished without a trace. Meanwhile, I continued to play the part of the interested customer, although I damn near blew my cover when Kevin smacked her in front of everyone. But Lucille stopped me, reminded me of the bigger picture."

I notice the defiant flicker in Lucille's eyes and realize she didn't just stumble into this mess. She chose to stay. Part of me wants to respect her bravery, while the other part wants to wring her neck for putting herself in danger.

"What's the bigger picture, Trace?" I grind out. "Because all I see is that Lucille is hurt and you're hiding behind some bullshit bureaucratic red tape."

"If I go in there, guns blazing, without solid evidence, not only will I lose my job, but that piece of crap walks. Lucille's been integral in collecting intel, and we're close to taking the bastard down, but her current situation complicates things." Trace's gaze shifts to her stomach, and the pieces click into place.

Still doesn't answer *my* biggest question.

"Speaking of that," I point at Lucille's belly. "Let's back up a minute. How did I get named as the father again?"

"I didn't plan it," Lucille blurts out, the desperation thick in her tone. "When Kevin started hitting me the other night, demanding to know what I'd done, I panicked. I didn't know what *it* was. If he found out I was working with Trace, I'd be dead—no doubt about it. So, I played the only card I had—I broke down crying and told him I was pregnant. He called me every name in the book—whore, bitch, cunt—and then, as calm as you please, he proclaimed that you *must* be the father. Like he'd solved a puzzle. Was almost smug about it. He said that made me someone else's problem now." She pauses, hanging her head. "I seized the moment and ran with it."

Holy shit.

"You agreed I was the father?"

Lucille nods, seemingly unaware of the shitstorm she's thrown my way. "I was so afraid I'd lose the baby if he didn't stop."

But two and two are *not* equaling four. "Why doesn't Kevin think the baby could be his?"

"He had a vasectomy years ago. Didn't work, obviously, but the truth doesn't matter to Kevin when it fails to suit his narrative."

I stand and pace the length of the grimy, threadbare carpet, sucking in a lungful of the stale motel air. "So, what now? What's your end game here, Trace?"

"Lucille moves in with you under the guise that you two are having a child together."

I screech to a halt and look at Trace, my jaw slack. "You're fucking kidding me. There *must* be another option."

"I put Lucille into witness protection, far beyond Kevin's grasp."

"Great idea," I reply, motioning toward her. "Request somewhere tropical. You love the beach."

"If we do that," Trace continues, "then Kevin may grow suspicious and shut down his operation. If Lucille stays local and visible, it lends credence to her story that you two are having a baby. It keeps his focus on her—and you—and off the trafficking."

Lucille shifts in her seat, wringing her hands. "If I disappear, those women will vanish, too."

"Jesus Christ," I mutter, yanking a hand through my hair.

The weight of what they're asking crushes me. They don't just want me to lie—they want me to become part of this fucked-up charade.

"We need you," Trace says, his tone firm. "If Kevin thinks the baby is yours, it buys my team time. Time to finish the investigation. Time to keep Lucille safe. And time to stop the women at the club from disappearing."

"This is insane." I scrub a hand over my face, my pulse pounding in my ears.

Trace's voice hardens. "I won't lie to you—it's dangerous. Guys like Kevin think they're untouchable, but they all slip up, eventually. If we pull this off, we can shut Kevin down for good. Countless women are depending on that."

"And what's the plan after that?" I inquire, my voice dripping with sarcasm. "Am I supposed to raise his kid, too?"

"No one's asking you to do that." Trace shakes his head,

the exhaustion etching lines into his face. "But we need your help to keep Lucille safe."

I understand how much is riding on Trace's investigation, and I've watched the documentaries—girls, some barely teenagers, stolen from their homes and sold into a life of sexual slavery.

Doesn't change the magnitude of their request.

"You really can't do this without me?"

"Brother, I wish we could. Trust me, I don't enjoy involving civilians in my work. Right now, Kevin doesn't know what to believe. That's why he's digging into your business. He's trying to figure out if Lucille's pregnancy claim is a setup. If you play along, act like the stand-up guy helping the woman he got pregnant, it might throw Kevin off the trail."

"Or he might shoot me in the street." I bite out the words, although at this point, anything is possible.

Trace shakes his head. "Kevin is a lot of things, but stupid isn't one of them. I'm hiding you two in plain sight. Everyone knows you in Sparkwood, Ash. If something happens to you, the whole town will be out for blood—and Kevin knows it. He'll make your life hell, but he's not stupid enough to risk collapsing his entire operation by taking you out. His house of cards is wobbling, and he knows one wrong move will bring it all crashing down."

"You've thought of everything," I mutter, the whiskey threatening to make a reappearance. "How long is this for?"

"Six weeks, maybe less. There's been talk of a new shipment within a month."

"Shipment meaning—"

"Girls," Trace states, the words falling clipped from his lips.

Yep, that whiskey is definitely coming back for round two.

Focus, Ash. Fucking keep it together.

"Trace said, hiding *us* in plain sight. Are you moving to

Sparkwood?” I ask Lucille, knowing my brother will have a conniption when he learns that piece of information.

“Yes. You and I must put up a unified front. Show the town, and more importantly Kevin, that we’re together.”

“So, you’ll live at my place?”

Please say no.

She nods. “And work at Black Lotus.”

“And we tell everyone the baby is… ours?” My voice cracks.

“You two have history,” Trace says, pulling his phone from his pocket. “Plus, there are photos of you two hanging out recently. It’s plausible.”

I drag a hand over my beard, my brain not fully comprehending this insane situation. “Shit, I hate this, but I get how big this endgame is, so I guess I’m in. But I need to talk to Ori and Braden first—let them know the situation.”

“Not a possibility. On either count,” Trace replies without hesitation.

“What the fuck do you mean?”

“This is on a strictly need-to-know basis. We need both of them—and their reactions—to be believable. Trust me, Kevin Duncan is watching, just waiting for someone to slip up.”

“You want me to lie to my girl?” I sputter out the words, shaking my head and hands in tandem.

“I understand what you’re feeling—”

I cut Trace off, slicing my hand through the air in a cutting motion. “No, you don’t. You’re asking me to lie to my girlfriend and claim my *ex* is having my baby.”

“That is what I’m asking,” Trace states, his gaze fixed on mine.

“I can’t do it. I’ll lose her.” Don’t either of them understand the gravity of this situation—of *my* situation?

“Maybe not,” Lucille chimes in. “If she realizes I’m not a threat—”

I smack my hand against my forehead. I swear, Lucille can

be so dense sometimes. "Which would be a hell of a lot easier to accomplish if I could tell her the truth. Explain how I'm working undercover and that it isn't my baby. There's no way she'll understand the alternative."

Trace leans back, arms crossed. "You and Ori have been dating three months, right?"

A muscle jumps in my jaw. "Should I bother asking how you know that?"

"Trust me, Ash, I don't give a damn about your social life —except where it intersects with this case. I'm right, though, aren't I? Three months?"

"Just about."

"Well," Trace points at Lucille, who sits silently, her face unreadable, "she's fifteen weeks. So whatever happened was before you and Ori got together."

"It doesn't matter. If I go along with this, I'll lose her." My voice cracks, the raw emotion threatening to take over. "She'll never forgive me."

"And you'll never forgive yourself if something happens to her. Look, Ash, you don't have much choice. If Kevin suspects this is a setup, it's not just Lucille or those girls in danger. It's everyone connected in any way with this case—and that includes the woman you love."

He slides a few photos across the table to me—Ori at her shop, Ori walking down Main Street, Ori at the grocery store.

"Did you take these?" The words fall from my mouth like shards of ice.

"Kevin did," Lucille says. "Or one of his guys. I found them in his desk drawer right before I left. I knew then he was watching you because I recognized the sign for *Black Lotus*."

But I'm not worried about my safety. It's the sight of Ori's face in those photos that hits me like a gut punch—each one a stark reminder of how close this bastard is to destroying everything I care about.

"He's watching her."

"And waiting," Trace says grimly. "You saw what he did to Lucille's face. He's capable of far worse."

"But why Ori? She has nothing to do with this."

"Because Kevin feels you took something that belonged to him." Trace jerks his thumb toward Lucille. "Even if he's glad to be rid of her, he won't forgive the perceived slight. He'll go after something you care about, just to make a point. Pretty obvious who that is."

"I can't do this." The words come out rough, a plea I don't even recognize as my own.

I never thought anyone would make me want to take a chance on the future again, but then Ori walked into my life. And now my past is demanding I throw it all away?

Trace's expression hardens, his tone cutting through my hesitation. "You think this is about your relationship? About whether Ori forgives you? Wake up, Ash—it's about keeping her safe. Kevin's already circling. If you step out of line, she's his next move. You help me, and I'll make sure Kevin doesn't get anywhere near her."

My hands tighten on the back of the chair, my knuckles white from the force of it. Anger simmers just beneath my skin, but Trace doesn't let up.

"You love her? Fine. Then protect her. You want to keep her safe? This is how."

"Fuck. Fuck. Fuck." I mutter the word over and over, desperate to awaken from this nightmare.

But it's not happening.

"Ash, I hate that you're involved. You're innocent in this. So are the people you love. I promise I'll keep all of you safe, but I need your help to do that. What do you say?"

The weight of Trace's words settles over me like a vise, squeezing tighter with every passing second.

I have no choice. To protect the woman I love, I have to lie to her.

I have to break her heart. Shatter any belief she has in me, in us, and in the future we could have had together.

They say you don't know what you've got until it's gone. Well, I know *exactly* what I've got with Ori—and what I'm about to lose. The thought makes me want to vomit.

But one thought rings louder than the rest.

I love you, Ori. Fuck, I should've told you that sooner. I should have said something on that first day. That first week.

Now, I may never get the chance to give her the life she deserves.

I thought losing Lucille was bad? It's nothing compared to giving up the woman I adore. But Trace is right, I'll lose my damn mind if harm befalls Ori.

I take another swig of whiskey, slamming the glass on the table. "Fine. But when this is over, I'm done and you two will get the fuck out of my life. No questions asked."

If keeping Ori safe means ripping my heart out and handing it over, then so be it. But Kevin? That bastard won't make it out of this unscathed.

Trace nods, his expression grim. "Fair enough. But for now, we play the hand we've been dealt."

Chapter 16

Breakfast in Bed ... For Three?

Ori

Ash isn't the only one capable of surprises.

The man has been burning the candle at both ends, running on a few hours' sleep per night and subsisting on whatever food he can grab on the fly. So, I'm bringing him breakfast in bed.

I'm fully aware he won't stay there for long, but at least it gives him a healthy start to the day. Plus, I'm worried about him. Even with his insane schedule, he always took the time to text me goodnight, even managing a few sexy comments to keep me sated during our time apart.

But last night? His reply was brusque—cold, almost.

Since I know I haven't done anything to anger him, something else must be upsetting him, and I intend to figure out what.

I pull up to his farmhouse, my gaze falling on an unfamiliar sedan parked next to Ash's truck.

That's odd.

But I shake off the thought and grab my basket of goodies from the backseat.

I stroll up the walkway and ring the bell but freeze when the door opens.

Standing on the threshold is a woman wearing a curious expression.

Trust me, lady, I'm wondering who the hell you are, too.

First thing I notice? She's tall, at least 5'9", and towers over me. The second thing? She's stunning. Her bright pink hair tumbles over her shoulders, and her eyes are an almost jarring shade of blue. Tattoos travel the length of both arms and across her chest in a colorful floral motif, all accentuating her impossibly ample tits.

Yes, I look. No doubt with the shirt she's wearing, that's exactly what she intends.

Then I notice the third thing about this gorgeous stranger —her slightly distended belly. It's not over-the-top obvious, but as a woman, I can tell.

She's pregnant.

Guess that whole pregnancy glow isn't a myth.

"Can I help you?" she asks, leaning against the doorframe.

I hope someone can, because I have a million questions about why Braden is dating a pregnant woman. Namely, is it *his* baby? If so, this discovery will devastate poor Mina.

Can't say I blame her because I'd feel the same way.

I lift the basket of breakfast food. "I came to see Ash. Is he here?"

A soft smile touches her lips. "You must be Ori."

"I am. And you are?"

She extends one hand, her grip friendly and firm. "I'm Lucille."

Just like that, the bottom of my world drops out.

Lucille is not a common name. There's zero chance that Braden is dating someone with the same name as the woman who broke Ash's heart all those years ago.

Which means this is Ash's Lucille—aka, his one true love.

Fuck, I need answers.

"Umm… are you visiting?" I stammer, my voice cracking under the dread.

"Staying here for a while. We wanted a safe place for the baby and me."

We wanted a safe place? We, as in her and Ash?

I need to leave because I'm milliseconds away from a total meltdown. My chest tightens, and I can't seem to get any air into my lungs as the reality of the situation settles over me.

Lucille is back, and she's carrying Ash's baby.

I need to go.

Now.

The familiar sound of Ash's boots echoes down the hallway, growing louder until he steps into the doorway. His eyes widen when he sees me, and he sucks in a sharp breath. "Ori, you're here."

My lower lip trembles, but I force my voice to sound normal, unaffected by the blow just dealt to my heart. "I was worried about you not eating right, but… I see you're fine. I'm leaving now."

Tossing the basket aside, I race down the walkway, tears blurring my vision.

"Ori, wait." Ash grabs my arm, spinning me around to face him. "Please, let me explain."

"Explain what?" My voice cracks, raw with emotion. "Your great love is back, and she's brought reinforcements. Congratulations on that, by the way. Banner day for you."

Ash's jaw tightens, his expression grim. "Trust me, you don't understand. Come inside so we can talk."

"You were with her last night?"

His gaze drops to the gravel, his voice a low rumble. "Yes. I didn't know until yesterday."

"Did you cheat on me?"

"Never. This was… before you and me."

I wipe my eyes, but the tears keep falling, hot and relentless. "You told me you two had slept together, but I didn't realize it was a few months ago."

He drags a hand through his messy hair, the tension radiating off him. "It just happened. We're not together."

Is that supposed to make me feel better?

"Well, you should be," I snap. "You're having a baby. You're a family."

"It's complicated."

At that moment, I realize it's not.

"No, it's simple. You love Lucille. It's only ever been her, and look how lucky you are—dreams do come true for some people."

Ash's hands slide along my face, his touch firm, forcing me to meet his gaze. "No way. I don't love Lucille."

His words hang in the air, doing nothing to soothe the ache in my chest.

And now I feel like even more of a fool for proclaiming my love for Ash during our vacation.

"Well, we both know you don't love me."

"Ori—"

I throw up my hands, cutting him off. "Honestly, just stop talking. Nothing you can say will make this situation feel any better for me. I'm just another name in your long line of women while you waited for Lucille's return. I see that now."

"You don't see—"

"Shut up," I hiss, anger flooding my veins. "Just stop with the bullshit, okay? I was a fool for believing this meant something. That *I* meant something."

"You mean everything to me."

How is it that the vision in my head is so drastically different from reality? I knew Lucille destroyed Ash, but I never guessed he still carried a torch for her. There's a fool born every minute, and this time, it's me.

Dragging a hand under my nose, I turn and walk to my truck, but Ash is hot on my heels. As soon as I reach for the handle, his hand covers mine.

"I'm begging you. Please don't walk away from me. You're all I've got."

"You don't need me, Ash. You never did."

"This was before you and I got together. If I had known—"

"Don't go there. Don't wish that, ever."

"You know what I mean. It's been a fucking horrible night."

I finally meet his gaze, peering into the green depths. He looks exhausted—dark circles under his eyes, worry lines creasing his forehead. He looks utterly haggard.

Neither of us has the energy to hash this out right now. Not that there's anything left to discuss, aside from returning the few personal items we've left at each other's places.

Hell, it took Ash a month to invite me to his home. It took Lucille one night to receive an all-access pass to live here.

The writing is on the wall. It's likely always been there—I just didn't want to see it. But my eyes are open now.

"Little one, I can't do this alone." His voice is low, trembling with emotion.

Damn me and my soft heart, but the man looks petrified. I want to hate him, but it's not that easy.

"You don't have to," I reply quietly.

His eyes search mine, a glimmer of hope lighting them. "You mean that?"

"Of course. You have Lucille, and I'm sure your parents will help however they can."

"What about us?"

"There is no us. I don't think there ever was."

"Please don't say that. Don't walk away from me now—I'm begging you."

I pull open the truck door and climb inside. "I need time, Ash. Time to process this. When I'm ready, we can talk. But until then, I need space."

I don't wait to hear his reply. What can he say that will change any of this?

Although I'm crumbling inside, I slap on a false front of bravery. Years of mourning my father's abandonment taught me how to fake it. It's not for Ash's sake—he has Lucille to lean on now.

No, this is for me. I deserve to leave here with the last shreds of my dignity. My heart is another matter. That I'll leave at Ash's feet, where he can walk over it a few more times, should the desire arise.

I put the truck into gear and glance through the windshield. Ash hasn't moved. His eyes remain locked on me, sadness etched deep into his features.

Or maybe that's just what I want to see.

Doesn't matter either way.

My time with Ash is over. He's going to be a dad, and I'm not the mom.

How stupid was I to think I'd ever have a starring role in Asher Hammond's life? I was nothing but the understudy.

I pull onto the main road, my entire body trembling as a mixture of shock, rage, and heartbreak courses through my veins.

Now what? How do I coexist, working next door to the man I adore—a man who's having a baby with his first love?

It's too much to think about. All I can do is get back to the shop safely, throw myself into work, and seriously reconsider moving back to the city. Avoiding Ash at all costs is now my top priority.

Do I hate him? No. If what he says is true, this happened when my only interactions with Ash were angry glares and muttered curses.

So, he's not an asshole who hid the truth while simultaneously wooing me.

It's simply something that happened before Ash and me… not that there ever was an Ash and me.

I see that now.

And, oh joy, I get to add one more thing to my to-do list: get tested. If he had unprotected sex with Lucille and me, there's no telling who else might be in the mix.

Today keeps getting better and better.

I know I should get it over with, but I can't bring myself to handle one more blow right now. What difference will a week or two make?

If I develop symptoms, I'll go immediately. Otherwise, I'll wait until it doesn't hurt to breathe.

Good plan. Actually, it's a terrible fucking plan, but right now, it's all I've got. Future endeavors are on hold until I figure out what the hell to do next with my life.

I have a terrible poker face, as evidenced by the concern crossing Mina's features, when I walk into *One More Page*. She rushes over but says nothing. Instead, she envelops me in a hug, her embrace warm and comforting.

I need that comfort now.

Pulling back, she thumbs under my eyes. "What in the world happened? Don't you dare say nothing."

See? Terrible poker face. The worst.

"Where to begin?" I huff, slogging toward the coffee bar. I need caffeine. Gallons of it.

Hey, it's better than whiskey, and trust me, that thought crossed my mind too on the way here.

I grab a mug and fill it, shaking off Mina's offer of sugar.

Black and bitter, just like my soul.

"Judging by your face, you've heard the news."

I twirl on my heel, forcing a smile for Braden as he leans against the coffee bar. "I just came from there."

"What news?" Mina interjects, her wide-eyed gaze bouncing between Braden and me. "Care to fill me in?"

"My brother knocked up Lucille," Braden mutters, tugging a hand through his hair. "I couldn't believe it when he showed up at the farm with her in tow."

Ignoring Mina's shocked gasp, I focus my attention on Braden. "I take it you're not a fan of hers?"

"Not even close. She fucked with my brother big time, and it took him years to get over her."

"Apparently, that never happened."

Braden shakes his head, accepting Mina's offer of coffee with a thin-lipped grin. Seems smiling is as difficult for him as it is for me right now.

"He did. When he met you."

I am *not* hearing this nonsense right now.

"Trust me, Braden. I was just another woman to your brother."

"That's not true. You were so much more. You brought the old Ash back." He takes a long drink of his coffee, his expression darkening. "And now I'm stuck watching him repeat the same damn cycle. Lucille pulls him in, chews him up, and spits him out. It's exhausting. I can't believe I have to live with the woman. Hell, she's making this big dinner tonight and asked me to join them. As if a meal could change my opinion of her. I told Ash I wasn't going. In fact, I might need to find a new place to live."

She can cook, too. Why am I not surprised?

Do I agree with Braden? On every count, but layering on insults will not help the situation.

"Go to the dinner, Braden. Your brother needs your support. No doubt he's terrified, even if he won't admit it. I think he'll be a great dad, though."

My sentiment is true. I know Ash will be top-notch in the parenting department. I just hope he hangs up his philandering ways and settles down with his family.

Their baby deserves that, because I know how painful it is to grow up wondering why you weren't enough for them to stay.

Pretty much the way I'm feeling right now.

"What are *you* going to do?" Mina questions, wrapping an arm around my shoulder.

"What do you mean? There's nothing to do. I'm going to finish with the inventory for the shop and then speak to Eddie about the house renovations."

Both Mina and Braden focus their gazes on me. Seems I'm not worming my way out of an answer.

Mina's voice softens, her hand squeezing my shoulder. "Whatever you decide, you know I'm here for you, right? You don't have to face this alone."

I glance at her, my throat tightening. "I'll be his friend. At least, as much as I can right now."

"You don't think you two can work through this?" Braden asks.

While we wouldn't be the first couple to endure an outside pregnancy in the early stages of a relationship, I have zero desire to peg my love against Lucille.

I'm not a fan of losing, and that bet is a surefire loss.

"Honestly, I'm not up for that level of drama in my life. I have enough to worry about, and so does he. We're better off as friends, or whatever we are now."

"I totally disagree. Hell, I figured you two would get married and have a few kids."

How wrong you are, Braden.

"The players have changed, but the game is the same. What did your parents say?"

Braden's eyes widen at my question. "No idea. I'm sure as hell not telling them. My folks hate Lucille more than I do. They're going to be pissed because they love you."

"They don't know me."

"But they know how you changed Ash," Braden replies. "They also remember what Lucille did to him. Fucking bitch."

I lean against the counter, trying to find a silver lining in this scenario. Trust me, it's not easy.

"Look, it sucks, right? And I plan on drinking heavily and eating cartons of ice cream for the foreseeable future. But you're going to be an uncle, Braden, and that's amazing."

"I just wish it was with someone else."

You and me both, buddy.

Enough of this. I need to focus my attention anywhere but on the festering pile that once was my heart.

Except I *can't* escape it. The man I love—and his drama—are literally right next door. Every time I see his face, it will twist the knife a little deeper. Proximity isn't just salt in the wound—it's the whole damn shaker.

Lifting my mug of coffee, I motion toward my office. "The books are calling, and I must go. Thanks for checking on me, Braden."

He leans across the counter, pecking me on the cheek. "Don't give up on him. Maybe you two can figure something out."

That's the thing. I don't want to figure out some work-around regarding this situation. Even if Ash claims to want that, I'd always feel like the other woman standing between Lucille and Ash's family unit.

I know how it feels to be on the receiving end of that scenario.

Do. Not. Recommend.

Come to think of it, I don't recommend love much anymore, either.

"Talk soon, Braden." I watch him stroll next door before turning my attention to Mina.

"I love you, but I don't want to discuss it. Not yet, anyway. Just let me work through it, okay?"

I don't give Mina a chance to answer as I head for my office, sure of only one thing.

Love stinks, and I have zero desire to ever participate in this game again.

I'm knee-deep in organizing my new shipment of books when Lucille walks in, making a beeline for me.

Fuck my life. No doubt she's here to remind me to stay far away from her man, lest I want a beating.

Okay, that might not be her plan, but I wouldn't put it past her to issue a claim of ownership.

It's Asher Hammond, for God's sake. Women line up for his attention, but she's the lucky bitch carrying his spawn.

Not that I would ever attempt to interfere in their… situation. I'm many things, but pathetic isn't one of them. At least not outwardly. I'm a hot mess on the inside, but neither she nor Ash will ever know.

Might as well get this over with so I can return to the unnecessary rearranging of my store.

Hey, a woman needs something to keep her mind off life, and Mina has forbidden me from having any more coffee today. Apparently, my jitteriness was off-putting.

Better that than taking a sledgehammer to the breakable objects in the store—or to Ash's handsome head.

"Hi, Ori."

"Something I can help you with?" I brace for the inevitable warning, but Lucille turns her attention to the shelf, running her long fingers along the spines of the books.

"Baby books? I have zero knowledge on the subject, and Ash said you're brilliant with pretty much everything."

How quaint. I'm now the Girl Friday for Ash's baby mama.

Dusting off my pants, I crook a finger at Lucille. "We have several on the subject, and I can always order more for you."

I lead her to the baby section, an area I laid out with all the touches expectant and new mamas might want: stuffed animals, soft hues on the furniture, rocking chairs.

Sadly, I based it on my ideals of motherhood, an area I'd hoped to explore one day. That concept is now further off than ever.

Pulling a book from the shelf, I hand it to Lucille and motion to the rocker. "Have a seat. Would you like some tea?"

But she doesn't sit. Instead, she grasps my wrist, holding me fast, her blue eyes boring into mine.

Here it comes.

"I know this must be hard for you, Ori. I hope you understand that neither of us wants to hurt you."

Oh, but you did. In fact, you decimated me.

Plastering on a smile, I pull my hand free. "It was definitely a surprise, but Ash and I were never serious."

Is it a lie? At least on my end, but I have to maintain face. I refuse to acknowledge that Lucille's reentry into Ash's life has destroyed all the plans I had for the two of us.

"That's not true. He's crazy about you. You're all he talks about. He says you're his best friend."

Best friend? The words land like a punch, wrenching something deep inside me.

Not a girlfriend. Not a partner. Just… a best friend.

Wait a damn minute. How often were they talking? And why would he bring me up to her?

"What an interesting topic of conversation," I reply dryly.

Lucille's expression softens, and for a moment, she appears almost sad. "You're important to him, Ori. More than you probably realize. This situation—it's breaking him."

Breaking him? What about me?

Her gaze drops to the floor, her voice barely a whisper. "He's trying to do the right thing. For everyone."

Damn it, I want to hate the woman, but there's something so earnest about her. She doesn't seem like the heartless bitch Ash and Braden talk about. She seems lonely, and a bit lost.

But looks can be deceiving.

"Braden says you're fixing them a big dinner tonight."

Lucille sighs, forcing a smile. "It's the least I can do since they're letting me stay there. You're welcome to join us."

Thanks, but I'd rather drink gasoline.

"I'm busy." I pause, wringing my hands as I work up the courage to tell Lucille what I know she needs to hear. "Ash will do the right thing, Lucille. He's a stand-up guy."

"I know, but this isn't what he wanted."

Ouch. That even hurts *me* to hear.

Giving her hand another awkward pat, I muster a calming tone. "Give him time. I'm sure it shocked him to learn he's going to be a dad."

Sure as hell floored me, but I'm no one in this situation.

I hand her two more books. "Let me know if you need anything else."

"Ori?"

Once again, I brace myself, unsure what Lucille might have left to say. "Yes?"

"Thank you for understanding. For being nice to me. Most women wouldn't in your situation."

A curt nod is all I can manage, and even that is a struggle. Winding my way around the piles of books I've strewn across the floor, I make a beeline for my office and shut the door.

Inventory can wait.

Right now, I need to fall the fuck apart.

When a knock sounds at my office door, I groan and press my forehead against the desk, the words spilling out before I can stop them.

"Not now. Please, not now."

Chapter 17

Whiskey & Ice Cream

Ori

It's been twelve days since my world fell apart.

To some, I might seem ridiculous and dramatic. The world is not ending, and I will recover in time. Hearts get broken every day, and in far more painful fashion than mine.

My brain repeats these facts countless times, but my heart has demanded at least a couple of weeks to wallow in misery after learning my boyfriend is going to be a father, and I'm not part of that equation.

Ironic that the man who hates the idea of happily ever after somehow muddled his way into one, while I sit on the sidelines, watching the events unfold from the cheap seats.

Ash has called both the store and my mobile dozens of times and texted twice that many, but I'm not ready yet. He's lingered by the coffee bar in *One More Page* and in the parking lot, but I squirrel myself safely out of sight until he leaves.

I don't know what to say to him—perhaps I never will.

I don't hate Ash. Trust me, it would be easier if I did. But love, mixed with supreme disappointment over the recent turn of events, are my overriding emotions.

If he had cheated on me, hate would have come easily, and

I'd likely be engaging in some serious revenge sex with any number of hot Sparkwood men right now.

But Lucille and Ash's fling happened before our fateful night in the basement. I can't hold it against him unless I'd like someone to dredge up my past decisions and hold them against me.

It was far easier when I was a teenager and could parade about, cutting ties and burning bridges without a backward glance. But the years have enlightened and softened me to the reality of the world.

Nothing is black and white—just muddy, drab shades of gray.

I'm certain Ash wants to remain friends—even Lucille mentioned the fact that I was Ash's best friend—but what does that look like?

When you strip away the physical attraction, which I'm not sure how the hell to do, is there enough common ground to build a friendship?

Better question is, do I want to attempt that? Wouldn't it be easier to walk away?

A ton of questions with no answers.

All I know is I miss him terribly.

Mina, as always, is my rock—steadfast in her support. Hell, even Braden has dropped by several times to check on me, although that might have more to do with Mina's good looks than with my plight.

At least I slept last night, and I didn't drink a drop of alcohol. I did, however, finish off a pint of chocolate ice cream.

Sue me. Who cares about cellulite now? No one's looking.

Figures. The best sex of my life, and I'll never have it again.

What a gyp.

Time to get to work. The busier I stay, the less I'll think about Ash and the future we don't have.

Tossing my hair into a messy bun, I shove my glasses up

my nose and head out of my office. *One More Page* sparkles, thanks in part to my rash of deep cleaning to keep the wolves at bay. My apartment is equally as tidy, and I'm considering offering my services free of charge to anyone in town, so long as it keeps me from ruminating on my broken heart.

Winter refuses to release her grasp on Sparkwood, so many of her residents continue to seek out my store for its glowing fireplace, book stacks, and hot cocoa. I'm blessed to own a bustling business, even if it is next door to the man I'm no longer allowed to love.

My gaze falls on a massive bouquet sitting on the front counter. Seriously, it might be the largest I've ever seen—a collection of daisies and irises in every color of the rainbow.

And I know who it's from.

Ash has sent flowers daily. I guess he considers it his penance. The first day, I damn near threw it out in the dumpster, but then I changed my mind and left it to brighten the front counter.

Might as well add some color to these drab days. Plus, I don't have to see it as much up there.

I haven't thanked him for a single one, because that would involve speaking to him. I also haven't read any of the cards, because my heart can't handle that right now.

But as I move closer, I see there are two bouquets today. Guess Ash is upping the ante.

"I see he's doubling his quota," I mumble to Mina, nodding toward the smaller collection of dark red roses.

"Those aren't from Ash."

"Who are they from?"

Mina plucks the card off the vase and hands it to me. "See for yourself."

I pull the card from the envelope, noting the elegant penmanship.

Beauty like yours should never go unnoticed. Always watching—K.

"Who the hell is K?"

Mina shrugs.

"Maybe they're not for me," I mumble, gliding my finger along the rose and stabbing myself with the thorn. "Ouch. Dammit." I suck the drop of blood from my finger.

"Are you okay?"

"Not hardly. No idea who K is or why they're sending me flowers."

"A secret admirer, I guess." Mina pulls a stack of cards from the front counter drawer. "These are the cards from Ash. Do you want to read them?"

I shake my head, tapping the mystery card against the counter. "What could he possibly have to say?"

"A lot, actually. I know you told me to chuck them, but I couldn't do it. They're here, if you want to have a look."

"I don't, Mina." My words emerge with more bite than intended. She means well, but over the last several days, her stance has shifted from killing Ash to me reconciling with him.

So glad she considers me living as the runner-up in Ash's world a possibility.

"I won't throw them away. They're heartfelt. Ash is trying, and he's terrified he's lost you forever."

"Please, Mina. Just stop." I hold up my hands, the desperation creeping into my voice.

She nods and returns Ash's notes to the drawer before motioning to the coffee bar. "How about some coffee?"

"No. I'm jumpy enough."

Plus, the idea of anything as caustic as coffee sounds terrible. Seems my stomach has gone on strike after a steady diet of alcohol, sugar, and heartache.

I've battled nausea all day. Maybe it's the stress. Maybe it's the flowers. Or maybe the universe has decided to throw the flu at me, too. Just for kicks.

Mina pulls me into a tight hug, holding me until I relax in her embrace. "I love you. So many of us love you."

I pull back and offer a tearful smile, but I know her words aren't true. At least not where Ash is concerned.

He doesn't love me.

He never did.

The bookstore is dark and quiet when I emerge from my office. No surprise, since it's our early day, but where the silence felt comforting before, it now only serves to enhance the loneliness surrounding me.

Mina hounded me to grab a few drinks at the local pub, but I'm not in the mood. Some things whiskey can't fix, and my trampled heart is one of them. Besides, I don't need the pitying glances from any of the locals.

They don't say anything—at least not to my face. They don't need to—Sparkwood is a small town where gossip spreads faster than a brushfire, and everyone gets their turn in the spotlight. My guess is Lucille is doing little to squelch any conversation involving her and Ash.

I pivot to lock the office when I catch sight of the note stuck to my door. Grabbing it, I feel a surge of emotions well inside me.

> *Don't leave. Come downstairs, no matter what time. I'm waiting for you.*
> *—Ash*

My finger traces the words as tears fill my eyes.

Ash, you need to stop doing this.

But a larger part of me is grateful for his continued efforts, even if I don't know when I'll be able to look at him as anything other than the greatest love I never had.

I stop by the front desk to grab the door keys and pause, my gaze falling to the stack of cards from Ash.

With a sigh, I grab them and turn on the desk lamp, its golden glow illuminating the pile.

Mina claims they're heartfelt, but let's get real. Ash is hardly known for his romantic sonnets, unless claiming I have a delicious pussy counts.

Here goes nothing.

Every day without you feels wrong. I want to fix this, if you'll let me.

You're the best part of my messed-up life, little one. I miss you.

Please don't give up on me.

I toss the rest of the notes back into the drawer, a few now wet with teardrops. The wet smudges blur his words, making them as hard to decipher as my own feelings. Mina is right—they *are* heartfelt.

I shoot a glance toward our shared hallway and the entrance to the speakeasy.

Stay. Go. Stay. Go.

Should I ignore or heed Ash's request? My heart and hormones scream out their choice, but it's not that simple anymore.

I still need time, though I'm not sure for what. I need to process the news of Ash's impending fatherhood, not that the outcome will change.

Never mind the jealousy gnawing in my core that the woman carrying his child doesn't deserve his affections—not after what she did to Ash's heart.

But fairness never plays into love stories. He's getting his happily ever after ending, and I'm back to square one.

I know that's not how Ash describes their situation, but let's get real. It's only a matter of time.

They're having a baby. Lucille is living with Ash. Let's throw in how she's also the only woman he's ever loved.

It doesn't take a rocket scientist to figure out the ending to that scenario.

Basically, my heart and future plans are fucked... or not, as the case may be.

Still, it's rude to leave him waiting downstairs. The least I can do is give him a heads up that while I appreciate the offer, I'm tired and begging off on any social gatherings for the foreseeable future.

Then I'll go home and attempt to drown my sorrows in a bubble bath of whiskey and tears and pray my stomach understands this last transgression.

I swear I'll eat vegetables and drink copious amounts of water tomorrow. Just let me have tonight.

Good plan.

The heavy oak door to the lower level opens with little effort, thanks to some newly installed hinges. A pang rushes through me as I finger the shiny brass handle, realizing that the dingy basement where we first began our journey is no more.

Much like Ash and me.

I realize, in the rational parts of my mind, how silly an idea it was to fall headfirst into loving Asher Hammond. The man told me, time and again, that he didn't buy into the whole happily ever after idea. At least, not since Lucille.

Even if she hadn't returned, I would have grown weary of playing second fiddle to a ghost. Now, I have the luxury of a real live human to compound my angst.

I think I prefer ghost stories.

Descending the polished steps, I pause, my gaze drinking in the changes since I last visited the speakeasy.

Dark wood tables and chairs are stacked neatly in the corner, awaiting their final placement. Vintage-style lanterns hang above the bar, casting a warm glow over the polished wood.

The bar is partially stocked, with an ornate tap installed and ready to pour libations for eager customers. Behind the bar, an empty space awaits the perfect centerpiece—a mirror. I know just the one. The ornate mirror Ash found in a room at the Dean Estate. He loves that thing.

He should have it.

"You came."

My gaze shifts to Ash, standing in the doorway of his office. His shirt is wrinkled, his hair a mess, and he's clutching a half-empty glass of whiskey.

"I barely recognize the place," I say, glancing around.

He nods and walks toward me, his steps heavy. "It started out as a dream, but it's turned into a hideout from my reality."

Something in his tone softens my emotional armor. I've never heard Ash sound so defeated, and although I know he's been drinking, there's a sorrow surrounding him now that no amount of whiskey can erase.

It wasn't just my life that got turned upside down.

"You've been working crazy hours the last couple of weeks, little one."

I avert my gaze, running a hand along the smooth wood of the bar. "Tax season."

"But that's not the reason."

"No, it's not." I sigh, already weary of how this conversation will play out. "How are you and Lucille?"

The words feel jagged as they leave my mouth. My eyes dart to the stairwell, torn between the urge to comfort Ash and the need to flee.

He drags a hand through his hair, his face gaunter than it

was just a week ago. Dark circles shadow his eyes, and for the first time, I see how deeply this is affecting him.

"I don't want to talk about Lucille," he mutters.

"She's the giant rainbow-striped elephant in the room, and you want to avoid discussing her?"

"We're not together. She's pregnant and needs a place to stay. That's it."

Of course, that's *not* it. But there's no point arguing semantics.

"How is she feeling?"

"Do you really care?"

I throw up my hands, my voice rising. "Honestly? I have no fucking idea. I'm supposed to care about how a pregnant woman is feeling, right? Make sure she's happy, healthy, and drowning in chocolate? But Lucille ruined my life, so forgive me if I'm battling the overwhelming urge to back her over with a bus."

Ash's lips twitch into a grin. "Damn, Ori. I didn't know you had it in you."

I bury my head in my hands and groan. "I'm an asshole, I know. And I don't mean it. Lucille is not my favorite person, even though I have no right to hate her. She loved you first."

"She didn't love me."

"Fine. You loved her."

"Past tense. I definitely do not love her now."

But their situation is very much the present, and it's mucked up *my* future. Sorry that I can't toss those facts aside as easily as Ash can.

"Since neither of us wishes to discuss Lucille, what shall we talk about? The weather? My favorite hockey team… what is their damn name again?"

"How about us?" He drops his voice, as if sharing an intimate secret. "And how I'm going to fix us."

I wave my hands, warding off that conversation. "No, no, no. I need to go—"

But Ash blocks my exit. "Can you not run away from me right now? I know you're scared and confused. Well, so am I. But, Ori, you've been my port in the storm since day one, and I really need that safety now."

But what about *my* safety?

"I don't sleep. I'm barely eating," Ash continues, his face lined with worry. "I thought if I could see you, life might make sense again."

I swallow, trying to contain the swell of emotions threatening to break free. Time to be his friend. "I'm here. Might as well have a drink. Just water, though."

Ash pours a glass and slides it over, our fingers brushing, that ever-present spark lighting up the cells in my body.

Hopefully, one day, that spark will extinguish.

"I'm sorry I've been avoiding you," I whisper. "It's just… hard."

"Trust me, I know."

But he doesn't. He has a future, even if he isn't too keen on it at the moment. I have sleepless nights and an empty bed.

I glance at the wall behind the bar, desperate to change the subject. "Remember that mirror you found at the Dean Estate?"

He narrows his eyes at my random segue. "The gilded one? Yeah, why?"

"You should hang it here. I'll have Eddie bring it to you."

Ash frowns. "You sure you don't want to keep it?"

"No. The more time goes on, the less I like that place."

Ash slides his glass in slow circles on the bar. "I thought you might say that, so I have an idea."

"Let's hear it."

"We get married, and I take over the restoration. You won't have to worry about it anymore."

My mouth drops open, my jaw slack at his offhanded marriage proposal.

I step onto the bar footrest, leaning forward to glance behind the counter. "Did you hit your head back there?"

"No."

I motion between us. "You just suggested marriage. Don't worry, I know it's the whiskey talking, but you'd better slow down before you propose to the whole town."

"I'm not drunk." His jaw tightens as he looks away. "I'm just… trying to tell you how I feel."

"You don't want me to sell the Dean Estate. Got it."

"No." He hits the bar with the side of his fist, the glass wobbling on the wood. "That's not it. Fuck, Ori."

I push away from the bar. "Maybe I should go. This wasn't a good idea."

In a flash, Ash rounds the bar, caging me between it and his arms. His eyes burn with desperation—a turbulent sea of emotions.

"You always begged me to open up, and now that I am, you're shutting me down?"

I jerk my head away and focus on the floor. "I'd rather not talk about something I'll never have."

But Ash will not let me hide. He grasps my chin, forcing me to meet his gaze, our mouths mere inches apart. "Name it and I'll make it happen."

"We both know that isn't true."

"You want your fairytale. Your happy-ever-after. The ring, the wedding, the baby. I'm right, aren't I?"

"Ash, please." Tears stream down my face.

"You think you know how I feel about you? You have no idea. I'm crazy about you. You're my true north—the only thing that makes sense in this messed-up world. So yes, I'll make it happen. Everything you want, I'll give you."

I tremble in his arms, but not from fear. There's such intensity in his words, such raw conviction.

I believe he's terrified of many things, losing me among

them. But despite sharing his fear, I can't relegate myself to second best. Not with Ash.

Although his words are the closest he's ever come to a declaration of love, they don't negate the fact that he's having a child with Lucille—which will solidify a lifetime bond between them. It's one thing to date a single father and quite another to date someone whose baby mama is actively pregnant.

That's not just a different ballpark; it's a totally different league.

Some women can handle it, and more power to them, but I'm struggling to come to terms with his new reality. Our new reality, if we even have one at all.

"I would do anything to keep you safe, even if it breaks me into a million pieces." Ash's words emerge in a hoarse whisper.

"I'm safe, Ash. My heart is broken, but the rest of me will survive."

His hands slide along my jaw, his fingers gentle, but his eyes are anything but. A turbulent mix of emotions swirls in them, and I can't look away.

"Yours isn't the only heart broken. Please don't give up on us. I swear on my life, I'll give you a fairytale ending."

I cover his hands with mine and force a smile, even though my heart feels like it's splintering. Finally, I dare to speak the words that have haunted me for weeks.

"I'm afraid of this new normal. Afraid of being second best. Afraid of you falling back in love with Lucille and leaving me shit out of luck."

"That's not going to happen."

"How do you know?"

"All the spots in my heart are already filled. By you."

Damn him. The man said nothing remotely over-the-top romantic in all the months we dated, but now he's a regular Shakespeare.

"Ori, I'd tear this whole damn world apart and build it back just to give you everything you've ever wanted."

Tears stream down my face as I run my fingertips over his bearded jaw. "Why couldn't it have been you? I wanted it to be you so badly."

"Mark my words, it's going to be me. You're mine, Oriana Thorne. *You're mine.*"

Ash captures my mouth in a fiery kiss. Shockwaves shoot through me as my knees threaten to buckle beneath me. His tongue glides against mine, low moans rising from his chest as he reclaims my body as his own.

He knits his fingers in my hair, edging closer, his length flush against me. Daring me to run from the only thing I know is true: I'm forever in love with Asher Hammond.

And I don't know what to do about it.

I slide my hands along his chest, breaking out of the kiss. "Ash—"

But Ash doesn't want to hear my arguments. His hands slip around the nape of my neck, drawing me back into the moment.

Releasing a heated groan, he lifts me onto the bar, his fingers fumbling with the buttons of my blouse as his tongue dances along every inch of my exposed skin. All the while, he murmurs my name like a prayer, soft and reverent.

"Ash? Are you down here?"

A woman's voice calls from the basement stairs, and I rip away from him, covering my mouth with my hand.

Ash shakes his head with a muttered curse. "I'm down here. What's up, Lucille?"

Her footsteps echo on the stairs as she descends, and I scramble off the bar, desperate to make it to the bathroom before she sees me.

No such luck.

Lucille's face registers surprise when she spots me. "Hi, Ori. I didn't realize you were down here."

On the plus side, there's no anger in her tone. On the negative side, she looks more pregnant than ever—a cutting reminder of who she is and what she carries inside her.

"I wanted to see the, uh, speakeasy. The renovations. And I have a mirror for Ash." I stumble over my words, much like a student caught without their homework.

"It's beautiful down here, isn't it?" Lucille runs a hand over the paneled wall, her gaze lingering on Ash before flicking back to me.

"What do you want, Lucille?" Ash barks, pouring himself another glass of whiskey.

Lucille tilts her head, her hand settling instinctively on her belly. "I just got back from the doctor, and the roads are getting bad, so I figured we should head home. Leave the car here and take the four-wheel drive."

Oh my God. Ash missed her doctor's appointment to hang out with me?

I feel sick.

"You should go," I mumble, glancing down at my blouse, still half open from Ash's earlier exploration. Heat rushes to my cheeks. "I'm just going to use the bathroom."

Ash follows me, his steps close behind as I push the door open. His face is awash with remorse as he punches the newly hung sheetrock with a muttered curse.

"You need to go," I say quietly, refusing to meet his gaze as I button my blouse and twist my hair into a bun. "She's right —the storm's supposed to be nasty tonight."

"I can sleep on the couch here. You can stay with me."

"Definitely not."

"Ori—" He grabs my arm, pulling me close, his whiskey-tinged breath warm against my ear. "Give me five minutes to walk her out. I promise I'll spend the rest of the night making love to you. That's all I want."

And therein lies the problem.

I press my hands against his chest, creating the distance I

desperately need. "It doesn't matter what you want. Or what I want. It's not reality. Not anymore. The reality is the woman you once adored is living at your house and carrying your baby. No other way to spin that story. I don't have a place in it, and I have to be okay with that."

I press a kiss to his lips, soft and lingering, before pulling back. God knows I want to fall into him and never surface.

But reality stands on the other side of that door, waiting for the man I longed to call mine, but who has always belonged to her.

"I need to go."

I pull open the door, sighing when Ash forces it shut again.

"Ash, you have to stop."

"I've only adored one woman in my life."

"I know."

"It isn't Lucille."

God help my heart.

I force back the tears and lift my head to meet his gaze. His eyes are soft, vulnerable—the same look he reserves for moments when it's just the two of us. It's the glimpse of the man he was before time and life broke him apart.

A man I thought I could help piece back together.

Turns out, I wasn't needed. The star of his show is back, and it's time for me to bow out.

Ash trails behind me as I walk back into the bar, sending Lucille an embarrassed smile.

Even though he claims to be single, her presence is that of a woman who knows she still has some claim to him. Meanwhile, I feel like the home wrecking harlot.

Good times.

"Ori," Ash's voice is thick with emotion, but there's nothing left to say.

Like I told him earlier, there's no room in his life for me now.

Perhaps there never was.

Chapter 18

Fuck Sweet

Ash

Holy hell, what a morning—and it's barely nine o'clock.

Doesn't help that my head's pounding or that I'm running on about fifteen minutes of sleep. Top it off with a thirty-minute car ride with a woman I want nothing to do with, and you've got a banner start to the day.

"Do you need me to stop for coffee?" Lucille asks, concern lacing her voice.

I glance at her briefly, biting back my irritation. Look, I'm not mad at her for yesterday—not exactly—though she ruined what could've been a perfect reunion between Ori and me.

She feels terrible. Or so she claims. A part of me wonders if she got some twisted satisfaction from barging in and breaking up my private moment with Ori.

But my anger isn't directed at her. I'm mad at the mess I'm in—how I've landed the starring role in what can only be described as a drug-fueled melodrama featuring my cheating ex, her jilted husband, and a psycho ex-boyfriend who's now gunning for Ori and me.

Universe, if there are karma points, I'd better be racking up some serious ones for this.

"Have you spoken to Trace?" I ask, leaning my head against my hand to avoid the sun's glare off the snow.

"I did. He said things are moving along, and Kevin wants him to drop by the club this evening."

"So, it's happening tonight?"

Lucille shrugs. "Honestly, I'm not sure how it works. Kevin used to have a monthly 'hiring' the third week of the month. Now I realize what he really meant by that term. If that schedule hasn't changed, it won't be for another couple of weeks."

I groan and punch the visor. "Fuck. It's never-ending."

Lucille leans over, placing a hand on my arm. "I know it feels that way—"

"Trust me, Lucille, you don't know how I feel."

She parks the truck in the lot but leaves the engine idling. "No, but I know what it feels like to be carrying the baby of a man who treated me like garbage. Who punched me for fun and got away with it because he's rich and powerful. So, no, I don't know your feelings, but I know hopelessness."

Damn.

I glance at her, and for the first time in a long while, I feel something new for Lucille—sympathy. I've been so twisted up in my nightmare that I never considered hers.

Still wish I were a million miles away from all this bullshit, though.

Leaning over, I wrap an arm around her shoulders and press a quick kiss to the top of her head. "We'll be okay. Somehow."

When I climb out of the truck, the arctic chill bites my face, and the crunch of frozen snow echoes underfoot. Feels mighty nice, if we're being honest.

At the far end of the parking lot, a floral delivery truck pulls onto Main Street, and I smile, knowing Ori's daily flower delivery has arrived.

Hey, I paid top dollar to make sure it reaches her first

thing in the morning. Anything to make her smile, even though she hasn't said a word about the other dozen I've sent.

Won't stop me from trying. It's not going to fix things, but it's a start. Let the world know she's loved.

Getting Ori to acknowledge it will be far more difficult.

Especially after last night.

"Whoa," Lucille gasps, grabbing the hood of the truck as her feet threaten to slide out from under her.

"Hey, hang on." I walk around the truck and grab her arm, steadying her as she catches her breath. "Are you okay?"

"I'm glad you were here."

Lucille grips my arm tightly as we traverse the icy path.

It's then I see Ori. She's spreading deicer on her front stoop, her breath visible in the frigid air. Her movements are sharp and deliberate, her gaze cutting through me like the winter wind.

The worst part? I know how it looks to her. Lucille clinging to me, her protruding belly on full display as we walk together into Black Lotus after a ride in from our shared home.

Trust me, I *know* how crappy it looks. And how shitty it's making Ori feel.

But if we can just get through another couple of weeks, I'll give her everything she's ever wanted.

I raise a hand in a feeble wave, but Ori turns on her heel and stalks inside without a word.

The sharp slam of her door echoes through the cold morning air.

So much for a good morning.

"I can talk to her," Lucille offers, her pace cautious as she navigates the walkway.

"Somehow, I don't think that's going to help."

And I know I'm right.

Ori's face burns in my mind—the way her eyes flicked to

Lucille's belly, the way she bolted from me last night like I was poison.

I know, in the long run, I'm doing the stand-up thing. But I'm not sure my heart—or my brain—can take much more.

Another two weeks feels like an eternity without the woman I love.

The word flashes in my mind, as it always does when I think of Ori. A word I swore I'd never use again for an emotion I didn't dare feel.

But love doesn't seem like a strong enough word for Oriana Thorne. She's my entire universe.

And though she's angry and hurt—rightfully so—she kissed me back last night.

There's still hope. And that's all I'm clinging to.

I shuffle into *Black Lotus*, muttering a grunted greeting at Zane and Braden.

Hey, it's the best I can manage right now—not that Braden has been overly talkative since my ex took up residence at the farm.

I get it. He hates Lucille for what she did to me, and just like Ori, he's in the damn dark about why this woman is suddenly back in my life.

I wouldn't speak to me, either.

Unlocking my office, I step inside, barely making it to my desk before the door flies open, slamming against the wall with a thud.

I tear my gaze upward, startled to see Ori standing there, a bouquet clenched in her hands and fire in her eyes.

Not quite the reaction I hoped for.

"Hey, beautiful. You got the flowers."

Nothing like stating the obvious, Ash.

Her glare could level a building as she stomps forward, slamming the vase onto my desk so hard that water sloshes over the rim.

"Cease and desist," she hisses.

"I was just about to head over there and grab a coffee—"

"Find somewhere else to buy your brew because I can't handle it anymore. I can't do this insanity."

"Hang on. Please." I step forward and close the office door, motioning toward the chair. "Come on, sit down. Let's talk."

But Ori has no intention of following orders. She plants her hands on her hips, her foot tapping an angry rhythm against the floor. "I don't want to talk. What is there to talk about?"

"Last night, for starters."

Ori rolls her eyes, a mirthless laugh escaping her lips. "I already know. You were drunk. You said a bunch of things you didn't mean. Yada yada."

Wait, what?

"That isn't—"

Her body trembles, every inch of her vibrating with restrained rage. "I can't do this anymore. Can't you see that? Can't you see what your situation is doing to me? If you care about me at all, please leave me alone."

"I get it, but I promise there's nothing between Lucille and me."

"That's not what the entire town of Sparkwood thinks."

"Who the fuck cares what they think?"

Ori points to herself, tears streaming down her cheeks. "I do! Imagine how I feel in this scenario—this reality television, fucked-up, beyond-all-recognition scenario. I thought dating you would be exciting, but it's literally hazardous to my health."

"Will you please sit down for a few minutes?" I fumble

through my desk drawer, desperate to find an aspirin. "And can we take the volume down a notch? My head is blasting."

"That's what happens when you down a bottle of whiskey and spout a bunch of lies and half-truths. Life catches up with you, Ash. Eventually, everyone has to pay the piper."

My hand finally closes around the aspirin bottle, but my nerves are so shot I can't get the damn top off. Next up? A hammer to smash the thing open.

Ori grabs the bottle and pops it open with ease, dumping two pills onto the desk.

I can't help it. That slight gesture, even at the height of her anger, makes me smile.

Unfortunately, smiling is the wrong move.

"I'm glad you find this amusing."

"I don't, but I appreciate that even though you think I'm a total asshole, you still give me the aspirin. You're sweet, Ori."

"Fuck sweet, Ash. I'm tired of this… whatever *this* is. I'm tired of people whispering when they pass me, knowing full well what they're saying. Do you know I overheard the florist discussing us last night? She felt sorry for me, clinging to hope while you string me along. And this morning, I had to smile at her and pretend it didn't gut me."

"I'll call the florist."

"Are you going to yell at everyone in town? Because everyone is talking. This is the biggest damn story around for this stinking storybook village."

"Ori—"

"I'm not done." She tears the card from the flowers and throws it onto the desk. "What the hell does *that* mean?"

I pick up the card, running my finger over the words. "Exactly what it says. I meant every word. Everything I told you last night—I meant it."

I hope my admission will soften her, but no dice. If anything, it fuels her fury.

"You meant every word? Which part? The part where you

aren't capable of loving? Or the part where I shouldn't get my hopes up? Which one did you mean?"

I open my mouth to respond, but she throws up a hand, silencing me. She isn't finished—not by a long shot.

"I really believed I could change your mind. That loving you enough would make you realize what we had. Turns out, there's a fool born every minute." She shakes her head, her voice cracking as fresh tears spring to her eyes. "I was right there the whole time, and you didn't believe in it. Didn't play that way. Then you knock up your ex-girlfriend, and suddenly you're all about giving me what I want. What you don't want is to lose."

That's it. I close the distance between us, sliding my hands along her jaw and forcing her to meet my gaze.

"You're right. I don't want to lose you, little one. Do you know why? Because you made me believe in love again. You did. I didn't want to, but I didn't stand a chance. I want to give you everything you want—a family, a home. Whatever it is, it's yours."

Her voice breaks as she pulls away. "What is it you think I want? A sympathy fuck and a pity baby?"

"That's not what it would be—"

"Well, that's how it would feel. And that's what everyone would think." She swipes at her tears. "What does it matter anyway, Ash? You don't believe in love, marriage, or any of those stupid novelties, do you? Funny thing is, you made me stop believing in them, too."

"Ori, there's nothing funny about that."

She stares at the floor, her voice trembling. "I know."

A soft knock sounds at the door, and Lucille pokes her head in. "Hi, sorry to disturb—"

Seems Ori has had enough of us both. She whirls around, her voice rising in a strangled cry. "You're *not* sorry. Not one bit. You're loving every second of this, aren't you? Well, guess what, Lucille? You win. I'm done."

Her words slice through me, leaving nothing but a hollow ache in their wake. I can't move. I can't breathe.

Ori's given up. On me. On us. And that terrifies me more than any of Kevin's threats or Lucille's secrets ever could.

"Ori, don't do this. Please."

Am I begging? Damn right. I've seen Ori's temper before, but never like this. Never at a point where I couldn't talk her down.

She throws her hands up, her gaze bouncing between Lucille and me. "Looking at you two, I get it. You're a perfect fit. I was the one who didn't make sense. I see that now."

I slump into my chair as my world shatters around me. "You're different. I always said that."

She pauses, a bitter smile tugging at her lips. "You break hearts every day, Ash. What's one more?"

Her words hang in the air like a final nail in my coffin as she storms out of the office.

This time, I know she won't come back.

I open my mouth, but the words choke me. She can't hear them, anyway.

I've broken hearts, yeah. But yours? Yours is the only one that would break me.

"Ash, I'm so sorry," Lucille whispers, her hand gripping the doorknob as she closes the door. "Let me go talk to her."

"Just stop," I groan, my head thumping like a goddamn marching band.

"What can I do?"

I lift my head and scoff. Is she serious? "You've done enough." I jab a finger toward the door. "Ori loved me. I didn't deserve that love. I didn't deserve *her*. And thanks to you, she's gone. I hope you're happy—you've cost me more than I can even fathom."

Lucille's lower lip quivers, but I'm done playing nice. Twice, this woman has stomped on my dreams. The first time, it was just my heart that broke, but this time, she destroyed Ori too—and I won't abide anyone hurting my woman.

I can't blame Ori for walking away. This situation is beyond fucked, and if the roles were reversed, I'd be insane with jealousy. Hell, I've damn near punched Eddie out just for standing closer to Ori than I deem acceptable.

It's the strangest thing—I was never a jealous guy. How could I be? I had fun with the women I hung out with, and most of them were having fun with other guys, too.

It made sense because I always swore I'd never settle down.

Now, those words taste like acid.

"I really messed things up, didn't I?" Lucille asks, her gaze drifting to some far-off point. "Seems that's what I'm best at —screwing shit up. But I'll fix this. I promise."

"How? The woman I love hates me. Wants nothing to do with me. I told her I'd give her everything—marriage, babies, the whole damn fairytale. She doesn't want it. She doesn't want me anymore, and I can't fucking blame her."

I pitch my water bottle across the room, the cap flying off as water sprays everywhere.

"Answer me this," I snarl, my temper barely leashed. "Do you love destroying things? Because you are a goddamn train wreck, Lucille. Have you ever loved anyone, or was it all just a game to you?"

"You love to hit people when they're down, don't you?" Lucille whimpers, her body trembling.

"This isn't some long-lost reunion. You dragged me into your mess, and now my entire world is upside down. Forgive me if I'm not rolling out the red carpet for you."

"I know."

Her blasé response snaps something inside me. "That's all you have to say? I know I fucked up your life, but here's my half-assed apology? You have got to be kidding me."

"I didn't mean to mess up your life."

I laugh bitterly. "Sure you didn't. But I'm the asshole for agreeing to help you. I should've left you to your own devices. No doubt you could have handled Kevin Duncan just fine."

"Yeah," she spits out, her voice cracking. "Those bruises proved how well I handled Kevin Duncan. You think I'm enjoying this? My life has been uprooted too. But Trace thought this was the only way out, and I trust him."

I cut her off, my chest heaving. "Enough. I don't care to hear any more of your sob story. The woman I love walked away this morning. I've lost her, Lucille. And you helped make that happen."

Her hand trembles as it drifts to her belly. "Everyone, you and Trace included, thinks I'm a horrible person. A screw-up. And I've earned that title. I don't deny it. But this little life…" She rubs her stomach gently, her voice breaking. "He doesn't know that. He only knows that I love him. And I just want a chance to show the world I'm more than the home wrecker people see. I can be a good mom, Ash. But not if I'm running for my life."

I've never seen Lucille this raw. She hides her emotions behind a tough-as-nails exterior, never willing to admit when she's scared. What she doesn't realize is that vulnerability makes her human.

"You don't owe me anything, Asher Hammond," she continues, running a hand through her hair. "You have every right to call Trace and tell him it's done. Kick me out of the farmhouse. I deserve it. But I think I finally realize how fucking scared I am. How goddamn alone."

Part of me wants to keep raging at her, to let her feel every ounce of anger I've been bottling up for a decade. But you don't kick someone when they're down. At least, I don't.

Doesn't mean I forgive her for what she's done. Not even close.

Scrubbing my hands over my face, I let out a noisy sigh. "I might live to regret saying this, but you're not alone."

Lucille's features crumple as fresh tears spill down her cheeks. "Yes, I am."

I could feed her a few lines about hope and friendship, but the truth is, she's right. She *is* alone. Without Trace and me, she'd be pushing up daisies.

This stress isn't healthy for her or the baby. It's hell on *all* of us.

Lucille wipes her eyes and straightens, her shoulders squaring like she's readying for battle. "I'm going to fix this, Ash. I don't know how yet, but I'll figure it out. Let me help you win Ori back. She's a good woman, and I'd like to have her on my side."

She leaves my office on that note, but her words linger in the air, pressing down on me.

Lucille's wrong about Ori. She's not just a good woman. She's the greatest woman I've ever known.

The worst part? Ori *was* all in from the moment we met—100% present, no hesitation. If she was ever afraid of love, she sure as hell never showed it.

Until now.

After Lucille leaves, I slam back another bottle of water and rest my head on the desk, willing the pain away.

Although nothing in the world will make the ache in my heart stop.

Not that I'm giving up on Ori—not by a long shot.

As soon as this god-awful situation is wrapped up and that

piece of shit Kevin Duncan is behind bars, I'm going to pursue Ori until I wear her down and she says yes—to all of it.

I just have to survive until then.

My office door opens, and I grumble, "What now?"

"He's here."

Lucille doesn't have to elaborate—I know who *he* is.

I tug a hand through my hair and push to my feet, gesturing toward the chair. "Sit down. Drink some water."

"What are you going to do?"

"Did he see you?"

Lucille nods, tears slipping down her cheeks. "What if he hurts me again?"

"Not fucking happening. Not on my watch." I glance toward the front of *Black Lotus* and sigh. "Close this door and call Trace. Let him know—if he doesn't already."

"Be careful. He's dangerous, Ash."

"So am I, Lucille."

I pass by Braden's office and lean in. "Do me a favor?"

"What?" Braden asks, not bothering to look up from his computer.

"Take care of Lucille for a minute. She's really upset."

Braden tosses his pencil down, glaring at me. "Seriously? Now I'm on ex-babysitting duty? Isn't that *your* job?"

I smack the office wall, my patience fraying fast. "Just do it, man. Stop giving me grief."

Braden crosses his arms, his jaw tight. "You know what? Keep screwing up your life, Ash. Just don't expect everyone else to clean up the mess."

Normally, I'd get into it with Braden, but not today.

Today, I have a meet-and-greet with my new nemesis.

And his name is Kevin Duncan.

Kevin stands in the reception area, his high-dollar suit clashing with the bright, offbeat designs of Black Lotus.

His cold gray eyes sweep the shop, pausing on a sketch of an intricate floral tattoo, before locking on me. A smirk tugs at his lips as he extends a gloved hand. "We haven't been formally introduced."

I straighten to my full height, letting him feel every inch of the fifty pounds of muscle I have over him. "I know who you are, and you know who I am. That's good enough."

"Is that how you greet all your clients?"

"You're not a fucking client. What do you want?"

Kevin removes his gloves with deliberate precision, snapping them against the counter like a challenge. "Consider this a business call."

"I don't have any business with you."

"But your lady friend does. Ms. Thorne—such an intriguing woman. Stunningly beautiful."

"Stay away from her."

Kevin's smirk widens as he leans against the counter, his tone dripping with mockery. "Aren't you a little busy dealing with my leftovers?"

My fists clench at my sides, my pulse hammering in my ears. "Don't make me drag you outside and wipe the parking lot with your ass."

His laugh is sharp, calculated, and meant to get under my skin. Trust me, it's working, too.

"Ah, there it is—that temper. I do enjoy poking it." He pauses, running a finger along the edge of the counter. "My representative at McGwyer Holdings mentioned your connection to the Dean Estate. Funny thing, though—your name doesn't appear on the deed."

My stomach twists, but I force my expression to remain impassive. So this is who's been after Ori's property all along. Kevin Duncan.

"What do you want with Ori?"

"To get to know her better, of course. I hope she liked the flowers I sent."

I lean in, my face close to his, letting him smell every ounce of the fury roiling in my core. "She would never have anything to do with a lech like you. She's out of your league."

"Or so you hope. One can never be too sure who a woman might seek out for comfort." His smirk deepens as his voice drops into a conspiratorial tone. "She's heading to the city later this week, isn't she?"

My chest tightens. *What the hell?* How does he know Ori's plans when I don't?

"How do you know that?"

Kevin leans in, his voice smug. "I know everything, Mr. Hammond. And I know far more about Oriana Thorne than you realize. I even dropped off tickets to the symphony for her this morning. She's a lover of the arts, isn't she? Perhaps I can persuade her to love other things as well."

It takes every ounce of restraint I have not to grab him by the throat and end this right here, right now.

"Time to go," Braden's voice cuts in, sharp and unwavering. He steps to my side, his usual irritation replaced by something more sinister. He might not know the details, but he's my brother, and he reads the situation—and me—well enough to understand this guy is trouble.

Moments later, Zane flanks my other side. Together, we form a solid wall of six-foot men with no patience for smug assholes like Kevin Duncan.

Kevin's smirk falters for a second, but he recovers quickly. "Have a pleasant afternoon, gentlemen." His tone drips with false politeness as he slips his gloves back on.

He pauses at the door, glancing over his shoulder. "Oh, and Mr. Hammond? Good luck keeping up with her."

I don't move until the door closes behind him, my fists trembling at my sides. He's not just a threat—he's a predator, and now I know for certain that Ori is in his crosshairs.

Braden crosses his arms, his brow furrowed. "Who the hell was that?"

"No one you need to worry about." My voice is tight,

clipped, but inside, my thoughts are racing. Ori doesn't know how dangerous this guy is, but she will.

And if Kevin thinks he's going to get anywhere near her, he's dead wrong.

I watch Kevin back his car out of the lot and rush over to One More Page. Mina glances up from behind the counter, her expression wary, no doubt wondering if a Second World War is about to break out between Ori and me.

"Hi, Ash."

I smack the counter, anxiety coursing through me as I spot the bouquet of red roses. Seems the bastard wasn't lying about sending them to Ori, and I swallow the urge to sweep them onto the floor in a million pieces. "Did Kevin Duncan leave something here?"

Maybe it's the wild look in my eyes, but Mina doesn't press me for information. Instead, she reaches into a drawer and pulls out an envelope. "He brought Ori tickets for the symphony—really great seats, too."

"Give them to me, and don't mention it to Ori."

Mina's eyes narrow at my demand. "No way. Ori could use a pick-me-up right now."

I really don't want to dive over the counter to wrest them from Mina's hands, but I'm not above it. Not at this point.

"Mina, I'm not asking. Give me the damn things." My voice raises, drawing the attention of a few customers.

Wonderful. If I don't rein in my temper, the cops will probably show up, and that's the last thing I need.

I jerk a hand through my hair, trying to figure out a way to let Mina in on the situation without telling her the entire story.

Turns out I don't have to.

"You don't like Kevin Duncan, do you?" she asks, her voice low, as if she's unsure who might be listening.

Dragging a hand across my face, I shake my head. "I hate him. He's not a good man, and his intentions with Ori aren't honorable."

Mina arches an eyebrow. "Is this one of those have-your-cake-and-eat-it-too situations? You want both Lucille and Ori?"

"Not even close." I grasp Mina's hand, my eyes searching hers and imploring her to understand. "I know you love your friend and want to protect her. So do I—more than anything in the world. Please help me do that."

Mina stares at the tickets, her teeth worrying her lower lip. Finally, she slides them across the counter. "I won't tell her about the tickets, but don't make me regret this."

I race into the parking lot of *The Camelot Inn*, my tires screeching against the pavement, drawing a few curious looks from the resident derelicts.

Trust me, you do not want to mess with me right now.

Jumping out of my truck, I storm toward room #7, which is quickly becoming my least favorite number. I bang on the door, barging inside the moment Trace cracks it open.

"When the fuck are you taking him down?" I demand, pacing the floor in angry, unrelenting strides.

Trace raises his hands, signaling me to cool it. Fat chance. "You want a drink?"

I stop pacing long enough to glare at him. "No. I want my life back. Did you know that son of a bitch stopped by *Black Lotus* today? He knows all about Ori—the house she's restoring, her love of the symphony. Hell, he knows she's going to the city next week. I didn't even know that!"

Trace pulls a flask from his jacket pocket and holds it out to me. I snatch it and take a swig, but the whiskey burn only fuels the fire raging inside me.

"I told you Kevin would make your life hell."

"This isn't about my life. He's following Ori."

"He's letting you think he is. Trust me, Ash, my guys have been tailing Ori, and Kevin hasn't been near either of her homes. He's just trying to get under your skin."

"Well, fuck, it's working."

"You're right. It is." Trace perches on the edge of the bed, rubbing his grizzled jaw. "Your little rendezvous with Lucille has thrown chaos into Kevin's perfectly coiffed world. He's so focused on pissing you off that he's not paying attention to me or my guy in the club. This is a good thing."

"Forgive me if I don't see it that way." I sink into a chair, pressing my head into my hands. "How much longer?"

"A couple of weeks. I know it's hard, but trust me, this is going exactly how I hoped it would. Just keep doing what you're doing."

"Losing my mind?"

Trace chuckles. "That's women for you. I've got a guy looking out for your girl, okay?"

I shake my head and push myself upright. "Not good enough. I need to ensure Ori is safe. It's *my* job."

"Lucille told me Ori wants nothing to do with you. What are you going to do—camp outside her apartment?"

Talk about a lightbulb moment.

Lucille is safe at the farm. Braden might hate her, but he'd never let anything happen to her. Plus, there's always at least one HSI agent watching her at all times—even if I've yet to figure out who they are.

She's covered.

And that leaves me free to take care of the woman I love.

Trace smirks, catching the shift in my expression. "You *are* going to camp outside Ori's place, aren't you?"

I take another swig from the flask before handing it back. "Damn straight."

Chapter 19

You Can't Stop Me

Ori

You know those days when all you want to do is go home, crawl under a blanket, and never emerge?

Well, stretch that out for a week, and you've got my life right now.

The past six days have been a special kind of hell—one long spiral of regret, anger, and heartbreak—ever since my final blow up with Ash.

But instead of escaping to a blanket fort, I've been bombarded by a rash of needy and clueless customers.

Most days, I love the people who frequent the store, along with their offbeat questions and requests. I really do.

Today is not one of those days.

Each person's cheerfulness grates on me more than the last, shredding my nerves until there's nothing left but a frayed, irritable mess.

Even with the onslaught of business, my brain refuses to stop spiraling over the pitiful state of my love life.

And if the chaos at the store and in my mind wasn't enough, Eddie has been hounding me daily with one small issue after another on the Dean Estate restoration. A loose floorboard here, a door that won't close there—little things that shouldn't matter but somehow pile up into one big headache. Every time I think things are finally under control, the house finds a new way to mock me.

And I'm ready to throw in the towel on all of it.

You'd think someone as smart as I am could handle all this without losing it. Seriously, I'm a bright woman. Top of my class in college—okay, one of the top, but still, I'm damn smart. And sensible.

Then I met Asher Hammond and turned into a googly-eyed teenager, hopelessly mooning after the unattainable stud.

A man with a storied reputation that reaches well past the borders of Sparkwood. *Everyone* knows about Ash's dating history—if you can call doing the horizontal mambo with six women in a week dating. Hell, even the elderly woman in the drugstore shot me a sympathetic look when she passed me in the aisle.

In Sparkwood, secrets travel faster than the speed of light. Everyone knows.

And because it's Sparkwood, no one can resist reminding me in the most passive-aggressive ways possible—pitying looks, fake concern, and thinly veiled gossip. It's suffocating.

Somehow, though, despite being surrounded on all sides by the truth, I was the last to see it.

I believed it might be different for Ash and me.

That I was different. That he'd wake up one day, realize I was exactly what he wanted and needed, and we'd share a life together.

A life which didn't include his former lover, their love child, and me as the third wheel on this cockamamie ride.

The worst part?

I can't tell if I'm angry at Ash for breaking my heart—or at myself for giving it to him in the first place.

I glance at my phone when it rings. Speak of the devil.

Do I answer it or ignore it and let him stew? Trust me, my juvenile side begs for the second option. He's been calling all week without leaving a single message—just letting my phone buzz as if I'll chase after him like some lovesick puppy. Fat chance of that.

But maybe I need to remind him what the term cease and desist means. Otherwise, this game will never end.

"I told you to leave me alone," I growl into the receiver.

Look at that, my voice sounds almost normal, as if the man on the other end of the line hasn't turned my entire life inside out.

"It's about time you answered the damn phone."

"I didn't answer it because I didn't want to talk to you."

"How many times has Kevin Duncan been in your store?"

I pull the phone away from my ear, shooting it a curious look. Odd segue. "Who?"

"Kevin Duncan," Ash snaps, his tone sharp enough to cut glass. "About our age, dark hair, spends more on his suits than most people make in a month, and always sniffing around first editions like he actually knows what the hell he's looking at. *That* guy."

I'm tempted to keep playing dumb, to frustrate Ash and make him sweat a little, but something in his tone warns me this isn't the time for jokes. "A few times. Why?"

"I don't want you helping him anymore. Read me?"

"He's a customer, Ash. I can't just ignore him."

"Let Mina handle him. You see him walk in, and you go straight to your office. Promise me."

"Why should I? He's a nice guy—"

"No, he isn't," Ash bellows, his voice reverberating through the phone like a thunderclap. "Just stay away from him."

"I don't need this shit. I'm hanging up."

"Ori, wait. Please. I know he seems charming, and he's got more money than God, and he's interested in you. Plus, you'd love nothing more than to stick it to me by dating him, but I'm *begging* you to stay away from him."

So, it's not about me. Once again, it's about Ash and his feelings. Well, fuck that.

"You don't get to dictate who I do and do not see. Besides, what makes you think you were even a thought in my head when he asked me to dinner?"

Am I being nasty? Absolutely.

Silence rings out on the other side of the line. Seems I've finally stunned Ash into speechlessness.

"You're not going to dinner with him," he finally growls, his voice low and threatening.

"You can't stop me." Do I want to go on a date with Kevin? Not at all, but Ash doesn't need to know that.

"Ori, I'll handcuff you to me if that's what it takes."

"What would Lucille say?" My voice turns icy. "If you've said your piece, I've got a busy day."

"Ori, don't—"

But I've already ended the call, and somehow, I'm even angrier than when the day started.

What did I expect? That he was calling to beg me back? No, all he did was beg me not to go out with another man.

Not that I had planned on dining with Kevin Duncan— though now, I might do it out of pure spite.

My phone rings again. Time for round two.

"What do you want?" I snap, my irritation carrying over from the last call.

"Is this Ms. Oriana Thorne?" an unfamiliar female voice asks.

Shit. I wince at my unprofessional greeting. "Yes, sorry. I thought you were someone else."

"No problem. This is Dr. Mazer's office calling regarding your test results. Can you please come into the office at your earliest convenience?"

Double shit. My day has officially gone from bad to worse. I shudder, my mind already spiraling. What could it be? Something serious? Something incurable? God help me—it's another glaring reminder that men, specifically Asher Hammond, are hazardous to my health.

"That bad, huh?" I ask, managing a strangled laugh.

"Ma'am, we can't disclose any information over the phone."

"Got it. I'll be right down."

With a sigh, I lower the phone and turn my gaze to the ceiling. How much worse can today get? Probably best not to ask that question.

I head for the parking lot and slide into the driver's seat of my truck, my mind a tangled mess of worst-case scenarios.

I swear, this is the last time I let a man anywhere near me.

A soft knock sounds at my passenger window, and I jump at the unexpected noise. Glancing over, I see Lucille motioning for me to lower the window.

Universe, are you fucking kidding me right now?

I unlock the door, and she climbs in, her movements tentative, like she knows she's not welcome. She offers me a soft smile, which only increases my anxiety.

"Hi, Ori," she says, her voice hesitant.

"You seriously need to learn the meaning of boundaries," I grumble, gripping the steering wheel so hard my knuckles ache.

"You can hate me later, but I need to say this."

Huffing out a breath, I lean my head back against the seat, staring at the ceiling. "I don't hate you. Either of you. There. Feel better now? Can I go?"

Lucille reaches over and touches my arm. Her hand is cool, almost trembling. "There's nothing between Ash and me. Not for years."

I roll my eyes. "Except for a baby, which, last time I checked, isn't nothing."

"It's complicated," she whispers, looking away.

"Right. He stuck his dick into you, and you got pregnant. Seems pretty damn simple, actually."

"That's not how it is." Her voice tightens, and her hand retreats as she clasps her fingers in her lap. "Don't hold Ash accountable for my mistakes."

"You're both guilty on this charge," I reply, my voice sharp, "but don't worry. He's got plenty more issues that belong solely to him. If you have something to say, just say it."

"Give him a chance," she blurts out, her voice trembling. "Let him love you."

I release a bitter laugh, the sound scraping my throat. "Let him love me? That's the trouble. He *never* loved me. I should know. I told him several times, and his response was always the same—he couldn't say it back. You're the only woman he's ever loved, even though you don't fucking deserve him."

Her face crumples, and for a moment, she looks like she's about to cry. "I never did," she whispers, her voice barely audible. "And trust me, he doesn't love me. He loves you."

"No, he doesn't." How much longer is she going to subject me to this ridiculous argument?

Lucille shakes her head. "Just because he can't say it doesn't mean it's not true. Besides," she murmurs, "he told me he loves you."

Another mirthless laugh escapes me. "Fucking figures. You get everything, don't you? His heart, his love, his baby, hell, even his admission that he loves me. You get it all, and I get nothing."

Lucille's lips part, and she leans forward as if to argue, but I cut her off. "Don't bother. Look, I appreciate you trying to keep the peace, but I'm not up for girl talk today. And we're never going to be friends, Lucille. I don't want to commiserate over shared dating disasters or braid each other's hair. The best I can offer is that we coexist as cordially as possible."

She averts her gaze, nodding. Her hands twist nervously in her lap. "I'm not worried about me. I'm worried about Ash."

"And for the first time in a long time," I reply, gripping the steering wheel tight, "I'm worried about me. And only me."

I mean it, too. Ash has ruined my view of fairytales forever. From now on, I'll align with the crusty witch hiding in the forest, far beyond the clutches of heartless men.

Fuck love.

Love is messy. Treacherous.

Mostly, love hurts, especially when someone you love with all your heart doesn't love you with any of theirs.

So, no matter how many fuzzy kitten somersaults my heart does whenever I see Ash, it's not love.

He was just a mistake I kept making.

An hour later, I walk back into my store and make a beeline for my office, shutting the door behind me.

I'm so over today. And this week. And this month.

I curl into a ball in the corner and bury my head in my hands, trying to rein in the emotions swirling inside me.

"Are you okay?"

"Nope," I reply, my voice muffled. I don't bother to look up as Mina's footsteps echo across the room.

She crouches beside me, her concern palpable. "What's going on? Are you sick?"

"Not at the moment, although I've felt flashes."

"What?"

With a sharp exhale, I lift my head to meet her worried gaze. "I just got back from the doctor. I got tested for STDs after… Ash."

Her expression hardens, and she stands abruptly. "What did that motherfucker give you?" she demands.

"A baby," I mutter, dropping my head back into my hands.

"What?"

Groaning, I push my hair out of my face and sit up straighter. "I'm pregnant."

Mina's eyes widen, her jaw slackening. "You're… wow. Holy… wow. Congratulations."

"No, not congratulations," I groan. At her confused expression, I release a heavy sigh. "It's Ash's baby."

"Yeah, I figured that."

"Did you forget he's already got a baby mama? You know, his one true love? Well, now he's got two. I'm the backup."

"Stop it, that's not true."

"What part of what I said isn't true? It's *all* true. What am I supposed to do?"

Her voice softens. "What did Ash say?"

"I haven't told him." I hold up a hand to cut off her response. "Don't give me that look, Mina. I will tell him, but I need time to figure out my approach and what I'm doing."

"Are you keeping the baby?"

I nod, my hand resting instinctively on my stomach. "Yes. Even if Ash wants nothing to do with us, we'll be okay."

"Why don't you think he'll be happy?"

"We've gone over this," I say, exasperated.

"Hear me out. He's sent you over a dozen bouquets and called you a ton of times. He's pretty damn determined to see you. Maybe you should spend some time with him. It's obvious how he feels about you."

But it's not. Despite everyone—his baby mama included—telling me how much Ash cares, I've never heard the man utter a word.

Well, that's not true. He spouted a bunch of shit when he was drunk. Lucky for him, I'm not holding him to it.

"I'm not hanging out with him again. I tried that once last week, and it didn't end well."

"What happened?"

"Lucille happened," I bite out. "She walked in and asked Ash to drive her home. *Their* home."

"What did Ash say?"

"Begged me to stay. Said he wanted to spend the night… you know."

Mina's eyebrows shoot up. "Ooh, give me all the juicy details."

"Sorry to disappoint but all I did was kiss him and that was a dumb decision based on heartache and hormones. It won't happen again."

"Yeah, right."

"No, it can't. This situation is already so murky and muddy."

"Is it, though? Look, I get that this baby mama drama is no fun, but Ash swore to me he's not with Lucille. They don't seem like they're intimate."

I groan, the thought making my stomach churn. "Can you not put that image in my head?"

"And all those notes with the flowers? So desperate to hang onto you."

"So desperate he said a bunch of things he doesn't mean."

"How do you know?"

"He was drinking."

"So? People tell the truth when they're drunk. What did he say?"

I wave a hand dismissively. "Nothing."

Mina shoots a narrowed glare at me. "What. Did. He. Say."

Rolling my eyes, I relent. "He mentioned us having a family. Some crap about fairytale endings. Told me he'd only adored one woman in his life, and it wasn't Lucille. But then he proceeded to go home with Lucille. So, yeah, I'm thinking he was full of shit. Oh, and copious amounts of whiskey."

Mina crosses her arms. "I think he meant it."

"Life with Asher Hammond has been a rollercoaster, and it has to end."

"Or it continues forever, and you two get married and have a dozen kids, just like you wanted."

Isn't she adorable with her chronic optimism? "Can you get out of my office now?"

"Sure. By the way, Kevin Duncan called, looking for you."

Only a day ago, her message wouldn't have caused a ripple, but after Ash's stern warning, I wonder if the man is up to something. "Likely wanted that book he ordered."

"I mentioned the book, but he insisted you call him back personally." She hands me a slip of paper with his number, her lips pressing into a thin line. "I don't like him, and neither does Ash."

That's an understatement. Ash seems hellbent on killing the man if he so much as breathes too close to me.

"Noted. Anything else, or can I return to my pity party for one?"

"Go tell Ash." Mina crosses her arms, her tone firm. "That way, you won't have to worry about how he'll react. If he's a shit about it, then fine. You go on with your life and forget he ever existed while I fashion him some cement shoes. But if he's great about the news, then you don't have to do this alone."

"I'm not ready."

"You'll never be ready, Ori. Doesn't change the fact that you're having a baby with him."

"Give me an hour to process, and then I'll talk to him. Fair enough?"

Mina skews her mouth to the side before relenting. "Fine."

"Zip your lip until then."

"Let me know when you tell him so I can start planning the baby shower."

"I've only been pregnant five minutes. You've got time."

How is she so damn excited? I'm terrified.

Mina winks before exiting my office, leaving me alone with my emotions. And trust me, I have *all* of them right now.

On the plus side, I have money and a successful business. I'm thirty-nine, and I've always wanted children. How many more chances will I have?

On the downside, the father is already expecting his first child with his first love, which leaves me—and our baby—a bit of nowhere.

Mina doesn't understand why I'm hesitant to tell Ash. I know he'll do the stand-up thing and be there for his child, but that's not the point. It's not because he *wants* a family. Hell, aside from that drunken tirade the other night, he's always made it abundantly clear that settling down isn't in his DNA.

Ash hates the idea of a white picket prison—or so he's long claimed. Even though Lucille is carrying his child, he hasn't shown a speck of excitement about it. I get men aren't usually into the nitty-gritty details, but this is his first kid. You'd think he'd at least mention the baby or Lucille's pregnancy. Instead, he damn near grimaces every time I bring them up.

Maybe he's trying to spare me.

But now, instead of one child he didn't plan for, he's got two. From two different women. Talk about a juggling act in a circus he never wanted to attend.

Hence my hesitation.

So, I sip my herbal tea and wait for a sign from the universe—or at least the courage to approach my baby's father.

Too bad whiskey isn't an option while pregnant. I mentioned to the doctor that I'd had a few glasses over the past couple of weeks. She assured me it happens all the time with surprise pregnancies, but suggested I enjoy the memory of it because I'm on the wagon until my delivery date.

Which feels like a million years from now.

What to do? What to do?

My gaze lands on the book Ash bought me at the beginning of our relationship. We hadn't gone on a single date yet, but he remembered how much I adored *Jane Eyre* and purchased a special edition copy.

Reaching out, I trace the hand-painted spine, the intricate design smooth beneath my fingertips.

Maybe he'll be okay with the news. Maybe I won't feel like a third wheel—or in this case, a fifth.

And it's not like I can hide the pregnancy forever. He'll find out eventually, unless I pack my things and return to the city.

I stand, a resolute feeling tearing through me. I'm going to tell him and rip off the bandage. Then, like Mina said, it's done.

Not that I believe in fairytale endings anymore, anyway.

My phone buzzes. Damn Grand Central Station in here.

Ash: We're ordering pizza over here, and I added a pie for you and Mina. The roads are getting icy, and I don't want you driving out to get food.

Damn him for being so endearing. This is the side of Asher Hammond most people don't see. Oh, they know he's hot, charming, and wickedly funny, but they don't get the cute moments where he's this big, tatted teddy bear.

I lived for those moments.

Okay, universe, good enough.

I push myself to standing and suck in a deep breath. I can do this. I've done far harder things in my life.

Strolling over to *Black Lotus*, I grin at Zane as I walk through the door. "Where's the boss hiding?"

"In his office. How are you doing?"

"Okay." For the first time in a while, I mean it.

I've got this.

But as I round the corner and raise my hand to knock on Ash's door, I pause. Voices filter through the other side. Two of them.

It doesn't take long to identify the female voice.

Lucille.

Of course.

"At least you haven't cracked any fat jokes," she says, her laugh light and annoyingly flirtatious.

"How stupid do you think I am?" Ash asks with a chuckle.

There's a pause, and then Lucille speaks again, softer this time. "I'm worried, Ash. How am I'm going to do this?"

His response is immediate. "You're going to be fine. You've got me."

My stomach twists, and I press a hand to it instinctively, as if that will somehow stop the hurt from spreading.

You've got me.

But where does that leave me?

I can't compete with her. She has all his firsts, and now I'm more aware than ever that I'm relegated to the role of runner-up.

I back away from his office door, my pulse pounding in my ears as I pass Zane.

"Where you off to so fast?" he asks, his eyes narrowing at my hurried stride.

"Gotta go," I mutter, keeping my head down as I push through the door of *Black Lotus*.

Maybe the universe thinks it's time to tell Ash about the baby, but I'm not ready for that yet. Not now. Maybe not ever.

I just need space. Space to breathe, to think, to figure out how the hell I'm supposed to move forward when my heart feels like it's barely holding together.

I'm so deep in thought that I don't notice Eddie standing there until I collide with his chest.

"Hey, you okay?" He reaches out to steady me, his brow furrowing as he studies my face.

"I'm fine." My voice is strained and quiet, and even those two words feel like an effort. "What's up?"

"I wanted to talk to you."

Something in me snaps, the frayed edges of my control unraveling all at once. I spin on my heel and toss my hands up. "Let me guess—there's mold or fungus or some rare bacteria growing in the furthest reaches of the house. Something that will cost a mint and take a million years to repair. Am I close?"

"No, it's not about—"

"I've got an idea, Eddie. Just burn the fucking place down. I'll buy you the matches."

The words barely leave my mouth as the tears arrive, hot and relentless. Mumbling a broken apology, I race to my office and slump into my chair. My arms drop to the surface of the desk, my head falling forward to rest against them.

Maybe if I stay here long enough, I'll melt into the wood and disappear.

I hear the heavy thud of Eddie's boots as he enters, but I don't look up. Eddie's never been good at taking a hint. Why should today be any different?

He pulls up the chair across from me, the scrape of it loud in the silence. A box of tissues lands on the desk near my elbow. "Whose ass do I need to kick?"

I swipe at my face, still not looking up. "What makes you think it's about a man?"

He barks out a laugh. "It's not my first rodeo, Ori. Besides, anyone who hurts my big sister is going to have to tangle with me."

"Thanks, Eddie, I..." I trail off as his words settle over me.

My heart stutters, disbelief cutting through the haze of my emotions.

What did he just say?

I lift my head, sniffing as I wipe my eyes. "Did you just call me your sister?"

He leans back in his chair as his lips twitch into a faint

smile. "I did. And I've got a million things to tell you about our dad."

Chapter 20

Family Secrets

Ori

"**Y**ou made coffee. Good man," I mumble to Eddie as I pad into the kitchen. "Shit. I can't have it, though."

"Sure you can. It's decaffeinated. I grabbed it at the store."

"You're the best." I smile as the warm liquid hits my lips. "Tastes almost as good as the real thing."

Eddie grins, giving me a light punch in the arm. "Only nine more months before you can return to the dark side."

Yes, Eddie knows I'm pregnant. It came up during our hours-long talk-a-thon last night, when he disclosed he was far more than just the local handyman.

It's funny how I never saw it before, but now that I know we're related, I see the similarities. We have the same honey-brown eyes, the same inappropriate humor, and the same dry wit.

He's far softer than I am, emotionally speaking, but he also concedes that growing up in my world would harden anyone.

I'll admit, when he first told me we were brother and sister, all I wanted to do was grab the closest bottle of whiskey and hide in a cave for the next year. Too much, too soon. My heart didn't think it could handle any more surprises.

I wasn't ready to discuss our father. I'd clung to my anger for so long, and hearing a different side of the story was a new pain. But it also turned out to be therapeutic.

My dad hadn't forgotten me. Quite the opposite.

Eddie had a vast sea of stories to tell. He shared how our father talked about me all the time, even setting a place for me at every holiday dinner—not that I ever bothered to attend or RSVP.

But my brother wasn't mad about my absence. He understood the pain I suffered, how distance was the only salve. Still, he longed to know his sister. And when our father was on his deathbed, he made Eddie promise to look out for me.

My brother took that promise seriously, and that's how he wound up in Sparkwood.

Of course, I was skeptical at first, wondering if there was a more insidious reason behind his sudden appearance—mainly my inheritance. Turns out, that wasn't the case. Eddie received the same amount from our father.

Then he brought out pictures, and that's when the tears arrived. Memories of days I chose not to be a part of because I never wanted my mother to question my loyalty.

Look, one stroll down memory lane won't erase the scars, but I feel better than I have in years. Plus, it feels good to know my brother has my back regarding the baby, even if he agrees with Mina that Ash needs to know.

"I'm going to jump in the shower," Eddie calls from the bathroom.

"Don't use all the hot water."

"No promises."

With a laugh, I slip on my coat and shoes. "I'm running out to get the mail. I'm waiting on a package."

Spring is finally making her way to Sparkwood, albeit slowly. The mountains love their winters and aren't quick to release her for another year.

But the snowdrops have broken through the ground, and

soon the daffodils and tulips will follow. New life is springing forth everywhere.

Including inside me.

Imagine that.

Pulling the package from my mailbox, I glance up and notice something unusual.

Ash's truck sits parked next to mine—and Ash is in the truck.

What the hell?

As I get closer, I see he's asleep, so I knock gently on the windowpane. Ash jerks awake, shooting me a surprised look as he rakes his hand through his hair.

After a beat, he cracks the window, his gaze flicking to mine. "Hey."

"What are you doing here?"

"You're here."

"Have you been here all night?"

"Yeah. I planned to slip away before the sun came up."

I shake my head, trying to decipher the meaning behind his actions. "You planned this? Sleeping in my parking lot?"

He nods, shifting uncomfortably in his seat. "I'm worried about you. After you hung up on me and didn't respond to my text, I stopped in the shop. Mina told me you were out to dinner."

Ah, *there's* the reason. Do I disclose I was dining with my recently discovered half-brother or let him stew?

Stew, it is.

"You were spying on me?" I fold my arms across my chest, unable to keep the bite out of my voice.

"No, I was afraid you went to dinner with Kevin Duncan, and I don't trust the fucking guy. I don't trust any man with you."

"What about you? Do you trust yourself with me?" I lean in slightly, challenging him with a raised brow.

He hesitates, and when he speaks, his voice drops, rougher

than before. "I know the things I want to do to you. And I guarantee a lot of other men feel the same way. But I'll break them at every joint if they try it."

I blink, stunned by the forcefulness of his statements. "You can't say things like that."

"It's true. No one touches you but me. I told you that." His jaw tightens as if the words are etched in stone.

Once again, Ash's well-intentioned remark rubs me the wrong way. I step back, trying to put distance between us. "Does that work both ways? Apparently not, considering your baby mama is probably frantic with worry. Go home, Ash."

He grips my wrist, holding me fast, and leans forward, his breath warm against my skin. "That's the thing. Where you are… that's my home."

I shake my head as the emotions swimming inside me threaten to drown me whole. "You can't say things like that."

Even if it is a ridiculously sweet sentiment.

Ash's gaze softens. "Not even when they're true?"

I swallow hard, trying to push away the warmth spreading through my chest. "What's that?" I ask, pointing to a sketchbook lying on the seat next to him.

"My drawings. I was working on the mural for *Rum & Ruin.*"

My eyes widen, and a hint of a smile breaks through despite everything. "Really? May I see?"

He waffles for a second before sighing and handing me the book.

I flip to the page, marked by a pencil, and my heart stutters as I stare at the drawing. "Is that—"

"You? Yes." His voice is low, almost reverent. "It's my favorite picture of you."

The sketch captures a version of me I rarely let others see —vulnerable and free. "I remember that day," I whisper. I also remember how desperately I loved him then.

We'll ignore how desperately I still do.

Ash runs a hand along his jaw, his gaze drifting toward the sketch. "It was sublime, from our breakfast that morning to my dessert that night. The first time I took you raw. The first time I felt all of you. Utter perfection."

My breath catches, hearing him recall the memory with such longing, and I struggle to maintain my strong facade. Still, I need to tread lightly.

"We were playing a dangerous game."

Ash's eyes flick back to mine, steady and sure. "Not for me. I'd do it all over again." He motions to my bedroom window, the only one visible from the parking lot. "You aren't sleeping."

"How do you know?" I glance over at the window, embarrassed. Damn, are the bags under my eyes that obvious?

Ash shrugs, his gaze focused on the third-story window. "Because I've been here every night for a week. I see you getting up, wandering around. You slept great with me."

"You've been in the parking lot every night for a week? Ash, it's been frigid outside," I exclaim.

"The truck has heat, and like I said, I'm worried about you. This way, I can ensure you're safe and still give you the space you need. Although, this is a nice change of pace." He dares to reach out, drifting his fingers along my cheek. "Why aren't you sleeping, little one?"

"I've had a lot on my mind."

Understatement of the century right there.

Ash nods and skews his mouth to the side—always an adorable look for him. "I get that."

But he doesn't. He can't. Ash doesn't know the secrets I'm carrying, and I'm terrified to tell him.

I swipe at the tears gathering in my eyes. "No, you don't."

"Then talk to me. I'm here to help you. To protect you. I'll do anything for you, but you have to open up and let me in."

I run a finger along the side-view mirror, trying to collect my thoughts.

How do I broach this topic? I'm not ready—not by a million miles.

Ash tips my chin up, forcing me to meet his inquiring gaze. "I know things have been beyond fucked lately, but there's something else, isn't there?"

I nod, willing the tears back. It's time to tell him.

"Beautiful, I can't do all the talking here."

As if on cue, a blast of wind cuts through me, and I shiver, gathering my robe tighter around me

"Shit, you're freezing. Get in the truck."

I smile and shake my head. "I'm going back inside."

Ash huffs out a breath and smacks the steering wheel. "Yep, I guess I deserve that. I'm here if you change your mind."

"You need coffee."

"I do. And a shower. I'm a bit ripe."

I shoot him a playful wink. "Lucky for you, I have both. Come inside."

"Will you join me in the shower?" Just like that, Ash's flirtatious side comes into play.

I really missed this side of him. Hell, I miss *every* side of him.

"Can't. I'll be busy making you coffee."

"If it comes down between you and coffee, you win every time."

"Baby steps, Ash."

I stop, realizing my Freudian slip.

But then it hits me—Ash has no reason to think I'm pregnant.

Although that will change in about ten minutes.

Ash grabs his phone and shoots me a dimpled grin. "I have to make a quick call, but I'll be right in, okay?"

I smile and tap on the truck door. "Don't keep me waiting."

Ash grasps my fingers, bringing them to his lips. "Never."

I stroll up the walkway, pulling in a lungful of crisp air.

Okay, Ori, you can do this. Ash obviously cares about you. Just take a deep breath, tell him about the baby, and reassure him he doesn't need to do anything.

Easy, right?

I may need to throw up first.

Eddie opens the door as I'm walking back, his laptop bag slung over one shoulder. "Hey, I wondered where you went. Shower's all yours. I'm heading out."

I engulf my brother in a hug, grateful for the unexpected kinship. "Be careful."

"Of course. You sure you don't mind me crashing here until I find a new place?"

"Not a bit. Better than that damn motel."

"True," Eddie says, adjusting the brim of his ball cap. "I'll see you when you get back from the city. Call me to let me know you arrived safely and have fun at the conference."

"Absolutely—" I pause as Ash's truck drives out of the lot. No warning. No goodbye. Nothing.

What the fuck?

"Was that Ash?" Eddie asks, confusion lining his face.

"Yep."

"What was he doing here?"

I shrug. "Claims he was watching over me. He was supposed to come in for coffee, but I guess he had to get home to Lucille."

"Christ, what a cluster," Eddie mutters, shaking his head.

"Seriously. Okay, see you later this week."

Once inside, I grab my phone and dial Ash's number, but it goes straight to voicemail. Another four calls also go unanswered.

With a grunt, I head for the shower, figuring he'll call me by the time I get out. Something must have come up, right?

Wrong. Because all my calls and texts remain unanswered an hour later.

"You know what, Asher Hammond," I hiss at the phone, tossing it onto the couch. "I've had about enough of your games."

Then I head into the bedroom to pack for my conference.

Looks like I'm on my own with this one.

Chapter 21

Rigged To Detonate

Ash

Fuck love. Fuck it in all its iterations.

I'm through with the concept.

I damn near inked the words across my face as a reminder should I ever be stupid enough to risk that emotion again.

Thankfully, Braden talked me out of that idea, although we've almost come to blows a few times in the last few days.

He wants to know why I'm being a belligerent prick. As if I owe him an explanation.

Oh, I'm out of my mind, and the scary part is… I kinda like it.

At least I'm not moping around like a lovesick cow anymore.

Now I'm a raging fucking bull, and if you see me coming, get the hell out of my way.

I knew something was up with Eddie. I knew it, and I called Ori out on it, and the woman denied it time and again.

She claimed there was nothing between them. Eddie wasn't overly attentive or caring. He was just a contractor, hired to restore her house.

Sure. More like they're playing house.

Hell, she didn't even try to hide her affection for the asshole—hugging him as he strutted from her apartment after doing God knows what to my woman.

The way she embraced him like he was her lifeline—or her lover. It didn't matter. It was enough to light me up.

Wait. She's not my woman. Not anymore.

Must keep reminding myself of that fact, as if the sting ever dulls.

Does Oriana Thorne really think I can't find somewhere else to hang my hat and get my rocks off?

Have we met?

I have a black book that's thicker than a phone book, for Christ's sake.

A long list of women who want to fuck me, and trust me, I'm all about the hate fucking right now.

Casey from *Ink Spot* called yesterday, claiming she had some business to discuss about the tattoo tour, but I saw it for what it really was. A business facade for a night of pleasure.

I damn near caved.

Why the hell not, right?

I even accepted her offer… and then canceled an hour before arriving at her suite.

Why?

Because of Oriana fucking Thorne, that's why.

The woman has destroyed me for other women.

Destroyed me, period.

How stupid can one man be? Honestly? I thought Ori's teary expression and hesitancy to disclose her innermost thoughts had something to do with us.

I guess in a way it did.

She had ended any chance of our reconciliation without bothering to let me in on the knowledge. Then she had the audacity to flaunt her new man in front of me.

I hate her for wrecking me like this. It's easier than admitting I still want her.

That I'll probably always want her.

Like I said. I'm done with love.

The only upside? I've thrown myself into work and cranked out two weeks' worth of labor on *Rum & Ruin* in three nights.

That's what love will do for you. Break your heart and make you break a damn sweat, right after you're done breaking a few walls.

Three new pieces of sheetrock are hanging as we speak, replacing the ones that met an untimely demise courtesy of my fists. At least I didn't hit a beam. Small mercies, right?

But my mind won't rest, no matter how hard my body begs to shut down. It circles back to memories of Ori and me, taunting me with happiness I was never meant to have.

Braden, Zane, and Lucille have steered clear of me, which is smart. I'm a powder keg with a short fuse. Just ask the UPS guy. Poor bastard left a package on the floor, and I went off like I was auditioning for a reality show about angry neighbors. He nodded, backed toward the door, and probably filed a mental note to avoid this address.

Truth is, I'm a mess, but I won't stop long enough to let that fact sink in. To let it break me.

Trace says it's only a week or so before he nails Kevin's ass to the wall. I should feel relief. Instead, it's like standing in front of a ticking bomb, waiting for the explosion.

And while I want Kevin gone for good, I'm in no rush to get there. There's nothing left to look forward to anymore.

I've had women over the years ask why some men are so opposed to love.

This. This is why, ladies.

Because getting your heart ripped out and stomped on by the one person you thought might save you will destroy your faith in fairytales.

One thing's for damn sure—I'm never falling again. My heart is now rigged to detonate if anyone dares come near it.

I haven't seen the petite heartbreaker since that morning at her apartment, but when she finally decides to face me like an adult, there won't be any friendly camaraderie. Not anymore.

We'll go back to ignoring each other's existence.

Guess we had it right the first time.

For now, my focus is on the speakeasy and getting her ready for the final inspection before opening night. One guarantee: I won't have just one gorgeous woman on my arm that night. I'll have my own personal harem.

Not that they'll come close to the magic of Ori.

Shaking off thoughts of her, I grab the putty knife and set to work. That's the thing about menial tasks: the rhythm is soothing, and I need that now more than ever.

That and blasting metal music.

Take that, *One More Page*. Hope you enjoy my song selection.

When a hand touches my shoulder, I jump, the putty knife skittering across the floor with a metallic clang.

Spinning around, I see who the hand belongs to, and my anger flares back a hundredfold.

"What the fuck do you want?" I bark at Eddie.

"Can you turn the music down?" He motions to his ears.

No, because that would drown out your screams while I pummel you into the ground.

With a scoff, I kill the music, crossing my arms against my chest. "Better?"

"Yeah. I've been calling your name, but you didn't hear me. No surprise, right?"

"What do you want?"

Eddie points to a large, draped object by the door. "Ori wanted you to have this. Said you two talked about putting it in the speakeasy."

"And she sends *you* to drop it off? Unbelievable. I don't want anything from Ori."

"You sure? It's a great piece." He pulls off the tape and blanket, revealing the etched mirror I'd admired all those months ago.

My chest tightens at the sight of it, but I force my voice to stay cold. "She should sell it. It's worth a lot of money."

"She wants you to have it, so I'm leaving it here. Do whatever the hell you want with it." He wipes his hands against his jeans, then leans casually against the bar, his gaze sweeping the room. "Looks good in here. Real good."

"Don't expect an invitation."

"I guess my sister shouldn't expect one, either, huh?"

I freeze as I bend to grab the putty knife. "Do I know your sister?"

For half a second, my brain shoots off in the worst direction. Did I fuck his sister? I've been with a lot of women, but surely, I'd remember one related to this asshole.

Eddie chuckles, cutting through my spiraling thoughts. "Quite well. Oriana Thorne is my half-sister. We only recently came into each other's lives."

Wait. *What?*

The ground beneath me shifts. Eddie. Ori. Sister. The anger I've been clinging to suddenly feels hollow, like a weapon with no target.

"Your... sister?" I repeat, dumbfounded.

"Yeah. Same dad," he says, casually inspecting a dent in his knuckles like he didn't just drop a bomb at my feet.

"How the hell did I not know this?"

"She didn't either. Not for a long time. I knew Dad leaving was a sore spot, so I wanted to ease her into it."

I drag a hand over my face, trying to make sense of it all. "But you don't have the same last name."

Eddie shakes his head. "I use my mother's last name in business, since there's already a well-known Edward Thorne."

"Oh yeah, that fucking psycho serial killer." Talk about an unlucky coincidence.

"That bastard pretty much killed my namesake," Eddie says with a faint smirk. "Thanks to that asshole, I've got to introduce myself like I'm not about to steal your wallet or bury you in the woods. Not exactly a great opener if you're trying to land a job."

"Good point. Wait a minute. You're not after Ori's money, are you?" I ask, my voice still sharp, even though my earlier assumptions about Eddie are unraveling fast.

"I've got plenty of my own." Eddie smirks, holding out his hand. "Still hate me?"

I stare at him, the pieces falling into place. Without saying it outright, he knows exactly why I lost my shit every time he came around.

"Fuck, man. I feel like an asshole." I shake his hand, then pull him into a quick, brotherly hug. "I thought—"

"I know," he says, cutting me off with a knowing grin. "But you've got nothing to worry about from me. Unless you hurt Ori. Then we have a problem. A *big* problem."

The mention of her name sends a pang of regret through me.

"She probably hates me right now," I admit, running a hand through my messy hair.

"Nah," Eddie says, his lips twitching. "But she's pissed as hell at you."

"I wish she'd told me."

"Would you have listened?" Eddie raises a brow. "I was there, man. You saw me and were gone in sixty seconds flat."

I tug at my beard, hating how right he is. My jealousy blinded me so completely I couldn't see the truth staring me in the face.

"I'll fix things with her," I say firmly, the resolve settling in my chest. "And you're always welcome at *Rum & Ruin*. VIP all the way."

Eddie nods, his approval clear in the small smile tugging at his lips. "I'll take you up on that."

"How is she?"

The grin falls from Eddie's face. "Tired. Overwhelmed. Defeated. She's asked me to find a buyer for the Dean Estate. Said there's no point in continuing the repairs."

My heart sinks at his words, especially since I know that I'm a central perpetrator in her angst. "You got work on the books right now? I'd like to hire you."

Eddie glances around the speakeasy. "To help out here?"

"No. I want you to get the carriage house at the Dean Estate and the adjoining courtyard pristine and move-in ready. How long would that take?"

Eddie considers my request, working figures in his head. "About a week, ten days, if I worked two crews around the clock."

"Can you do that?"

"I have the guys, but that's going to cost a shit ton of money."

"Let me worry about that."

"But Ori wants to sell."

"And I want a life with Ori. She loves that house and deep down, she still loves me. I want to do this for her—for us—to show her I'm serious. But I know she'll say no, so can you just do it for me? Stall her for two weeks. Make up whatever bullshit excuse about getting the house or investors ready. We got a deal?"

Eddie hesitates, the conflict clear on his face. His jaw tightens as he glances toward the mirror, then back at me. "You're really all in on this, huh?"

"All in." I've been dancing around the idea of forever for years, but it's different with Ori. She's different. That house might be where I finally put a ring on her finger. Tonight, I'll start looking. It's time she knows I'm done running.

Eddie exhales, finally shaking his head with a small grin. "You know this is going to blow up in your face if she finds out, right?"

"That's my risk to take. Can you do it?"

He lets out a low whistle, then extends his hand. "Fine. But if this backfires, you're on your own."

I grip his hand firmly, relief flooding my chest. "We got a deal?"

"One condition," he says, his grin widening. "Free drinks on opening night."

I chuckle and smack him lightly on the shoulder. "You got it. Hey, are you living with her now?"

Eddie nods. "Yeah. She invited me to crash on her couch after my short-term lease expired. I don't think she wants to be alone. This whole situation—you, her, and Lucille—bothers her way more than she'll admit."

It bothers me way more, too, but I keep that to myself.

"I'm glad you're there with her," I say. "Watching over her. My life's been so intense lately I haven't been around as much as I want, even before this misunderstanding. Thanks for taking care of her."

"It's what we do." Eddie gives a mock salute before turning toward the stairs. Then he pauses, looking back at me. "She loves you, man, but I think that idea terrifies her. So, be careful with her, huh? She's been through enough."

That's an understatement.

As soon as Eddie leaves, I walk over to the mirror, running a thumb along the etched edges. It's worth a small fortune, but Ori gave it to me. Even after everything.

The truth is, she's given everything of herself this whole time, while I've dodged and weaved around the idea of love like a professional boxer.

Now she's more scared of love than I ever was—and with better reason.

But I'll be damned if this is how our story ends.

I walk upstairs into *Black Lotus* and knock on the reception desk, the sound drawing everyone's attention. "I want to apologize for being an asshole the last few days."

Braden cocks a brow at me, crossing his arms. "You want to tell us why?"

"Misunderstanding," I say, keeping it vague, though the heat rising up my neck betrays me.

Lucille and Braden exchange glances, matching smiles spreading across their faces.

"Ori," they say in stereo.

Fuck, am I that transparent?

"Yes, Ori," I admit, rubbing the back of my neck. "I messed up, and now I'm trying to fix it."

Zane leans back in his chair, smirking. "I think Ash should buy us all dinner as an apology for being intolerable. What do you guys think?"

"Yes. I'm craving steak," Braden says without hesitation.

"Ooh, and lobster," Lucille chimes in with a wide grin.

"Bunch of savages," I mutter, shaking my head but smiling for the first time in days. "Fine. We'll go after closing, okay?"

As I turn to head toward my office, Braden's voice catches me again.

"Hey, Ash."

"Yeah?" I glance back.

Braden leans casually against the counter, his grin mischievous. "What are you buying Ori to make it up to *her*?"

I hesitate for a beat, my gaze flicking toward the floor before meeting his. "I don't know yet. A diamond ring, maybe."

Braden whistles low, his grin widening. "Shit. You're not messing around, are you?"

"Not this time," I reply, my tone firmer than I expected.

"Welcome back, man," he says, the teasing edge softening into something more genuine.

"Thanks." For a moment, the weight I've been carrying feels lighter. I feel lighter, too.

Now I have a new mission—finding Ori the perfect ring.

Two days later, I suck in a deep breath and walk into *One More Page* right before closing, determined to right this latest in a string of wrongs.

I just wish I could tell Ori everything.

Soon enough.

"Hey."

Ori glances up from behind the counter, a half-smile flitting across her face. "Hey yourself."

"How was Manhattan? The conference?"

"Fine. It was nice to get away."

Code for: nice to get the hell away from me.

My nerves threaten to overtake me. I feel like a teenager asking a girl on a first date. Hell, I wasn't this nervous at the jeweler last night, though I nearly lost it when they assumed the ring was for Lucille.

I've been mired so deep in this crap I couldn't see how it felt for Ori—how much this charade has torn her apart.

There's a sadness in her now—she's withdrawn, quiet.

I pull out my phone and glance at the photo of us on the beach in Florida. We'll get back there again if it kills me.

"Do you need some coffee or something?" Ori asks, startling me.

"No, I need to apologize."

Ori clicks her tongue against her teeth. "Go ahead."

"He's your brother?"

"Yep. Shocked the hell out of me, too. And if you hadn't driven off like a lunatic, I would have introduced him as such."

I wince, her words cutting deep. They're deserved. "How much groveling is required to make up for my behavior?"

"Don't worry about it." She waves her hand dismissively and averts her gaze.

"But I am worried," I insist. "I was an asshole."

"Agreed."

"And I want to make it good. Make us good."

She sighs, her shoulders slumping. "We are."

"No, we aren't."

"Ash…" Ori runs a hand across her brow. "We're fine."

Screw this distance.

I step behind the counter, moving closer to her. I wrap my arms gently around her waist, resting my chin on her shoulder.

"See, that's the trouble," I murmur. "Fine means we're decent, tolerable, getting by. But I want us to be incredible. Amazing. Like we were in Florida, where there was nothing but the two of us. I replay those days over and over again."

"Why?" she whispers, her voice barely audible.

"Because I miss you, Ori. I miss us." I tighten my hold, the feel of her anchoring me. Despite her size, she makes me feel safe. "You know, it's my birthday on Friday."

"Don't know if you're getting a gift this year. You've been a bit of an ass."

I chuckle softly, the tension between us easing just a fraction. "You're all I want for my birthday."

"Still an ass," she mutters, but there's a faint lilt in her voice.

For a moment, she leans into me, and I swear I feel her soften. It's fleeting, but it's there.

I glance at her hand, bare and delicate, and wonder if

she's ready for what I have planned. Hell, if I'm ready. But it doesn't matter. I've already decided—she's it for me.

"Still yours, too," I whisper.

Her body stiffens, and she steps out of the circle of my arms. Her eyes shine with a raw pain. "Sometimes it's easier not belonging to anyone," she says quietly. "I think you had it right all along."

The words hit like a fist, and before I can respond, she sighs and moves further away. "I have a headache, so can we talk tomorrow?"

Just like that, the vault on her emotions slams shut, and I know I have no one to blame but myself.

Like she said the other morning in the parking lot—baby steps.

Ori needs to be handled with care now, and that's just what I'll do.

I step to her side and brush her hair from her face, my fingers lingering against her cheek. Leaning in, I steal a tender, lingering kiss, gentle enough not to spook her.

"I'm here when you're ready, Ori. You're worth the wait."

Chapter 22

Wily Investors

Ori

"Ori, you have a visitor."

I gaze up from my desk, noting the tense expression on Mina's face.

Wonderful.

"Who is it?"

Lucille steps around Mina and into my office. "The unwelcome wagon."

"Those books are due in tomorrow. I'll run them over when they come in."

I hope my disclosure ends our awkward chat, but Lucille has other ideas.

"That's not why I'm here," she states.

Like I said, wonderful.

I stiffen and nod toward a chair on the other side of my desk. "What can I do for you?"

Although Lucille and I have hashed it out, so to speak, I'm still wary of the woman. It was actually a pleasant reprieve, heading to Manhattan for the week and putting some distance between me and the drama of Sparkwood.

She sinks into the chair, her movements slower than usual, and I notice how much she's popped since the last time I saw her. I hold myself back from saying as much. Yes, pregnant women are beautiful, but no one wants to be told they look like they've swallowed a beach ball.

I also realize that will be me one day.

Lucille breaks the silence. "Ash's birthday is tomorrow."

"I know," I reply, turning my focus to the computer screen and typing nonsense just to look busy. Anything to act like this entire situation isn't a giant cluster.

"I'm throwing a party for him."

How fucking quaint.

I bite back the sarcasm and manage a curt nod. "That's nice of you."

She exhales, her gaze fixed on her hands. It's the first time I've seen her look genuinely uncomfortable, which, frankly, throws me off. "Please come."

"That's not a good idea."

"Ori, you mean so much to Ash. I know my arrival has turned your life upside down, and I'm sorry for that. Sorrier than you know. But it won't be his birthday if you're not there."

I glance at my calendar, running my finger over the date. With a sigh, I lean back in my chair. "I don't know, Lucille. The last thing any of us needs is more tension."

"There won't be. Just good food, good drinks, and good people. All celebrating a good man. What do you say?"

"Is he a good man, though?" I grimace as the words escape before my brain can pull them back.

Lucille bites back a laugh. "He most definitely is, even when he behaves like a horse's ass."

I giggle, realizing she's got him pegged. "Spot-on description there."

"But we can let him slide for one day, right? Come on, say yes. I bake a mean manicotti."

I stare at the calendar again, weighing the pros and cons.

Skipping this would be easier, but Lucille's offer feels almost sincere.

Almost.

With a sigh, I relent and nod. "Sure. I'll be there."

I instantly regret accepting Lucille's invitation and spend the next few hours ruminating over how to get out of it. As I place the new inventory on the shelves, I run through a range of excuses from car trouble to an emergency root canal.

Then it hits me.

A doctor's appointment. I need a checkup, especially since I've been wrestling with this stupid dizziness for the last week.

"It's a perfect and honest excuse."

"What is?" Mina asks, scrunching her brows at me.

Crap. Didn't mean to say that aloud.

I wave my hand, dismissing my words. "Nothing."

"So, what did *she* want?" Mina doesn't elaborate on the subject of her question. She doesn't need to, though she has far more colorful names for the love of Ash's life.

"Lucille invited us to Ash's birthday party tomorrow."

Her eyes widen. "She's throwing him a party?"

I shrug. "Some might say it's a nice thing to do."

"Or calculated. Are you going?"

"I told her we were, but now I'm trying to figure a way out of it."

Mina taps her finger against her chin. "Actually, it's perfect."

"As a torture venue?"

"Your opportunity to tell Ash."

"Tell Ash what?" a familiar voice asks from over my shoulder.

My heart drops to my stomach as I turn around, wondering how much Ash overheard of our conversation. "Hi."

"Hi, yourself." He smiles, pulling his bottom lip between his teeth. "What did you need to talk about?"

Mina jabs me in the ribs, and I wince, earning a glare from her. "Tell him," she mouths.

Sorry, Mina, you're not winning this round. I need Ash seated and calm when I break the news.

Possibly comatose.

"Lucille told me about your birthday party."

Ash rubs the back of his neck and shifts his weight. "Yeah. She insisted. You're coming, right?"

"Probably not."

The smile falls from his face, and his jaw tightens as he averts his gaze. "How come?"

Let me count the reasons. How much time do you have?

Instead, I hem and haw, all legitimate excuses flying from my mind. "I… well, see I'm…" I huff out a breath and force myself to meet Ash's gaze. "It's been a long week."

"For all of us. All the more reason to spend some quality time together."

Yeah, you, me, your baby mama, and your poor friends who have no idea who to root for in this situation.

A slight wave of dizziness hits, and I steady myself against the counter. Ash notices immediately, his protective instincts flaring as he steps closer and grips my elbow.

"Are you okay?"

This is another perfect entry point into the pregnancy conversation, which I'm also choosing to ignore.

Chicken shit extraordinaire, at your service.

"I'm fine. Just a bit tired."

"Maybe because you're running yourself into the ground?"

"Likely that's the reason. It's probably nothing."

"You should get checked out. I'll take you to the doctor," Ash offers.

"Why would you want to spend an afternoon in a doctor's waiting room just to hear I need a nap?"

He frowns slightly, his concern visible, before a grin softens his face. "Because I like you a whole hell of a lot."

There's that damn word again. Like. He likes me. He *really* likes me. A whole hell of a lot, even.

Too bad it's the wrong L word.

The bells jangle above the shop door, and I seize my opportunity to escape the stilted silence. "That's a sweet suggestion, but I have to go. There's a customer waiting."

But when I turn, I realize it's not a customer. It's that damn investor again, and even though I'm seriously considering throwing in the towel with the Dean Estate, I don't appreciate the way the man keeps pushing me to decide.

I groan and mentally steel myself for another round of fending off McGwyer Holdings.

"No way," Ash booms behind me, storming toward the well-dressed man. "Get out of here."

The man doesn't flinch, adjusting his tie as he pulls a stack of papers from his briefcase. "I have a new offer for Ms. Thorne, which I think she should seriously consider."

Ash steps closer, anger radiating from his aura. "What part of no don't you understand? Now, before I drag your fat ass out of this store, I suggest you leave and never come back. As for your boss, you let him know to stay away from Ori. Do you understand what I'm telling you?"

The man barely spares Ash a glance, his smug expression unwavering. "I am under strict orders to speak to Oriana Thorne, and *only* Oriana Thorne."

Ash clenches his fists at his sides, his voice dropping to a dangerous growl. "Well, as her future husband, I'm telling you to speak to me. Don't you bother her again, or I will hunt you down. Now get out."

The man's composure finally cracks, his face reddening as he fumbles to close his briefcase. Without another word, he hurries out the door, no doubt leaving with an extra stain on his trousers.

I stand frozen, watching Ash take this investor down, peg by peg.

I don't want to miss a second of my man defending my honor, even if it's against a pasty, paunchy middle-aged man who's likely never seen a fistfight in his life.

My man.

Seems my heart is still set on that idea.

Ash turns and huffs out a breath, shooting me a rueful smile. "That felt fantastic."

Yeah, it sounded fantastic, too.

But it's not the case. Ash and I aren't getting married. Hell, we aren't even together anymore.

And although I'm extremely turned on by his dominant alpha showing, he also just pushed away an investor who might have allowed me to unload the Dean Estate.

I bite back a smile and force myself to appear stern, shaking my head at his outburst. "What if I want to sell the house?"

"But you don't."

That's not entirely true.

"Ash, I'm so out of my depth with that place. Eddie is busy on some secret project, I can't find another contractor, and the repairs are endless. I never should have bought it."

He takes a step closer, hesitating for a moment before framing my face in his hands, his touch warm and comforting. "We've got it, Ori. You and me."

But there is no you and me.

I swipe at a stray tear. "I can't ask that of you. It's not fair."

Ash nods, a strange smile crossing his face. "You're right. It's a lot to take on."

"Exactly."

"So, like I told you before. We'll get married."

Excuse me while the earth tilts on its axis.

"Wha-what?"

"You heard me. We get hitched. Then it's something we handle together. Done and dusted."

He shrugs and offers me that crooked grin I love so much, but all I can manage is a blank stare as his offer seeps into my brain.

"I have a client, but I'm right next door if you need me, okay?"

I nod, snapping back to reality just before he walks out the door. "Ash?"

"Yeah?"

"I'll stop by your party."

His grin widens. "You better. Have to have my wife there."

Then he's gone, disappearing into Black Lotus.

"Holy shit, Ori. Did I hear him correctly?"

"What?" I jerk my head toward Mina, her face awash in shock. "Um, yeah. Ash doesn't want me to sell the house."

"Not that part. The part where he referred to you as his wife."

"Oh, that." I wave a hand dismissively and focus on straightening a stack of flyers on the counter, my tone intentionally casual. "He just wants to make me feel better."

Mina grabs my hand, squeezing it tightly, and starts bouncing on the balls of her feet. "I want to make you feel better, too, but I'm not proposing marriage."

"He didn't propose, Mina." I yank my hand free and busy myself with the flyers again, shuffling them unnecessarily.

"Or did he? Either way, now you know how he feels."

"Do I?"

"Ori, you are not *that* blind." Mina leans in, forcing me to meet her wide-eyed gaze. "The man is in love with you. He offered to marry you."

"To save the house," I interject. "Not because he loves me."

"Why does it have to be one or the other? Why can't it be both?"

"Because Ash doesn't believe in both." I exhale sharply and cross my arms over my chest, desperate to shut down the conversation. "At least not with me."

"What happened to the woman I knew a month ago? The one who knew Asher Hammond was her soulmate and was going to prove it to him? Where did that Oriana go?"

"She left when Lucille arrived." My voice drops, and I shrug, avoiding Mina's gaze. "She didn't leave a forwarding address."

Have I ruminated on Ash's offbeat proposal? Only every spare moment. Okay, every moment.

For the past twenty-four hours, I've thought of little else. Ash, for his part, hasn't mentioned it again, although he asked me to join him for dinner and drinks in the speakeasy.

I begged off, claiming I was buried in work after the conference.

But that's only partially true.

A pall hangs over the speakeasy ever since Lucille walked in on us, making me feel like an intruder in my love life. Despite Lucille and me clearing the air, I'm still pretty gun-shy.

Am I horny? All the damn time, but that's why I have a vibrator, remember? Let's just say it's getting its fair share of use.

I've also rolled through a billion different excuses for skipping the party tonight, although none sound plausible—especially not after I told Ash I'd be there.

Unless you count the fragile state of my heart and how distance is key to my survival.

"All closed up," Mina announces, dropping the key into the drawer. "Are you almost ready?"

I fake a cough and shoot her a pitiful look. "I'm sick?"

"Nice try, Ori, but I'm dragging you there even if you test positive for the flu."

"Damn. I thought we were friends."

"We are. And I love you enough to push your stubborn ass into doing what's right. I'm tired of carrying this secret around, worried I'll slip up and say something and then I'm the bad guy. You're pregnant. Deal with it."

She's none too happy that I've yet to tell Ash about our impending arrival and takes every opportunity to nudge me ever so gently in that direction.

So far, I've been a billy goat—stubborn and unrelenting.

It's not that I don't want to tell Ash. Okay, that's not entirely true. I dread telling him for so many reasons, not least of which is the disappointment and shock I fear I'll see when he learns he's got not just one, but two baby mamas.

Some stories are too hot even for reality television. Sadly, ours is one of them.

Let's not forget how Ash has been a bit of a horse's ass lately, what with going postal over Eddie and not bothering to wait around to learn the truth.

Yes, he apologized. Several times. But I can't help feeling irked that he seems to think his dimpled grin and remorseful expression will buy his way out of the doghouse.

Even when it works like a charm on every other woman in Sparkwood.

Sue me, I'm not every woman.

Throw in his random marriage proposal, and I'm so twisted, I don't know which end is up.

"Well?" Mina is not letting up. Not this time. "It's the perfect opportunity."

"Is it, though? It's his birthday. He's going to want to kick back and have some drinks, not hash out custody agreements."

She shoots me another glare, which raises my rancor.

"This isn't easy, Mina. I have to walk into his home, the one he's sharing with his pregnant ex, and announce he's having another kid."

"I know how hard it is, but I also know you. You've already got yourself convinced he's going to tell you to leave and that you're out of luck. He won't do that, Ori. Enough is enough."

I can continue arguing or cede defeat. Dropping my chin, I offer a nod. "I'll tell him tonight."

"Good woman."

Mina pivots, and I roll my eyes behind her back, grumbling under my breath.

My friend snorts, catching my expression out of the corner of her eye. "Real mature."

"Never claimed to be." It's the truth. When I feel cornered, I regress to sarcasm and biting wit.

Right now, I feel like a rabbit hemmed in by ravenous coyotes.

Mina slides a cup of tea to me before reaching across to give my arm an affectionate squeeze. "Give the man a chance."

I shake my head as the steam wafts up to warm my face. "A chance to what? Break my heart again?"

"Maybe this time he'll heal it instead. Ever think of that?"

Yes, Mina, all the time. At least until he introduced me to the love of his life. That encounter swayed things a bit.

Still, the man deserves to know. It's only right, no matter his reaction.

"Promise me you'll keep an open mind. Deal?"

I snort and nod, knowing full well Mina will not relent until I've completed my quest. "Deal. So long as you say nothing about me eating two pieces of pie."

"You are eating for two."

"And you'll keep that info to yourself."

"I think he'll surprise you. Ash will be shouting it from the rooftops. Mark my words."

Do I doubt that scenario? Entirely. Although the romantic in me still clings to the faintest of hope.

The issue is when I tell him, and he is disappointed instead of overjoyed, that hope disappears into the ether.

I need hope, no matter how pathetic it may seem to others.

Plus, I've got some time before I start showing.

I am the queen of excuses.

Lifting my cup in a mock salute, I motion toward the back of the store. "I'm heading to my office. We'll drive out together?"

Suddenly, my stomach lurches, and the edges of my vision blur. I grip the counter, my tea sloshing over the rim as my knees threaten to give out.

"Not again," Mina mutters, her voice sharp with concern as she rushes to steady me.

I squeeze my eyes shut and swallow hard, trying to ward off the faintness. "Just give me a second. I'll be fine."

"You're not fine," Mina says, easing me into a chair. Her hands stay firmly on my shoulders, keeping me steady. "When are you seeing the doctor?"

I take a few deep breaths, blinking away the dizziness. "I planned to go today, but now I have to attend a birthday party."

That statement earns me another withering look. Lucky for me, I can blame hormones for my petulant behavior. It sounds better than blaming a broken heart.

"We'll stop by Ash's for an hour and then head to urgent care to have you looked at, okay?"

I understand my friend's concern, and I'll admit to having worries of my own. After all, mine is a geriatric pregnancy.

Boy, oh boy, but hearing that really chapped my ass. I damn near called the doctor out into the parking lot to hash it out and show her just how 'geriatric' I am—before she mentioned how much she despises the term, too.

So, yes, there's a higher risk because apparently, thirty-nine is as old as dirt. But my doctor assured me everything looked fine.

Still, a part of me is scared.

But like everything else in my life, I put my head down and keep going. If I focus on it too long, I'll just end up more terrified that something is wrong with the baby.

I pat her hand and offer a small smile. "The doctor said this can happen, Mina. Everything was fine at my last visit. But I think I can handle an hour with Ash and Lucille. Besides, it gives me an easy escape route when he loses his mind after learning I'm pregnant."

Mina wraps an arm around my shoulder, her expression softening. "You can do this, Oriana Thorne. And you will. Today."

Chapter 23

Birthday Surprises

Ori

I can do this. I'm a strong, independent woman who has survived far worse than spending an hour with my ex-boyfriend and his baby mama.

An ex I desperately love.

A man whose baby grows in my belly.

A baby he doesn't know about… yet.

Screw strong and independent. I'm fucking terrified.

Mina and I walk into the farmhouse, offering smiles to the people hanging out in the converted garage space. I'll give it to the Hammond brothers—their house is always ready for a good time.

A pool table takes center stage in the room, while Zane works the small bar in the corner, mixing drinks like a pro.

"Did you know Zane was a bartender?"

Mina shrugs, glancing around the room. "I'm not surprised, with the way the man parties. You'd think they'd tire of endless drunken nights."

It's the oddest thing. Mina is only twenty-five, a good eight years younger than anyone else here, but in terms of lifestyle, she's an old soul. All she wants is to find the perfect man and settle down.

And she has her sights set on one man in particular—Braden Hammond.

I can't blame her in the slightest. Braden is gorgeous, like his brother, and a genuinely decent human being.

Unfortunately, Braden thinks Mina is too young, and he'd never use her for a one-night stand or as a casual plaything.

That's not his style—especially since he knows I'd use his body in a science experiment if he ever tried.

Mina's face lights up the moment she spots Braden, but the excitement fades just as quickly when her eyes land on the woman clinging to his arm.

"You're way prettier," I say, giving her a gentle nudge. And I mean it—Braden's flavor of the moment might be attractive, but Mina is stunning. Not that I'd ever admit I'm biased because I love the woman.

"You're a bad liar."

"Good thing I'm not lying. Ready to leave?" Hey, I'm just being a supportive friend here.

Mina wags her finger at me. "You think you're slick, don't you?"

"Not at all, actually."

"Well, we can leave as soon as you tell Ash your news."

I tip my head back and groan. "You suck."

Braden appears at our side, grasping Mina by the elbow. "Hey, I need a favor."

"Anything." Mina's voice is even, but I see her cheeks flush from Braden's touch.

Actually, I think this is the first time Braden has managed more than some casual pleasantries to Mina. Per Ash, Braden has a shy streak, too.

Seems a few beers have loosened his tongue. Hell, I might be watching love unfold in front of my face.

I could use a good romance right now, especially considering the state of *my* love life.

"See that woman?" Braden swings his gaze across the

room. "She's been hanging on me all evening. Keep me company in the greenhouse?"

I raise my brows and bite back a smirk.

Subtle, Braden.

Still, I'm glad he's giving my friend a chance. She's an amazing woman.

If he hurts her, I'll kill him.

Braden smiles at me, nodding toward the kitchen. "Ash is inside. I know he's waiting for you."

"Great." I flash a wide grin.

Is it fake? One hundred percent, but so is Braden's claim.

I highly doubt Ash is waiting for me, but I might as well get it over with before the night gets any darker and the party-goers fall further into their cups.

I stroll into the kitchen, my feet heavier with every step as I clutch Ash's present in my arms.

Ash glances up from where he's leaning against the counter, a whiskey glass in his hand. His lips curve into a faint smile as he sees me. "You came."

"Well, you invited me. Happy Birthday." I thrust Ash's gift into his hands. "I didn't think it would arrive on time."

"Thank you." He runs a hand along the edge of the box, his thumb lingering on the ribbon for a moment before setting it aside, unopened, on the counter.

"Aren't you going to open it?"

"Truth is, Ori, you're all I wanted for my birthday. The rest is gravy."

His sweet words take direct aim at my heart, but my armor is intact and ready. It has to be; the last time I let myself believe in his promises, Lucille walked in and reminded me where I stand—on the outside, looking in.

"Or in this case, whiskey."

Ash narrows his gaze. "What?"

"Open your gift. I ordered it especially for you. For *Rum & Ruin.*"

Ash tears into the wrapping paper, his eyes widening as he pulls out the sleek, dark glass bottle. The custom label catches the light, with *Rum & Ruin Reserve* embossed in bold, elegant lettering over a minimalist design. The deep amber liquid gleams inside. He turns the bottle over, studying it.

"Holy shit."

"It's your own brand. Aged for five years, and the entire stock belongs to you. This is just a sample. I thought it'd be cool for the bar to have its own blend."

"This is the best gift I've ever gotten. You are the queen of awesome presents." He grins, setting the bottle down like it's the most precious thing he's ever held. "Come on, let's sample the wares."

I shake my head. "I'm driving soon, so I'll pass. But please, go ahead."

I follow Ash to the bar, where he proudly shows off his gift. A few of his friends glance my way, nodding their approval, and I manage a polite smile.

It's then I realize how strange this must be for them—Ash's baby mama and his most recent ex, together at a party.

And yet, none of them seem fazed. Maybe they're used to watching Ash juggle women with effortless charm, as though relationships were accessories he could switch out at will.

To think I wasn't nauseous until this very moment.

Lucille sidles up beside me, one hand resting on her belly. "Well done. That's the greatest gift I've ever seen."

"Hardly. I just thought it would be cool for him. How are you holding up?"

"Bumping along. Don't believe anyone who says pregnancy is the best time of your life. They're liars."

Tell me about it.

Ash's voice breaks through the moment, warm and inviting. "Oriana Thorne, this is incredible. Come on, have a sip."

I wave my hand, declining his offer. "I tried some when I bought it. Glad you like it, though."

He walks over and pulls me close, seemingly oblivious to Lucille standing right next to us.

His lips find mine with an urgency that steals my breath. His hands grip my waist as his thumbs brush along the curve of my hips. The heat of his touch seeps into me, making it impossible to think straight. Whiskey lingers on his tongue, smoky and heady, and I almost drown in it.

Almost.

But then reality claws its way back in and I pull back with an embarrassed laugh, shooting Lucille a stilted smile. "Don't let the whiskey go to your head."

"I'm not," Ash chuckles, his hands still firmly clinging to my body. "This is all about you."

Before I can respond, his lips claim mine again, slower this time, deliberate. His tongue traces the seam of my mouth, teasing, coaxing, until my knees nearly give out.

Do I want to lose myself in him? In this moment? More than my next breath. But things have changed, and we must change, too.

Pushing out of his arms, I press my hands against his chest. "You better behave."

"Why?"

Oh, so many reasons, not least of which is your baby mama standing three feet away. It doesn't matter that she seems unfazed by the display.

I'm affected by her presence in our private moment.

Hell, I'm affected by her presence in our lives. Period.

Ash senses my discomfort and laces his fingers with mine, giving them a squeeze. "Come on."

Without a second glance at Lucille, he leads me into the house and down the long hallway toward the back bedroom.

We pause outside the closed door, my heart hammering in my chest. "What are we doing?"

His smirk says it all. "I have a ton of ideas. Let me show you."

But it's not that simple.

He's not my man.

Not anymore.

And if I'm honest—really and brutally honest—he never was.

That was never an occupation Asher Hammond wanted.

At least, not with me.

No amount of kisses, however public or reassuring, are going to change the fact that the woman he once adored is carrying his baby.

Oh yeah, and so am I.

See? Once again, I'm relegated to second place. The runner-up. Or, as I lovingly call it, breadfruit.

I groan, realizing a split second too late that the sound needed to stay in my mouth.

Ash's gaze widens. "Not the reaction I hoped for."

"Sorry. It's not you. It's… life."

He strokes the hair from my face, his fingers gentle against my skin. "Are you okay?"

For a man as big and burly as Ash, he's also the king of the gentle caress.

Shrugging off the malaise, I force a smile and hope it doesn't border on maniacal. Let's get real—my psyche has lived through the wringer these last few weeks. "Absolutely. Just a bit sleepy. And wondering what we're doing outside the bedroom."

He winks at me before pulling me close and pressing that gorgeous mouth to mine once more.

"Anything you'd like," he murmurs against my lips, his hands sliding to my ass and pulling me flush against him.

I stiffen, my hands flying up to push him away, but he doesn't budge. If anything, his grip tightens—a silent reminder that, in his eyes, I belong to him.

Do I want to cave to his ministrations? Of course. But that's not the point.

I don't share my lovers or my loves.

"Ash, stop," I whisper, my voice cracking.

His lips linger for one last moment before he finally pulls back. His eyes search mine, and I see the hint of frustration living there.

"I'm sorry," he says quietly, stepping back with a sigh. He hesitates, like there's something more he wants to say, but opens the door and motions toward the bed sitting in the center of the room. "I thought you might want to say hello to Merlin."

For the first time since I arrived, a genuine laugh bubbles from my throat. I bound to the bed, leaping next to the bundle of fluff snuggled on the blanket. "Merlin, you lazy, fat cat."

The black cat awakens and gives me a sleepy yawn, reaching out a paw to coax me into more pets.

Like he even has to ask.

Ash sprawls across the bed on the opposite side of Merlin, resting his head in his hand. But his gaze never wavers from me.

At this point, it's unnerving.

It's more than the man undressing me with his eyes. It's like he's trying to peer straight into my soul.

"Such a spoiled boy," I murmur, rubbing Merlin's stomach. "I've missed him."

"He misses you, too." Ash gestures to the three of us. "Our little family."

His words pierce the armor around my heart, and I blink back tears.

If only...

My mind races at his intimation, wondering if he knows.

Is that possible?

If I was brave, I'd take this moment and run with it. Tell him we're expanding the family.

But my tongue is tied in knots.

Time to change the subject. I'll circle back later.

I sit up, wringing my hands, trying to still the tremors reverberating through my body.

"How are things with Lucille?" I blurt out.

Ash's eyes widen briefly before he rolls onto his back with a groan. "Why do you always have to bring up Lucille?"

"She's your family, too."

"No, she isn't. She's just a woman who can't seem to avoid trouble, and I'm the lucky one who gets to clean up her mess." He scrubs a hand over his face, his frustration giving way to guilt. "I don't mean it like that, but this situation has turned my life upside down. And not in a good way."

"Sometimes the best things in life are unexpected," I breathe.

"Her situation is not one of them." He leans over Merlin to place a soft kiss on my lips, his voice dropping to a murmur. "However, you are an entirely different story."

"How so?"

"I told you. You're my true north."

I chew my lip, a small smile breaking free as Merlin scampers off the bed to chase a foil ball.

Ash reaches out, tucking a stubborn strand of hair behind my ear before scooting closer on the bed. "You look tired."

"Is that a nice way of saying I look like crap?"

He snorts, dragging his fingers lightly along my side. "I'm not that stupid."

I glare at him, but he holds up his hands in mock surrender, chuckling. "You're gorgeous, woman. But you look tired. Are you okay?"

There's another opening.

A perfect opportunity to tell Ash the reason for my exhaustion.

A moment I let slide by—*again*—as the blood pounds in my ears.

With a sigh, Ash pulls me into his arms, burying his face against my neck.

For a moment, I forget the outside world.

For a moment, we're back on that beach in the Keys again.

I heave out a sigh, gearing myself up for the discussion. "Ash, can we talk?"

He nods against my skin, his beard a delicious tickle. "Just give me a second. I'm lost in you, and I'm not ready to leave."

I settle into his arms, allowing myself the luxury of contentment for the first time in weeks.

The truth is, I'm happy staying right here forever. Reality be damned.

But reality isn't content to wait outside.

"Ash, are you in there?" Braden's voice comes from the other side of the door before it cracks open. "It's not locked, so yell if you're naked."

"What do you want?" Ash asks, refusing to release his hold on me. "Can't you see I'm busy?"

Braden sighs, shaking his head. "Lucille was wondering where you went. She picked up some fancy cake for you and wants to sing happy birthday. Figured I'd track you down before she did."

Ash groans, his aggravation clear. "I'll be right there."

Just like that, the glitter falls away from our brief interlude.

Once again, I'm reminded that another woman lives with the man I love.

"You'd better go."

"Nah, I'm happy here." Ash's arms tighten around me, his lips brushing my temple as if to prove his point.

"Ash, she's pregnant."

"I'm aware."

I'll bet you are.

"How far along is she?" I ask, even though I don't care to know the answer.

He shrugs, his gaze flicking to the ceiling. "I'm not sure. Nineteen weeks, I think?"

"You think?"

"I don't keep track," he says flatly, dragging a hand through his hair.

"Huh." I cross my arms, bracing myself. "What room are you making the nursery?"

His brow furrows, confusion clear in his expression. "None. She's moving in with her cousin in a month or so."

"Really?"

"Yep. In California."

"That's so far away."

"That's why they built planes," he replies dryly, a frustrated tone to his voice.

"Won't you miss them being here?"

He groans, leaning back against the headboard. "No. Not at all. In fact, if we're being honest, I'm sick to death of her being here."

My eyes widen at his biting remarks, and I press my lips together to hold back the sharp retort bubbling in my throat.

So much for Ash being a doting dad. Hell, he sounds like he'd be happier never seeing his child.

"Sorry," he says after a moment, his voice softening as his gaze meets mine. He reaches out, brushing a hand over my arm. "I'm just tired of her coming in between us."

But... she'll always be between us.

"Ash?" Lucille's voice echoes down the hallway, eliciting another groan from him.

"Yeah," he snaps.

She peeks in, offering a small smile. "Sorry, but a few of the guys have to leave, and I wanted to do the cake."

Ash nods curtly. "I'll be right there."

Lucille's gaze flickers to me, and she offers a polite wave before retreating.

"Want some cake?" Ash asks, standing and running his hands over his beard.

"Actually, I have to get going."

A muscle jumps in his jaw. "Why?"

"Long drive," I say, keeping my tone light.

"Stay here and you won't have to drive."

"Honestly, I'm ready for a nap, so I'd be a buzzkill."

He motions to the bed, his voice softening. "Go to sleep. Want me to kick everyone out? I will. Just say the word."

It's another sweet gesture, one of many from Ash, but this time, it isn't enough.

His icy demeanor regarding his impending fatherhood has turned me cold on the idea of telling him. It's obvious he wants nothing to do with being a father, and I refuse to ruin his birthday with such an unwelcome announcement.

"I hope you have a great night. Time for me to track down Mina."

As I turn to leave, Ash grabs my wrist. "I wish you'd stop running."

"Only way to stay safe," I mumble, my voice and heart heavy.

Sadly, this time, I know it's the truth.

I find Mina perched on a barstool, a glass of water in her hand.

"You ready?" I ask, nodding toward the door.

"Are we leaving?" Mina grasps my elbow, her expression concerned.

"You don't have to, but I'm tired, and it's a bit of a drive."

"What did he say?"

I feign nonchalance, fishing my keys from my bag. "He loves the whiskey."

"Ori, what did he say?" Mina's voice sharpens as she steps in front of me, her eyes locking on mine.

"I didn't tell him, okay?" I cry, the words spilling out before I can stop them. My voice cracks under the weight of my emotions, and I press my lips together, trying to rein them in. "We were talking, and I asked about Lucille and the baby, and he was so blasé about it."

I blink rapidly, willing the tears to stay back. "He doesn't know any details about her pregnancy and doesn't care to know. Told me he couldn't wait for her to move with her family so he could get his life back."

My chest tightens, and I choke out the next words. "I figured at that point, telling him my news was a bad idea if I hoped for any type of positive reaction."

Mina places a hand on my arm, her voice soft and cautious. "Maybe that's not what he meant."

I shake my head as the tears roll down my cheeks. "Or maybe it's exactly what he meant."

I need to leave—now.

A sharp wave of dizziness hits, and I sink to a squatting position, clutching the edge of the bar for support. A few partygoers glance my way, their faces a mix of curiosity and concern. I wave them off, forcing a weak smile.

No doubt they think I'm drunk. If only it were that easy.

"That's it," Mina says, her tone firm as she kneels beside me. "We're going to the doctor right now."

I know better than to argue. "Good."

Wrapping an arm around my shoulder, she helps me to my feet and guides me toward the door. "Shit, I forgot my bag. I'll be right back. Are you okay?"

I nod, but it's not the truth.

I'm so far from okay, I don't know when I'll see that emotion again.

With a sigh, I slide into the passenger seat, crank the engine, and lean back against the headrest, closing my eyes.

Maybe I just need a rest. Hell, a ten-minute nap sounds perfect right about—

The passenger side door jerks open, and my eyes snap open just in time to see Ash turn off the car and pull the keys from the ignition.

"Change of plans," he says, his tone leaving no room for argument.

Chapter 24

You're What?

Ash

I love her, but I'm kicking her ass for this latest stunt.

I knew something was wrong with Ori. She's looked absolutely rundown the last few weeks, and even though she's the queen of burning the candle at both ends, this was different.

She was different.

Hearing from Mina that she's so damn tired, she's fainting?

A different animal, entirely.

Ori has a hands-off approach to her life. She can handle it. She's got it.

Well, I've got a newsflash for her.

Now, I've got it.

And I don't give a damn what argument she has at the ready.

I tear open the door to her truck, trying hard to rein in my emotions. Those beautiful eyes widen at my abrupt gesture, but I'm in no mood for her protests.

"Ash, I mean it. I'm too tired for any more partying tonight. I just want my bed."

I jerk my thumb over my shoulder. "Hop out. We're taking my truck."

Ori shakes her head, her lips pressing into a thin line. "I don't need an escort. Go back to your party."

She can keep stalling, but I'm done playing games with this woman.

My woman.

Besides, I'm so frustrated right now that I'm tempted to toss her over my shoulder and haul her out of the truck if she doesn't cooperate.

"We're going to the doctor, but we're taking my truck."

"You're not leaving your own party," she argues, her tone sharp.

"Want to make a bet?" I reach across and unlatch her seatbelt, extending my hand. "Don't make me come in there after you, Oriana Thorne."

"Ash—"

"Just stop, okay?" I soften my voice, but the frustrated edge remains. "I'm already angry."

With a defeated sigh, she slips her hand into mine. "Fine. We might as well get this over and done with."

We settle into my truck, and I waste no time heading toward the urgent care center in town. Every few seconds, I glance her way, but she keeps her gaze locked on the trees beyond the passenger window, her jaw tight.

Enough of this nonsense.

"Why did you lie to me? I asked you not an hour ago what was wrong, and you claimed you were just tired." I emphasize the word with air quotes.

"I am tired," she says quietly, her focus shifting to her lap as her fingers toy with the strap of her purse. "But I also happen to be pregnant, which is something Mina shouldn't have told you. It wasn't her place."

I open my mouth to respond, but the words catch in my throat as her statement registers.

What. The. Fuck.

Swerving to the shoulder, I ignore the honks of irritated drivers as I throw the truck into park and whip my head toward her. Grasping her chin, I tilt her face toward mine. "You're what?"

Her brown eyes meet mine, wide and brimming with unshed tears, her chin trembling. "I'm pregnant. Why do you look so surprised? Isn't that what Mina told you?"

I hear her words, but they sound distant, muffled—like I'm underwater, and they're only just surfacing.

Leaning back against the seat, I tug a hand through my hair. "She told me you were sick. That you've been dizzy and that you need my help. She didn't mention a baby."

My head spins, a dozen thoughts firing at once, none of them coherent. With every second, my anger simmers closer to the surface.

With a grunt, I smack the roof of the truck before scrubbing my face with my hands. "That's fucking great."

The sound of the door handle clicking pulls me out of my spiraling thoughts. I jerk my head around to see Ori trying to escape.

"I told you I'm fine," she says, her voice icy, her shoulders rigid. "Just leave it alone. I don't need any help."

"Fucking stop, Ori. Okay? Just stop." My voice cracks as I drum my fingers against the steering wheel, the weight of her news threatening to crush me. I suck in a breath, trying to will the anger away, but it claws at me, relentless.

And then, it all comes out.

"How long have you known?"

"About two weeks," she mumbles, her long hair falling like a curtain between us, shielding her from the fire in my voice.

"Two weeks?" I huff out the question, an exasperated laugh bursting from my lips. "When I was camped outside your place, you knew?"

"Yes."

"And let me guess—Mina and Eddie knew before me, too. Am I right?"

Ori nods, her shoulders sagging as she slumps in the seat.

"Unbelievable." I shake my head, hitting the steering wheel with my palm.

"This is why I didn't want to tell you," she whispers, her voice cracking. "I knew you'd be angry."

"Damn straight," I snap, my tone sharper than a knife. "This is the most important news of my life, and I find out after your employee? Like some second-class citizen?"

Ori drags the back of her hand under her nose, still avoiding my gaze. "Welcome to my world, Ash," she mutters bitterly.

Her words hit me like a gut punch, but I can't allow them to derail me.

"How could you keep this from me?" I demand, slamming my fist into the steering wheel once more.

That does it.

Ori bursts into tears, her sobs raw and jagged. "Because I didn't know how to tell you!"

"How about this?" I shoot back, my voice rising. "You're going to be a dad, Ash. Now get busy doting on me for the next nine months."

"I don't need you to dote on me," she grumbles.

"Yeah, that's really apparent by our destination right now."

She whips her head around to look at me, her tear-streaked face twisted in defiance. "I didn't want to ruin your birthday with a hospital visit. That's why I left."

"No more of this shit, Ori. No more secrets." My tone is firm, final.

She lets out a shaky exhale, her gaze darting back to the window. "Just drop me off, okay? Go back to your party and forget all about this."

"No way in hell." I grab her hand, squeezing it tightly.

"I'm hearing from the doctor's mouth that you and my baby are safe. Don't argue with me on this, either. You won't win."

"Never do," she whispers, an air of defeat coloring her words.

I glance at her again, her fingers trembling in mine. "Despite what you think, you being pregnant didn't ruin my birthday."

"Yeah, right. Just what you need. Another baby and another baby mama. Banner year for you, alright."

"It *is* a banner year for me. True, the baby is unexpected, but it's hardly unwelcome."

She sniffles, her eyes red from crying. "I'm sorry."

Those two words break something inside me, splintering my anger and leaving only raw emotion in its wake. The woman I'm in love with is apologizing for carrying my child.

If only she knew the truth about Lucille, maybe it would allay her fears. But letting Ori in on the secret puts her in *more* danger, and I won't risk that—especially now that we're expecting a baby.

The only thing I know for sure is I have to keep Ori safe.

At *all* costs.

That, and we must keep quiet about the baby. Trace is certain there are several leaks in Sparkwood. One wrong word to the right person, and this entire house of cards collapses— with Ori and me at the bottom.

And Kevin? He's already too close. If he suspects that Ori and I are back together, let alone expecting a baby, it'll give him leverage I can't afford to let him have. The man plays dirty, and he won't hesitate to use her—or our child— against me.

But first, I need to reassure my woman that I'm not mad. Actually, I'm pretty fucking excited.

I reach over, tucking her hair behind her shoulder. "Look at me."

But she doesn't.

Her gaze stays fixed on her lap, her fingers still fidgeting with her purse strap.

I unfasten my belt and lean over, brushing a soft kiss against her neck. "I know you're scared, little one, but you're going to be the best mom. We've got this."

"We?" Her voice is quiet, almost disbelieving.

"Obviously."

She finally looks at me, her eyes shining with unshed tears. "Thanks for saying that. Sorry I ruined your birthday."

"You haven't," I reply, my voice steady. "And it's going to be the best on record once I get word that you two are okay."

But she doesn't believe me.

Hell, I don't know if she believes *anything* I say anymore.

I pull back onto the highway, but this time, I'm overly cautious. Every car, every shadow, feels like a potential threat that could strip my family from me.

My mind races, caught in a loop I can't break.

I'm going to be a dad.

Holy shit.

I'm going to be a dad.

I couldn't have picked a better woman than Ori. She's the entire package—fierce, brilliant, and beautiful. And now she's carrying my baby.

When I pull into the urgent care lot, I realize I've been silent for the last ten minutes of the ride. Judging by Ori's expression, it's scaring the hell out of her.

I get it. I'm terrified, too—but not for the reasons she thinks.

Sure, the idea of being responsible for another life is over-whelming, but isn't that the point of this crazy ride? You fall in love, they love you back, and then you create tiny versions of yourselves to drive you up the wall for the next eighteen years.

Good times.

I park the truck and glance at Ori. "Do you need a wheel-chair?" I ask, my voice brimming with nervous energy.

"No. I'm fine." Ori's already out of the truck and headed toward the entrance, her pace brisk and determined.

I easily overtake her. It helps that I have over a foot on the woman.

"Will you wait a minute?"

She whirls around, her eyes blazing, hands clenched into fists at her sides. "For what? To keep looking at that petrified, disappointed look on your face? I told you, I'm fine on my own."

Typical Ori. When she's scared or insecure, she throws up armor so thick it's damn near impenetrable. I saw it during our first six months—those horrible days where instead of loving her, I was glaring at her.

But then she let me in. She removed her armor for me.

For a while, it was perfect—until Lucille showed up.

Since then, her emotional armor has been locked in place, and I don't have a damn key.

But it won't stop me.

Even if I have to scrape it off inch by inch.

Ori checks in, even going so far as to put a seat between us as she fills out the paperwork.

Me? I'm not sure what to say.

Patting my thighs, I stand and rest a hand on her shoulder. "I'm going to get coffee. You want something?"

Ori doesn't bother to look up from the clipboard. "I'm fine."

Another fine. I'm beginning to hate that word. She's not fine. Neither of us are. We're both so far from it, we can't even see the damn road back.

Plus, we're both exhausted. Between juggling my businesses and worrying about Ori, I'm running on fumes.

Now that worry has multiplied a million-fold.

When I return to the waiting room, coffee in hand, Ori is nowhere to be seen. My chest tightens as I scan the room. "She better not have left."

"They took her back, sir," the receptionist says, her voice clipped.

"Great. Can you buzz me through?"

She hesitates, her gaze darting away. "Ms. Thorne figured you'd rather leave or stay out here."

She did, did she?

"Ms. Thorne figured wrong. I want to be back there. With her. Please buzz me through."

"I'll have to check with her."

I grit my teeth, forcing a smile. "Look, let me back there, and if she tells me to leave, I'll go."

"Really?"

No. Not really. But I nod anyway, because there's zero point in arguing with this woman.

Mainly because I'll be arguing with Ori in about thirty seconds.

She's trying to push me away, but I'm not leaving without a fight.

Ori sits gowned on the exam table when I step inside the room. She looks at me and crosses her arms, a mixture of annoyance and overwhelm dancing across her face. "What are you doing back here?"

"*You're* back here. I will not sit out there while you're in here." I pace the small space, my boots echoing against the floor.

"Just go, Ash. Everyone is waiting for you at the farm."

"No chance in hell. I'll leave when you leave. Where is that damn doctor, anyway?"

"That damn doctor is here," a voice says as the door opens. "Although I prefer Dr. Fulton. Ash, didn't expect to see you here."

"Trust me, neither did he," Ori mutters, earning a sharp scowl from me.

"She hasn't been feeling well. Dizzy spells. Tired." My

gaze narrows on Ori. "Or so I hear, since she didn't bother telling me until today."

Dr. Fulton chuckles nervously, shifting his focus to the chart in his hands. "Do you two need a minute?"

"We're good," I reply. "Let's get her checked out."

Am I overriding Ori? Absolutely. With every passing second, my concern for our baby grows. Dizzy spells every day —there's no way that's normal, right?

The doctor clears his throat. "Okay, well, I need Ori's consent before we continue. Do you want Ash to stay, or—"

"I'm not going anywhere. Don't even think it," I cut in, my tone firm.

"She has to be okay with it," Dr. Fulton says, his gaze flicking to me.

"It's fine," she mumbles, her voice barely audible. She doesn't meet my eyes, convincing no one in the room.

"We good here?" the doctor presses, looking between us.

"Oh, I'd say *good* is a stretch," I mutter under my breath, earning a quick glare from her.

Dr. Fulton sighs, glancing between us before setting the chart down. "I'll give you two a moment to sort this out." He pauses by the door. "Let me know when you're ready."

Can't blame the man for wanting to hightail it to safety.

Ori throws up her hands in resignation before flopping back on the table. "How is it you're so cool and collected regarding your baby with Lucille, but with me, you're a bundle of nerves?"

I'm ready with a withering remark when I stop, realizing the truth—she doesn't see the difference. And why would she? She's in the dark about the entire Lucille situation.

Crossing the small space, I place my hand on her stomach, my voice softening. "Because it's you."

Her lips tremble as she looks away. "I'm not going to break, Ash. You can go."

"Don't you get it?" My voice tightens, thick with emotion. "All I want is to be here with you."

Seems my words finally break through as tears slide down her cheeks. "All I want is for you to be here, too."

My resolve softens as I take her hand in mine. "Then there's no problem."

I poke my head into the hallway. "We're ready."

"Now we're good?" Dr. Fulton asks, a smirk tugging at his lips as he steps back into the room.

"Absolutely. Even if she is a royal pain in the ass."

"*Me?*" Ori's jaw drops, a look of feigned shock on her face.

"Yes." I lean down, brushing my lips against hers in a soft, lingering kiss. "You. Let's check on our baby, and then you can go back to fighting me on everything. Deal?"

Ori chuckles, and for the first time in forever, it sounds genuine. She tilts her head up for another kiss before nodding toward the doctor. "Deal. Go ahead, Doc. What's the plan?"

While the nurse draws Ori's blood, I slip into the hallway and find Dr. Fulton at a workstation, typing notes into a computer. His fingers hover over the keyboard as he glances up, his brow lifting when he sees me approach.

Thankfully, we've been friends for years, so I'm banking on him agreeing to my plan.

"Can you do me a favor?"

Dr. Fulton stops typing, turning his chair slightly toward me. "I can try."

"Can you recommend Ori rest for a week or so?"

"Bed rest? That's likely unnecessary, unless there's something you're not telling me," he says, his tone cautious.

"No, but here's the thing—she won't rest. The woman

works 24/7 and never stops. Ever. But if you mention it to her, she'll listen."

Dr. Fulton leans back, folding his arms as he considers my request. "You want me to recommend bed rest to a woman who doesn't medically need it?"

"Not bed rest," I clarify, running a hand through my hair and glancing down the hall toward Ori's room. "Just rest. I want to take care of her, but she has to stop moving for a hot minute for me to do that."

Dr. Fulton's serious expression softens into a faint smile. "I can phrase it in a way that'll get through to her. If she's really overextending herself, then yeah, she needs to slow down."

"Exactly. So technically, you're just telling her the truth." I shove my hands into my pockets, releasing a loud sigh.

"Anything else, Ash?"

I hesitate, clearing my throat as I glance at the computer screen. "Yeah, actually. Is it safe for her to, uh, you know—" I gesture vaguely, feeling like a kid in junior high asking about the birds and the bees.

Dr. Fulton pauses mid-keystroke, turning to smirk at me. "You're asking if it's safe for her to have sex?"

I shrug, trying to act casual. "I mean, look at her. Can you blame me?"

His smirk widens, and he shakes his head, returning his attention to the computer. "Assuming her labs and ultrasound results come back normal, there's no reason to avoid it. But you might want to let her take the lead—she may not feel up to it."

"Fair enough," I mutter, rubbing the back of my neck. "Just checking."

And I'm damn sure going to stoke those embers smoldering between us—so long as it's safe, of course.

Dr. Fulton chuckles softly, finishing his notes before swiveling back to me. "Any more questions, or are we good?"

I grin, leaning in a little. "That custom ink you wanted? It's on me. Just take care of her."

Chapter 25

Where's My Cloak of Invisibility?

Ori

I manage a smile for the nurse, but it's so fake I feel like my face might crack. Between worrying about the baby and fretting over Ash's reaction, I'm a bundle of nerves.

She's drawn about a million vials of blood, only to replace them with a giant IV bag of fluid now filling the veins she just drained.

The joys of modern medicine.

"The doctor and I will be right back to do the sonogram. I'll send your husband in," the nurse states before stepping out of the room.

Please don't let Ash hear you call him that. I'll never see the man again.

I have to give Ash credit. He's taking the baby news in stride—although, to be fair, he's likely still in shock about the entire situation.

Lord knows I was when I learned the news. I warned him we were playing with fire. Turns out, I was right.

"Okay, we have a plan." Ash says as he walks into the room and grasps my hand. His palm is warm and comforting, even if the rest of him seems like a live wire.

"Who's we?"

"Dr. Fulton and me. Normally, he'd want to admit you for a few days of observation, but I talked him out of it. Barring any problems, of course. Not that there will be problems. Everything is going to be fine."

The man is talking a mile a minute, and it would be adorable if I thought the speed of his diction was because of excitement rather than sheer terror.

I motion toward the exam room door. "The nurse said Dr. Fulton will be in to do the ultrasound. I guess you're getting used to these."

Does it gut me to utter those words? Damn right it does. But let's be real. He's got more than one baby mama, and she's weeks ahead of me. Everything Ash and I do together with this child, they've already done.

Once again, I'm breadfruit. Maybe that's the tattoo I need—not that I know what the hell breadfruit looks like. Probably as appetizing as it sounds.

Yuck.

Ash shakes his head, his focus snapping to the door as Dr. Fulton and the nurse enter with the ultrasound machine. "I've never seen one before."

"What about with Lucille?"

Another shake of his handsome head. "Nope. Wait. That's not true. I had one for kidney stones about ten years ago."

"This is a bit different," Dr. Fulton jokes as he pulls on a pair of gloves. "Now, this is a transvaginal ultrasound, which sounds scarier than it is, but I promise it won't hurt a bit."

"Is it safe?" Ash asks, squeezing my hand, his voice tight with worry.

The nurse nods as she positions herself at the end of the table. "Absolutely. We use it all the time, especially in early pregnancy. Ms. Thorne, can you scoot down a few more inches?"

"Sure." I grit my teeth and comply, sliding down the table.

Nothing like having my lady bits on display for an audience. "You're positive it won't hurt?"

Yes, I'm a novice at this. The closest I've come to this machine is seeing one in a medical drama, and even then, it was only used as a backdrop while the main characters had sex against it.

No one ever said Hollywood was realistic.

"Not at all. I'm going to estimate the gestation of the baby and let you hear the heartbeat. Just give me one second."

Terror slices through me, and I hesitate to look at the screen. What if something *is* wrong? What if I've messed this pregnancy up with too much worry and work?

"Hey," Ash whispers, leaning close to place a kiss on my forehead. "It's going to be fine."

"Promise?" A tear slides down my cheek, and Ash sweeps it away with his thumb.

"There's your baby," Dr. Fulton says, his voice steady and reassuring. "Right as rain."

Never have words sounded so sweet. My head turns toward the screen, a smile breaking across my face at the sight of the tiny little alien in my stomach.

"She's fine?" I ask.

"It's a little early to tell the sex yet," Dr. Fulton replies, his tone light. "But your baby looks great." He flips a switch, and the room fills with a pulsating sound. "Strong heartbeat."

"See? I told you everything would be fine," Ash says, shooting me a devastating grin.

"I'm glad when you're right."

"I'm *always* right." He smirks, leaning back in his chair and giving an exaggerated tap to his temple, as if pointing out his superior intellect.

"On that note, I'm leaving again," Dr. Fulton interjects with a laugh before printing out a strip of sonogram photos and handing them to us.

"Escaping to safety, huh?" I joke, clutching the photos in my hand.

"Absolutely. I'm no fool." Dr. Fulton washes his hands, pausing by the door with my chart. "Everything looks great, but Ash informed me you have a tendency to run yourself down."

Thanks for throwing me under the bus, Ash.

"I'm busy with the store."

Dr. Fulton nods. "I understand, but your dizziness is concerning. It's likely due to a combination of hormonal changes, low blood sugar, and dehydration, which are all common in early pregnancy. However, stress and overexertion can make it worse. I want you to take a few days off. Get some rest. Let someone else do the heavy lifting for a change."

That's where things get tricky. How can I manage that when I live alone?

Eddie still has a few things at my place, but my brother's been working crazy hours on a construction project he's under the gun to finish. I haven't seen the man in days, although I'm grateful he's got work after I put the kibosh on restoring the Dean Estate.

So, I'm sans help, unless I hire someone to wait on me—and that is definitely not my style.

"She's coming home with me," Ash states matter-of-factly.

"I'm what?" No, that's not possible. I shake my head, but Ash is undeterred by my objections.

"You'll stay at the farm so I can take care of you."

"No," I hiss, the dread rising into my throat. "I can't stay with you."

"If you don't want to stay there, I can admit you for a few days," Dr. Fulton says. "But we need you to rest. This is a crucial time, and you're not doing yourself—or the baby—any favors by pushing too hard."

Fuck you, Dr. Fulton.

"My choices are the hospital or home with Ash?"

"Yes. We need to get you back to one hundred percent. What's it going to be?"

Groaning, I scrub my face with my hands. "I'll go home with Ash."

"Smart move. The hospital food is terrible. Trust me, I know." Dr. Fulton smiles as he jots something down in my chart. "Follow up with your OB-GYN in the next week and be sure to eat and hydrate regularly. No heavy lifting, minimal stress, and plenty of rest. Have a good night, you two. Congratulations."

As Dr. Fulton steps out, I glance at Ash, who is sitting back in his chair with a self-satisfied smirk, arms crossed like he just won a prize.

"Don't look so smug," I mutter.

"I'll be right back." Ash dashes out the door as his phone rings, leaving me to contemplate my next move.

Since there are no egress windows and I left my cloak of invisibility at my apartment, it looks like I'm headed home with Ash... and Lucille.

Even Hollywood couldn't invent this level of soap opera drama.

I pull on my clothes and finger-comb my hair into a loose bun. Elegant, I am not, but I'm too tired to bother with my looks.

Ash pops back into the room, a satisfied smile on his handsome face. "Hey, beautiful. Let's go home."

"You're letting me go home? Thank you."

He wraps his arms around me, dropping a kiss on my mouth. "Correction. *My* home."

"I don't think that's a good idea."

Actually, I *hate* it.

"Well, I think it's fabulous, and I'm the one with the vehicle here. Plus, there's a ton of food at the party. I'll even let you beat me at darts."

"I thought I was supposed to stay in bed." I duck under

his arms and make a beeline for the exam table, giving me a few feet of breathing room.

"We can find plenty to do there, too."

"Nice try."

Although, some sexy time with my sexy man might be just what the doctor ordered. Just not in the same house as Lucille.

Talk about throwing cold water over a hot fire.

"It might not be safe to do what you want to do, Ash."

"It is. I checked with the doctor."

I blink, heat creeping up my neck. "You asked Dr. Fulton if we could have sex?"

Ash shrugs, his smirk turning wicked as he steps toward me. "Damn straight. You're gorgeous, and I'm horny as hell. Plus, I think you like me, too."

I roll my eyes, but I can't stop the grin tugging at my lips. "Your tongue has its merits."

"What about the rest of me?"

I meet his gaze, feeling the familiar tension that always simmers around Ash flare to life. "Not too shabby."

"I'll show you 'not too shabby' as soon as we get home."

"Oh no," I cut in, narrowing my eyes as I lean back against the exam table. "We are *not* having sex. That's how we got into this mess."

His grin widens as he advances, his steps deliberate and confident. "It's a beautiful mess."

"Wonderful. We're a stunning disaster with glitter bombs instead of orange cones."

"Ori?"

"What?"

"Less talking. More kissing."

"Absolutely not. We are friends."

"We are *not* friends." His voice drops to a low rasp, sending a shiver skittering through me as he reaches the table.

"You need to stop," I whisper, though my voice falters as

his hands slide along my ribs, leaving a trail of fire in their wake.

Ash leans in, his lips grazing the sensitive spot just beneath my ear. "Ori, shut up and kiss me," he murmurs, his breath warm against my skin.

"No." My fingers grip the edge of the table for stability as his mouth moves to the hollow of my collarbone, planting slow, deliberate kisses. I tip my head back, giving him greater access. "You want me so bad, you better take the lead."

His eyes flash with amusement as he pulls back slightly, his devilish grin never wavering. "I'll take more than that," he murmurs, his hands tightening on my waist, his thumbs brushing lazy circles that make me squirm.

Before I can argue further, he hoists me onto the table and steps between my legs, his body pressing against me, firm and unapologetic. His lips hover just above mine, his unrelenting gaze locked on me.

"I'll take everything," he breathes, his voice rough and full of promise. "Hours and hours of worshipping you. That's part of the fairytale, you know."

"Not the ones I've read," I whisper, my breath catching as his lips drift tenderly across mine.

"You've been reading the wrong ones."

Then his mouth claims mine, his hand sliding around to cradle my neck. The kiss starts out slow and tantalizing, as if he's savoring every second. But the moment a low moan slips from my throat, Ash tilts my head back and deepens the kiss, demanding all of me.

I gasp as his hands weave into my hair, loosening the bun I'd hastily thrown together. His fingers thread through the strands, angling my head for better access. His body molds to mine—solid and unyielding, his heat seeping into me, awakening every nerve.

My fingers twist into his shirt, clutching the fabric like a lifeline. My heart races as his lips leave mine to explore my jaw, tracing down to the tender hollow beneath my ear.

"How wet are you right now, beautiful? Maybe I should tear these pants off and have a closer look."

"You wouldn't."

"Like hell I wouldn't." His voice darkens, sending a shiver straight through me. "I'll mark every inch of you as mine."

He rests his hand on my stomach, his expression raw with hunger. "Forever mine."

I bite my lower lip and pull him closer, the feel of his beard against my skin sending a wave of sparks through me. "Ash," I breathe the word on a sigh, the wall around my heart crumbling to let him in.

The door bursts open, and the nurse walks in, a surprised smile on her face. "I'm sorry. I thought you two had left."

"We're leaving now," I stammer, my cheeks flaming as I leap off the exam table.

She closes the door, and Ash lets out a grunt, adjusting himself with a wince.

"Problem?" I tease, unable to hide my smirk.

Ash laughs, though it comes out strained, his hand subtly adjusting his erect cock. "That's putting it mildly. I've got one addiction in this world, and I've been without it for weeks."

"And what's that?"

His gaze locks with mine, his voice dropping to a low rumble. "You."

Heat flushes through me, my breath catching at the raw honesty in his tone.

"Damn, that was good."

"True, too," he replies, his lips curling into his infamous cocky grin.

"Even better."

"Okay, finish getting dressed, and I'll meet you outside," Ash says, stepping back, his hand lingering on the door handle. His grin widens. "Otherwise, I can't be held responsible for my actions."

Ash is chatting with Kiki, a friend and local realtor, when I walk out of the exam room.

She smiles as I approach. "Hey, Ori. Hope your head is feeling better."

My what?

Ash pivots to me, his smile tight. "Kiki was worried about you, but I told her your migraine is better now. You get them from time to time."

I nod, clutching my bag tightly against my body. "Right. My... head."

The nurse passes us, pushing the ultrasound machine out of the exam room.

Now, I might have limited medical knowledge, but I'm pretty sure ultrasounds aren't used to diagnose migraines.

Judging by Kiki's raised brow at the machine, she's clued in to that fact, too.

"Well, migraines are the devil," Kiki says, patting my hand. Her gaze flicks to the machine again before returning to me, her lips quirking. "Didn't realize they used those for migraines these days."

It seems Kiki has decided to let it slide and go along with Ash's story—at least for now.

She walks off, and I whip around to Ash with a sharp glare. "A migraine?"

He drags a hand through his hair, his sheepish expression doing nothing to quell my irritation. "I didn't know what to tell her. She cornered me and wanted to know if we were okay. I had to make something up on the fly."

Instead of telling the truth, I guess.

Ash falls into step beside me, his voice dropping. "I love Kiki, but the woman is a terrible gossip. We don't need everyone in Sparkwood knowing our business."

"Oh, yes, that's right. You prefer *discretion*." My words drip with sarcasm as the memory of our first night together flashes through my mind. Ash used the same term when his brother walked in on us, and it sits just as well with me now as it did then.

Like a thumbtack in my ass.

"Ori—" Ash grabs my arm, but I pull it free, quickening my pace.

"Let's go. Although I certainly don't require care and tending at your house for a migraine. I'll just head home."

"Hey." Ash steps in front of me, cutting off my escape. "It's early, okay? I'm just being careful."

"Careful about what? Us?"

"No. About you." He rests his hand on my stomach, his eyes locking with mine. "About our baby. Random people don't need to know yet."

I exhale, my frustration ebbing as his words sink in. Damn it all, but he's right. "Sorry. My hormones are out of whack."

"Maybe spending some time together will help," he says, his voice warm and coaxing.

I can't help but giggle, shaking my head at his persistence. "I suppose we can give it a shot."

Ash slips an arm around my shoulder and pulls me close. "Let's get the hell out of here."

Ash hops into the driver's seat and leans over to steal a kiss before backing out of the parking spot. "How are you feeling?"

"Better."

In truth, I feel immense relief. Not only is Ash supportive, but he actually seems excited.

Granted, it's not a normal family situation, but it could be far worse.

Far, far worse.

Ash rests his arm on the center console, and I wrap my hand around it, resting my head against his biceps. I smile when he presses a kiss to my hair.

"What do you think everyone will say?" I ask.

"About what?"

About your choice of breakfast food, Ash. What the hell do you think I mean?

"The baby?" I lift my head to look at him, but he keeps his eyes on the road.

"We're not telling anyone yet, remember? It's still early."

"Right, but what about Braden… and Lucille? They live at the farm. They have to know why I'm staying with you."

I bite my lip, desperate to keep my voice steady. I understand not wanting the whole town to know, but Braden is his brother, and Lucille is already tangled up in this mess. Keeping it from them feels… wrong.

Ash tightens his grip on the wheel, his knuckles whitening. "We tell them the same thing we'd tell anyone else—that you're exhausted, overworked, and need a break for a few days."

"That's not the whole truth, though."

"Ori." His tone softens, but there's tension in the way he says my name. "It's not about lying. It's about timing. We need to keep this between us for now, except for whoever you've already told. And they need to keep quiet, too."

"But—"

"Ori, please don't argue with sme about this. I'm just trying to protect you."

The words hit me like a dull thud. Protect me. From what, exactly?

I slump against the seat, the elation I felt just moments ago now gone. That cold, hollow feeling? She's here to stay.

I turn toward the window, shifting in my seat so Ash won't see the tears sliding down my cheek.

Wiping them with the palm of my hand, I nod, determined to put on a brave face. "That's fine."

"Hey." Ash's voice is soft and pleading. "It's not perfect, but it's safer this way. Just for now."

That's when I realize the truth.

He's not worried about protecting *me*. He's worried about himself.

Of course, he doesn't want anyone to know.

How would it look? Two baby mamas in six months?

Honestly, I'm shocked Ash hasn't been in this situation before, considering his reputation.

Stupid woman, thinking he was going to change because you loved him. Because you were different.

I've had this exact conversation with countless friends over the years, counseling them on the futility of betting on someone changing.

Newsflash: people only change for two reasons. They want the change for themselves, or they're left with no other choice.

We all know which category these pregnancies fall into for Ash.

Will he do the right thing? Of course, because despite being a man whore, he's a stand-up guy. He's not going to leave a woman he knocked up in the lurch.

Not his style.

And knowing Ash's prowess and charm with the ladies, even two baby mamas won't ruin his chances with the women of Sparkwood.

That's some kind of power.

"Ori, are you okay?" Ash reaches for my hand, but I inch away and flip down the passenger-side mirror to apply lip gloss.

I might be breadfruit, but I'll be the best damn-looking one this side of the Mississippi.

"Just fucking fabulous."

The sarcasm drips off my words, but I'm done playing nice.

In fact, I'm done playing at all.

Chapter 26

Black Cat Magic

Ori

Ash pulls into his driveway and gives my arm a gentle shake. "We're here."

"I see that."

"Did you have a nice nap?"

I release a slow breath and shake my head. "I wasn't sleeping."

Ash gazes out the windshield, but I catch the furrow of his brow. Is he afraid I'm going to have a meltdown in front of all his friends?

Don't worry your pretty little head, Ash. I know how to behave like an adult.

"You didn't say a word the last twenty minutes," he says, running a hand over his jaw.

"Not much to say."

Actually, there's a ton to say, but what's the point?

"Looks like most people have left." I wave a hand at the few remaining cars parked in the drive. "Seems I ruined your birthday, after all."

Ash opens his mouth to retort, but I'm out of the truck before he can get a word in. I don't need to hear his objections or some well-worded reassurance to make me feel like I matter.

Actions speak louder than words, and Ash's message about our impending arrival is clear: say nothing, pretend everything is normal.

Like that's a possibility.

I screech to a halt and throw up my hands in annoyance. "I don't have clothes here."

And if you tell me Lucille will lend me some, I'll shoot myself right now.

Ash smiles, dragging a finger along my jaw. "We won't need any."

Nice try, but you'll have to find a new dirty secret to fill that role, Ash.

When I don't respond, Ash sighs and pulls me into a hug. "I'll lend you a T-shirt and boxers. We'll grab your stuff tomorrow. Come on, let's get you fed."

"Fine."

Must remember it's his birthday and despite being pissed at the man, I've caused enough upheaval for one day.

We walk into the finished garage, where Braden, Zane, Lucille, and a handful of others are chatting and lounging around.

"There you are. Everything good?" Braden asks, his gaze darting between us.

Oh, let me field this question, Ash.

"I'm fine. Just been working too much lately. The doctor says I need rest, and your brother was kind enough to let me stay here for a few days."

"Mi casa, su casa," Braden says, gesturing around the room. "Want a beer?"

"No, thanks. Where's Mina?"

Braden clears his throat and grins. "I drove her home. She felt a bit out of place, and I couldn't convince her otherwise."

"Maybe you should have tried harder," I reply with a wink.

A hint of color rises in his face. "Trust me, I did."

My poor friend. I'll have to apologize for deserting her and then have a serious sit-down about missing opportunities with hot, tattooed men.

"There are some more gifts for you, Ash." Lucille motions to the stack of presents at the end of the bar.

"No one had to get me anything."

"Fine, I'll take them," Braden says, reaching his hands toward the pile.

Ash shakes his head and moves between his brother and the gifts. "Back the hell up. Should I open them now?"

The remaining partygoers nod, and Ash tears into his gifts, while I stand stiffly to the side. Have to hand it to his friends, they have good taste. He scores with a new pair of motorcycle gloves, a mixology book dedicated to the 1920s, a gift card to the local motorcycle shop, and some new needles for his tattoo machine.

It's a damn fine haul.

"Last one," Ash says, grabbing a gift bag.

"That's actually not a birthday gift," Lucille interjects, snatching the bag away.

"Okay," Ash replies, confusion furrowing his brow.

Lucille looks at me and then at Ash, a tremulous smile on her face. "It's for the baby. Kathy made it." She pulls a soft yellow blanket from the bag and passes it to Ash. "Cute, right?"

Shoot me now.

Ash nods, his tense smile doing little to conceal his uneasiness as he glances at me. "Yep."

But his discomfort is nothing compared to what I'm feeling. I can barely force the air into my lungs as I stare at the blanket.

To most people, it's just a soft, downy present for the new

arrival. But for me, it's yet another glaring reminder that while Lucille and Ash's baby is well known amongst family and friends, my baby is a secret.

My baby isn't good enough to share the limelight.

And neither am I.

It doesn't matter what slick lines Ash uses when we're alone. What counts is how he treats me when I'm standing in the bright sunlight, visible to all.

Tears spill down my cheeks, but I duck my head and swipe them away.

I hate crying with an audience. Even worse is crying in front of people who likely think I'm a moron for attempting a romance with Asher Hammond, particularly when his first love is now back in the picture.

That's enough. I can't hang out here pretending this is okay—or that I am.

I want to go home and crawl into bed, but I know Ash will fight me on it. At least I can escape this room—the air suffocates me.

"I'm going to lie down." Pivoting, I glance at Ash. "Where can I crash?"

"We'll go to my room."

Oh, so *fucking* me isn't a secret—just the outcome of that act.

Lovely.

Seems my anger is worsening by the second.

"That's a terrible idea. I need to rest, and you're a distraction. Plus, it's your birthday, and your friends are here to celebrate. So, drink up and be merry."

Boy, I'm laying it on thick.

"I enjoy being a distraction," Ash says with a grin. "And I want to celebrate my birthday with *you*. Rewriting those fairytales, remember?"

Usually, his charm would work. I'm a sucker for the man, and my hormones are firing on all cylinders.

But knowing that the baby and I are secrets Ash wants to keep hidden swiftly overrides any carnal desires.

Besides, I feel Lucille boring holes into us as we talk, undoubtedly curious about the tension between us.

Lucille and I might be cordial, but we're far from friends. And although they both claim there's nothing between them anymore, I have a hard time believing it.

Hell, if that were true, why is she living here?

See all the things you're willing to overlook in the name of love?

Love is a stupid, no-good, very bad idea.

And I'm over it because, no matter what Ash says, Lucille is the one woman he gave everything to.

Me? I'm breadfruit, at your service.

I still don't know what the damn fruit looks like, but if I ever find one, I'm taking a sledgehammer to the thing. Just for kicks.

"I'll take the back room where Merlin is sleeping. No one's staying there, right?"

Ash shakes his head, clearly aware the conversation has gone silent as his friends watch our exchange. "You can sleep back there, if that's what you want."

"Thanks. Goodnight, everyone."

"I'll be in soon."

"No need," I reply with a dismissive shrug. "You have fun, Ash. Happy birthday."

I'm freezing my ass off back here.

Even though the temperatures during the day hit near sixty, it still dips close to freezing at night, and Ash's farmhouse, though gorgeous, is drafty as hell.

How come I never noticed the chill before? Oh, right—probably because I was too busy overheating during my numerous sexual escapades with Asher Hammond.

Hey, he knows how to keep a woman's blood pumping… for hours on end.

And Merlin is an unwilling snuggle partner, especially since I'm intent on stealing the warm spot he's created in the middle of the bed.

"You have fur. I guarantee you're warmer than I am."

Yes, I'm arguing with a cat, and judging by the side-eye he's throwing my way, I'm losing.

"Fine," I mutter as Merlin curls tighter into his space, clearly unmoved by my plight. "See if I bring you tuna treats again."

The door swings open, and Ash steps in, huffing out a breath. "Well, this won't do."

"What?" I snap, sitting up and shooting him an annoyed look.

"It's too cold in here."

Of course, he's right, but I'm in no mood to admit it.

"I have blankets."

"That's not enough. I'll sleep in here. You can take my bed."

"Ash, I don't need rescuing. Go enjoy your night."

He pauses, tilting his head as if trying to decide whether an argument is worth it. But then he rubs the back of his neck, a common tell that he's reining himself in. "All right. I'll grab you extra blankets, though I'm a much better heater."

No argument there.

"Thanks," I mutter, glaring at the quilt like it's personally offended me.

Ash sits on the edge of the bed, tipping my chin up with his hand. "Hey. Smile, beautiful."

"What for?"

"Aren't you excited?"

I was, but you ensured that emotion didn't last long.

"No, because I'm breadfruit."

Ash blinks, his brow furrowing. "Huh? What the hell does that mean?"

"Nothing. Inside joke. Ignore me. Probably just hormones."

"Ori…" He leans closer, his expression softening. "Please be excited. We're having a baby."

"I know."

He takes my face in his hands, his thumbs brushing gently over my cheeks. His breath hitches for a moment, like he's weighing every word. "We're having a baby. You and me. How fucking incredible is that?"

Despite my inner turmoil, I smile, the warmth of his touch breaking through my defenses. "Pretty damn incredible. Thank you."

"For what?"

I avert my gaze, plucking at a thread on the quilt. "For being supportive. I know this whole situation must be overwhelming for you. Not one, but two babies—with different mothers, neither of whom you're dating. If it's hard for me, I can't imagine how much harder it is for you. So, thank you for being here."

I chance a peek at Ash, just in time to see the smile fall from his face. Guess the truth hurts.

He presses a kiss to my forehead, lingering there for a few seconds. "I'll grab some extra blankets. Get some sleep."

At the doorway, he pauses, resting his hand on the frame. "It's only ever been you, Ori. No matter what other narrative you're convinced is true."

With a small shake of his head, he smacks the doorframe and walks out, leaving me alone once more.

I can't move.

Something is standing on my chest.

Something fat and furry, purring loud enough to wake the dead.

Blinking open my eyes, I chuckle and scratch Merlin's ears, earning a pleased mew.

"You are quite the snuggle bug, aren't you? Let me guess—you're starving. Haven't eaten in decades. Am I close?"

The sun streams through the blinds, and as I sit up, I catch the faint aroma of coffee wafting through the air.

Lord love caffeine… which I can't have for another seven months.

Fuck my life.

With a groan, I push back the covers and swing my legs over the side of the bed. The extra blankets Ash piled on kept me cozy, and I must've been more exhausted than I realized.

Mine was a heavy, dreamless sleep—a welcome reprieve from the chaos of my reality.

Gazing to my right, I notice a blanket tossed across the chair beside the bed.

Strange. I don't remember doing that. Did Ash come in after I fell asleep? Either way, I'm too groggy to care.

I grab my phone and wince at the six missed calls from Mina.

Damn. I forgot to check in last night. She probably thinks I'm furious with her.

I dial Mina's number, and she answers on the first ring. "Are you okay?"

Code for: Are you pissed at me?

"Yes, I'm fine. The doctor wants me to rest for a few days,

but I need to stop by the shop to grab my laptop. I'll be there in an hour or so."

"I can bring you the laptop."

"No need. Hey, why did you leave last night? Braden said he couldn't convince you to stay."

Mina laughs, but it rings hollow. "A few women showed up and showered him with affection. I felt like a third wheel."

Welcome to my world.

"I think he was disappointed you wanted to leave."

"Trust me, he was too busy with those women to care."

Somehow, I doubt that, based on Braden's version of events. Still, I'll always back Mina first.

"Bastard. I'll have a word with him."

"Don't bother. I'm just glad Ash isn't like that with you."

If you only knew.

"Are *you* okay?" I ask, flipping my friend's initial question back on her.

"I'm fine."

Damn, but we love that answer, don't we?

Wrap your pain in a bow labeled 'fine' and hope no one notices you're falling apart.

But I don't argue with her response. We can hash it out in person, and then I can decide if Braden deserves to be strung up by his pinky toes or if he gets a reprieve—this time, at least.

I throw on my clothes from the day before. The one benefit of being on the sobriety bandwagon? My clothes don't smell like smoke or beer.

I'll take the win where I can get it.

After taming my hair into a braid and shoving my glasses onto my face, I peek in the mirror hanging above the dresser.

World, this is as good as it gets. Please lower your expectations accordingly.

Now watch—I'll run into everyone I've ever met between here and the store.

Lucille sits at the kitchen table, sipping a cup of coffee. She smiles, but it doesn't quite reach her eyes. Tension lines her face and the worry wafting off her is palpable.

No doubt she's not thrilled Ash has another woman roosting here. Who can blame her?

"Good morning, Ori. Want some coffee?"

"I'm good, thanks."

"You sure? Although it is decaf, so it lacks the kick." Her tone sounds innocent enough, but I think she knows far more than she lets on about my sudden appearance at the farm.

But Ash wanted to keep everything a secret, so I'm Fort Knox. "No thanks. I'm headed to *One More Page*."

"I thought you were supposed to be resting."

"Just need a few things from my office. Are you working today?"

Lucille nods, her gaze drifting out the window. "Working from home. Be safe driving."

Another innocuous reply, but it sticks in my craw—a reminder that I'm the runner-up, and as long as Lucille is here, I'll always be on the outside looking in.

Time to hit the road. Dr. Fulton wants me to rest? Fine, but I'll do it from my apartment. Staying here is far too stressful, and he did say stress is bad for the baby.

Don't you love logic?

With a wave, I duck out the door and make a beeline for my truck. Funny how, only a month ago, this farm brought me such a sense of peace. Now it feels like enemy territory.

Truth be told, I'm the trespasser. Time for me to accept that fact.

I almost made it—I was *this* close to escaping.

If I hadn't taken those extra fortifying breaths before shifting my truck into reverse, I would've missed Lucille's frantic wave as she hurried toward me.

Stupid breath work. Totally overrated.

With a sigh, I lower the window. "Are you okay?"

"Can I ride in with you? I forgot a sketch at the parlor, and there's no sense wasting gas. Besides, this gives us a chance to catch up."

I nod, though I'd rather stick a burning poker in my eye than endure a thirty-minute ride with Ash's baby mama.

Correction: his *other* baby mama.

I stifle a groan and force a smile as Lucille eases into the passenger seat.

She's silent for the first ten minutes of the drive, humming along with the radio and gazing out at the first signs of spring cropping up along the highway.

I settle, hopeful it'll stay this way for the duration. What would we talk about, anyway?

But then she speaks.

"So… you're staying at the farm now," Lucille hedges, her gaze sliding toward me.

"Yes. It's stupid, really. The doctor wants me to rest, and Ash doesn't think I'm capable of it."

"Are you okay?" Her voice holds a note of concern, but I can't tell if she's sincere or fishing.

"Fine. Just tired."

"Then shouldn't you be resting instead of going to work?"

I shoot her a side eye. "Now you sound like Ash."

Lucille chuckles, running a hand over her belly. "Heaven forbid."

That's enough focus on me. Let's put her in the hot seat.

"How are *you* feeling?"

"Enormous, and I know it's only going to get worse. Plus, I have constant heartburn, and everything is swollen."

"Do you know if it's a boy or a girl?"

Do I really want to know? No, but these are basic questions, right? Shooting the shit about the weather, work, and baby mama drama.

"It's a boy."

I bite back a sudden flood of emotion, my eyes fixed on the road.

"A little boy. Ash must be excited."

"He's been amazing. But you know that about Ash." She shifts slightly, her gaze narrowing. "When are you planning on joining this club?"

I choke on air, struggling not to swallow my tongue at her pointed question.

If she only knew.

How am I supposed to answer that question? Everyone knows I'm a terrible liar, and when I'm nervous—like now—it shows on my face.

"One day," I croak, sending up a silent prayer of thanks when I turn onto Main Street. "I joked with Ash that I wanted twelve kids. Damn near scared the man into the priesthood."

Lucille giggles. "Could you imagine him with a dozen babies?"

Sadly, I wouldn't be surprised—not with Ash's sexual history. But Lucille will always be first.

"Honestly, I have a hard time imagining him with one."

"I know it's a lot to handle, but you've been great, Ori. Thank you for making this such a smooth transition for me."

What other choice did I have? Were there other options on the table?

"Are you two ready for your son's arrival?"

"No, but is anyone ever ready? I'm fully prepared for this little guy to turn my world upside down. He already has—but in the best way."

I park my truck and offer her a smile. A genuine one, this time. Even though she represents everything I'll never be in Ash's life, she deserves a modicum of happiness for her role in providing the first Hammond heir.

"You'll do great, Lucille. I've no doubt."

My driver's door jerks open, and I glance up into Ash's face. His very perturbed face.

"What the hell are you doing here?" Ash snaps.

"Relax. She was giving me a ride," Lucille offers, her tone light. "Letting this pregnant woman rest."

Wrong choice of words, Lucille.

"Is that so?" Ash drums his fingers against the door, his green eyes glaring holes into me. "*You're* supposed to be resting, Ori."

"I'm fine."

"We had a pleasant chat," Lucille remarks, stepping out of the truck.

"About what?" Ash demands, his tone pointed.

Lucille's grin widens. "Girl talk. You know, marriage, babies. All that shit."

Then she strolls into *Black Lotus*, leaving me alone with a walking hissy fit named Ash.

"Did you tell Lucille anything?"

My anger flares to life at his accusatory tone. I jump out of the truck and grab my bag from the back seat. "Not a word. Just discussed *your* impending arrival."

"I'm serious. This isn't a joke."

No shit, it isn't.

"Ori," Ash presses, grabbing my elbow. "Did you say anything to her?"

I jerk my arm free, shooting him daggers as tears sting my eyes. "About me? Not one damn word."

Then I stalk into *One More Page* without a backward glance.

Screw Asher Hammond and his moral high horse.

It's not as if I impregnated myself.

Mina slides a mug of coffee toward me as soon as I step into the store. "A special decaf blend I created this morning."

I release a satisfied moan as the warm liquid hits my throat. "You need a raise. This is fabulous."

"Tell me everything. How did Ash take the news?"

I shrug, still furious with the man after our parking lot altercation. "Fine."

"That is not an answer."

"He took it quite well, considering. Wasn't angry or throwing things. He was sweet about it. Overprotective, even."

"He loves you."

I bark out a dry laugh, shaking my head. "No, he doesn't. He's just acting as a well-intentioned human being."

"Ori, he loves you. You don't see the way he looks at you, but I do. You've *never* seen it."

"I wish that were the case, but you're mistaken, and I have proof."

Mina cocks her head to the side, her eyes narrowing. "Do tell."

"Ash has requested that we not mention the baby to anyone. This includes Braden and Lucille. No one can know. Even you and Eddie need to zip your lips."

Her jaw slackens in disbelief. "How come?"

"You'd have to ask him. I'm simply following orders."

"That's kind of messed up, isn't it?"

"Tell me about it. Likely doesn't want to kill his groove by having the town catch wind he's knocked up two women. Even groupies have their limits."

"Fucking men."

"*Amen.*" I take another sip of coffee, desperate to change the topic. "Spill it. What happened with Braden? Why did you leave?"

Mina shrugs, looking down at her hands. "Nothing happened. He's always nice, but I have to face facts. He thinks

I'm too young, and he will not go there. To him, I'm just a kid."

I set the mug down, leaning forward to intersect her gaze. "Honey, trust me. The only time being too young is an issue is when your fake ID fails you. Otherwise, it's the most amazing time, and you are beautiful, sweet, and talented. Screw Braden."

Her lips twitch into a faint smile. "Is that an option?"

"Not a good idea if your heart plans on getting involved."

Sadly, I know my words are true.

After all, I'm living it.

And it's a living hell.

Chapter 27

One More Item On The To-Do List

Ash

I keep shooting glances out the parlor window, growing more aggravated by the second.

Why?

Because my woman's truck still sits in the lot.

Even after Dr. Fulton warned her to take it easy. Doesn't matter if the doctor thinks I'm overreacting. Ori's safety isn't negotiable.

I crack my knuckles, the sound echoing through the quiet shop. Time to push Ori's stubborn ass out the door and back home.

But I don't make it three steps.

Kevin Duncan strolls through the entrance to *Black Lotus* like he owns the place, his smug expression already setting my teeth on edge.

I freeze, my pulse quickening.

"Be with you in a second," I bark, my voice tight.

I glance toward the back to warn Lucille, but Kevin raises a hand, stopping me in my tracks.

"Don't bother. Lucille walked across the street ten minutes ago. She looked well, by the way. Must be the company she keeps." His smirk widens. "Though she's not why I'm here."

Fuck.

Clearing my throat, I shove my hands into my pockets, hoping the maneuver will keep my fists from flying into this prick's face. "What do you want?"

Kevin strolls over to the reception desk, tapping his manicured fingers on the edge as he surveys the room. "You're not very friendly to your clientele, are you?"

"You're still not a client, so I'll repeat—what do you want?"

Kevin's smirk deepens as he leans casually against the desk. "I hear congratulations are in order."

A chill races down my spine, but I keep my expression neutral. "If you're here to congratulate me about Lucille, save it. She's not your problem anymore."

"Hardly." Kevin chuckles, the sound low and grating. "I'm well rid of that one. She's trouble, you know."

"Then what are you congratulating me for?"

Kevin's eyes narrow, and his voice drops an octave. "You know exactly what I'm talking about."

I step closer, closing the gap between us. "You don't know shit."

Kevin tilts his head, his sneer sharpening. "Don't I?"

My fists clench in my pockets, every muscle in my body coiled tight.

Kevin holds his ground, an air of arrogance surrounding him, his overpriced cologne assaulting my senses. "The better question is, *how* do I know? And the answer, Hammond, is that I know everything."

I grind my teeth, trying to keep my voice even. "If you're here to play games, you can leave. *Now*."

Kevin chuckles again, the sound like nails on a chalkboard. "Relax, Ash. I'm just saying it pays to know who your friends are—and where their loyalties lie. Sparkwood's a small town, after all."

My heart slams against my ribs. He knows. He fucking knows.

"I will kill you," I growl, my voice cold and firm, every word laced with barely restrained fury.

"For what?" Kevin's grin widens, his tone dripping with mock innocence. "For pointing out the obvious? For suggesting you keep your house in order? It's not a crime to be observant."

I step forward, glaring into his gray eyes. "Get. Out."

Kevin raises his hands in mock surrender, but the smirk never leaves his face. "Message received, lover boy. No need to get so worked up. Just be careful. You've got a lot of moving parts to manage. Wouldn't want them all to fall apart now, would you?"

His words hang in the air like noxious smoke as he strolls out, the door swinging shut behind him.

I stand there, frozen, Kevin's words looping in my head like a ticking time bomb.

He knows.

About Ori. About Lucille. Maybe even about Trace.

There's a goddamn leak.

Before I can think, the fury explodes from inside me. I whirl and slam my fist into the wall, the sheetrock caving beneath the force. Pain radiates up my arm, sharp and searing, but I welcome it.

"Jesus Christ, Ash!"

Braden's voice cuts through the haze, and I glance up to see him rushing toward me. His gaze volleys between the jagged hole in the wall and the blood dripping from my knuckles.

"What the fuck?" he snaps, his eyes blazing.

I shake out my hand, ignoring the sting as I press it against my thigh. "It's nothing. Just leave it, Braden."

"It's nothing?" He points at the hole in the wall, his jaw tightening. "You just put your fist through the wall and your hand's bleeding all over the damn floor. What the hell is going on?"

"I said it's *nothing*." I bite out the words, desperate to get my brother off my ass.

Braden tosses up his hands in resignation. "I'm so over this goddamn drama. What is happening to you?"

I don't answer. There's nothing I can tell him. At least, not now.

My brother steps back, his expression hardening. "You're not going to tell me, are you?"

I meet his gaze, my chest heaving with unspoken words, unspoken fears. "It's better if you don't know."

His face falls, disappointment etched into every line. "I'm done. Whatever this is, I'm done with it, and with you."

"Braden—"

"No." He holds up a hand, cutting me off. "Figure your shit out. Before you lose everything."

He storms into the back as I stand there, blood dripping from the cuts on my knuckles.

What he doesn't realize is I'm terrified I already have.

After Kevin's surprise visit, I don't waste a second.

I clean up my hand and the mess on the floor, hanging a random photo to cover the hole in the sheetrock. One more repair to add to my ever-growing list of things to do.

I call Trace, my voice sharp and shaking. "Meet me at *Black Lotus*. Now. No questions asked."

But even as I hang up, my mind is somewhere else— on Ori.

I march over to *One More Page*, my chest tightening with every step.

God help Kevin if he's gone anywhere near her.

The bell above the door jingles as I step inside, but I barely notice the few customers milling around. My eyes zero in on Ori, perched at the coffee bar, sipping her drink like the world isn't crumbling around us.

I can't let her see how wrecked I am. I have to hold it together. For her. For our baby.

But the second I open my mouth, my thin veneer of control snaps. "We need to talk. *Now*."

She turns, startled by the edge in my voice. Her eyes widen as they sweep over me—my bandaged hand, my disheveled hair, the barely concealed panic vibrating from every pore.

"What happened to you?" Ori asks, her voice laced with concern.

"Don't worry about it," I bite out.

Her gaze drops to my hand, her brows knitting together. "Your hand—"

"It's fine." I wave her off and grab her elbow, steering her toward her office.

But no place feels safe anymore

"Ash—"

"I said don't worry about it." My words emerge harsh and sharp, as the fear inside me roars like an unrelenting beast.

Once in her office, I shut the door behind us, leaning against it for a moment to catch my breath.

Her arms cross over her chest as she glares at me. "What do you want?"

"Who did you tell?" The words fly from my mouth, driven by the panic raking at my throat.

"About what?" she fires back, her eyes narrowing.

"Don't play dumb, Ori. Who else knows?"

Her mouth falls open at my insulting remark. "No one. I've been here less than half an hour."

I tug a hand through my hair as my frustration mounts. "Why can't you just listen for once?"

"Play along, you mean?" she counters, her tone dripping with sarcasm. "I'm not telling *anyone*. Don't worry, I'm used to being second rate. It's the theme of my life."

Her words damn near derail my perilously dangling emotions. "Ori, that is incredibly unfair and untrue."

"Is it? Keeping things quiet was your idea."

"Just for now," I say, desperation creeping into my voice. "And I am."

"You need to understand—"

"No." She steps closer, jabbing a finger into my chest. "*You* need to understand. You act like I'm set to blab this baby news all over Sparkwood, but the truth is, I didn't even want to tell *you*. It's hard enough standing in line with the rest of your women, but I won't do that to my child."

Her words are a knife to my chest. She has no idea how much I want to tell her everything—to let her know she's my whole goddamn world. But I can't.

I drop my gaze to my hands, my knuckles raw and aching as I crack them.

She presses her palms against her eyes, her shoulders slumping in defeat. "I hate that anger is the only thing I seem to feel anymore. It's no good for any of us. I'm going back to my apartment. I'll rest there. Don't worry about me—or us."

I step closer, my voice trembling. "That's just it, Ori. You're *all* I worry about. This isn't me being a controlling asshole. It's about protecting the most important things in my world."

Her eyes search mine, filled with frustration and hurt. "Ash, you don't want anyone to know about our baby, but *everyone* knows about Lucille. She broke your heart, and yet here she is, reaping the rewards. Well, I won't be your dirty secret."

"Beautiful, I never hid you." The emotions course through me, threatening to break loose and drown us both.

"No." Her voice softens, her gaze locked on mine. "You hid your heart, which is worse."

"Ori—"

She steps back, wrapping her arms around herself as if to shield against the storm brewing between us. "Choose. For once in your life. Me or her. I'd rather live alone than like this anymore."

"Can we please talk—"

"No." Ori shakes her head, tears brimming in her dark eyes. "I'll get that fairytale if I have to build it myself. But I refuse to subsist on the scraps of affection you toss my way. I want it all. I deserve it all. And I finally see—I'll never get it from you."

Her harsh demands leave me speechless, and I know I can't argue with her about them. Not now, at least.

She reads my silence and lifts her chin, the sheer strength in her gaze shattering the last vestiges of my composure. "Stop toying with my heart when all you intend to do is break it."

Then Ori points to the door, her message clear: the conversation is over.

"Promise me you'll go straight to your apartment and lock the door." My voice cracks, but I bite back the anguish threatening to claw its way out of my chest.

"Fine."

Her tone is clipped, the anger radiating off her in waves. She's furious, and I can't blame her.

But that's fine—so long as she listens to me. So long as she's safe.

One day, she'll understand why I had to lie to her. And how every word, every omission, damn near broke me.

"This is a bad idea," Trace mutters, sinking into one of the newly installed booths in the speakeasy.

He's not wrong, but I've been super careful this past month, and everything still went sideways.

Now, I've got bigger problems than his damn case. Problems involving the woman I love and the baby she's carrying.

"Couldn't be helped," I reply, sliding into the seat across from him and Lucille.

The construction crew cut out early after running out of material, and I figured this was the most secure place to talk. Not that anywhere feels safe right now.

"What's going on?" Trace asks, his sharp gaze darting between Lucille and me.

"There's a leak," I say, drumming my fingers on the table.

Trace's eyes narrow. "What do you mean? How do you know?"

I throw up my hands, my frustration boiling over. "Those aren't the right questions. How about *why* is there a leak, and what the hell are you going to do about it?"

"Relax, Ash," Lucille says softly, placing a hand on my arm.

I rip my hand from her grip and shoot her a scathing glare. "I can't relax, Lucille. You know why? Because my world is upside down right now, and you're the common denominator."

Lucille leans back, her shoulders slumping. "I know. I'm so sorry you're involved in this mess."

Her voice carries the same exhaustion and guilt I've been dragging around this past month. She means what she says, and it's not her fault. Not really.

We're all at our breaking point.

Trace knocks on the table, calling back my attention. "What makes you think there's a leak?"

I flex my aching hand, the stiffness worsening by the minute. "Ori is pregnant."

Lucille gasps, her hand flying to her mouth. "Really? That's wonderful, Ash. Congratulations."

I bounce my foot against the floor, unable to keep still. "It would be, right? Except I've sworn Ori to secrecy. She thinks it's because you're pregnant with my baby. She believes she's second best in my life, and I can't tell her otherwise."

Trace leans forward, his voice threaded with aggravation. "Congrats on the baby, but that *still* doesn't answer my question. Why do you think there's a leak?"

"Kevin dropped by this morning."

"What did he say?"

"He offered his congratulations on our impending arrival."

A muscle jumps in Trace's jaw. "How the hell does he know about the baby?"

"Exactly my question." I slam my fists against the table, the wood vibrating beneath the force. "How the fuck does this psychopath know anything about Ori and me?"

Trace rakes a hand through his hair, and I can almost see the gears and switches flipping in his brain. "I need you both to think. Think hard. Have you let anything slip?"

"No," Lucille states. "We've been careful, Trace. We know what's at stake."

"How much longer do we have to keep this shit up?" I ask, desperation edging my voice.

Trace's hand taps out an erratic rhythm on the table. "The shipment's set to arrive tomorrow night, but now I'm not sure it'll happen. Not if Kevin has insider information. Fuck, I hate dragging civilians into this shit."

"Hey, we haven't said anything," I bark, motioning between me and Lucille. "We've *been* careful."

Trace's nostrils flare, his jaw tightening as he growls,

"Well, someone said something. What about your guys upstairs?"

"Zane doesn't know a damn thing."

Trace sharpens his gaze on me. "What about your brother?"

Before Trace can respond, a new voice slices through the air.

"What about me?"

I whip my head up to see Braden standing in the doorway, his expression a volatile mix of confusion and rage.

"What's up, Braden?"

"You tell me," Braden says, his heavy, measured steps echoing across the floor. "I come downstairs to talk about a client, and I overhear some stranger throwing my name around."

"It's nothing," But I know my response is futile. My brother is past the point of walking away.

"Bullshit." Braden's glare hardens, volleying between Lucille and Trace. "This whole situation stinks. You and I never keep secrets from each other. *Never*."

"Braden—"

"I'm not done," Braden bellows, jabbing a finger at me. "It's your life. If you want to screw it up with Lucille, fine. But it becomes my business when I hear my name in some stranger's mouth, questioning my integrity."

Trace rises, extending his hand in a calm greeting. "We haven't met. I'm Trace."

Braden's lip curls as he crosses his arms over his chest. "Why the fuck should I care who you are?"

"Because you know him—or at least know of him," I reply, my head pounding like a marching band has taken up perma- nent residence in my skull.

Braden's eyes go wide as he looks between Trace and Lucille. "Wait. You're *her* ex-husband? You're that Trace?"

"One and the same," Trace says, his expression devoid of emotion.

Braden passes a hand over his eyes. "What the hell have you gotten yourself into, Ash?"

Trace gives me a subtle nod and I motion to the seat beside me.

"Sit down, Braden." My voice is steady despite the overwhelming fear coursing through me. "It's time to fill you in."

It's not even ten in the morning, and my brother looks like he needs a drink. Hell, he might need an entire bottle.

The man sits shell-shocked, trying to process the truth behind the situation with Lucille and me. To be fair, it's the same expression I've been wearing for the past month.

Braden scrubs his face as he absorbs the barrage of revelations thrown his way.

"Shit," he mutters.

I clap a hand on his shoulder. "Braden, I hated not telling you."

He shakes his head as if that might bring clarity to the craziness. "I appreciate the truth. Lucille, Trace—sorry for lashing out."

That's the thing about Braden. He's got a temper, but he knows how to apologize—and mean it.

Best guy on the planet, no doubt.

"No worries. You have every right to hate me," Lucille says, offering a faint smile.

"I don't hate you," Braden argues.

"You all do, and I get it." Lucille shrugs, her expression resigned, as if forever cast in the role of harlot and home wrecker.

"Actually, Cilly," Trace interjects, using a nickname I've never heard before, "it takes tremendous courage to do what you're doing. You took a hell of a chance, and I'm going to make sure you're somewhere safe once this is over."Lucille nods, but I see the lost little girl inside her—hopeless and alone.

And in that moment, I forgive her for not loving me back all those years ago and breaking my heart into a million pieces.

If she hadn't, I never would have gotten the chance to love Ori and I know without a doubt that she is the love of my life.

Trace pivots toward my brother. "Braden, I know these two trust you, but I'm not thrilled you know this much about the investigation. So, here's the deal for all of you: keep your mouths shut. If this case gets compromised because of loose lips, I'll make sure the law comes down on you harder than you can imagine. Understood?"

"I think I liked him better as the head of an MC," Lucille mutters, clearly unfazed by Trace's show of authority.

"Cute," Trace responds dryly. "But no joke, guys. Mouths shut, or this all falls apart."

"Fine." I stand, giving my brother a clap on the back. "Do me a favor. Clear my afternoon."

"Where are you going?" Braden asks.

"To be with my woman. But hey, Braden..." I pause, letting the weight of the moment settle. "There's another secret I've been keeping from you."

Braden rests his chin on his hand and smirks. "Let me guess—Ori's pregnant."

Talk about silence.

After a few beats, Braden's eyes go wide. "Holy shit, is Ori pregnant?"

I can't hold back the grin quirking my lips. "Yeah, she is."

A smile spreads across his face, slow and genuine. "See? Now *that* makes sense. Congrats, my brother."

"We'll celebrate soon. But first, I need some quality time with Ori."

"I thought she wasn't speaking to you," Lucille calls out, twisting in the booth to look at me, a slight glint of mischief on her face.

"I have a few ways to convince her. Right now, I just need to be near her. Trace, do you think you guys can handle the rest of this case without me?"

Trace snorts and waves me off. "It won't be easy, Hammond, but I'll manage somehow."

Hey, we need to end this on a positive note, right? Because we *will* take Kevin Duncan down.

He will pay for the lives he's ruined.

Anything else is too unbearable to consider.

Chapter 28

The Truth Shall Set You Free

Ash

I knock on Ori's door, huffing out a breath as I prepare for my woman's wrath.

Trust me, I know I've got it coming.

True to form, she cracks open the door and shoots me a glare. "God, I'm in no mood. What do you want?"

"We need to talk. Now."

"How about I don't work around your schedule? How about I don't feel like talking? How about—"

"Beautiful, open the damn door."

Ori's lips press into a tight line, and she leans against the doorframe, clearly ready to ride the petulance train as far as it will take her. Can't say I blame her.

"No."

Okay, time to change tactics. Trace warned me to keep quiet, but Ori needs to know. I can't stand another minute away from the woman I love, and if facing Trace's wrath is the price, I'll pay it without hesitation.

I glance around the parking lot, praying no one is within earshot. Paranoia is a bitch, and it grows worse by the minute.

Here goes nothing—and *everything*—all at once.

I shove my hands in my pockets and rock back on my heels. "It's not my baby."

A growl rises from Ori's chest as she slams the door shut. For a second, I think I've screwed this situation up even worse, but then the latch slides off, and she throws the door wide open.

"You are such a jerk. I can't believe you'd say that."

Is it an asshole move? Sure, but it worked.

"Got me in the door," I reply, stepping inside and kicking the door shut behind me. My fingers twist the lock into place, ensuring no one can follow.

"Get out," Ori grunts, pounding her fists against my chest.

I easily fend off her blows and scoop her into my arms. "I'm not leaving."

"What do you think you're doing?" she demands, wriggling against me.

"Just be quiet for a second, and I'll tell you." I carry her into the bathroom and set her on the vanity before turning the shower on full blast. "Now, as I was saying, it's not my baby."

Ori releases a howl of frustration, jabbing a finger toward her stomach. "This is your baby. You want a paternity test? Fine, but I'm not risking the pregnancy now, so you'll have to cool your heels until the baby is born. Don't worry, I won't say a word about the baby's daddy until then. Maybe I'll invent some raucous story about how the father is a stripper in Vegas with a ten-foot dick."

I cross my arms and lean against the sink, unable to hide my amusement. The more she goes on, the funnier it becomes. She's five feet of terror wrapped in an adorable package, like one of those maniacal chihuahuas that screech and howl at every dog, no matter the size.

Best not to mention that fact right now.

"Is this funny to you?" she snaps, throwing up her hands in disgust. "You're a bastard, Asher Hammond. You need to leave."

She slides off the vanity, but I step forward, caging her in my arms.

Sorry, little one, but this is all the space I'm giving you now.

"Yell at me all you want. I'm not leaving your side."

"You're sure as hell not staying here."

"Will you listen? After I'm done, you can decide if you'd like to continue yelling at me."

She juts out her chin, her glare sharp enough to cut glass. "What more could you possibly have to tell me? You swear me to secrecy, demand my love and understanding for your first baby mama, and then top it all off by asking for a paternity test."

I rest my hands against her stomach, letting the warmth of her body calm my frayed nerves. "Ori, I know this is my baby."

"Then why would you say that it isn't?" Ori buries her face in her hands, her body shaking. "Ash, you heard the doctor. I need to reduce my stress, and you being here is doing the opposite. So, please, say what you have to say and go. Just go."

"Lucille's baby isn't mine." I hiss the words in her ear, still terrified of who might be listening to our conversation.

Ori's jaw slackens, and she shakes her head as if to clear it. "Did you take a paternity test?"

"No need. I haven't slept with the woman in years."

Her gaze narrows at me. "Then why would you think you were the father? Ash, you understand how this process works, right?"

I shoot her an exasperated look as I drag a hand through my hair. "Don't worry. I understand the basics, beautiful." I exhale sharply, trying to gather my thoughts. "Lucille and I are working undercover."

"You're what? With whom? Some underground tattooing ring?"

"Homeland Security."

"Of course. Homeland Security." Ori's gaze drifts to the far wall, her palms pressing together as if trying to grasp the weight of my admission. "Come on, you're not serious."

"Actually, I am."

She presses her fingers to her temples, exhaling sharply. "You never stop, do you? Spinning some ridiculous story about working with the government. What's the point?"

"I'm serious."

Ori slips from the vanity and turns off the shower. "Can we please stop wasting my water?"

As soon as she steps away, I throw the spray back on. I don't give a damn if I run up a $500 water bill. I'll gladly pay every dime. "No, because I'm not sure who's listening."

Ori groans and rolls her eyes. "Please stop. I don't know what crazy crime drama you pulled this plot from, but it's enough now."

Gripping her shoulders, I force her to meet my eyes. "Ori, I've never lied to you—except about what Lucille's presence meant in my life. And I'm sure as hell not lying now."

I'm not sure what finally breaks her defenses—my steadfast stare, my unwavering posture, or her own intrinsic understanding that I'm telling the truth.

She sags against the vanity, her face awash with confusion. Then she lifts her hand, giving me the floor. "Spill it, Hammond. What the hell is going on?"

"Lucille got mixed up with the wrong guy, and I mean the *wrong* guy."

"This wrong guy is her baby's father?"

"Yeah." I brace my hands on the counter, my knuckles turning white with the force. "Anyway, she started suspecting her boyfriend was running girls—you know, trafficking them through his club. One night, her ex-husband came in to sample the wares, if you catch my drift."

"Wait a second. Both her boyfriend *and* her ex-husband

are involved in sex trafficking? Jesus. She's picked a couple of winners."

I shake my head, tension tightening my jaw. "No, her ex works for Homeland Security. He reached out to her after he learned she was mixed up in this mess and asked for her help. She became his inside person."

Ori's mouth twists into a grimace, her fingers tapping against the countertop. "That's super risky for a pregnant woman. But how did *you* get involved?"

"It got very dangerous, and her ex had to pull her out and get her somewhere safe. That's where I came in."

She tilts her head, skepticism flickering in her eyes. "I still don't understand."

"Lucille's boyfriend accused her of cheating with me after some pictures of us at the convention in Vegas surfaced. Nothing happened—it was totally professional—but he didn't see it that way."

"Was it, though?" she asks, hesitancy lining every syllable.

I grasp her chin, capturing her dark gaze. "Yes, Ori. Since our first night, I haven't been with anybody else."

Ori covers her mouth with both hands and releases a deep breath. "I needed to hear that." She waves her hand, prompting me to continue. "Sorry, back to your story."

"Her boyfriend beat her pretty badly, and Lucille was scared she would lose the baby if she stayed any longer. Since he already believed I was sleeping with her, we decided to make that the public front. It got her out of his way and gave him something else to stew on while Homeland Security finished their investigation and prepared to take him down."

"So, you know her boyfriend?"

"Yes." My teeth clench as a fresh wave of tension rushes through me. "And so do you. Who did I demand you stay away from?"

Ori's eyes widen, horror dawning on her face. "Kevin Duncan."

I nod, taking her hands in mine. "That's why I was so desperate to keep you from him."

"Is that why he was hanging around me? Because of you and Lucille?"

"Pretty much. He wanted to get even with me by hurting the most important person in my world."

Her breath catches as she stares at me, tears shining brightly in her eyes. "Why didn't you tell me all this a month ago?"

"I wanted to, but Trace swore me to secrecy. Braden didn't know, either. No one did. Trace worried if you guys knew, then your reactions might give it away. Kevin is a piece of shit, but he's no fool. He was sniffing around, just looking for anything to prove this was a ruse. I had to ensure you believed it was real, too."

Her tears earn their due, sliding silently down her cheeks. "Trust me, you gave a hell of a performance. This was the worst month of my life."

I reach over, sweeping her tears away with my thumbs. "Mine too."

"So, why are you telling me now? Did they get him?"

"They're closing in tomorrow, and I'm taking an enormous risk telling you, but I couldn't go another minute with you, not believing that you are everything to me."

Ori ducks under my arms, shaking her hands as she tries to digest the deluge of information. She paces a few short steps before stopping, her head tilting up to meet my gaze. "My head is spinning."

"Are you okay?" I step closer, my stomach tightening with worry.

"Metaphorically speaking," she replies, waving a hand to brush off my concern.

I exhale sharply, the tension easing from my shoulders. "Don't scare me like that."

"Sorry. So that's why you showed no interest in Lucille or her baby?"

"Yep."

"And why you've been so ridiculously overprotective of me?"

"Exactly."

She removes her glasses and pinches the bridge of her nose, releasing a shaky breath. "Makes sense."

"Look, I want Lucille safe, but she's not the reason I agreed to play along with this ruse. Trace and Lucille informed me that Kevin was watching you. They had photographic proof, and I knew he had been hanging around. I figured he had a thing for you, because a lot of fucking men do, but when I learned his real reason for staying close, I knew I had to protect you. Taking him down was the only way to keep you safe."

Ori huffs out a small laugh, her lips quirking into a half-smile. "Are you done now?"

I chuckle at my woman's thinly veiled annoyance, realizing how good it feels to laugh again. "Keeping you safe? No. Never."

"With your undercover work."

"Yes, I'm done. Hopefully, for good."

Her shoulders sag as the tension slides from her body. "You're a good friend to Lucille."

"She's not my friend, but she's no longer my enemy, either. Besides, you help people when they're in trouble. That's how my folks raised me."

"They raised you right. Thank you for protecting me, even though I spent most of this month thinking you were a total asshole. Also, I may have bought a book on black magic."

"Shit. Did you read it?" I really hope she's kidding, but with Ori, you can never be *too* certain.

"You're still here, aren't you?" Her reply is blasé, like I'm off the hook for now—but I'm pretty sure that book is staying in her nightstand, just in case I screw up again.

"I almost told you everything that night in the speakeasy, when I was drunk."

"I *knew* you were drunk." Ori points a finger at me, but I catch the wicked gleam in her eyes. Damn, I've missed her mischievous side.

I'm hopelessly addicted to it—and to her.

"Still meant everything I said." And I did—now more than ever. "But I kept quiet, even though I hated the distance between us. I couldn't risk you acting out of sorts or saying something that might raise Kevin's suspicion."

Ori plants her hands on her hips, shooting me a mock glare. "Are you saying I don't have a good poker face?"

"You're the worst liar in history, but I love that about you."

The words slip out before I can stop them, although I'm not sure my pseudo admission counts. Somehow, those three little words—*I love you*—don't seem nearly grand enough for Ori and our baby.

"I am *not* the worst liar," she grumbles.

She doesn't bring up my mention of the L word, but I see her edges softening as she grants me entrance to her heart once more.

I raise my hands in mock surrender, a smug smirk coloring my face. "Hands down, the worst, but that's what makes you perfect. Do you honestly think, for one second, I wanted to be away from you?"

"It was a lot more than one second. It was about a million of them."

"I hated every day we were apart, but it made me realize something important. See, I didn't think I was ready for you, Ori, but I've realized that's not the case. I've been waiting my whole life for you."

A slow smile spreads across her face, lighting her up from

the inside. "That was good, Ash. Really good. So, you're ready for me now?"

"Absolutely."

"And you're ready for this?" she asks, pointing at her still-flat abdomen.

"Without a doubt. So, are you still mad at me?"

Ori bobs her head, considering my question. "Yes."

Then, in a totally unexpected move, she pulls off her shirt and twists her hair into a messy bun, her movements unhurried and deliberate.

"What are you doing? Not that I'm complaining about you stripping down." My voice thickens with desire as I drag my tongue across my lower lip.

If I had my way, Ori would be naked 24/7—for my eyes only, obviously.

"The water's warm," she says, motioning to the steam swirling thick in the air, as if she isn't ignoring the important question I just asked. "I'm taking a shower."

She slips her hands under the waistband of her sweats and slides them down in one fluid motion. Her bare skin glistens as she tosses them aside and steps under the shower spray.

Fuck, my cock is desperate for a piece of this action. I grunt and adjust myself, realizing it's been far too long since I've made love to my gorgeous woman.

Hopefully, that drought ends tonight.

"Seriously, you forgive me, right?" I ask, peering around the shower curtain and dragging my gaze slowly over every inch of Ori's form.

She flashes me a cheeky grin as she runs her hands along her body, ensuring I have a front-row seat to every one of her delectable curves. "Forgive you for keeping me in the dark while you try to rid the world of vermin? I don't know. It's a big ask, Hammond, but I might let you try to convince me. That is, if you're interested."

"Fuck yes, I'm interested."

"Then get the hell in here."

My woman doesn't have to tell me twice. I've never stripped down so fast in my life.

Once beneath the warm spray, I grab Ori to me, enveloping her slight frame in my arms. Her body melts against me and I close my eyes, allowing the moment to sink in.

Home. I'm finally home again.

Ori tips her face up, and I waste no time claiming those luscious lips. Her love eases every hurt, every pain my heart has known.

No, *I love you* isn't nearly good enough for a woman like Ori. They haven't invented a word to describe this emotion yet—or maybe there simply isn't one that could encapsulate this overwhelming need to protect and adore her.

Despite the steadily growing inferno inside me, I maintain an easy pace as I reclaim the parts of her I feared were lost forever.

Her hands glide across my chest, and her tongue tangles leisurely with mine, the heat between us building with every soft caress.

I frame Ori's face with my hands, dropping delicate kisses across her cheeks and forehead. "I missed you so much."

"How about you never have to miss me again?"

"That's the plan," I reply, sealing my promise with another kiss.

Ori steps from the shower and wraps a towel around her body. "Come on. Hero or not, you still owe me big time."

I grab a towel to dry off, loving my lady's hooded gaze when it falls on my fully erect cock.

Yes, beautiful, he's all for you.

"I'll give you anything you want."

Her eyes widen. "Be careful there, Ash. You're leaving yourself wide open."

I pull her into my arms, her towel falling to the floor. "Anything. You. Want."

Ori bites her lower lip, the playful curve of her mouth faltering. Her brow furrows slightly, and the sparkle in her eyes dims as seriousness takes hold.

"So many options," she murmurs, her gaze focused on the floor. "You mean it? Anything I want?"

"Yes." It's not a lie. No matter what demand she puts on the table, I'll give it to her—gladly.

She interlaces our fingers, and I feel the slight tremble running through her.

"You'll answer me honestly?" she asks, her voice barely a whisper. "Not just say what you think I want to hear?"

"Of course."

What in the world is going on in your head right now, beautiful?

Ori rolls her shoulders and meets my gaze, her eyes once again bright with unshed tears. "Are you mad?"

"About what?"

"Me having a baby."

I trail my fingers gently along her temple, desperate to ease the worry from her mind. "You mean *us*? Can I be included in this scenario, too? Oriana Thorne, I knew the risks when I tossed the condom. I did it anyway. Then I did it again, and again, and again. So no, I'm not mad. I knew."

A flash of levity crosses her face as she nods. "I knew, too. Guess we're equally guilty."

I tip her chin up, hoping she can read the truth in my eyes and this time, know beyond any doubt that I'm for real. "I wanted it with you, even if I didn't know how to say it. You weren't the only one."

A single tear glides down her cheek, and I lean down to kiss it away.

"No more tears, beautiful."

Ori has endured enough pain and heartache for one lifetime. Now, it's time for adoration and worship to claim the starring role.

Sweeping her into my arms, I carry her to the bed, placing her across the soft blanket. When her eyes meet mine, I see everything I've searched my entire life for—everything I damn near lost forever.

I settle between her thighs, my lips dusting kisses along her abdomen and hips. Her soft sighs fill the room, and I swear they're my favorite melody. "You're so beautiful. So perfect."

My tongue traces a languid path along her breasts and up her throat, savoring the soft warmth of her skin, every movement as slow and reverent as if discovering her for the first time.

When I reach her mouth, her lips eagerly claim mine. She tangles her hands in my hair as we reacquaint ourselves with a chemistry so powerful it could burn the world down.

My thumb circles her clit, slick with her arousal, teasing her open with deliberate strokes. My fingers slide inside her, curling and stroking, pulling soft gasps from her as her body tightens beneath me. Just as she starts to tremble, I slow, dragging her back from the brink before starting again.

Yes, I'm keeping her on that edge, riding that razor, and taking back every single minute I lost over the last month.

"You know, Mr. Hammond," she teases, "it's almost unfair how good you are at this. How am I supposed to survive without you for even a day?"

"You won't have to ever again." I pause, brushing my lips over hers as the truth pours out of me. "Even though I can breathe without you, Ori, I never want to. Life without you isn't living. You're my reason for everything."

Her eyes shimmer with unshed tears as she cups my face, brushing her fingers along my jaw. "You're mine, too."

Ori's reassurance is all I need. Now, it's time to reclaim what's mine.

My cock teases her entrance, savoring how wet and ready

she is for me. I've always said she has the most perfect pussy on the planet, but I was wrong. Every inch of her is perfection —and every inch belongs to me.

Her hips lift in an unspoken plea as she cups her breasts, teasing her nipples into hard peaks.

"Please don't make me wait any longer," she begs.

What my lady wants, she gets.

When I thrust deep inside her, she releases a guttural moan, her nails raking down my back as she pulls me close.

A flash of overwhelming emotion rushes through me, and I pause, basking in her tight warmth.

I slide my hands under her shoulders and pull her close as I move slowly inside her, savoring every second.

This is so much more than sex. So much more than making love. This *is* love. This is us rediscovering every inch of each other.

Ori whimpers, her body trembling as she nears release, but I won't rush one second of this. My gaze locks on hers, a smile tugging at my lips as the pleasure sweeps across her face.

She arches into me, her whole body trembling as she unravels, her muscles clenching around my cock and pulling me dangerously close to the edge.

Ori moans my name as she clings to me, her nails scratching temporary tattoos into my skin. Let her mark me everywhere because I know one thing—I belong to this woman.

No one else will ever stand a chance.

When a second orgasm crests through her, Ori thrashes beneath me. "Ash, fuck, it's too much."

But it's nowhere near enough. I silence any protest with my mouth, kissing her deeply, my tongue tangling with hers in a slow, sensual rhythm as my shaft glides through her slick heat.

When her cries soften, I pull back, savoring the moment before resuming my slow, deliberate rhythm.

"Does it feel good for you?" Ori murmurs, her voice a soft purr of satisfaction.

"You're perfection. Utter perfection," I whisper, pressing my lips to her temple.

But she knows, after months of our wild and crazy sex life, that I'm taking it easy.

Ori strokes her fingers along my bearded jaw, a knowing smile curving her lips. "You're so slow and gentle tonight. Are you afraid of hurting the baby?"

I nuzzle my lips against her neck, smiling when she releases a low chuckle. "I know our baby is safe, but I don't want to miss a thing."

"Ash?"

"Yes, my love?"

"I missed you." Her arms tighten around me, and I melt into her embrace.

With a sigh, I rest my forehead against hers. "I've only ever been right here, waiting for you."

I know how lucky I am that Ori has given me another chance. That through some twist of fate, her unrelenting understanding and enormous heart still have room for me.

She'll never have to question my loyalty—or my love—again.

"I needed that," Ori murmurs against my chest.

"Understatement of the year." I tuck a hand behind my head, my other arm draped protectively around her. "See? This is yet another reason why you should've accepted my marriage proposal. Fantastic sex on demand."

Am I messing with her? Yes—and no. I'd like to know where Ori stands on walking down the aisle, especially since I may have dropped a small fortune on a vintage engagement ring.

Ori props her chin on my chest, quirking her brows in surprise. "When exactly did you propose and how did I miss it?"

"I talked about it that night at the speakeasy—"

"When you were drunk," she reminds me.

"Minor detail," I chuckle. "And then again, on that day with that investor prick."

She bites her lip as a cheeky grin threatens to break across her face. "*That's* your idea of a proposal?"

"I think it's pretty good."

Ori's laughter bubbles between us, light and warm. "It's terrible, actually."

"Thanks a lot."

She peppers kisses across my chest, her fingers trailing idle designs on my skin. "I should've agreed to all of it, though, just to throw you off."

"You should have, because now you'll have to ask me," I tease, smiling up at her. "And you will, too."

"Is that a fact?"

"It is, because I'm the total package. Good in bed, good job, nice guy—"

"Eh, I don't know about all that."

"Oh, you're going to pay for that." I tickle her sides, laughing as she squirms against me, her delighted squeals filling the room.

With an exaggerated harrumph, she fixes me with her dark gaze. "You're an amazing man. You've built two incredible businesses, and as for your skills in the bedroom..."

"Well? Go ahead, you can say it."

Am I being a cocky bastard? Of course, but here's the thing. Ori loves that side of me, just as much as she loves the sweet teddy bear side.

"Best time I've ever had."

"Damn straight." I tug her close, my voice thick with emotion. "And you're mine."

The heat simmers between us as we stare at each other. Two people couldn't be more different and yet, we make perfect sense. The yin to my yang. The light to my shadow.

I roll on top of her, capturing her lips in a slow, teasing kiss that quickly deepens, threatening to consume us both in its heat.

"This counts as bedrest, right?" Ori asks, wrapping her legs around my waist as I settle between her thighs. "I mean, we *are* in bed."

"It counts. Besides, Dr. Fulton never said you needed bedrest. I convinced him."

She smacks my chest, her huff making me grin. "Real nice."

"I'll show you just how nice," I murmur, sliding into her again, consumed by the need to have her one more time.

Seems I'm always desperate where Ori is concerned.

But just like earlier, I take my time. Yes, I want to ravage her, but more than that, I want to hold her. To feel her warmth surround me in an unspoken whisper, knowing that this time, my heart is safe.

Safe to love her. Safe to love this life we've built together.

Chapter 29

Everything Is Gone

Ori

"Are you hungry?" I murmur, pressing a kiss to Ash's chest.

We've lazed around in bed for hours. Sue us—we had some serious catching up to do.

"Starving," he replies, his hand absently tracing patterns along my shoulder.

"Let me get dinner started."

Ash catches my wrist before I can leave the bed. "You're supposed to be resting. I'll pick us up some food."

"You said that whole bedrest thing was a crock."

"Bedrest, yes. Resting, no. Dr. Fulton wants you to take it easy."

"That's no fun. I want to cook."

Ash shrugs, his grip firm on my wrist. "And I want you safe, so I win."

"You're full of great lines today."

"I was saving them up, showing you what a catch I am."

"I think the entire world knows you're a catch."

"See? This is why you should ask me to marry you."

"Right," I mutter, rolling my eyes. Don't get me wrong, it's a hell of a one-eighty to hear Ash discussing marriage, but I need to play this one cool.

"You know you want to." He props himself up on one elbow, his grin widening into that signature cocky smirk.

I'm 99% positive the man is messing with me, but that 1% is *mighty* interested in this recent development.

Shaking my head, I smack a kiss to his mouth. "Sadly, I'm not brave anymore where you're concerned."

But Ash doesn't miss a beat. "I'll be brave enough for both of us, and Ori—you *will* marry me."

I lean back, wagging a finger at him. "Laying down a demand doesn't qualify as a proposal, either, you know."

"Since you're such an expert, why don't you show me how it's done?"

"Nice try," I reply, swinging my legs out of bed. "I'm going to hose off. Order me some fettuccine, please? I'm craving carbs."

"At least it's not pickles and ice cream."

"Yet. Give it time."

"Hey Ori, one day you're going to regret not jumping on this marriage deal while it's still on the table," he calls after me.

"Don't hold your breath," I reply in a sing-song voice. "Ash, your phone is ringing."

He waves it off, content to lounge in the bed a few minutes longer. "They can wait. I'm too busy enjoying this moment."

I duck into the bathroom and turn on the shower. Although I might have laughed off Ash's persistent hints about our betrothal, every single one hit the bullseye of my heart, leading me to one undeniable fact: he loves me.

Maybe he can't say those exact words, but he's told me in so many other ways.

And yet, there's still a niggling voice in the back of my head, reminding me that Ash doesn't believe in love. He's told me this on numerous occasions.

What if this is all just an elaborate way of keeping me close without risking anything deeper?

I try to dismiss the thought as lunacy, but it lingers like a bruise that's only tender when you press it.

Then again, does it even matter?

How could I not love him? He risked everything—his reputation, his business, his life—to save those girls. He also risked losing me to keep me safe from the same monster.

Maybe I *should* ask him to marry me, though if this is some kind of new game, my heart won't recover this time.

I stroll out of the bathroom after a luxurious shower to find Ash on the phone, tension radiating off him in waves.

"*Everything* is gone? And you didn't see her leave?" he snaps into the phone.

Uh-oh. I pull the towel from my head, my ears perking up at his heated conversation.

"Shit, Braden. Just search high and low for a note or anything, okay? Yeah, I know you already did, but can you do it again? Thanks."

Ash ends the call with a frustrated sigh. He tosses the phone on the counter, raking his fingers through his hair.

"Everything okay?"

Not sure why I bother asking when I already know the answer is a definitive no.

Ash shakes his head, his hands drumming an erratic beat against the counter. "That was Braden. He went to check on Lucille. All her stuff is gone from the farm—every stitch of clothing, all her toiletries, everything."

"Did she say she was leaving?"

"No, which has me really fucking worried." He runs a

hand over his jaw, another sigh escaping his lips. "Come on. Take a ride with me to *Black Lotus*."

"What are we looking for?"

"She kept all her tattoo gear there. I want to see if it's gone, too."

"Let me get dressed."

I'm ready to go five minutes later, although I look like a hot mess in my oversized sweats, my damp hair twisted under a hat. "Don't say a word about my appearance," I warn Ash as I slide on my coat.

I mean for it to lighten the mood, but it falls on deaf ears. Even though Ash doesn't love Lucille anymore, the thought of harm befalling her is more than he can bear.

I grasp his hand and offer what I hope is a reassuring smile. "Let's go."

My apartment is less than five minutes from *Black Lotus*, but we're not even halfway there when blue lights flash behind us.

"What the hell?" Ash grumbles, pulling to the side of the road. "I'm doing thirty."

"It's probably some bullshit reason."

The officer knocks on the window, and Ash rolls it down, irritation playing across his face. "Seriously? What's up, Drake? Since when does the chief play traffic cop?"

"Hey, Ash. Sorry to startle you, but I wanted to let you know you have a taillight out."

Ash glances over his shoulder, his brow furrowing. "No problem, I'll fix it tomorrow. Are we good?"

Drake taps the truck door, ducking his head to shoot me a smile. "Oriana Thorne. We've yet to be officially introduced."

Ash motions between us with a sharp jerk of his hand. "Ori, this is Drake, the police chief. He's married to Kiki."

"I love Kiki. She has worked a few fabulous real estate deals for me," I reply, leaning across Ash to shake the man's hand. "Tell her I said hello."

"Will do. Oh, and I hear congratulations are in order. About time, Hammond. You've got a good woman in Oriana Thorne."

The smile drops from Ash's face, his expression hardening. "Yeah. Thanks."

"Alright, well, drive safe." With a last nod, Drake walks back to his car and pulls past us on Main Street.

Ash grips the steering wheel like a vise, staring at the road ahead like it's suddenly a battleground.

"Are you okay?" I ask, noting the rigid set of his shoulders.

"Fuck no. I think I found the leak."

What the hell is he talking about? "What leak?"

"Someone here in Sparkwood is working with Kevin Duncan."

"And you think it's the police chief?"

"He knew about you being pregnant, which he would have heard from Kiki after she ran into us at urgent care."

"Right, but I'm not connecting the dots."

Ash exhales sharply and smacks the steering wheel. "Kevin knows you're pregnant. That's why I lost my shit this morning. I knew someone was feeding him information about us—where we were, what we've been doing. Since I doubt it was Dr. Fulton, and you haven't said anything, that leaves one person—Drake."

"Jesus," I mumble, my heart thumping against my ribs. "You hear about dirty cops all the time on TV, but you don't expect them in your town."

"Think about it," Ash says, his voice vibrating with barely restrained anger. "How else is Kevin getting the girls in and out of Sparkwood without anyone noticing? Drake controls the police routes, the patrols—everything. If he's in Kevin's pocket, the whole town is compromised. And what are the odds the chief is handing out tickets tonight? He was waiting for us."

I swallow hard as the reality of Ash's words sink in.

"Do me a favor. Hop out and tell me if a taillight is out."

When I walk behind the truck, both taillights are fully lit. I'll be damned—Ash is right. "They're both working."

"Fucking bastard. He was toying with me."

"Maybe he was stalling you?"

Ash's jaw clenches. "Or sending a message. Let's get to *Black Lotus*. I need to call Trace."

Ash races to the tattoo parlor, and we hurry inside. He heads straight for Lucille's temporary office. Sure enough, all her belongings are gone.

"Fuck," Ash yells, pulling his phone from his pocket. "Pick up. Pick up. Dammit—voicemail."

I need to calm Ash down because flying off the handle never helps in any situation, even one as dire as this.

"Hold up a minute. If Kevin's guys had grabbed Lucille, why would they bother taking her things? That makes no sense. Is there any possibility she cleared out without telling you?"

Ash stops, considering my words. "I mean, it's possible, but knowing the danger, wouldn't she get word to me somehow?"

"Maybe she can't right now. Keep calling, and hopefully, we'll have an answer soon."

Ash's phone buzzes, and he grabs it on the first ring. "Thank God. Where the hell are you? Okay, I can do that. I'll be there in twenty."

He hangs up and motions to the door. "We need to take a ride."

I slink down in the seat as Ash pulls into the seedy motel parking lot.

"What is this place?" I grumble.

"A shit hole," Ash answers, smiling at my horrified expression.

"Why are we here?"

"You'll see."

He parks and walks around to open my door, wrapping a protective arm around me.

A couple of people, high on God knows what, yell something in our direction, and I scrunch closer to Ash's side.

All my senses are on high alert, and I just want to leave and never return.

Ash strides to room #7 and knocks on the door.

Moments later, a man with dark blond hair and a beard opens it and ushers us inside. "You made good time."

I glance around the room, at the dingy, outdated furniture and threadbare carpet, and the seed of unease in my stomach grows.

But then I see Lucille emerge from the bathroom.

"You're okay," I cry, not bothering to stand on ceremony.

She walks over, giving me a quick hug. "I'm fine. Sorry to worry you."

"You scared the shit out of me," Ash interjects as we sit around the rickety table.

"Couldn't be helped," the man replies, turning his attention to me. "I'm Trace. It's nice to meet you, Ori."

"You're the agent?"

He nods. "Something like that."

"What's going on?" Ash asks, resting his forearms on the table.

"I'm moving Lucille somewhere safe," Trace replies.

"But I thought it was all going down tomorrow. Aren't you taking a risk moving her now?"

Trace clears his throat and gazes at the far wall. "I lied. See, I didn't know who the leak was, so I fed you and your brother some fake info. Needed to figure out the answer real fast."

"Dude, are you nuts? I was working with you," Ash argues.

But Trace is unaffected by Ash's surge of anger. "You know how many good guys actually work both sides? I couldn't risk it."

"Well, it wasn't me, but I know who it is," Ash says. "The police chief."

Trace nods, his expression grim. "We had a feeling he was involved. Caught him and Kevin together too many times for it to be a happy coincidence."

"So now what? That's it? It's over?"

Trace stretches, rolling his neck to work out the kinks. "Yes, and no. We intercepted the shipment of girls, and they're safe, but Kevin has fled the country."

Ash groans and lowers his head to the table. "Holy fuck."

"He's in the UAE. We'll monitor him, but their laws make it nearly impossible to extradite him, which he knows. For now, he's out of reach."

Ash frowns, a muscle jumping in his jaw. "And what about Ori and me? Are *we* safe now?"

Trace leans back in the chair, his expression softening slightly. "Yeah, you're safe. Kevin knows you didn't know anything. To him, you were just collateral—something to keep Lucille in line. He's not going to bother you."

"Are you sure about that?" Ash presses.

"What can he get from you? You don't know anything. I made damn sure of that fact. Trust me, Ash, I'm not going to say you're safe if you aren't."

Ash nods and glances at me. "That's something, at least."

More than something, Ash. It's our safety.

"But what about Lucille? Is she safe? What if Kevin comes back?" I ask, fully aware I play no part in this scenario but desperate for answers. Hey, this turned my life upside down, too.

"That's why I'm getting Lucille out of here, although I doubt Kevin will want anything to do with her now that his operation is shut down. Plus, he knows I'll be watching Lucille, and the second I hear he's in the country, I'll be all over him."

"Sounds like a lot of what-ifs and maybes," I state, worrying my lower lip with my teeth.

Lucille offers me a sad smile. "Trust me, it's not an optimal ending, but Trace has assured me he'll take care of me. His word is good."

Ash rubs his chin, the exhaustion wearing lines into his face. "What do I tell everyone? You know people talk in Sparkwood."

Trace shrugs as he pulls out his phone to check the time. "Tell them the truth. You were helping a friend who ran into some trouble. Now, she's heading to a new spot to prepare for the birth of her baby."

"Where *are* you going?" Ash asks, grimacing when Lucille and Trace exchange glances. "Let me guess—need-to-know basis, right?"

"Yeah," Trace says. "But Lucille insisted on saying goodbye first. So, let's make it quick because I don't want to waste any more time."

Lucille and Ash move to one side of the room, and I give them their space. I'm not sure what they have to say to one another, or if this is the last time we'll see her, but they're closing a chapter in their lives. They deserve that privacy without my interference.

"Thank you," Trace says, giving me an awkward pat on the shoulder.

I widen my eyes. "For what?"

"Understanding this situation and why we had to play it this way."

"I'm just glad I'm not in the dark anymore."

"Do me a favor? If you hear or receive anything from Kevin Duncan or McGwyer Holdings, call this number, yeah? Doesn't matter what it is, or how insignificant. This bastard loves to play games, and you were his favorite pawn." He slides me a card with some numbers scribbled on it.

"Is this your number?"

"No, but they'll know how to reach me."

"Cloak and dagger," I mumble. "Kevin always gave me an uneasy feeling. He never did anything, per se, but there was an air about him."

"Luckily, that's *all* he gave you."

Truer words have never been spoken.

I slip the card into my pocket. "Will you ever return to Sparkwood?"

Trace shrugs. "Eventually. I'm not giving up on catching that son of a bitch, but for now, I need to protect Lucille. Kevin thinks he's gotten away with this, but he hasn't. We'll get him one day."

"I'm glad Lucille has you in her corner."

Perhaps my senses are off, but there's something tangible between Trace and Lucille. Ash mentioned they were once married. Who knows? Maybe this crazy-ass ride might rekindle their romance. Stranger things have happened, and the woman needs a good man to protect her. Seems like Trace is up for that job.

Lucille returns to my side, opening her arms. "Give me a hug, preggers."

I stand and embrace her. "Take care of yourself."

"You too—and take care of this guy, okay?" She glances at Ash, her eyes misty. "He's one of the good ones."

"You have my word."

"This isn't goodbye forever," Lucille says, giving Ash's hand a squeeze.

But I can't help wondering if that's exactly what it is.

Ash is quiet as we return to Sparkwood.

"Are you okay?" I ask, glancing at him.

He sighs and shoots me a half-smile. "Yeah. Just hard to believe it's done. Not the ending we hoped for, though."

"Hey, you helped save a dozen girls from a lifetime of slavery. That's a pretty damn good ending."

"But he's still out there. He can still come back."

I rest my hand on Ash's arm. "You and I don't have anything he wants. Like Trace said, we were pawns to him."

"I just wish they'd captured the bastard."

"They will. I saw the determination on Trace's face."

Ash exhales, his gaze fixed on the road ahead. "I guess."

I toy with the seatbelt, hesitant about asking my next question. "Are you okay with Lucille leaving?"

"I want her safe, and Trace will take care of her."

"That's not what I meant."

Ash glances at me briefly before returning his focus to the road. His free hand reaches for mine, his thumb brushing over my knuckles. "I told you, you're everything."

Tears sting my eyes, and my voice shakes. "I didn't believe it the last time you said it."

"It's always been true. It's always been you. *Sei sempre nel mio cuore.*"

My breath catches at the unfamiliar words. "What does that mean?"

The corners of Ash's mouth quirk up. "It means you'd better learn Italian."

"I'll get right on that and come back in a year with either a thoughtful response or a clever retort—just in case you insulted me."

He laughs, his thumb still tracing lazy circles on my hand. "I didn't insult you."

"Good to know."

"Just listen and you'll know what it means," he says, his voice dropping slightly. "*Sei sempre nel mio cuore.*"

Even though I don't understand the individual words, I feel their weight.

Once again, Ash has assured me that his heart is safely—and only—mine.

Chapter 30

Letting Go

Ori

um & Ruin has only been open for an hour, and it's already the talk of the town. A line stretches around the block, with people clamoring to get inside the intimate new hotspot.

Lucky for me, I have an all-access pass.

I wind around the crowd, shooting them a smile as I descend the steps into the roaring '20s.

A warm buzz of conversation weaves around me as I enter the speakeasy, mingling with the rich scent of aged whiskey and a faint smokiness in the air. The polished wood floor vibrates beneath my feet, the bass line from the jazz quartet thrumming throughout the space.

A few locals raise their glasses in greeting when I enter.

Doesn't hurt to know the owner, I guess. Even if I haven't seen the man in the last ten days.

After the Lucille and Trace whirlwind, Ash needed to get his head in the game if he wanted *Rum & Ruin* to open on time. He's been working around the clock, but like everything in his life, he makes success look effortless.

Still, I miss the man.

Twirling around, I take in all the details: the brass sconces throwing golden light onto the polished wood tables, the soulful jazz song crooning about love and loss, and the servers decked out in full flapper gear. Their sequined dresses catch the light as they glide between tables, fringes swaying in time with the music.

I scan the room, but there's no sign of Ash. He's probably somewhere behind the scenes, ensuring every detail is perfect.

One thing is for certain. F. Scott Fitzgerald would be proud.

"Ori, you're here." Mina rushes over, pulling me into a warm hug. "You look fabulous."

"Have to play the part, right?" I sway my hips playfully in my emerald green dress. I'd found this beauty at a vintage shop and knew it would be perfect for *Rum & Ruin*'s grand opening. Paired with T-strap heels and a string of pearls, I feel like I've stepped straight out of the Gatsby era.

I motion to my friend. "You're gorgeous, as always. Has Braden seen you yet?"

Mina blushes, waving a hand to dismiss my question. "He's got his fair share of admirers tonight."

I follow her gaze to where two women sit with Braden, hanging on his every word. But I also see something Mina doesn't—how Braden's gaze flits to my friend's form every few seconds.

"I think you should give them some healthy competition."

"No. I'm terrible at flirting," Mina protests.

But I'm not about to be dissuaded. I stride over to Braden's booth, flashing fake smiles at his two guests. "Hey, Braden."

"Ori. How are you?"

"Good. I'm off to find a drink, but will you keep Mina company?"

Braden smiles and slides out of the booth without hesitation. "Absolutely. I didn't think she wanted to talk to me. She's been distant lately."

"I wonder why." The sarcasm practically drips from my voice, but the younger Hammond brother doesn't pick up on it. "You make her nervous."

"Me? Why?"

"For the same reason she makes *you* nervous. Now scoot— I need a liquid refreshment."

I smile when I sidle up to the bar, noting the mirror from the Dean Estate hanging front and center. She looks perfect there.

"What can I get you, miss?" a familiar voice asks from the other side of the bar.

I turn and grin at Zane, who's fully embracing the 20s-era theme. "Moonlighting, huh?"

He shrugs. "Keeping the natives in line."

"Good luck with that. So, what do you recommend?"

"For you? It's obvious. There's only one choice." He mixes a few ingredients together and sets the glass in front of me.

"That better be virgin," Ash says over my shoulder.

"Don't worry. I'll always protect your mama bear," Zane replies with a wink.

I accept the drink and turn to face Ash, my breath catching at the sight of him. He's stunning in a crisp white shirt with the sleeves rolled up, dark suspenders framing his broad shoulders, and fitted charcoal pants that leave little to the imagination, highlighting every inch of his delicious physique.

"Don't you look incredible?"

He polishes his fingers on his shirt, offering me a flash of his dimpled grin. "Not too bad, huh?"

"Good enough to eat. Although, I thought we weren't telling anyone about our—you know," I say, arching an inquisitive brow.

Ash shrugs, his signature smirk firmly in place. "I might have mentioned it to a few people."

"Well, Zane is family. Has anyone asked about Lucille leaving?"

"Funny thing. Seems no one in town is surprised the baby isn't mine."

"I wonder why," I muse.

"Because I'm crazy about you and the entire population of Sparkwood knows it."

"Now *that* I like to hear." I take a sip of the drink, tasting the hint of peach on my tongue. "This is delicious. What's it called?"

"The Oriana."

"You named it after me?"

"Yep. She's our signature house cocktail. Sweet, delicious, and will put you on your ass if you're not careful."

"Sounds about right," I reply with a grin. "It's damn good."

Ash leans closer, his voice a husky whisper. "Doesn't taste nearly as good as you."

I shoot him a playful scowl. "You didn't really name it after me."

"Check for yourself. You're pretty damn important to me." He pulls a menu from the bar and points to the top of the drink menu. There it is—*The Oriana*. I'll be damned.

I bite my lip, fighting a grin as a rush of feelings sweeps through me. "So, you kind of like me a little, huh?"

Ash's expression softens, and he exhales, locking his gaze with mine. "No. I'm fucking in love with you." He drags a hand over his brow, a nervous chuckle slipping out. "Didn't mean to say it like that."

Holy hell, he just told me he loves me. He just told me he loves me. He... wow.

"Did you mean to say it at all?" I ask, my voice a throaty whisper.

Instead of answering, he smiles and presses his lips to mine in a tender kiss.

"That's not the only surprise," he murmurs against my mouth. "Look behind the stage."

I pivot, craning my neck to get a better view. When I spot it, my hand flies to my mouth. "That's me."

On the wall is a mural of me on the beach in Florida. The same drawing Ash once showed me in his sketchbook.

"That's you, little one," he says, wrapping his arms around me in a warm cocoon. "Can I just say how gorgeous you look tonight?"

"Like it?" I wiggle my hips, causing the fringed hem to swing against my legs.

"So damn much," he growls, his voice thick with desire. "Might have to take you to my office and show you exactly how much."

"Remember what happened the last time we played too much in that office," I remind him, biting back a laugh.

In a move that catches me totally off guard, Ash bends down and presses a soft kiss to my stomach.

"Best thing in the world," he whispers, his voice filled with reverence.

Universe, if this is a dream, I want to sleep forever. Deal?

The mayor walks over, also decked out, in period appropriate attire, and whispers something in Ash's ear.

"I'll be back. You okay?" Ash asks, his eyes fixed on me.

"I'm perfect." And at this moment, I am.

I scan the bar, noting how Braden and Mina look very cozy together in a corner booth. Good. It's about damn time.

Settling onto a bar stool, I sip my drink, my foot tapping to the rhythm of the music as I soak in the night's levity.

What a brilliant idea Ash had, restoring this place to its original glory. I'm so lucky to be a part of it.

"So, you're the reason Ash said no."

I turn on the stool, startled to see Casey, the scout from *Ink Spot*, standing next to me. "Excuse me?"

She motions toward the mural, a wry expression on her face. "Good likeness."

"He's a great artist," I reply, my tone cautious.

"He is, which is why it's such a damn shame he turned down the world tour."

The what now?

"What are you talking about?" I ask, my stomach sinking.

Casey's eyes narrow slightly as she leans closer, her voice dropping to a sharp whisper. "*Ink Spot* wanted to sponsor Ash on a global tour—twenty of the most exclusive tattoo parlors in the world. Live events, guest spots, maybe even a behind-the-scenes documentary. It was a golden ticket. The kind of opportunity every artist dreams of. And he turned it down."

My throat tightens. "Ash never mentioned a world tour to me."

"Really?" Casey raises a brow, her lips quirking as if she's enjoying my discomfort a bit too much. "He was raring to go. They even started planning the itinerary—Tokyo, London, Buenos Aires, Berlin. Hell, he was going to tattoo on a yacht in Monaco. Then, out of nowhere, he calls me and says the deal is off. Said he had too much going on here in Sparkwood."

The weight of Casey's words falls heavy around me. Granted, she *could* be lying about the entire thing, but isn't that a bit grandiose and detailed story to spin?

Besides which, what would be the point?

The answer? There wouldn't be, which means Casey is telling the truth.

"You're sure he said that?"

"Word for word." She tilts her head, shooting me a curious look. "Now I *definitely* know you're the reason behind it. Don't worry, it's his choice, but it's a shame. It would've made him an international superstar in the tattoo world."

"When was this supposed to happen?"

Casey shrugs, accepting a drink from Zane with a flirtatious smile. "A few months from now. He'd have been gone about twelve weeks."

"And he didn't tell you why he no longer wanted to do it?"

"It's pretty easy to figure out, Ori. You're his girlfriend. You're his priority."

Why the hell doesn't that make me feel better?

"How do you know I'm Ash's girlfriend?"

Casey smirks, her eyes gleaming with amusement. "Every woman east of the Mississippi knows that. Honey, when a man like Asher Hammond leaves the market, women notice." She winks and takes a sip of her drink. "Anyway, this speakeasy is amazing. The bee's knees—wasn't that what they used to say? I'll have to plan a photo shoot here. Catch you later."

"Wait." I grab Casey's arm before she can slip away. "If I talk to Ash and convince him to change his mind, will *Ink Spot* still agree to the tour?"

Casey considers my offer. "Honestly? I haven't told my bosses yet. I was hoping I could come here tonight and sway him myself."

We'll ignore, for a moment, the tactics she likely plans to employ to sway him to her way of thinking. After all, I remember all too well her handcuffs and lube comment that night at the restaurant.

But that's neither here nor there.

Sucking in a breath, I force a polite smile. "I'll talk to Ash."

"Are you sure?"

Am I? The thought twists in my chest. Letting Ash go means losing him to the global stage. And even though I know he'd come back to Sparkwood, I don't know if he'd return to me.

But I can't hold him here, either. That's the worst kind of prison—one built of guilt and obligation.

"I'm positive," I state, my voice steadier than I feel. "Just give me a little time."

"Great. Thanks, Ori." Casey clinks her glass against mine and disappears into the crowd, her cheerful demeanor firmly intact.

But my frivolity strolls away with Casey, leaving me with a growing kernel of doubt which threatens to eat away the tenuous happiness I've only recently built.

I'm not sure which bothers me more: Ash deciding against a global tour, something that would undoubtedly boost his prominence in the tattoo industry, or him never mentioning it to me.

All I know is I refuse to be the reason he stays. I won't be yet another obligation he has to fulfill.

Arms slip around my waist, and Ash's intoxicating scent washes over me as he nuzzles my neck. "Hey, little one. Sorry, it's so crazy tonight. I promise I will have more time for you two starting tomorrow."

His words are tender, and I know he means them, but I need to speak my piece—before I lose my nerve and bury the issue.

I turn in his embrace, resting my hands on his muscled forearms. "Never apologize. *Rum & Ruin* is a triumph, and I hope you're enjoying every second."

His gaze sweeps around the speakeasy, an affable smile on his lips. "Hard to believe this is where it all started, huh?"

"A new beginning."

"We've got lots of those happening," Ash murmurs, dropping a kiss beneath my ear.

We sure do, even if we aren't together for all of them.

"Can we talk?"

"Absolutely, but can it wait two minutes? I have to go up and say a few words to the guests. You know how it is."

"Of course." I rise on tiptoe to kiss him. "I'll be here when you get back."

Ash makes his way through the crowd to the small stage, accepting the microphone from the svelte singer with a smile. "How's everyone enjoying a taste of the Gatsby era?"

Applause sounds from around the speakeasy, and my heart clenches with pride as Ash works the crowd like a master.

"I can't believe I'm actually standing here. This has been a lifelong dream for me, and now she's here. She's real." He holds up his glass, his eyes locking with mine. "And I have one person to thank for that. Oriana Thorne, I never saw you coming. A lot of people here in Sparkwood probably remember how much we hated each other, but a faulty lock on a basement door changed all that. Some sexy lingerie didn't hurt, either."

Laughter ripples through the crowd, but Ash's grin softens as his gaze stays fixed on me.

"She loves lingerie. The sexier, the better. And she doesn't need an occasion—says it makes her feel sexy. I'll bet she's wearing some right now."

A few more chuckles rise up from the bar patrons.

"The thing is, Ori doesn't need anything to be sexy. She's the total package—brilliant, beautiful, and absolutely one of a kind."

He pauses, and for a moment, the crowd fades away, leaving just the two of us in the room. "You changed me, Ori. I heard every word you ever said, and I wanted to say them back. But I was a fool—I thought I had time to get my head straight. Then life went sideways, and you walked away. The color drained from my world, and I realized the only story I want to tell—the *only* life I want to live—has to have you in it."

Everyone in the speakeasy pivots to look at me, my eyes

bright with tears as I raise my glass in a toast. "Sorry to break it to you, Hammond, but you're not getting rid of me that easily. Besides, you make a mean cocktail and I kind of like you a little bit."

Actually, I adore you, which is exactly why I'm going to let you go.

Ash's face splits into a wide smile as he hands the microphone back to the singer and makes a beeline through the crowd for me. "Hey, little one."

"Hey, yourself."

"You wanted to talk? Let's go."

We stroll hand in hand to his office, and he latches the door behind us, turning to me with a mischievous grin. "What did you want to talk about? How to get you out of that dress?"

"Tempting, but I'm not up for this many voyeurs." I motion to the couch. "Have a seat."

"Time for a striptease?"

"Not quite."

Ash's eyes widen slightly as he sits down. "I hope I didn't embarrass you with the lingerie comment."

Resting my foot on the edge of the couch, I hike my skirt to reveal the thigh-highs and garter belt underneath. "You were spot on."

His gaze darkens, and he licks his lips, his hands tracing the contours of my leg. "Fuck, but you're pretty. Come here."

His touch sets my skin on fire, but I press my hands against his chest, stopping him. "Wait," I whisper, my voice trembling. "Let me say this first."

He leans back, a curious expression crossing his face. "Okay. The floor is yours."

"Why didn't you tell me about the world tour?"

Ash runs a hand along his jaw, his gaze flicking to the far wall. "Because I'm not doing it."

I perch on the edge of the couch, resting a hand on his knee. "But you wanted to go."

"Things change," he replies, a hint of resignation in his

voice. His eyes dart back to mine, and for a fleeting second, I catch the longing in them.

"That's why I need to say this." My voice shakes, but I press on. "I wanted you to be the one who saved me from myself. To build me a home in your arms so I could finally stop running. But that's not fair to you. It's not your job to save me, Ash. It's not your job to fit someone else's dream."

His brow furrows, and I force myself to keep going. "Promise me something. Live your life on your terms. Chase what makes you happy, and never let it go."

He studies me for a long moment, his expression unreadable. "No matter who gets hurt in the process?"

"If you don't follow your bliss, *you'll* end up hurting. And you deserve better than that."

Ash clicks his tongue against his teeth as he processes what I said. "Let me get this straight. You want me to put aside everything everyone in my life wants in favor of what *I* want? Disregard Braden, my folks, the people at Black Lotus... even *you?*"

I nod, despite the tightness in my throat. "Exactly. Do what makes you happy."

"Do you really mean that?"

"I do."

And at that moment, I realize it's the truth. We can't force anyone to stay anywhere. The best we can hope for is that certain people might want to journey by our side, but there's no guarantee of how long they'll stay.

There's no guarantee, period.

I think I finally understand how my father felt, breaking free of a life that didn't fit him in order to pursue the one that did. Maybe now I can finally work on forgiving him.

Ash reaches for my hand, lacing his fingers through mine and returning me to the moment. "Thank you."

"For what?"

"For loving me that much. Enough to let me go."

I smile as my vision blurs with unshed tears. "Anything less isn't love. The best stories are the ones with endings you never see coming. Where the narrative shifts, and you see everything in a whole new light. You're my favorite plot twist, no matter our ending."

I smooth my dress and take a few slow, deep breaths, Ash's gaze never wavering from me. "I'm going to head home. This place is magnificent. *You're* magnificent. I'm so glad I know you. Really glad I'm allowed to love you."

He bites his lip, and I know, without him saying a word, that he's equally overwhelmed with emotion. "We close at two, so it'll be a few more hours before I can leave."

"Okay." I lean down to place a lingering kiss on his cheek. "Casey is sticking around. She wants to talk to you."

Ash nods, but before I can step away, he pulls me onto his lap and buries his head in the crook of my neck. "I do not deserve you."

We need to lighten the mood. My disclosure, however necessary it may be, has hung a pall over the night, and that will never do.

So, as is my nature, I opt for levity—and a little sarcasm. "True. You got damn lucky with me."

Ash laughs, delivering a soft nip to my skin. "Woman, what am I going to do with you?"

"So many things. And remember, I spent a pretty penny on this lingerie. You'd better make sure it's put to good use."

"I locked the damn door, little one. I'm ready now."

But I giggle and squirm free from his grasp. "Too many interruptions tonight. And you know I like it when you take your time. See you later, handsome."

As I exit the speakeasy, I realize something—I didn't let go of Ash tonight. I gave him the freedom to choose. And maybe, just maybe, that's the kind of love that lasts.

I awaken to the jingle of keys in the lock and jerk upright, glancing at the clock.

2:45.

Ash appears in the bedroom doorway, a rueful smile tugging at his mouth. "Damn, I didn't mean to wake you."

"What are you doing here?" I ask, rubbing the sleep from my eyes.

He jiggles the keyring before tossing it onto the dresser. "I told you I was coming home after the opening."

"I thought you meant *your* home."

"You're here. Our baby is here. That's home to me." He pauses, a flicker of mischief in his eyes. "Plus, I have a surprise for you tomorrow."

"A surprise?"

"Yeah, and it's a big one."

The last one with Lucille was a pretty damn big one, too.

Ash unbuttons his shirt and walks over to drop a kiss on my mouth. "I'm hopping in the shower."

"Okay."

I watch him disappear into the bathroom, my thoughts swirling like a whirlwind. I wonder how things played out with Casey and the upcoming tour. Although I'm desperate for details, I'll give him a few minutes to unwind first.

Ten minutes later, he emerges in a cloud of steam, a towel hanging low on his hips, droplets of water glistening on his skin.

"Better?" I ask, my eyes slowly trailing over his tatted physique, drinking in every inch. Damn, he's a work of art.

Trust me, the man knows exactly what he does to me—and to the female population at large.

"Much." He drops the towel and slips into bed next, wrapping his arms around me and pulling me against his chest. "I've barely slept the last two weeks. Apparently, insomnia is my new best friend."

"Now you can get some well-earned sleep. How was the rest of the night?"

But Ash doesn't answer me.

"Ash?"

Seems sleep has finally claimed him.

I press my lips to his in a soft kiss before settling my head against his chest. Looks like our chat will have to wait for another day.

"Goodnight, Ash."

And then I hear it, so faint it's almost unintelligible.

"Love you, Ori."

But when his arms tighten around me, I know that regardless of our future, he means what he says. He loves me, and somehow, that will be enough.

Chapter 31

Are You Ready?

Ori

"Hey, time to wake up." Ash nudges me gently, his beard tickling my skin as he drops soft kisses along my shoulder.

"Do I have to?" I grumble, rolling over and snuggling further into the blanket.

"You do, and although you're going to hate me for this, I hope you'll understand why it's necessary."

Huh?

I blink up at him, confused. "What are you talking about?"

"This." Ash grabs the blanket and yanks it away in one swift motion.

"If this is your idea of foreplay, we need to have a serious talk," I mutter, curling into a ball. "Be nice to the pregnant woman."

"Trust me," he whispers, scooping me up in his arms. "I plan on being *very* nice to you."

"What's going on? I figured after all the craziness of the opening, we'd lounge around today."

Ash shakes his head. "No can do. Too much happening."

He carries me to the bathroom and turns on the spray. Judging by his appearance—freshly showered and dressed—

he's been up for a while. He's also got this anxious energy buzzing through him, which doesn't bode well for me.

But I'm too tired to analyze it—much. Best to wake up before I start freaking out over contrived scenarios.

"I'm picking up breakfast for us. You want an omelet?"

"Sure," I mumble, stepping into the shower. "And tea, please."

"You got it." He leans his head into the shower, shooting me a dimpled grin. "Dress casual but nice."

"So, no sweatpants? Is that what you're telling me?"

"That's what I'm telling you."

"Damn. Fine." I smack a kiss on his mouth before shooing him from the room.

The warm water does its job, loosening the knots in my neck. As I glide my hands along my body, I pause when they slip over my abdomen. Glancing down, I notice it.

I'm showing.

It's barely noticeable and only when I'm naked, but it's there—the faintest bump, the first undeniable sign of this new life growing inside me.

Wow.

I stand there, my hands resting on my belly, allowing my mind to wander. I picture the next several months: late pregnancy, a baby shower with piles of cute gifts, strange cravings, midnight runs for pickles and ice cream, the first kick, and Ash's head resting on my belly as he talks to our baby.

But what if Ash isn't here for any of it?

That thought opens a floodgate of bittersweet images: decorating the nursery alone, picking out the crib, prepping my hospital go bag.

Me. Me. Me.

God, I hope I made the right choice in telling him to go.

"Well, Ori," I say aloud to the steamy tiles. "No take backs. We're going to be okay, no matter what. There's enough love in this little town to carry me through the darkest nights. And Ash will—"

"What will Ash do?" His voice cuts through my thoughts, and I whirl around to see him poking his head in the door, barely visible through the steam.

Shit. I didn't realize he was back already. How long have I been in here, musing about my future?

"You okay, little one?" Ash asks, pulling back the curtain slightly. "You almost done?"

I shut off the water and offer a rueful grin. "Lost track of time. That's what a lack of caffeine will do to you."

"Come on. Let's eat, and then it's time for your surprise."

Ash is usually cool under pressure, but right now, he's vibrating with so much restless energy, I feel like I should offer him a stress ball. Whatever this surprise is, it's got him twisted up in knots—and now it's doing the same to me.

I walk out to the kitchen, marveling at how Ash has set out our food, even going so far as to include a single tulip in a bud vase.

"Look at you," I remark, fingering the petals of the pink tulip. "Who are you, and what have you done with Asher Hammond?"

He shrugs, a grin splitting his face. "Consider this the upgraded version. Ash 2.0."

I giggle and bite into my omelet. "Can't wait to take you for a spin."

"Oh, that's happening. I've had entirely too little Ori in my life for the six weeks."

I shovel food into my mouth, but notice Ash is only drinking coffee. "Aren't you hungry?"

He shakes his head, his fingers drumming a beat on the table. "Not really."

"Are you okay?"

"Yeah, I'm great." But the incessant tapping continues as he downs his coffee in big gulps.

He's definitely nervous.

And he definitely doesn't want to talk about it now.

Even though not talking about it is sending *my* anxiety skyward.

Breathe, Ori. You'll be okay. If he leaves tomorrow or in two months, you'll be okay.

I huff out a breath, feeling my body calm. For the first time since I gave Ash the chance to leave, I believe my words.

"Put this on." Ash hands me a blindfold, and I stare at him, my eyes wide.

"Why?"

"For the surprise."

I hold the blindfold, worrying my lower lip with my teeth. "Do I have to wear it?"

He huffs out a sigh. "Yes." Then, with practiced ease, he slides it over my eyes and steals a quick kiss.

"What do you have planned?"

"You'll have to wait and see." His voice is full of mischief, but a gentle squeeze of my hand reassures me.

The soft hum of music fills the truck a moment later—a playlist of my favorite oldies, likely meant to calm my nerves. It works... a little.

"Can I at least have a hint?" I ask after a few minutes, shifting in my seat.

"Nope. Then it's not a surprise." His hand clasps mine, his fingers entwining with my own. "Trust me, little one."

Twenty minutes later, the truck slows to a stop, and he kills the engine.

"Can I look now?"

"No. Stay put and don't peek," he warns as my fingers twitch toward the blindfold.

"Fine," I grumble, knotting my hands in my lap. "This had better be good."

I hear him chuckle as my door opens. He loosens my seat-belt and helps me down from the truck, his hands steady.

"I think it's better than good. Don't worry. I've got you. You're safe. Step up... and again."

I follow his lead, pausing when I hear the jingle of keys and the creak of a door opening. Warm air brushes my skin, carrying with it the faint scent of cinnamon apples.

"Are we at *Rum & Ruin*?"

"Definitely not," he replies, a teasing lilt in his tone. "Hopefully later today, though."

He guides me further inside, his hands never leaving me. "Ready?"

"I guess."

"You're going to have to do better than that," he murmurs, his lips brushing my neck.

"Abso-fucking-lutely," I exclaim with an excitement I don't fully feel.

Hey, give me some credit. Surprises are not *always* happy.

"Much better." His chuckle is rich with anticipation as he lifts the blindfold.

I blink against the sudden light, my vision adjusting.

And then I realize where we are.

I spin around, my heart pounding as my mind struggles to reconcile what I'm seeing.

We're at the Dean Estate, standing in the fully completed carriage house apartment.

But it's not possible, is it?

"How... how is this finished?" I twirl slowly, my eyes taking in every detail, half believing that if I blink, I'll wake and find it all a dream.

"Come on," Ash says, grabbing my hand. "Let me show you around."

He gestures to the main living space, drenched in natural light from three massive windows lining one wall. "We kept the exposed brick and beams but laid down new hardwood floors. And there are those Tiffany pendant lamps you liked."

"It's incredible," I breathe, still unsure that any of this is real.

He walks us to the kitchen, a perfect blend of modern convenience and vintage charm. "I know you love cooking, so we made sure there's plenty of room to whip up your fabulous feasts. And there's space for a table for when friends come over."

I run my hand along the cool quartz countertop, marveling at the stained-glass insets in the cabinet doors, each panel capturing natural scenes of the mountains. "It's fantastic. I can already see myself cooking in here."

"So can I." He smiles, taking my hand again and leading me to the master bedroom. "We added crown molding and a tray ceiling, plus a walk-in closet for all your stuff."

"Smart man," I murmur, a permanent grin etched on my face.

"And this," he says, guiding me into the second bedroom, "will be the baby's room. I didn't decorate it completely—I figured you'd want to help with that."

The future nursery is painted a soft, calming green, with a large oak crib already set in the corner. Above the crib, in Ash's perfect calligraphy, is a familiar term: *Sei sempre nel mio cuore.*

"That's what you said to me the other day."

"You're always in my heart," Ash murmurs. "That's what it means and Ori, you are."

"I can't believe you did all this," I whisper, a few tears slipping down my cheeks.

Ash brushes them away with a tender swipe of his thumb. "Hey, come on. You haven't seen the best part yet."

He guides me to the bathroom, pointing out the clawfoot soaking tub and dual shower, but it's the atrium that steals my breath.

What I never told anyone is that the atrium and gardens—despite their shoddy appearance—were what sealed the deal for me when I bought the Dean Estate. I envisioned them fully restored, bursting with life and color. Turns out, my imagination pales compared to the reality Ash has created.

Sunlight streams through the glass walls, warming the space, while flowering vines climb a trellis that sits above a two-person glider rocker. In the corner, a rock pond gurgles as water splashes down from a delicate waterfall.

"Ash…" My voice falters as I take it all in, my chest tight with emotion.

He wraps me in his embrace, and I melt against him, the world beyond disappearing from view. "I decided, instead of a bouquet, I'd get you a garden. Something that keeps growing, bringing you new surprises every day."

I plant my chin on his chest, beaming up at him. "It's perfect. But how did you do all this?"

"Your brother. Turns out, you were right. He's one hell of a craftsman."

"Wait a second—*you* were Eddie's secret project?"

"Yep. I knew you wanted to throw in the towel, that you were overwhelmed. But I wanted to show you that, together, we can do it all, beautiful."

He leads me back into the living room and gestures to a box on the table. My breath catches when I realize it's no ordinary box—it's my wish box.

The one covered in stickers and doodles, packed with a lifetime of knick-knacks, each one representing dreams of my future wedding, baby, and happily ever after.

"My wish box," I whisper, my voice quivering.

Ash traces his fingers along the edge of the box. "You need to open it, because I plan on making every one of these wishes come true."

My lips tremble as the realization hits me—through all those days I thought Ash had moved on, he was really waiting for my return. Just like he said.

Ash points to the floor to ceiling bookshelf. "I also bought you the first book for your newly restored bookshelf."

I cross the room and pull the special edition book out, my heart skipping at the sight of the gorgeous cover—an infamous rose encased in glass. "Beauty and the Beast."

Ash is by my side in an instant, a faint flush coloring his cheeks. "You're my Belle. Smart, beautiful, stubborn, and absolutely perfect. And this book? It has the fairytale ending you deserve."

"Ash—"

"I'm not done." His voice cracks, his green gaze locked on mine. "That's the *only* acceptable ending, and I'm going to give you that. I swear on my life I will, if you'll let me."

I burrow my head against his chest and cry, releasing years of pent-up emotion and grief. Ash's embrace stays strong and unwavering, his arms a haven from the often cruel world.

After a few minutes, I pull back and wipe my tear-stained cheeks, shooting him a rueful grin. "This is too much. It's perfect—and *way* better than your last surprise."

Ash's brow furrows. "You didn't enjoy the Keys?"

"God, yes. I meant when I met Lucille. You told me you had a surprise for me, remember? That was *not* a pleasant one."

He chokes out a laugh. "I can see why, but that was *not* the surprise I had in mind."

"It wasn't?"

"No. I was going to ask you to move in with me so we could work on this place together." Ash gestures around the pristine carriage house interior.

"Is that still the plan? Moving in together?"

Because cohabitation with this gorgeous hunk of man sounds pretty damn nice.

Ash skews his mouth to the side and shakes his head. "Nah."

"Oh," I murmur, trying to mask the sting of disappointment.

"I'm going to ask you to marry me instead."

I freeze, my eyes scanning his face, waiting for him to laugh it off and claim he's joking.

But he's not laughing.

"You… you don't believe in marriage," I stutter.

"I believe in you. I believe in us. You made me believe in forever, Ori. And since you're having my baby, I'd really like you to have my last name, too."

He drops to one knee on the hardwood floor, his fingers shaking as he pulls a small velvet box from his pocket. My chest tightens, a surge of emotions rushing through me so fiercely I clutch the edge of the bookshelf to steady myself.

"Ori—"

"Wait." I cut him off, grabbing his hands as I sink to my knees beside him.

Ash's eyes widen, a muscle jumping in his jaw. "Wait?"

I need him to understand he's not bound by any obligation —not to me, not to anyone.

I squeeze his hands, my voice shaking. "You don't have to marry me because of the baby."

The tension melts away from Ash's face as he releases a sharp exhale. "Fuck. Don't scare me like that, Ori. Just so you know, I bought this ring before I knew about the baby."

He flips open the box, revealing an exquisite vintage ring —a masterpiece of delicate filigree and sparkling diamonds. At its center sits a stunning Asscher-cut diamond, flanked by two deep green emeralds, their hue almost identical to Ash's eyes.

I hope our baby has those eyes, too.

Although his hands tremble, his voice remains steady. "This ring was made in the 1920s. He was a writer, and she was his one true love. He bought this as a testament to that love. I thought it was fitting. Maybe he could provide the words I often can't find."

My eyes flit between his face and the glorious ring, as a smile lights up my face. "Personally, I think you're doing pretty great."

"What do you say? Be Mrs. Hammond? Marry me?"

Tears blur my vision as I cup his face, my voice quivering with emotion. "Yes, Ash. A thousand times, yes. But don't you see? You've already given me my fairytale ending."

Ash slides the ring onto my finger, and I admire the way it sparkles and shines in the light of our newly restored home. He's taken my broken life and made it beautiful.

Perfect.

Just like him.

And then, unable to hold back any longer, I pounce, gently pushing him back as I straddle his waist. "I love you, Asher Hammond," I murmur, claiming his mouth as my tongue dances with his in a perfect, unbreakable rhythm.

His arms wrap around me, locking me in his embrace. His hands tangle in my hair as he deepens the kiss, promising me without words that I'll never be alone again.

But then I pull back, because I have a surprise for him, too. Something I hope he'll enjoy seeing.

"I want to show you something," I say, lifting the hem of my shirt.

Ash smirks, his eyes sparking with mischief. "I like where this is heading."

I laugh as he slides his hands to the waistband of my pants. "You're going to have to wait a few more minutes for *that* brand of attention. Look." I guide his hand to my abdomen. "I'm starting to show. Just a little, but... isn't that crazy?"

Ash falls silent as his fingers splay across my abdomen, but I see the brightness in his eyes.

"You're so beautiful," he whispers.

"I thought you might like to see."

He sits up and wraps his arms around me, pulling me tight against his chest. "I don't want to miss another second, Ori. You two are my entire world. Nothing else matters. Don't you get it? You're my home."

"You're mine." I frame his face with my hands, depositing a multitude of kisses across his cheeks and mouth. "But don't worry. I'm going to take a ton of videos throughout this whole pregnancy, so no matter where in the world you are, you'll still be a part of it."

Ash quirks a brow at me. "Where exactly am I going?"

"The world tour, remember? Casey said—"

He grins, ducking his hands beneath my shirt to cup my breasts. "Nope, not until next year. I delayed it. Works out better this way—more time for them to plan, and I get to take my wife and baby along with me."

"You want me to come, too?"

"Ori, I want you by my side every second of every day. Being away from you this past month taught me something— you put me back together. And I plan on spending every moment showing you how grateful I am that you took that chance."

His sweet words blend with the sensual caress of his hands, sparking a firestorm inside me. I drag my nails along his shoulders, my body trembling with every touch.

And boy, does Asher Hammond know *exactly* what he's doing to me.

A wicked grin spreads across his face as his hands slide lower, curving around my hips.

"You know pregnancy makes a woman really horny, right?"

Ash's grin deepens. "Tell me more."

I bury my face against his neck, delivering a small nibble to his throat. "How about I show you instead?"

"Perfect." Ash pops to his feet, sweeping me into his arms. "Let's try out our new bed, shall we, Mrs. Hammond?"

Glancing at the ring sparkling on my finger, I shoot him a coy smile. "I'm ready for everything you've got to offer, Mr. Hammond. Question is, are you ready for me?"

"Beautiful," he says, his voice low and filled with desire, "I've never been more ready for anything in my life."

We fought countless battles to get here, but as I gaze into his eyes, I know he was worth every teardrop.

Our love isn't perfect. No, it's better. It's ours—imperfect, messy, and undeniably real.

Epilogue: Did Someone Say Wedding?

Ash

Mina rushes over the second Ori and I walk into *Rum & Ruin*, her bright smile bordering on exasperated. "Where the hell have you two been? We've been waiting for hours."

Braden laughs, lifting his beer in greeting. "I know *exactly* where they've been."

Raising my hands in mock surrender, I shoot my brother a smirk. "I'm not saying a damn word."

"Well, I will." Ori holds out her hand, flashing her engagement ring. "The world has officially shifted on its axis. Hell has frozen over. And somehow, I managed to get lucky enough to land Asher Hammond as my husband."

Our friends admire the ring, each offering us heartfelt congratulations. They witnessed the battles we fought to get here.

They know we deserve this happiness.

But it's the joy on Ori's face as she snuggles into my arms that makes it all worthwhile.

"So, how did we do on the carriage house renovation?" Eddie asks, giving Ori a quick side hug.

Ori waves her hands, her excitement palpable. "It's perfect. Actually, no. It's better than perfect. Although I have a serious question for you two. What are we going to do with all the space in the main house?"

She's right. The carriage house is more than enough space for our little family, but I have a few plans for the main part of the Dean Estate.

Hopefully, she's on board with my ideas.

"I figured I might set up a private studio there, if that works for you."

Ori nods, her eyes lighting up. "Brilliant idea. Plus, you could use a couple of rooms for photo shoots, too."

A wicked grin spreads across my face. "Now that you mention it, I could go for a photo shoot with you in that lingerie from last night."

Mina groans at my candid remark, while Braden sputters his beer, laughing.

"You're unbelievable, Ash," he says.

"Hey, my woman—my wife—is gorgeous," I reply, unapologetic. Plus, that burgundy lace number she wore last night didn't hurt, either. It hugged her curves like it was created especially for her.

Lucky for me, the little siren wore it again today.

And I took full advantage.

Which is why we're two hours late.

Am I sorry? Not one fucking bit.

I always said Ori's pussy was magical, but the truth is, *she's* magical.

More importantly, she's mine.

Zane resumes his unofficial role as bartender, sliding a celebratory mocktail into Ori's hand.

"Only seven more months until I can have one of these delicious cocktails with all the alcohol," she says, releasing an exaggerated sigh.

"Unless I knock you up again," I tease, leaning on the bar beside her.

She arches a brow, her lips quirking. "I don't think so."

My grin widens. "Sounds like a challenge, and you know I love a good challenge. Haven't lost one yet."

"This little one," she says, pointing at her belly, "was a happy accident. Now you're planning a sequel?"

"Beautiful, when the original is that good, you can't leave it at just one."

She reaches her hand up, gliding her nails lightly across my chest. "I hate how good that sounds. Stop stirring up my pregnancy hormones."

"You don't hate how good I am, though."

"No," she says, her voice softening. "I love it. I love every damn thing about you."

And I know, as I steal a kiss from her pouty lips, that Oriana Thorne hasn't just pieced my heart back together. She gave me a life. A purpose. A future.

I'll make damn certain she never regrets that fact. Judging by her hands creeping further up my leg, teasing me with the promise of a second round, she's as ready for this wild ride as I am.

"So, tell me, does anyone else have news?" Ori asks, her eyes bright with excitement.

But all eyes swing to Mina as she walks back into the room, her earlier smile replaced by a scowl.

Ori rests a hand on her shoulder. "Mina, are you okay?"

"Too much marriage talk?" I tease. "We can switch to football chat if you'd prefer."

"Apparently not *enough* marriage talk," Mina mutters, her gaze on the floor.

"What?" The single word echoes through the room, spoken in unison by me, Ori, and Braden.

Mina squeezes Ori's hand, offering her a thin-lipped smile.

"I'm thrilled for you and Ash. Really, I am. But... I have a situation. Never mind me, we can talk about it later."

"Or we can talk about it now." Concern etches Ori's face as she looks at her friend. "What's going on?"

Mina rolls her shoulders and meets our gazes, determination flickering behind the tension. "My great-aunt has offered to sell me her dance studio in town."

"That's amazing," Ori exclaims, clapping her hands together. "Mina, you can go back to dancing now. That's your dream."

Mina wrings her hands, pacing the area in front of the bar. "Yeah, but it's not that simple. See, my great-aunt has attached a stipulation to the deal."

"What kind of stipulation?" Braden asks, his brows furrowing.

Mina hesitates for a beat before exhaling sharply. "She wants me to settle down. As in, be *married*, before she'll sign over any of the paperwork."

"Whoa," Braden murmurs, taking a long pull of his beer.

"Crazy, right? Ridiculous, especially in this day and age."

"So, it would be a business deal?" I ask, hardly able to believe her great-aunt's offbeat request is real.

Mina nods. "I guess so, though she couldn't know that. But, it's always been my dream to own a studio, so... um, do any of you happen to know someone who might want to marry me?"

THE END

Preorder Your Copy of Igniting Sparks Today!

Don't Forget to Grab Sparks Fly, a Sparkwood novella that's free when you sign up to my newsletter!

Sparkwood Series

A Billion Sparks (Prequel Novella)
Secret Identity / Billionaire / Insta-Love
The First Spark (Book 1)
Enemies to Lovers / Forced Proximity / Opposites Attract
Chasing Sparks (Book 2)
Protector Role / Return of Ex / Surprise Pregnancy
Igniting Sparks (Book 3)
Fake Engagement / Age Gap / Forced Proximity
Sheltering Sparks (Book 4) *Preorder*
Friends to Lovers / Reverse Age Gap / Single Dad

A Billion Sparks *is exclusive to newsletter subscribers. Click the link to above to receive your free copy along with all the latest Sparkwood gossip!*

Also by M.L. Broome

Seasoned Hearts Series

Make You Stay

Friends to Lovers / Opposites Attract / Single Dad

Both Sides Now

Young Widow / Forbidden Romance / Love After Loss

Hook Up

Brother's Best Friend / Sports Romance / He Falls First

And Then Came You

Friends to Lovers / Slow Burn / Celebrity Romance

Alchemy Unfolding

Reverse Age Gap / Sexy Surfer / Medical Romance

Yuletide Acres

Yule Holiday Romance / Second Chance / Single Dad

Forgot to Tell You Something

High Angst / Surprise Pregnancy / Medical Romance

A Sinner's Memory (Lyrical Love Letters)

Rockstar Romance / Second Chance / Single Dad

A Series of Moments Trilogy Box Set

High Angst / Celebrity Romance / Medical Romance

It Must Have Been the Mistletoe

Christmas Romance / Second Chance / Snowed In Together

Keep in Touch!

Want important announcements, bonus goodies and exclusives, and behind the scenes peeks at my real life? Subscribe to my twice monthly newsletter!

Want preorder and new release alerts? Follow me on Amazon and Bookbub!

I'm always posting snippets from my books and upcoming releases on Tiktok, Facebook and Instagram. Be sure to follow me there!

About the Author

M.L. Broome is a bohemian spirit with a New York edge. She writes high-octane contemporary romance with plenty of angst and steamy, sexy goodness. Her characters are bitingly real, earning their happily-ever-after only after some emotional ass-kicking and personal growth.

When M.L. isn't writing or holding one-sided arguments with her characters (spoiler alert—they always win), she loves losing herself in nature on her micro farm, one of her rescue buddies by her side.

She adores dressing up and kicking back, a glass of whiskey with an equally stunning view, and experiences that make the soul—and senses—tingle.

For all the latest releases and exclusive goodies, subscribe to M.L. Broome's newsletter today at https://www.mlbroome.com.

9 798990 999145